MW01125001

MUSIC: THE GIRL IN THE BOX, BOOK 36

Out of the Box #26

ROBERT J. CRANE

Ostiagard Press

MUSIC
The Girl in the Box, Book 36
(Out of the Box, Book 26)

Robert J. Crane

Chapter 1

Nashville, Tennessee

Neon lights lit the sidewalks of Broadway, and music spilled into the night. Some of it rang out hard, some of it pitched sweet; all of it was loud, the competition on to get the attention of the tourists and locals moving by on the sidewalks. Broadway was like a piece of old Vegas dropped into Nashville, packed crowds bustling past. Honky-tonk bars lined the street, their windows pushed open and music blaring out like an attempt at an open air concert into the cool—but not cold—February evening.

Brance Venable came along Broadway at an easy saunter. His heart was thudding about a million miles an hour, warring against his attempts to keep cool as he went. He was a little taller than average, a little thinner than average, looked a little better than average, based on his luck with the ladies. The words of Alan Jackson's "Chasin'

That Neon Rainbow" were bouncing around in his head as he threaded his way through the teeming, living mass of humanity threatening to spill over the metal sidewalk barricades and into Broadway itself, where the traffic was at a complete standstill waiting for the next light. Brance noticed none of it; not the overripe tourist spitting a curse at the homeless guy next to him, not the scent of margaritas wafting off the loud bachelorette party passing by him.

Brance was focused on one thing, and one thing only.

Screamin' Demons was a honky-tonk on 2nd Avenue, just off Broadway. It was ahead. Everything else...well, everything else needed to be behind him right now.

Because this was it.

Brance had moved to Nashville a month ago from Cody, Wyoming. A month of craziness, of trying to get his crap unpacked in his tiny apartment in Germantown. He'd gotten the lay of the land in Music City, USA, and now he was ready to make his debut. He'd chosen everything carefully, figuring the optimal venue that he, a nobody, could succeed at. And he'd found it.

Open mic night at Screamin' Demons, which was a honky-tonk and a dive bar all in one.

The red neon lights off the Screamin' Demons sign were like the fires of hell, ominous and crimson, casting the glow out on the street. Screamin' Demons wasn't even a block off the chaos that was Broadway.

Brance slipped in through the open door of the honky-tonk, nodding at the big dude in black bouncing at the door. The bouncer nodded back, barely. It was the most human contact Brance had gotten since he'd moved here.

He bellied up to the bar as the lady on stage warbled a broken version of Patty Loveless's "I Try to Think About Elvis." Her voice broke on the chorus, and the crowd—

half full at best, mostly with young people out for a Wednesday on the town—evinced a collective disinterest, paying more attention to their drinks and conversations than her crackling vocals.

"What do you want?" the bartender asked. Guy looked about Brance's age, mid-twenties, buff.

"Mich Golden Light," Brance said, and chucked a thumb over his shoulder toward the stage. "And where do I sign up for that?"

The bartender pulled a beer bottle out from under the bar and popped the top, then pointed down the bar. Ah. A clipboard.

Brance made his way over, cold beer in hand, condensation working its way down his grip. The list on the clipboard was long, filled to five pages. He stared at it only a second before adding his name and settling back at the bar, squeezed between a couple and a lone dude who weighed about three-fifty and was fully done up in a cowboy hat and boots with a Roy Rogers shirt. Brance tried not to stare at the rhinestones as he sipped his beer. Talk about out of date.

Nashville nowadays was Dierks Bentley and Kacey Musgraves. Had it ever been that ostentatious? Maybe in the seventies, long before Brance's time. He chuckled in a self-satisfied way into his beer. Only a month and he was already thinking like a local.

The night dragged on as Brance waited. The crowd was good; they didn't boo when someone was terrible. Polite applause followed the ones that utterly bombed, voices cracking or lyrics forgotten. There were a couple of solid performers in there, too. One young lady did a pretty good rendition of Elton John's "Don't Let the Sun Go Down on Me."

Brance was still sipping that first beer two hours later, though it was really warm, when they called him up. He finished it in an easy pull, wiped the condensation of the beer mingled with the sweat onto his jeans, and made his way up on the stage.

"My name's Brance," he said. He'd decided his stage name was just one word. Like Garth. But without even the Brooks. "And I'll be singing an original song."

That didn't get much reaction. Most everyone was paying attention to their beers or whatever they were drinking. It was tough to see much beyond shadows through the stage lights.

Brance started up, a cappella:

"*I see you*
out there in the night..."

He really put some effort into his voice, tried to use the microphone to push it out there, project over the crowd and the buzz of people drinking, talking. A couple eyes watched him from the bar. Could they be someone from a record label?

He had to nail this.

"*...I see you*
at the end of my fight..."

Man, he sang. Voice projected to the rafters, all the soulful sound and feeling he could put into it. These were the daydreams he'd had for all the years of his life since the first time he heard someone singing on the radio one Sunday afternoon while his dad worked on an engine block in the garage. His foot moved in time with the music and Brance watched, tried to mimic it. Then, later, he tried to mimic the sounds, the words. And his daddy's leg just kept moving in time with the music as he sang.

"*...You were always thereeee*

always the one for meeee..."

This was it. Time to ramp up to the chorus and really give her hell. If he was on *The Voice*, this was the part where some chairs would start turning. He was all up in his own head now, perfectly focused on his lyrics, the music, hitting the notes perfectly as he sang. The outside world was just shadows he could barely see through squinted eyes, pure emotion on his face, the stage lights hot on his skin, beads of sweat popping out on his brow. The distant noise of the crowd was just a faint rumble.

This was the moment. His whole life had been leading to this. Ever since that time in the garage when he'd heard the music, and his daddy had smiled—

God, one of the only times it felt like he'd smiled at Brance—

"*...Like a desert dream*

Like a teenage queeeeEEEN—*"

There was a rising scratch in the back of Brance's throat. It caught him halfway through "queen." Something happened, something bad, and he hit a different note, real different—

Someone screeched loud enough that Brance jerked. The whole room seemed to be shaking gently, and the lights at the base of the stage all blew out in a blast of glass and sparks as Brance's eyes jerked open. The speakers blew, too, and Brance stopped singing as the noise in the room swept over him like a wave after a dam broke.

"Ohmigod—"

"Aiiiiiiee! Make it *stop*!"

The cacophony was painful, pained. His eyes open, the stage lights shattered, he could see the crowd now.

That standing ovation he'd hoped for? Wasn't happening.

Every single person in the place was on the ground.

Clutching ears, clutching their heads. Only a very few eyes were even on him at all.

Brance just stared for a moment, dumbstruck, then realized the microphone was still in his hand. "Are...are you all right?" he asked, then realized his voice wasn't magnified at all. Oh, right, the speakers.

Then he glanced down at the mic.

The entire top of it looked like it had been shredded off by a metal grinder.

"What the...?" The mic stand that had been parked in front of him was missing its top, too, smoking as though someone had burned it like a candle wick.

"What the hell did you do, man?" someone shouted from the crowd.

"I...I don't know," Brance said, clammy feeling falling over him, sweat drenching his brow. He stared out over the darkened bar, wondering what he should say.

"You almost killed us!" a woman's voice screamed into the silence. Distantly, Brance could hear the noise of Broadway, the crowd. It sounded normal, like nothing had happened there. Nothing like what had happened here—

"I...sorry," Brance said, and tried to shove the shredded microphone into the ruined stand a couple times before realizing it was futile. Staring at the strange object, he finally just dropped the ruined thing, stepping off the stage.

"Who the hell are you?" a man asked from his knees. "Were you trying to kill us?"

"I...I was just trying to..." Brance stumbled past him, past the others. He made it out the door just as people were getting to their feet.

There was a strange silence in his head as he ran—surprisingly fast—down 2nd, old brick buildings blurring past as he hurried back to Broadway and lost himself in the crowd.

This wasn't how it was supposed to go tonight. This was supposed to be his chance, his shot.

This was supposed to be the beginning of his dream.

Then why, Brance wondered, as he threaded through the noisy crowd, a ringing in his ears like distant sirens, did it feel so much like *the end?*

Chapter 2

Sienna
New York City

This was not exactly the stuff my dreams were made of.

"Sienna Nealon, do you swear to tell the truth, the whole truth, and nothing but the truth, so help you God?"

I stared down at the bailiff from the witness box, my right hand raised. "I do." So help me, God.

"Ms. Nealon," said District Attorney Michaela Girard, a petite blond lady with her hair in a tight bun, face in a tight smile, patience on a tight leash—yes, everything about Michaela was tight. "Can you explain, for the jury, what you witnessed the night of September 27th of last year?"

I glanced over at the jury box, where sixteen New Yorkers stared at me with various poker faces only slightly less friendly than Michaela Girard's. Girard had coached me for this moment, and now all I had to do was not screw it up. I drew a short breath and let 'er rip.

"September 27th, sure. Surprisingly balmy evening. The AC in my apartment wasn't working, so I was adhering to everything like Spider-Woman." I paused, considering. "Spider-Lady? Whatever. You know the humidity is bad when I'm wearing a spaghetti strap top and sticking to the leather couch." Someone coughed in the gallery. "Anyhoo, I was listening to a police scanner, and a call came through for a domestic not too far from my apartment—"

"Can you clarify for the jury what a 'domestic' is?" Girard asked. Still tight. Woman was going to sprain something if she didn't loosen up soon.

"Sure," I said, trying to display none of the uncertainty I was feeling here in my first jury performance in quite some time. "Domestic dispute. It's what cops call it when people living together get into a squabble. It often involves physical violence." I mimed a gentle punch in the air. "Usually it's the dude doing the hitting. Sometimes it's the woman. Notice I didn't say 'lady,' cuz a real woman uses her mouth, not her fists, to express her displeasure." I realized what I'd said and flushed a little. "Which I guess means I would not be Spider-Lady, in fact. Shocking, I know. Maybe Spider-Bitch—"

Girard cleared her throat. "The, uh...domestic, if you please?"

"Right," I said. "I go to the address and I find the, ahem, defendant—" I shot a glance at the sandy-haired dude sitting behind the defense table with his lawyer, not deigning to look at me "—straddling his girlfriend, with his knuckles bloody and his lady's face sporting a series of bruises and cuts. I beat the cops to the scene by, oh, two minutes, probably? And I, uh...separated them...until the NYPD showed up."

Michaela Girard's entire body looked like it was

holding enough tension that somebody could have plucked her like a guitar string and made her produce a decent note. "I see." She wavered for a moment, clearly trying to decide how to approach that revelation. "And from there...?"

"I assisted the NYPD in taking the defendant into custody," I said, "and...that was pretty much that."

Girard nodded, not looking at me anymore. "And you are certain you saw the defendant, Mr. Ivanovich, hit his girlfriend Ms. Petruchoff?"

"Oh, yeah," I said. "He punched her twice that I personally witnessed after I broke the door down. Both times to the face."

"Thank you, Ms. Nealon," Girard said, and retreated to her seat. "No further questions."

There was only a moment of silence, and the defense attorney shot to his feet like his hamstrings were spring-loaded. "Ms. Nealon? Ernie Groves, attorney for the defense—"

"Glad you cleared that up for me," I said, "because I was really sure you were here representing the State of Ohio."

Groves blinked a couple times, brain not quite catching up with his mouth. "Why would the State of Ohio need to be represented in this courtroom?"

"I just assumed that no one would want to sit next to your sleazeball, woman-beating client," I said. "My bad, for drawing the wrong conclusion. Huge oopsie on my part."

"Ms. Nealon," Judge Henry Rohrbacher rumbled from the bench. Rohrbacher was a large black man who looked like his appetite for taking shit was really low, as though even flushing a toilet near the man after dropping one would fill his quotient enough to send him over the top. "Stick to the questions."

"Yes, Your Honor," I said, trying to appear chastened. A couple guffaws came from the jury.

"Ms. Nealon," Groves said, adopting a very earnest, curious look, like a puppy seeking out bacon, "did you kick down the defendant's door when you arrived at his apartment?"

"Damned right I did," I said. "I had probable cause to enter the apartment because I heard a beating going on."

Groves tried to talk over me, but I was speaking and reacting meta fast, so I got it all out before he managed to cut me off. It was funny to see the words pass him quicker than he could shut them down, and his face fell a little as he realized I'd actually sped up my speech. Not so much it was indecipherable, but definitely a quicker cadence. "Ah, uh," he stuttered. "Have you often kicked down doors at crime scenes?"

"Whenever I hear a beating going on, definitely."

Groves looked pained. "Objection, Your Honor. Speculation."

"If I may, Your Honor," I said, before Rohrbacher even got his mouth open to reply, "if it pleases the court, I submit that I may be one of the world's foremost experts on beatings, having dealt and received many, many more than the average person or law enforcement professional, and at an intensity that few could claim given my powers."

Judge Rohrbacher's eyes flashed as he considered that, then looked at Michaela Girard, who had apparently been about to interject when I'd made my own case. "Overruled," Rohrbacher decided. "The court recognizes Ms. Nealon is in fact an authority on...violent interactions."

"It's nice to be recognized for your expertise," I said

lightly, causing someone in the jury to snicker. "Especially when I've suffered so very much for my craft."

"Ahem." Groves shuffled over to his table and leafed through a notepad, a line of questioning he'd planned to engage apparently cut off at the knees. "Ms. Nealon." He came back up, looking right at me. "Perhaps you can describe for us the time you burned a man to death."

Michaela Girard looked like someone had smacked her with an aluminum bat. Even the jury was silent.

I pursed my lips, pretending to think about it. "You're going to have to be more specific."

Groves got a gleam in his eye. "Why, Ms. Nealon...are you saying you've burned more than one man to death?"

"Well, yeah," I said. "There was the guy who was going to blow up an LA neighborhood, killing all its inhabitants. There were several mercenaries who had guns pointed at me—"

Once again my rocket-mouth had made a fool of Groves, spitting out all that before he had a chance to pick and choose what he wanted to play with. "Wait—no—the —no—ah—"

"Or that one mercenary who—"

"Objection, Your Honor!" Groves sounded like he was about to cry. "She's talking too fast!"

"No, you're talking too slow, Groves," I shot back before Rohrbacher could even draw the breath to answer. "I mean, really. Shouldn't you have at least done the research on this burning thing so you knew which one you wanted to ask about? Sloppy."

"Sustained," Rohrbacher said, giving me plenty of side-eye. Which I acknowledged, barely, out of the corner of my own. "Ms. Nealon, you are talking awfully fast."

"There's just so much ground to cover," I said, trying to sound innocent. "I like to be efficient. Also, I miss flying, so I try to replicate the sensation verbally from time to time. It's fun. Nice breeze."

Groves just stared at me, and a little hint of frustration vanished as he pulled out what I'm sure he thought was a winning smile. "How many people have you murdered, Ms. Nealon?"

I blinked, thinking it over. "None."

Groves's eyes popped wide. "None?"

"Yes," I said.

"Perhaps you'd care to explain your accounting on that reply," Judge Rohrbacher said, leaning toward me from the bench. "Because I don't think I believe 'none.'"

"Pretty simple accounting," I said. "He said 'murdered.' 'Murder' implies innocence of the victim. I have never killed an innocent person. The only people I've ever employed lethal force on are people that have in fact employed it themselves or were threatening to do so. Ergo, no murder." I shrugged.

Groves was trying to reply fast, but he just couldn't keep up. "Your Honor, this is not a good faith reply—"

"Ms. Nealon." Judge Rohrbacher wasn't even waiting for Groves to object. "Please answer the question without the semantic games."

Groves stopped mid-sentence and smiled, looking right at me. It was a look I was well familiar with by now; the look of a hawk about to swoop on a mouse. If self-satisfaction was electric energy, the man could have powered the whole of Manhattan for a couple years. Too bad he was mostly gas-powered instead of wind.

"I..." I tried to formulate a reply but failed. My brain locked, and I worked on my answer. There wasn't going to be a good one, not here, not with this question. Mostly because I didn't actually *know* how many people I'd killed over the years. "Uhm...I...ahhh..." And so I turned into a stammering mess, looking like I was doing the arithmetic right there. Which I was not, because there was no way for me to calculate this answer on the spot.

I looked at Judge Rohrbacher. There was not an inch of give in the man's eyes. I looked at Girard. Her gaze was on a notepad in her lap, probably trying to figure out the next move after this humbling bomb of a question blew up her key witness.

Groves was all triumph. Seriously, if I could have punched him right then, my uncountable murder number would definitely have gone up by one. Maybe two, because I wanted to hit him so hard his client—the nearest person to him and also a scumbag—would die from the concussive force of the impact.

Which brought my gaze around to Mr. Ivanovich. Who did not look back at me because, well...

When I'd found him battering his girlfriend, I'd hit him twice. Enough to stop him, I'd told the NYPD officers at the scene. Which was true.

It was also hard enough that I'd blinded him permanently from the impact of my fist to his skull. Oh, he wasn't brain damaged, exactly; he could still speak and think just as he had before. But I'd hit him so hard the fluid concussion in his brain had torn his optic nerves. And he'd been lucky I hadn't done worse, because seeing the state of his girlfriend had put me in an immediate killing mood.

"Uhh..." I said. "Uhhh." There was no answer to this.

No way out.

Except...

Footsteps in the hall outside the courtroom sounded through the quiet of the silent jury, attorneys, judge, court reporter and a pathetic shell of a defendant. I could even hear them over the steady rhythm of my own guilty heart.

The doors burst open and a winded cop in NYPD

blues was standing there, radio mic in hand, breathless, but managing to cough a few words out as he looked right at me in an utter panic.

"Hostage situation. Midtown. Biridelli Theater." He pointed out the door.

The silence of the courtroom hung for just another moment. "Sorry," I said, speaking up before anyone else could. "Call of duty."

"Ms. Nealon—" Judge Rohrbacher straightened.

But I'd already vaulted out of the witness box and was sprinting toward the open door, hurdling over the railing without waiting for the judge's reply. I was out the door in a hot second as the courtroom behind me dissolved into a wash of chaos at my exit.

Chapter 3

Reed
Eden Prairie, Minnesota

"Just bottom line it for me," I said, rubbing my temples. I sat at my desk, Miranda Estevez across from me and another, almost as familiar face staring back from next to her.

"You're still deeply broke," Ariadne Fraser said, her red hair catching the room's dim fluorescent light and magnifying it somehow. She didn't show any grey, and her only wrinkles were hints of crow's feet around her eyes. She slid the packet of papers in her hands around and slapped them onto the desk in front of me. "More broke than ever, in fact."

I stared at the indecipherable numbers printed on the spreadsheet she'd just slapped on the desk blotter. There were a lot of zeroes in there, ones with no numeral in front of them. I couldn't help it; I broke out in an impish smile. "Probably doesn't help that I had to hire you as a consultant just to tell me that, does it?"

She shook her head, no hint of amusement in her bearing. "Miranda could have told you for cheaper."

"Not for much longer, I can't," Miranda said, shaking her head. "In-house counsel is the next cut you're making."

"Then who's going to tell me which laws I can freely break and how much destruction and mayhem I can cause before trouble comes my way?" I asked, trying to hide that sinking feeling in my guts by making jokes. Of course, I often made jokes when I didn't have that sinking feeling, but here they seemed to take on a particular poignancy, in much the same way my ship was apparently taking on water.

"I suggest you consult an attorney on an as-needed basis," Ariadne said. "Looking at these numbers, there's a considerable amount of bloat still weighing you down. I mean, your office expense seems ridiculously high for what you're getting..."

I shrugged. "Rent gets higher when they find out you've blown up your last, uh...several...locations. And that insurance doesn't necessarily cover the damages."

"Be that as it may," Ariadne said, "personnel is your biggest expense. Payroll, I mean. If you want to remain afloat—"

"Well, I don't want to sink."

"We need to cut some more people," Miranda said, and boy, did that take the air out of the room. Not literally, because that was something I did, but...close. "Starting with me."

"Miranda..." I said, slumping my shoulders. "I don't want to—"

"Forget it," she said, making a cutting gesture at shoulder-level. "I'll be fine, okay? I came from a high-priced firm, only took this job because your sister needed someone she could trust to handle the start-up phase until you came on board." She smiled thinly. "Well, you're on board now. And you really don't need me all that much, at least on an ongoing basis. I'll head back to a law firm that'll pay me twice as much, and you can call me if you need something, okay?" Her expression darkened. "As long as it's not an everyday thing."

"What if we got a ton of business tomorrow?" I asked, trying to seize a thin hope. "I mean, these things always seem to come in gluts—"

"Doesn't matter," Miranda said, shaking her head. "The work you do, it takes sixty days before most of your clientele—the government agencies, state and local—pay out. You're already this far behind—" Ariadne obligingly leaned forward, flipped to a page and showed me a number that made me feel a little sicker "—and even if you got five jobs today—"

"I won't be able to make payroll this month," I said, cold, hard, brutal truth kicking its way through at last. "Or next."

"You got it," Ariadne said, and a tight smile flashed on her lips, wan and pitying. "You'd struggle to survive this year even if you manage to pick up five jobs a month between now and December."

"Which is a near-impossible pace lately, especially given how few people I'm going to be left with," I said, mouth drying out. "Damn." I let my hand drop to my side and stared out into the bullpen. "We're cooked."

"It's an unenviable position," Miranda said.

"Which is why you're bailing out?" I asked, a little coy.

She gave me a faint smile. "These are the perils of being the boss. You get all the glory when things go right and you also get the kick to the teeth when things go wrong."

I let out a low, whistling sigh. "Well, Miranda...thanks for—"

"You haven't seen the last of me, Reed," she said, rising. "I'll be back to help over the next couple weeks as you wind things down. I have my feelers out on a job back in Houston, so I won't be here forever, but..." She glanced down at the sheet in front of me. "Angel is still on there. She'll stay at half pay. She's right on the borderline of what Ariadne and I deemed 'essential' personnel." Her lips became a thin line. "I've hinted to her what's going on, because I suck at keeping secrets from her. I mean, she's basically like a sister to me, so..."

"I'll keep her if she's okay working for that," I said, looking at the line next to her name.

"It's still more than she'd make at just about any other job short of running a massively successful restaurant," Miranda said. "And she likes the work."

I nodded slowly. "Well...okay then."

"Okay then," Miranda said, and went for the door to my office. "See you tomorrow." And she was gone.

I stared at the sheaf of papers on my desk, deciding whether I wanted to flip any farther in the stack. "These cuts, Ariadne, they're..." I looked up at the older lady in front of me. "Scott and Kat are already working for free. Eilish and Olivia aren't doing much better. How am I supposed to break it to Augustus and Jamal—"

Ariadne nodded. "Sorry to be the bearer of bad news. But this is why you hired me."

"Yeah," I said, pushing at my hairline, as though massaging my scalp would make this headache—or this catastrophe—go away. "And it wasn't to nod and tell me I had no money problems."

"Good," she said, "because you have a heaping pile of money problems." She glanced toward the door. The offices were pretty quiet; Augustus and Jamal were home in Atlanta, Eilish had gone home for the night. Kat was in LA. The only people I could see out in the bullpen were Angel, and Olivia Brackett. "I know this is probably disappointing for you—"

"Yeah," I said, my thoughts stirred back to the people who worked for me. Scott Byerly popped his head up in the distance, and I heard him say something that prompted a round of laughter from those in the bullpen, but hell if I could hear it over the throbbing in my skull. "I mean, cutting Casey is fine. We don't really need a receptionist. But J.J.? Abby?" I gave her a pained look. "J.J.'s been with us forever. You know that, Ariadne."

She had some tightness in her jaw area, and I wondered if she did, in fact, remember that. She nodded, though, which told me she probably did.

"Excuse me, sir—sir—" The voice of Casey, the receptionist, carried down the hall and into the bullpen, causing me to sit up straight in my chair. "You can't go back there—"

"Don't worry, darlin', it's fine; I'm a friend of the family," came a deep voice. A man appeared at the far end of the bullpen, his stride confident and unerring. He didn't even hesitate or miss a step as he came into view, navigating through the place like he'd been here a thousand times before, even though—to my knowledge—he'd never even been here once.

"Did he just call Casey 'darlin'?" Angel asked under her breath.

"Who is this guy?" Olivia asked, on her feet. The air distorted slightly around her as she prepared to do...well, whatever it was she did to move things around her.

"Hey," Scott called after him, popping up from his cube, "you can't come back here."

"Hold your seahorses, Scotty," the man said, waving him off with a hand. That made Scott do a double take, then sag as he recognized the man making his way to my office as unerringly as if shot out of a cannon.

I rose, leaving my seat behind me. An unintentional pucker came to my lips, that sour taste like I'd gotten a bite of something really unpleasant.

Because seeing this guy here, right now? Probably wasn't going to result in anything good.

"Reed," he said, stopping a few feet from me. "Got a problem."

"I kinda figured it wasn't a social call when I saw you come in here for the first time in...ever," I said, looking him over. He seemed a lot more put-together than the last time I'd seen him, which had been in South Dakota, almost three years prior. "Team," I said, nodding to Olivia and Angel, who did not look remotely like they were ready to stand down, "I'd like you to meet Harry Graves." Blank looks greeted me, except for Scott, who had a faint burning behind his eyes. "You know...Sienna's boyfriend."

Chapter 4

Sienna

"Tell me what we've got, Welch," I said as I popped out of the NYPD cruiser outside the Biridelli Theater, just off Broadway. It looked like a classic movie house, complete with a red carpet stretched up to the front door. It was like Grauman's Chinese Theater, but with a more New York sentiment about the place. I might have liked it if I wasn't finding it at the worst of times.

Captain Allyn Welch of the NYPD stood behind a squad car that was parked on the curb. A waiting police cruiser had ferried me from the courthouse right to the theater, like Uber but with a police siren and lights to get me where I was going in a double hurry. Welch was an aging man, complete with a combover, his uniform the dress blues of New York's Finest. He surveyed me with squinty eyes that emphasized his crow's feet, as though daring to ask me why I was late to this party. "Hostage situation. We think it's actually a meta this time."

"Oh, actually *actually* a meta this time?" I asked, stepping up behind the police cruiser with him. "Not one of your fake meta calls designed to give me an excuse to intervene and solve all your problems for you?"

He shook his head, all serious. "Not one of the fakes, no. Or as I like to think of them, Metahuman Pretense Situations."

"That's too unwieldy. It'll never catch on."

He pointed at the ruins of some cell phones scattered around the red carpet, and at a limo that was turned over down the street. "We think the guy did that."

"And you're sure it's a guy?" I surveyed the damage with a wary eye, then looked down at my shoes. Steel-toed boots, the perfect fashion accompaniment for Sienna Nealon, ass-kicker to the stars. Excellent for almost all occasions.

"Not sure of much at this point," Welch said, gesturing at the scattershot cordon around the place. Only a half-dozen units had responded, which told me that they'd called me in right away, before they'd even had a chance to bring in overwhelming force and really seal this place off. "The theater was hosting the world premiere of a new movie. *Everybody Goes to the Valley* or something like that. Anna Vargas is the star." He looked down at me. "You know who she is?"

"Yeah, I went to one of her parties out in LA one time," I said, bending over to untie my boots. "Met the President. Got in a fight with a guy who could phase in and out of reality. It was a real hoot."

"Ha ha," Welch said without mirth. "Everything's always a joke with you—what the hell are you doing?"

I kicked off my shoes without booting them into the next county. "I'm not joking," I said, slightly nonplussed as I undid my belt and started shimmying out of it, careful not to drop my gun. Once I'd removed the pistol from the belt, I handed both to him without ceremony.

Welch took my pistol, holster and belt from me, eyes wide as I piled them onto his arms. "Seriously, what gives?"

I promptly added my cell phone and backup gun to the pile. "Getting rid of all the metal on my body." I nodded at the overturned limo, then the busted cell phones abandoned just off the red carpet. "See those?"

Welch's eyes looked like they were about to pop out of his head. The sergeant behind him had his gun drawn and was pointing it over the trunk of the squad car we were standing behind, but he was craning his head, probably to see if I was going to complete my little undressing game. I did, reaching to the back of my shirt and fumbling with the clasp of my bra beneath it.

"The hell, Nealon?" Welch hissed again. He looked like he was going to pop a vein in his forehead.

"Don't get all hot and bothered. It's a Magneto," I said, just tearing the damned strap off and pulling my blouse back down so I didn't flash the whole street. I slipped each arm in and finished removing the bra before I popped them back out, catching it in my hand and brandishing it in front of me before adding it to Welch's pile. "Underwire is metal and I don't want to get squeezed to death while I'm dodging whatever else he throws at me."

Welch's brow subsided a little as I tossed my cell phone and keys into his mounting pile and he struggled to keep from dropping all my stuff. "You could have just said that."

"I'm not a great sharer." I turned toward the theater, giving it a quick once-over. "How many hostages?"

"Lucky for you I am a great sharer," Welch muttered. "We don't have an exact count—"

"Then it really doesn't matter whether you're sharing or not, does it?"

"But it's in the fifty to a hundred range," Welch said, getting the other officer to open the car door for him so he could dump all my personal effects into the cruiser's seat. "The premiere wasn't scheduled to start for another few minutes, so the theater wasn't full yet. The big stars have already showed up, though."

I patted myself down, looking for any other points of metal. My blouse buttons were plastic, and thankfully I'd worn dress pants for court, complete with—to my shock— a button fly instead of a zipper. Small miracles, but this was what happened when I managed to shed my denim habit. "Okay," I said, thinking it through. "I'm going in." I beckoned to the cop behind Welch. "Nightstick? Is it metal?"

He shook his head and pulled it off his belt, tossing it to me. I turned and looked at another cop, who sighed and tossed me his as well. I brandished both and spun them; they were of the baton variety, complete with a handle sticking out at a right angle. The smooth, heavy industrial polymer was cool to the touch. The February air had a nice little chill to it, and I looked down. "Okay, I need to get this done quickly."

Welch nodded. "Right. There are people's lives on the line."

"Yeah, that," I agreed, turning my back as I headed for the door, "but also, it's cold and I'm no longer wearing a bra. Do the math on that."

"But...also the people's lives, right?" Welch called after me.

"Always," I muttered, waving one of my newly borrowed batons. "Always with the people's lives." And in I went.

Chapter 5

The Biridelli Theater lobby looked like it had been ransacked by a very angry poltergeist. The popcorn machines were overturned, the Slurpee maker was squirting neon blue out of a perforated plastic spinner and making an unhealthy grinding noise. It hit a pitch that made me cringe as I came in.

Ushers in tuxes were cowering along the sides of the room, a counterpoint to the well-dressed attendees. All were hiding, squatting behind potted ferns and under the popcorn buttering stations. I met the timid gaze of one of them as she stared at me, clad in a formal dress that had been split all the way up to the ass. "Which way?" I asked.

She pointed toward a door in the distance. There was some noise from within, but I couldn't decipher it over the rumble of the sick Slurpee machine.

"Get out," I said, jerking my head toward the door and surveying the room. There was a sudden motion as someone dashed for the exit, followed by a few others. I looked at the woman who'd cued me in. "Go."

She must have taken some courage from my invocation, because this time she ran, ass hanging out in the breeze like she'd had underwire in it that the Magneto had removed with his mind. Or maybe she'd just gone commando, which seemed like a bad choice given that dress, but hey. Starlet fashion choices: where you pay obscene amounts of money for barely enough cloth to cover your important bits, if that.

A quick glance around the lobby found I'd cleared the innocent bystanders here. The noise from within the darkened theater door was increasing, which was my cue to get moving. I had a real gut-churning feeling about this, and not only because I'd disarmed myself down to the damned bra before coming in here.

What the hell was I supposed to do when I got dragged back to that courtroom and had to answer the question about how many people I'd killed?

Also, I was about to face a master of the magnetic arts with nothing but a couple batons. But seriously, that wasn't as vexing as figuring out how to answer the question, "How many people have you killed, Sienna Nealon?" without sounding like a complete and total psychopath. "Only as many as deserved it," was not a valid answer.

There was no point pouting about it, though, and even less point in ignoring the fact I really had to get moving if I wanted to save the day. I charged into the darkness of the waiting theater and burst out at the bottom of a stadium seating arrangement. The place was about a quarter full, and all with people who were entirely too well-dressed to be anything other than brief guest stars in my working-class life.

Except for the one guy who was hovering ten feet in the air on a metal platform. He was wearing a cheap suit and wingtips with a haircut that screamed that he bought discount dandruff shampoo in five-gallon refill tubs.

"'Come live with me and be my love,'" he said, over the screaming of several women in the crowd, "'and we will all the pleasures prove'—"

He had a hand extended to a woman lurking below with a look on her face that could only be described as "horrified." Or possibly "gastrointestinal distress-y." Her long hair was perfectly coiffed, and her gown sparkled in a very classical style that made me wonder if her designer had made the entire thing out of diamonds. Even in the soft glow of the emergency exit lights, she was stunning.

Also, she was Anna Vargas.

"Hey, Marlowe," I said, twirling a baton and chucking it for the Magneto's head. "I don't think the lady's interested. Maybe thou shouldst learn to love the word 'no.'"

Our poet non-laureate (and also plagiarist) whirled on me, blocking my thrown baton with a hastily constructed shield made out of...

Little steel ball bearings?

"Oh, man," I grumbled under my breath, getting a bad feeling about the way this was going to go based on my foe's preparedness. He was standing on the equivalent power of a human claymore mine.

And he let it off at me, steel bullets spraying at me like a blast of shrapnel.

Chapter 6

Reed

"What the hell are you doing here, Harry?" I asked, staring out the window at the sun-dappled parking lot. Sunset was nearly here, and the snow that covered it was reflecting the glare. The heat was pumping from the vent above my desk, though it was nothing compared to the warm sense of annoyance I felt from sitting across from Harry Graves.

"It's a pleasure to see you too, Reed," Harry said, shifting in his seat and looking to either side like Olivia or Angel might come busting down the door to my office any second to "rescue" me from him. He did have predictive powers, though, so maybe they were going to do just that. "Especially with your wits about you again. Didn't like seeing you under the control of Harmon last time we met. That had to be rough, losing your senses like that."

"Yeah, it's just been a barrel of fun since I got them back," I said. I suppressed the twitch that threatened the corner of my eye; conversations with Harry had a tendency to go like that in my (albeit limited) experience with him. "Why are you here?"

"Well, there's a crisis, of course," he said. Like that answered everything.

"There's always a crisis," I said.

"Yeah," he said. "This is one you're going to need to get involved in."

I felt a laugh that was very lacking in mirth spring out. Forced, really. "Do you remember the first time we met?"

"Hard to forget."

"You killed a man," I said. "In cold blood."

"I was trying to save the world from a very bad man," Harry said, shrugging lightly, like it was no big deal. "I'd think you, of all people, would understand that."

"You and my sister really are a well-matched pair, aren't you?" I couldn't keep the annoyed grin off my face. "Kill anyone who threatens the status quo. I mean, you two just hold hands whistling right through the graveyard and leave the rest of us to clean up the mess—"

"Don't pretend you're that mad at her—"

"I'm mad at *you*, Harry," I said with a strange loathing, taking my voice meta-low to interfere with any bugs that might have been planted in my office. I'd had Jamal sweep it before he left, but that didn't mean someone hadn't planted one since then. "All this shit? Her working for the FBI? This whole godforsaken year?" I waved a hand. "This is you. I know it's you."

Harry made a show of examining his fingernails, then gnawed on one of them. He must have seen—or anticipated—me making a face, because he said, "Come on, we're metas. Germs don't affect us in the slightest."

"I don't see you drinking out of toilets to prove that point."

"Might have happened in the past," Harry said, examining the nail he'd just bitten off. "I've hit a low time or two. But that's neither here nor there." He stood, reached into his coat, and pulled out a newspaper clipping. "I'll leave this with you." And he let it flutter down on my desk. Aided by the vent above, it landed squarely, perfectly in front of me.

TENSIONS RISE AS LABOR DISPUTE UNLEASHES PASSIONS

"You son of a—" I stared at the clipping.

"Keep in mind my mom works for you," Harry said. He was already at the door.

I snatched up the clipping and stormed after him. "You cannot be serious," I called across the bullpen.

"Serious as you when arguing a civil libertarian position," Harry called back without turning.

I raised the clipping. "This is an article about a labor dispute."

"Keep reading." He disappeared down the hallway.

"Why would I—" I focused in on the second paragraph.

Oh.

...flooding at the warehouse, which is not anywhere near a flood plain, lends speculation that metahuman activity may be involved...

"You...utter and complete asshat," I muttered. The door thumped closed in the distance. Harry had already left.

I frowned, staring at the wrinkled newsprint. Why the hell had he given this to me?

Chapter 7

Sienna

A last-minute dive saved me from getting splattered by a shotgun blast of ball bearings as I sailed behind the cover of the first row of seats in the movie theater. I rolled end over end behind the concealment that the seats offered, ball bearings shredding through the wood and fabric behind me, and I didn't stop until I reached the end of the row.

"Leave me alone!" the Magneto screamed. "I just...I need her!"

"Aww, man," I muttered under my breath. "Obsessed fan, aisle two." Raising my voice, I called out to him. "Hey, I'm not looking for a fight here, but do you care at all what Anna thinks?"

"She doesn't know me yet," he called back, clearly social enough he felt he had to explain himself. That was good; if he'd been disconnected long enough to just write me off, he'd have grabbed her and been gone. While this storm of metal was not the greatest sign, like, say, him surrendering outright would be, it was a hint that he wasn't completely gone 'round the bend yet. Just mostly. "She needs a chance to know me. The real me."

"I don't want to know you, creeper!" Anna shouted, oh-so-helpfully. "You're a freak!"

"You...you don't know that," the creeper said, and the ball bearings disappeared, leaping from where they'd lodged in the floor and seats behind me. They arced up and toward Creeper, and I wondered what he was up to. "I need time—"

"Dude, this is not good," I called to him. "Come on. We're talking kidnapping here. Let's walk it back. There have to be better alternatives. Like, y'know, Tinder. That'd be a safer...ish...starting point in a companionship search than snatching up Anna Vargas and taking her to your love bunker or whatever, trying to trigger Stockholm Syndrome." I moved a little to the side, hoping if he decided to launch another blast at me, he'd do so where I'd just been speaking from. I clutched my remaining baton tightly.

"She'll see," Creeper said confidently. "I just need to give her a chance to see."

A hammering sound like a rock drill assailed my ears, but I didn't dare peek over the seats keeping me separated from Creeper. Besides, I knew to a ninety-nine percent certainty what he was doing, anyway.

He was using the ball bearings to chip away at the floor, hurling them with all his power into the ground. It was having roughly the same effect as a grinding drill bit, chipping away at the carpet, then the concrete sub-floor.

He was boring an escape tunnel out of the theater so he didn't have to go out through the cops. Which was either smart or cowardly, and judging by the fact he wasn't trying to pursue and destroy me, I had a guess it was a little bit of both.

"Come on, dude," I shouted, looking for any kind of help from the rows of seats above me. These Hollywood superstars were hiding like they were bugs trying to escape the exterminator. Smart, but not helpful. "My kingdom for a Steven Clayton among you assholes," I said under my breath. Steven Clayton was a Hollywood heartthrob but also a real action hero who'd helped me in the past. It'd have been too much to hope that he'd have been invited to this premiere.

"Just let us go!" Creeper called, and Anna Vargas screamed from somewhere near him. I guessed he had her bound up somehow, supervillain style. Probably gave her a belt of ball bearings and was hauling her along like a proper abductee. "I don't want any trouble!" There was a hint of pleading from him, one that bypassed my cold heart and made me feel a spark of sadness for Creeper. Dude had problems in the head. Needed a therapist.

Unfortunately, I was not a therapist.

I was the bullet sent to dispatch the problems no one else could seem to.

"You know we can't do that," I called back. "You're taking someone who doesn't want to go with you—"

"She doesn't know me yet!" Creeper shouted. "When she does, she'll love me!"

"That's really not how this works," I called back. "Please. This can't sound normal to you."

"Our love defies the bounds of normal!" Creeper screamed, definitely rounding the bend between sanity and insanity, if he hadn't already crossed over. "No one understands us!"

I cringed. This was not going anywhere good. "Please —" I started to say.

I was interrupted by ball bearings smashing through the seats around me, and I rolled again until I fell out into the aisle on the far side of the theater and almost tumbled down the steps to the floor level. Catching myself before I did, I looked up just in time to see the last of the ball bearings arcing into the air and retreating down into a hole in the floor the size of a municipal bus.

Cracking my neck from the constant rolling and its impingement on my spine, I slowly inched up to the gaping hole in the floor. Darkness waited below, and at its bottom, I could see train tracks.

The subway.

I let a brief noise of impatience, and the sound of Anna Vargas's screams echoed up to me from somewhere down the tunnel.

"Tally ho," I said, and down I went, into the darkness, chasing the Creeper and the starlet.

Chapter 8

The New York City subway was probably the least comfortable place I could imagine on the island of Manhattan, with the possible exception of Marina Abramovic's dinner table. The mechanical rattle of a train somewhere in the distance set me on edge, and the darkness was broken only by the faint light seeping in from the hole above and a dim glow somewhere in front of me.

I listened and heard a high-pitched grunt; Anna Vargas was struggling against her captor, but I doubted with much efficacy. I had my doubts about how well this would come out for her if she fought him too much, but I hadn't had time in our brief exchange of words to really delve into Creeper's psyche. My initial impression: he was nuts. Obsessed. Normal, well-adjusted people didn't use their superpowers to kidnap their celebrity crush during a movie premiere, after all, dragging them into the darkness of the underground afterward.

But hey, Phantom of the Opera here didn't play by the normal rules.

I sprinted along the center of the track, keeping an eye

out for the third rail in the little light I had. Getting zapped to death would put an end to my mission rather abruptly, and I didn't need that. Running with my shoes off (again) was forcing me to slow down and be a little more careful, especially given the ground was cluttered with debris. The last thing I needed was to catch a stray needle or stub my toe at superhuman speed and accidentally tear it off in the process.

"Stop following us!" Creeper screamed in the distance. He was waaaaaay out there, and I heard something whistling through the dark.

I dove for the ground and ball bearings smacked into the concrete and rails behind me, making an awful racket that rang through the tunnels like metallic thunder.

"Why won't you leave us in peace?" Creeper cried. He really did sound like he was on the edge.

"Do you know who I am?" I called, then leapt up and bounced off the nearest wall, vaulting into a sideways run then flipping against the opposite wall for a few steps before vaulting back. It was very *Matrix*-y, wall-running. Running on the ground down a small tunnel with the enemy in front of me was going to be dangerous—and predictable. Time to use my super strength and speed to defy conventions. And hopefully keep from catching a shotgun blast of ball bearings from turning me into a metahuman smoothie. "Peace isn't really in my repertoire. Not when someone's kidnapping."

"She just needs time to see who I am so she can love me!" Creeper shouted. His voice sounded a little rattle-y, but not just from the emotion. There was a distant light glowing in the tunnel past him, slowly getting brighter. Not a single source, like a bulb, but a glow like a...

A station. There was a station somewhere ahead.

But the noise? It wasn't just his voice. It almost went

over his voice, made him harder to understand. There was an echo that persisted even after he finished shouting too, like—

"Motherf—" I Samuel L. Jackson'd.

Light was refracting off the concrete walls around me, coming from behind.

A subway train was only a hundred yards back, and closing on me fast, as though it neither saw me nor cared that I was blazing down the damned tunnel trying to rescue Anna Vargas.

And in another few seconds, it was going to hit me.

Chapter 9

Reed

"This is the thing that drives me nuts about these future-seers and telepaths," I vented, loudly, pacing across my living room, a cushion of air beneath my feet for reassurance. "They never tell you the whole story." I was gesticulating wildly with my hands. "So Harry Graves shows up and just dumps this on me—" I flung the clipping he'd left with me toward Isabella in a twirl of wind, a little tornado of the sort I used to stir her hair when I was feeling mischievous "—and I'm supposed to...what? Take his word for it that I need to go to Murfreesboro, Tennessee and intervene in some penny ante labor dispute?"

Isabella Perugini was a woman who was all about the no-bullshit lifestyle. Somehow, too, she was all about me. How those two radically different forces reconciled, I had no clue. She was paging through a magazine while listening to me, and I knew from long experience she was paying very close attention to my every irritable utterance.

"Then don't go," she said simply, turning to the next page.

"Ah ha, but maybe that's what he actually wants me to do," I said, twisting my brain in another knot trying to figure out why Harry had inflicted this stupid directive on me. "He's not a normal guy, you know. Maybe he's playing three-dimensional chess—"

"Or maybe he told you what he needs you to know and anticipates you'll be a good guy and go intervene in the problem," Isabella said. So simple. So matter-of-fact.

So trusting.

I narrowed my eyes. "Or maybe that's what he wants me to think."

This made her pause, narrow her own beautiful, brown eyes, and look up at me quizzically. "But that's not what you think. You think he's working some scam on you."

"Because he's tricky that way," I said, popping off my air lift and slipping onto the couch next to her. "See, you don't know Harry. Hell, I don't really know him, except to know that I don't *like* what I know of him."

Isabella shrugged. "Sienna trusts him, plainly."

"Sienna has legendarily bad taste in men and they often betray her," I said. "Women too, actually. And you don't even like her, so I'm not sure why you're taking her side on this one—"

"I'm taking my own side on this one," Isabella said, flipping to the next page. I realized at last this was a fashion magazine she was looking at, and the article she was paging through was *27 Hot Looks for Spring!* Which was funny, because it was February and Minnesota, which meant spring was a good eight hundred months away by my reckoning and would only last two days before we were straight into the one day of summer and two days of fall before winter's ominous, reckoning return. "I don't need to listen to you sit and get spun up about this all night. You're chasing your own tail."

"I don't actually have a tail, and I don't think you're taking this seriously enough."

She closed her magazine with great ceremony, placing her hands in her lap for a moment before reaching out and grabbing one of mine, holding it very earnestly as she looked me in the eyes. "So you're worried your sister's boyfriend is trying to manipulate you into a mission that will be too dangerous for you?"

"Right," I said. Then paused. "Well, sort of. Maybe. I—"

"Mm, this is well thought out, I see."

"I'm really just concerned that there is something going on in his thinking that will be of negative repercussions for me," I said, trying to boil it down.

"Because you don't trust him."

"Right," I said. "He's asking me to do this Tennessee thing as a leap of faith."

"But you don't have faith," Isabella said, still staring right in my eyes.

"Exactly." I snapped my fingers at her. "I am faithless. Especially as pertains to Harry Graves."

"Well, it seems like your decision is made, then," she said, and patted my hand a couple times before letting it loose so she could pick up her magazine and get back to paging through the spring looks she'd get to wear in four to six years when that season came here to us.

I watched her study the magazine with great interest for a few moments, stewing in my own juices, before I finally burst out with, "But is it *really*?"

She slumped, head bowing in defeat as she cast aside her magazine again and turned to me with her *very serious* look, the one she put on right before delivering bad news to a patient or telling me that no, tonight intimacy was definitely not going to happen, before hitting me with her reasoning for said decision. "Reed. I love you, *mi amore*. I trust you, *si*?"

"Well, yeah," I said. "I hope so."

"I trust you because you have shown to be the kind of man I can respect." She landed one hand on each of my cheeks and I felt suddenly self-conscious that my five o'clock shadow was probably a little rough on her smooth, sweet-smelling hands. "You try so hard to make these things work, even when they are not working."

"Did you just bring this around to the agency?" I asked. Where the hell was she going with this?

She nodded. "It is a very determined approach you take. And I respect you for it. It endears me to you. It— and many other things in our history—make me trust you, yes? Because you are an honest man. Very forthright. And you trust the people that you are close to."

"Thanks. I think?"

"But I feel that you are going to drive me absolutely nuts with this business about your sister's boyfriend," Isabella said, still looking at me very seriously. "You don't trust him, fine. Decide not to trust him and be on about your business of trying to save the business, yes? Or decide to give him a shot and see if this Murveesburro—"

"Murfreesboro."

"Whatever. See if this thing is a real thing for you to deal with," she said. "Because this is, to my estimation, his first 'reach-out' to you." Her face was so very earnest, eyebrows all in a cute little V line. "He must know you don't know each other, really. He must know you are not a trusting person when it comes to strangers—"

"Or people I view as jerking my sister around for

strange and non-obvious reasons," I muttered under my breath.

"Exactly," she said, clapping me on the cheek. Her mother did the same thing when we met, and I found it a little patronizing coming from her. Isabella, thankfully, deployed it usually under much more pleasant and intimate circumstances, so she got some leeway on that whole condescension judgment. "You have suspicions. That's a fine thing. You should go into everything with your eyes wide open. But you should make a decision on whether you will try trusting Harry or not. And if the answer is not—"

I sighed, loudly enough to interrupt her. "I don't want to trust Harry."

"That much is obvious."

"This is not how I anticipated things would go when my sister finally got out from under the damned accusations against her," I said, vaulting out of her grasp and back to pacing. "She was supposed to come *home*. She was supposed to start running this damned agency instead of leaving me holding the freaking bag—"

"It is a heavy bag," Isabella agreed. "Like a Gucci filled with many medical texts."

"I'm watching it sink every day," I whispered, looking at her with this stark horror, afraid to even speak it very loudly. "I'm not sure I'm going to have anything to hand her when she gets back. And then Harry comes along with his damned warnings—"

Isabella waved me off. "She trusts him."

"I don't," I said, pausing, floating on air.

"Is it because you don't trust anyone?" she asked quietly. "Or because you don't like the message he gave her?"

I sighed again, deeper, and slumped 'til I was bent nearly double. "Can't it be both?"

She rose and came to me, put a light hand around my shoulders and pulled me gently from the air. I dispelled the gusts and let her wrap me in her arms, chin on my shoulder.

"It is very difficult to watch a dream die," she said, fingers threading through my hair. "Even worse when it's not your dream, but one you're watching for someone else."

"Sienna," I said, a little choked. "I wanted this to work for her. So she could get free of the damned government. But if she gets out and we're not even standing anymore by the time she does—"

"Shhhhh," Isabella said. "You are worrying too much."

"I'm not sure that's possible," I said, my fingers holding tight to her waist, her shoulders. She felt so good, so smooth. When she breathed I smelled the Lindor truffle she'd snuck before dinner on her breath. Dark chocolate and orange. My favorite.

"You will do the right thing," she said, and that was it. She just held me close for a while as we stood in the living room.

And I knew what that right thing was.

I was heading for Tennessee.

Chapter 10

Sienna

"The light at the end of the tunnel is a train," I muttered as the subway train thundered ever closer behind me.

Ahead was a kidnapper and his starlet kidnappee, not bound by the laws of gravity and probably slipping away— floating away? Flying away? By the second.

Behind me was death, chewing up the distance between us quite handily, moving at about twice the speed I could manage on foot.

The answer seemed obvious.

When the train was twenty yards behind me, I jumped forward as hard as I could. I was relying on my limited knowledge of physics, a study I had not really made in earnest since the day I'd busted out of my house into the dead cold of a Minnesota winter.

Fortunately, I'd done quite a lot of practical physics work since then, and I had a feeling this would work.

Or a hope. Probably a hope.

The train caught me mid-leap, my speed a little over half of its own. I slammed into the front window like a bug and hung there, grabbing a metal ridge in the front with one hand and catching the top with the other. My face was plastered on the windshield, staring in at the driver, who stared back at me with wide eyes and a jaw that was about ready to touch the ground.

I saw her shake out of her stunned reverie and start to reach for the gearshift to stop the train, but I smacked the spiderwebbed window with a palm and shouted, at the top of my lungs, "Don't slow down!"

She stopped, hand halfway to the gearshift lever, and just stared at me, vacant-eyed.

"Speed up!" I shouted, and you could just about see her brain freeze as she weighed that command against her instinct and training, which probably told her you're supposed to stop the damned train when you hit a person.

To hell with the training, I thought. Trains were for riding. And I meant to ride this one straight to my destination.

I tapped on the window again, hanging there, feet bracing me from falling and taking up most of my weight. "I need you to go faster," I said, throwing a look over my shoulder.

She just stared, and her lips moved. Over the sound of the rattling train echoing in the tunnel, I could barely hear her: "Why?"

I chucked a thumb over my shoulder. "Bad guy," I shouted, looking again. Sure enough, we were gaining on Creeper. Anna Vargas was clearly visible, legs bucking in mid-air as he hauled her along a good ten feet ahead of him. Creeper was casting nervous looks back, watching the train approach with clear worry. "When I tell you to, stop.

47

Fast. Emergency stop." I looked the driver in the eyes. "Understand?"

She stared at me for a second and I thought maybe I'd fried her brain. Then she nodded, and rested her hand on the lever.

The train's speed increased obviously, and I could feel its vibration in my bones. I flipped myself so I was facing forward, slipping in front of the door. There I rested my legs on the small step, and started to coil down into a partial squat, ready to spring.

There was a ding-dong chime within the train, and I heard the driver's voice echo through the carriages: "Please brace for an emergency stop. This is not a drill. HANG ON!"

"Good girl," I muttered, patting the cracked windshield. "Good thinking."

Creeper was only thirty feet in front of us now. I could see the next station, less than a mile away.

Physics. My mom had always drummed it into my damned skull, and I'd wondered where I would be finding any use for it at all locked in my house.

If only I'd known, I would have paid closer attention.

I looked over my shoulder and made eye contact with the driver. "Hit it!" I shouted. Creeper was twenty feet off and started to throw a hand back to stop us—

The train stopped, and boy, did I feel the deceleration. If I'd had a seatbelt, it would have yanked me back.

But I didn't. In fact, I pushed off from the train with both legs as soon as my hands broke contact, launching off in the ultimate leg press.

"Yeehaw!" I shouted as I flew through the air. My ability to control my direction was largely reliant on the push I'd given before I'd broken away from the train. Now

I was a bullet in flight, nothing but the useless flapping of my arms to give me any sort of rudder.

Creeper's eyes were like two dots of white growing larger and larger as I soared through the air toward him. He thrust a hand at me, panicking, but I didn't have a speck of metal on me for him to control. I flew closer and closer and he waved his hand more and more wildly, as though gesticulating with more force would suddenly allow him to throw me off my guided-missile-like course toward him—

Zoinks.

I crashed into Creeper midair and brought us both down. I pulled my limbs in as tight as I could considering I was gripped around him in a metahuman bear hug. I don't know whether panic overwhelmed him and he froze, or he just couldn't take the force I'd hit him with, but we both lost our breath and went tumbling without control.

He hit the ground shoulder-first and we bounced. The next impact was to me, drubbing my head into the concrete, which hurt. He got the next mini-landing, catching it all across the back of his neck, and I let him go at that point, flipping to my feet in a woozy landing in which I somehow, miraculously, ended upright. Bobbing slightly, legs woozy, but upright and standing.

Creeper made it a couple more rolls and landed face down, moaning. A second after that, he choked out a sob, and I knew he was hurting.

I bobbed closer to him on weak-ass legs. I was pretty sure I had the beginnings of a concussion, but I'd fought through worse. My head felt like it was underwater, and I was weaving a little with each step, but I stayed—and swayed—on my feet. A quick look back confirmed the train had, indeed, stopped. Go driver. Get down with your bad self.

"My arm!" A whine behind me revealed that Anna Vargas was indeed alive. "I think I broke my arm!"

"Stay right where you are; don't move or writhe," I said. She didn't answer, but switched to a quiet whimper and didn't argue, so I assumed she'd heard me and obeyed. "At all."

"You are...ruining...everything." Creeper pushed to all fours, sobs dripping out between his words.

"That's what I do," I said, stepping right up to him. I was keenly aware that he had a whole host of ball bearings somewhere in the tunnel behind me, and I was listening for the whistle of them over the ringing in my head. "Now...please. I'm begging you here. Are you going to surrender and come quietly or...?"

Nope. I heard the whistle, and it wasn't a train.

"You...are...ruining...*everything*," Creeper said, and he raised his face up so I could see the malevolence as he lifted a clenched fist in front of his face and got to his feet. "And I will not—"

I pushed him back a step, firmly, and his eyes snapped open in indignation as he realized he'd been shoved. He teetered, tottered, staggered, and finally caught his balance while on one leg. "You think that's going to stop me?" He looked at me like I was crazy, still standing on one leg. "I'm going to—"

"Put your foot down?" I asked. Probably a little flippantly. "Stomp me? Or stand there like a chicken on one leg and berate me?" The whistling behind me was getting closer, but I couldn't dodge. Not quite yet.

Right then, he realized that, yeah, he was standing on one leg. Yes, like a chicken. He looked down and realized, but didn't full stop to process that there was something beneath that foot that he hadn't put down.

Like a child I'd taunted into action, Creeper put his foot *down*.

Onto the subway's third rail.

Watching a person get electrocuted does not look quite like it does in the movies. There were some blue sparks, but they didn't course over his body like he'd been blasted by a Thor-type. They were restricted to where his foot made contact with the third rail, the fatal dose of electricity contracting every muscle in his body. He jerked and spasmed like someone had shoved a cattle prod up his ass—

And the whistling of the ball bearings?

Didn't stop.

It got closer and louder.

Very cognizant of the third rail I'd just goaded him into stomping on, I flung myself down and out of the way as much as possible. The wet smack of a hundred ball bearings being somehow attracted to him in his moment of death was as sickening a sound as I'd ever heard, followed closely by the groaning sound of his powers dragging the train in spite of its brakes.

Fortunately, all that stopped a moment later as the ball bearings finished rendering unto Creeper the fate that he'd tried—desperately—to put onto me a half-dozen times in as many minutes.

I looked up and found he was gone from the waist up, the remainder of him thrown clear of the third rail by the thousand impacts of his ball bearings.

"Ooh, hoist on your own petard," I said, then collapsed. I hit hard concrete all across my back, and the ache began in earnest.

"My arm is broken," Anna Vargas whined down the tunnel. "You broke my arm!"

"Think of the publicity this will get you, though," I

said, unable to command my limbs to move as the concussion sank in, along with the various and sundry pains one accumulated leaping from a moving train at sixty or seventy miles an hour and smashing into another human being. Hell, I was lucky to be alive.

So was Anna Vargas, though it seemed she didn't think so. Gratitude was such a lost art in our society.

"You ruined my premiere," she whined.

"Pretty sure Creeper did that," I managed to get out. Things were getting hazy.

"You're a murderer," she called. "And a homophobe."

I made a grunting noise in the back of my throat. "That second one is a lie. Damn you, Friday." I sighed. As to the other charge...

Whatever the number of people I'd killed was, we could add another with the death of Creeper, however little I'd actually had to do with the full execution of it. Honestly, I don't know how anyone could have expected me to keep track of these things.

Chapter 11

"What did you do this time?" These were Willis Shaw's first words to me as I strolled into his office at a leisurely pace and flopped down in the chair across from his desk.

"Me?" I played innocent. "Saved the day with my usual grace and aplomb. Kudos were handed out. I received some of them. And acclaim. Much acclaim. And also, there were—" I lowered my voice to a quick, barely coherent mutter "—almost—" raised it back up "—no fatalities."

Shaw just stared at me. His face had two settings: poker and irritable. He vacillated between the two now, and I wondered which I was going to get, the inscrutable Special Agent in Charge of my division, or the barely controlled anger of a boss whose employee was being a recalcitrant shitbag.

Then he flipped his computer monitor on its axis so I could see it, and boy, did I see. I saw Creeper's disembodied legs strewn across the train tracks in a photo that looked like it had been taken by one of the subway train's passengers as they were led out of the tunnel by rescue personnel. It was captioned *Slay Queen Strikes Again!*

"Hmm," I said, frowning. "I would have gone with, '*Slay Queen Holds Half-Off Sale.*' And I want to point out, in my own defense, I did qualify my 'no fatalities' thing with an 'almost.' Not my fault you normal people have terrible hearing."

Shaw just glared at me. "Injuries?"

"Maybe there might have been one or two."

"Oh?" He scrolled the screen down to another photo of the wrecked train, complete with first responders carrying people out on stretchers. It read *37 Injured in Subway Catastrophe.*

"Say..." I folded my arms over my chest. "If you already knew, why did you ask?"

"Because I wanted to see how your infantile ass would explain this monumental screw-up." Shaw's eyes were dancing with dangerous annoyance.

"I feel like you should reserve 'monumental' for when I break the Statue of Liberty, send the Unisphere off its axis at Flushing Meadows, or knock the Bull and Fearless Girl over on Wall Street," I said. "The subway is, after all, more of a 'fixture' than a 'monument,' technically speaking."

Shaw was surprisingly restrained given that I was intentionally antagonizing him. Was it possible that after all these months of working with me, he'd finally figured out that the quickest way to make me be a bigger asshole was to yell at me? "Today," he said, keeping his voice quite level, "you missed half a day of work going to court to testify in a case that was not our case. It was a local case. Not federal."

"I know all this. I would have thought you'd welcome a chance to get my happy ass out of the office for a half day, though."

"This——" Shaw waved a hand over the screen "——was also not your case. Similarly, it was a local case. For the local PD and local superheroes to handle."

I made a face. "Manhattan doesn't have a local superhero."

Shaw's face wavered a little. "What would you call Captain Frost?"

"An assclown. In yoga pants. I mean, really, there is visible moose knuckle there. It's horrifying."

He evinced a little reaction, a small twitch at the corner of his eye. "And Gravity?"

"Staten Island's finest, but not easily on call for the island of Manhattan or the other boroughs up here," I said. I shrugged. "Look, I do heroing, okay? I don't sit back and let shit go down without taking some responsibility."

"But you don't," Shaw said, strangely muted.

I had a bad feeling I knew what he meant. "Don't...what?"

"Take responsibility." Shaw slid the screen down the page of the newspaper a little farther. It had a picture of a crying Anna Vargas holding her hand. "You did this?"

"I did not, in fact," I said. "That happened when Creeper, as I had taken to calling the villain who'd kidnapped her, dropped her after I...uh, struck his body from the air with my own. After being launched from a train."

"Hm." Shaw sounded very matter-of-fact. He was usually a yeller. The lack of was disquieting. "How are you going about making things right for this young lady?"

I waved my hand at the weepy picture of Vargas. "I mean, I made sure she got checked out by EMS. Beyond that——"

He tapped the screen and I peered at it. There were subheads beneath the headline.

Anna Vargas claims Sienna Nealon has cost her everything!

'Three years ago she wrecked my house, tonight she almost claimed my life.'

'Next time we meet I'm afraid she'll kill me.'

"Now that's just unfair," I said, sagging in my chair. "I saved her life. That dude was kidnapping her for clearly odious purposes. She was definitely going to get the lotion on the skin, if you catch my meaning, because Creeper was just that kind of guy. As for her house, I did not plant bombs around it and blow it up, that was Redbeard—"

"Where do you come up with these names?" Shaw just shook his head.

"From my imagination. It's a fairly obvious leap with some pirate overtones."

Shaw made that hmph-ing sound again. "You're going to court again tomorrow?"

"Well, yeah," I said. "There's a conviction hanging on it."

Shaw nodded slowly. "You have an actual case waiting. One of ours." He spun his screen back around, tapped at the keyboard, then flipped it again. "Local authorities request assistance with a metahuman matter."

I stared at what looked the wreckage of a bar and a stage. "Where is this?"

"Nashville." He pursed his dark lips. "Been there?"

"Not sure. Briefly, once or twice on a layover, maybe?" I frowned. "This looks unpleasant. Any fatalities?"

"No," he said darkly. "Unlike your handiwork, just injuries."

"Scathing."

"The details are in your inbox," Shaw said, sliding his screen back. "You will not be attending court tomorrow. Your flight leaves in the morning."

"You could have just said that upfront instead of

making it a question, boss," I said, standing up and brushing myself off. I hadn't even realized how dirty I'd gotten during my little train chase. Also, there was a hole in the back of my blouse I was just now noticing.

"I'm not your boss," Shaw said, back to tapping away at his keyboard.

"But you keep giving me orders anyway," I said cheerfully.

"I mean I'm not your boss *anymore*, Nealon," Shaw said.

I froze in the door frame. "Beg pardon?"

Shaw stopped tapping and looked dead at me. "Transfer orders just came through. You, Holloway and West are being reassigned to DC to be supervised...more closely. Director Chalke thinks you need a firmer hand."

"Mmmm." I shook my head. "Firmer hands get broken around me. Squeeze me, I react badly. Like a Coke can in subzero temps."

"Be that as it may," Shaw said, "you're transferring as soon as you get back. Might want to make a start of packing your stuff before you leave for Nashville." He was so serious, so not yelling.

Now I knew why.

"Good luck, Nealon," Shaw said, and he looked back at his screen, our conversation—and reason to interact—apparently now over. "Because based on your record...you're definitely going to need it to survive in DC."

Chapter 12

Reed

The winds were clear across the midwest as I swept through the skies over Wisconsin, Illinois, Kentucky, and finally Tennessee. Snow-covered hills gave way to the brown flatlands of western Illinois, and somewhere just north of Kentucky it finally started to green, changing shades until just south of Nashville it turned really verdant.

Murfreesboro was a city of a little over 100,000 almost squarely in the middle of Tennessee. According to Wikipedia, it was one of the fastest-growing cities in the country, which was not something I'd heard. Flying gave me lots of time to enjoy the finer corners of the web, though, until my battery started to die as I was on final approach. Well-timed, that.

I'd heard of this company with the labor dispute only by reputation and news articles. The headquarters of Lotsostuff (actually their name, amazingly) was an immense warehouse on the outskirts of Murfreesboro. Also according to Wikipedia, it had been purchased by founder

Logan Mills for a relatively low price five or so years ago due to a downturn in the area. Property values had since rebounded, so if nothing else, he was sitting on a fortune just in real estate.

Plus it was filled with stuff.

It was also easy to pick out on approach due to its massiveness. The warehouse stretched the length of several football fields, way bigger than the Metrodome, for instance, though quite a bit shorter. It sprawled on the outskirts of Murfreesboro, a blocky superstructure of corrugated-roofed warehouses that was probably visible from outer space.

There was a crowd gathered at one of the entrances to the fence that surrounded the place, easily visible as I slipped down to a thousand feet or so of altitude. They looked like milling ants, and somehow a vague feeling deep in my detective instincts told me I'd found my labor dispute.

A small line of navy-clad cops had formed a perimeter just outside the fence, a pitiful firebreak on the milling, angry ants—or rather, laborers. I felt a pang of discomfort rolling into this. I had my natural sympathies, and they were with the guys on the line. But even from this height I could tell things were getting rough, some shoving going on. The cops weren't wearing SWAT gear, and they weren't wearing private security uniforms. They had real badges, and the cop cars parked nearby said POLICE in big white letters on a blue stripe with Murfreesboro smaller on the white paint of the car underneath. These were not rent-a-cops designed to break the strike.

I couldn't let the angry natives cause a riot with the local PD, so I separated them from the fence with a little...gust-o.

I know. A dad joke and I'm not even a dad. What can I say? My father taught me well before his untimely passing.

With a little twist of my hand, I sent bursts of wind strong enough to move the crowd. They were forced back —driven, really—stumbling, as I descended into the no man's land I had created.

The crowd of furious Lotsostuff workers watched me like they were standing under the blades of a helicopter. Some were maybe a little more irritable than others, even though I was trying to be gentle. I saw relief on the faces of the cops, as well as one guy in a shirt and tie that now had some seriously dust-covered shoes.

"Chill, people," I said as I let the gusts die down. "No need to get violent."

The crowd made a noise that sounded like they disagreed. I heard a lot of disparate shouts, some real disgruntlement coming out of them. Some profanities, but mostly muttered. They'd been quieted by my forceful entrance, I guess.

"Wow," said the guy with the shirt and tie. Clearly management. He looked up at me with glowing, watery blue eyes. I'd probably blown some grit into them. "Mr. Treston."

I nodded at him. It was kind of nice now that people knew my name. Sure, most of them knew me as Sienna's brother, but hey...my name recognition was rising. That wasn't nothing. "What's up?"

"You showed up just in time," the guy said. He had blond hair, looked to be in his mid-twenties. "It was getting pretty tense there."

I threw a look over my shoulders. Some of the workers —all clad in navy overalls with LOTSOSTUFF written on them; must have been the company uniform—were carrying baseball bats and lead pipes and other such lovely blunt instruments. The cops were outnumbered at least ten to one, which was not a good thing to be in a tense situation like this. It was getting a little mob-like. One guy clapped his bat into the palm of his hand; another, who walked with a limp, just glared at me through brown hair that hung in front of his eyes, apparently blown wild by my gusts. "It does look like you were dealing with some tension," I said.

"I'm sure Mr. Mills is going to be very relieved you've arrived," Mr. Shirt and Tie said, pushing open a gate and re-entering the fenced compound of Lotsostuff.

I just stared after him for a moment as he bustled back toward the warehouse. "Ah...uh...what?" I asked, then looked to the nearby cops. They weren't listening to our conversation, though, being too focused on the crowd and the danger they posed. After standing there for a moment, trying to figure out whether I should just stay here, I realized—aw, hell, I wasn't going to get anywhere with this thing if I didn't start talking to the major players. So off I followed Shirt and Tie, hoping to get some sort of answers about how this started and where it was going before it could turn into...

Into...

Well, whatever the hell Harry Graves had envisioned it was going to turn into.

Chapter 13

Sienna

"Ms. Nealon!" A thousand reporters descended on me as I stepped out of my cab and walked toward the terminal at JFK Airport. Someone had tipped off the world about my departure, apparently, because it felt like they were all here, all snapping pictures and calling questions at the same time. It was lucky for me that epilepsy wasn't a thing for metas, because the sheer number of flashbulbs going off around me would have triggered even the most latent case.

"Do you still stand by your homophobic statements, Ms. Nealon?"

"Do you people even journalism anymore?" I asked, rhetorically. "I mean, really. Attributing a quote to me I never even said—aw, forget it. You suck. Go get better at your job. Or find one that you would be better at. Have you tried being Stevie Wonder? Or is his sight-reading level just too aspirationally out of reach for you?"

"Ms. Nealon, how do you respond to Anna Vargas's complaints about you?"

"I don't," I said, stepping into the terminal, my roller bag clinking along behind me. Director Chalke had sent me a very lovely, formal email instructing me—in the parlance of our times—to STFU. Which I was not doing a very good job of now, but hey, try having your optic nerves obliterated by enough flashbulbs to blot out the sun while having ten thousand questions shouted at you, and see how you do at shutting up and taking it with dignity.

I rolled my way to the counter and chucked my suitcase at them, flashing my FBI ID at the attendant. "Got me?" She nodded. "Great. Send that on, will ya?" I caught a flicker of distaste on her face but, pursued as I was by the press, I decided to hightail it for the security checkpoint in advance of a thousand thundered questions and a million more flashes of blinding light.

When I got to the checkpoint I flashed my badge and sailed through with only a little glare from the TSA guys. I'd already checked my weapon in my bag, after all, and I had FBI credentials, so they skipped the invasive bodily searches and let me wander past. The press got stuck there, taking pictures and yelling questions until long after I'd gotten out of sight. I could still hear them trying a concourse away.

I caught a lot of attention on the way to my gate. Double takes were pretty common for me, even among the jaded New Yorkers who frequently saw celebrities in their midst, dining and brunching and whatever else. A few people commented. A few people muttered less than flattering things, mostly related to Friday's stupid ass Socialite post from months back. Chicken shits didn't even have the guts to say it loud and proud.

I bought the most touristy I HEART NEW YORK

baseball hat I could find in the gift shop, and matched it with a hoodie that bellowed that I was a supporter of the FDNY. Hood up, cap on, hair back and sunglasses dark as good coffee, I strolled toward my gate with my head down and my eyes up, scanning for trouble.

When I got to the gate I settled in with my phone, my earpods, an audiobook about criminology, and the soothing voice of the narrator lulling me as my eyes darted behind my sunglasses, looking for threats.

I still caught looks of recognition, though my disguise gave them enough doubt to hold them at bay, thankfully. When they called my flight, it was a sweet relief, and I boarded quickly into my window seat, positioning my hood so no one could see my face and settling in against the bulkhead for a mind-numbing flight, my audiobook's narrator my only company.

My head thumped against the bulkhead as the plane landed, surprising me out of a sleep I didn't know I'd entered. I guess the history of La Cosa Nostra circa 1935 hadn't been the eye-opener I'd figured it would be when I'd bought the book. Or at least not enough to counteract the lack of sleep I'd had the night before, wherein I'd basically packed a healthy portion of my apartment. I didn't know exactly when my move to DC would be required, but I'd made a decent start on preparing for it. Chalke had sent me a short email formalizing things. Vague enough that I didn't know the timetable, short enough to let me know she assumed full ownership of my ass. Like she hadn't already made that abundantly clear.

I smacked my lips dryly, staring out into the sunlit day as green grass stared back from beside the grey tarmac strip. It had been a while since I'd seen green, what with February being something of a dull, brown and snowy month in New York. Not quite as much as Minnesota, but still...dull.

The plane taxied up to an airport that looked not much different than any other I'd been to as the flight attendants announced we were now in Nashville, Tennessee, in the Central Time Zone. I yawned but kept my head down, glancing to my side only to make sure that neither of the people sitting to my right weren't giving me undue attention. The problem with the turtle strategy I'd employed was that it did leave me vulnerable, but I had to hope my disguise and the doubtful occurrence of being attacked on a plane would protect me. Apparently it had.

I debarked with all due speed, keeping my head down as I went. My phone lit up with messages as I turned it back on. I had a couple of *WTF?!?* messages from Holloway and Hilton, my remaining squadmates. I tentatively thanked my lucky stars neither had been assigned to go with me on this detail. I was tasked to help the locals, so I'd get state-level help from Tennessee rather than the FBI's federal-level assistance. If it kept me from having to deal with Holloway's aggravating ass or Kerry Hilton's overly chipper and enthusiastic one, good.

If, on the other hand, they paired me with some local yokel that was more concerned with protecting his little fiefdom, pissant territory than catching the bad guy? I might be praying for Hilton or Holloway before this was all done.

The terminal at Nashville Airport was pretty well maintained in my estimation, though the carpet was a reddish-orange horror out of the nightmares of any interior decorator with reasonable aesthetic sense. Still, I'd seen worse, and the place made up for it by having the aroma of barbecue wafting through the air as I passed a restaurant to my right. It smelled like heaven, and it was all I could do to keep my eyes front and try to recall that skipping breakfast was a smart move for caloric intake control but probably a terrible one given that my missions always resulted in me missing several meals and being extra crabby.

There was a guitar player singing some country song as I passed the TSA exit checkpoint, a bored agent leafing through a magazine the only protection against some terrorist bolting through and purchasing fried chicken from the Popeye's I'd spotted in the food court. I caught a few bars of the song and had to concede the singer was pretty good, especially for an airport performer.

Riding down the escalator to baggage claim, I steeled myself. I'd flown into and out of New York airports a few times, and whenever the press knew I was coming, it was a shitshow all the way. I was pretty sure I'd be dealing with paparazzi soon, especially given the level of fevered attention that had been on me when I'd left NYC. There was no way that level of heat subsided just because I left the Eastern Seaboard.

But when I got to the baggage claim, there was...no one. At least, not paparazzi or reporter-wise. The place was quiet, clean, people getting their luggage from the carousels and leaving without any undue fuss. I stared out the glass windows into the loop where buses and cars and cabs and Ubers picked up arrivals and saw...

Not a damned thing out of the ordinary.

No cameras.

No reporters.

Nada.

"Hm." Pleasantly surprised, I sidled over to my carousel to wait for my bag.

It never showed up.

Now, some thousand miles away from New York, my

brain put together the clues. The lady asshole behind the airline counter had flashed me some attitude that I'd blown off at the time. Now it seemed clear: she didn't like me, so she'd probably sent my bag somewhere else. A quick check with the apologetic agent behind the luggage counter confirmed it.

"I am so sorry, Ms. Nealon," she said, and she really seemed like it. "Somehow your luggage got sent to—well, I'm not sure." She folded her hands in front of her, and by the look on her face she seemed certain I was about to punch her into oblivion. "I am so, so very sorry."

"It has a gun in it, you know," I said. "Two, actually. Plus a knife or two. Maybe three. And a spring-loaded baton—"

The agent cleared her throat and turned her attention back to her computer. "Yes. Of course. Um. We have tracking on it. It's not lost. It's just...in the wrong place. I will get it here as quickly as possible. End of day, if I can." She reddened. "I have no idea how this happened."

Really? Cuz I had a sinking suspicion I did. "Just get it back to me," I said, sighing as I checked my phone again. My local contact had texted me a few times, just quick, to-the-point messages about where to meet them, which was just outside.

"Yes, ma'am," she said. "And again, on behalf of the airline—"

"You're sorry—yes, I caught that," I said, heading for the exit. The sun was shining, the sky was blue out there, and I tried to put the dark clouds behind me as I stepped out into the fresh, pleasantly cool-but-not-cold Tennessee air.

Chapter 14

My local contact was sitting in a black SUV with Tennessee government plates just outside the door. Crossing guard airport cops were buzzing around, making sure pedestrians didn't get run over in the busy pickup circle, which was, like most airports I'd been to, a sort of tunnel beneath the departing flights floor of the terminal. Since 9/11, though, the airport cops tended to shoo people along to parking lots inside the beltway road that banded most airports. It wasn't true of every airport I went to, but it was true of most, though some were more viciously aggressive about it than others. Depending on the day, Minneapolis/St. Paul airport cops could let you sit there for an hour or roust you less than a minute after pulling up to the curb.

A law enforcement SUV could sit there as long as it wanted, though, and that's just what my guy was doing. I could see he was a guy by his outline, though his texts hadn't given a name.

I walked up to the passenger door and hauled on the handle. It opened easily, sparing me from ripping open the lock and shearing it off in my annoyance at the baggage loss. My contact looked up, and his dark skin and slicked-back black hair stood out against wide, white pupils with nice brown irises. His surprise knocked his customary expression off his face, but to me it looked like he had smile lines.

"Hi, Sienna Nealon," I said, flopping into my seat and slamming the door. I flipped my hair as I entered, not because I wanted to but because sleeping with the hoodie up against the bulkhead had really messed it up.

"Chandler," he said, offering a hand to me.

I tried not to hit him with a suspicious look at the name. "Just...Chandler?"

He chuckled, and I saw his smile lines. "That's what they call me."

"But there's a story there, right?"

He looked like his breath caught in his throat. "Sure, but—"

"Hit me with it, Chandler. Let's do this 'getting to know you' thing fast, huh? Since you probably already know me."

"Okay, you got me," he said, smiling. "My name—full name—is Amit Chandrasekhar. Born in Hyderabad, came to Sweetwater, Tennessee—" he put on a perfect Southern accent for a few seconds "—when I was three. No one could say 'Chandrasekhar,' and *Friends* was huge back then, so I made it easy on them—Chandler. I'm funny, anyway, so it works."

"Oh, good, a partner who's funny," I said. "Haven't had one of those in a while." I flipped my finger forward in a point. "Let's roll, Chandler."

"Uh...do you not have any more luggage?" He eyed my total lack of a bag.

"The bitch behind the counter in New York got shitty

with me and 'lost' my bag," I said. "No luggage, no gun—if we run into trouble right now, I'm going to have to rip apart your car and beat someone to death with a tire."

"We can get you a gun at TBI," he said.

I frowned. "'TBI'?"

"Tennessee Bureau of Investigation."

"That's..." I twitched. "That's a thing?"

"Yeah," Chandler said, blowing it off as he put the SUV into gear. "You know how bureaucracies are. They went with the familiar name instead of going all original. I mean, what's the FBI going to do? Sue for copyright infringement?"

"You make a fair point there."

Chandler slid us out from beneath the tunnel of the baggage claim pickup and we started to cruise. Sunlight shone down from outside the tunnel area, blue sky just glowing out there. I hadn't noticed it being freezing when I'd walked to the SUV, so I looked for the external temp on the dashboard but didn't find it.

"What's the temp out here today?" I asked, peering at the dash, still looking for it.

Chandler tapped a number in the middle of the display screen. 72 degrees.

I blinked. I'd thought that was what the air conditioner was set to. "Nice," I said as we rolled along the airport ring road.

The grass was already greening from its winter fading, and as we came around a corner at the parking garage, a series of cherry trees in the median were covered in bright white blooms that seemed to have an almost surreal glow about them. I indicated the window button. "Do you mind?"

"Go right ahead."

I rolled down the window, hoping for a scent of cherry

blossoms as we went past, but didn't get anything but a faint aroma of it. I took another deep breath. Spring was actually in the air here, funny as that sounded. In February. Six more cherry trees in full blossom greeted us along the way out of the airport.

"Do we need to file a stolen weapon report with the ATF?" Chandler asked over the roar of the wind rushing in. "For your lost guns?"

"Not yet," I said. "They say it's not lost; that pissy attendant in New York just decided to detour my shit out of—hell, I don't know. Pique, I guess. I should have noticed her, but I was too busy speed-walking from the damned paparazzi." I shook my head, rolling up the window. Chandler was speeding up as we were leaving the airport's ring and riding a long, curving ramp toward a wide, eight- or ten-lane freeway. "I'm surprised they didn't pick me up on this side of my flight."

Chandler made a face. "We don't really do...paparazzi...here."

"Say whaaaaat?"

"This place is the home of the country music stars," Chandler said as we merged onto the interstate. It was mildly busy but not bad at all compared to, say, the Midtown tunnel or one of the bridges at this time of day. "Their privacy gets respected around here; we don't do the whole—cameras and craziness thing. If you're a local, it's considered kind of gauche to even go up to them, really." He shook his head. "I don't know what you're used to in New York, but I suspect here you'll be able to walk down the street and be mostly left alone."

I thought about all the yelling at me that had happened in the wake of the San Francisco mission, the occasional angry mob-like chants that broke out around me as I was walking down the streets of New York. In a way, it was reassuring that people felt comfortable enough that they weren't going to die horribly that they could safely chant nasty things at me about something I hadn't even done.

In another way, it was really aggravating to be eating lunch and suddenly have people shouting at you across a restaurant about how much you suck. It made me want to go back to being in disguise full-time, something I had dabbled with again in recent months.

Not having to worry about that? Hell, I could use a few days of calm.

Chandler must have sensed at least a little of what I was thinking. "Welcome to Nashville, Ms. Nealon." The car just rolled along the relatively quiet freeway, taking us toward the city.

Chapter 15

"Where are we?" I asked as we pulled up to...not a honky-tonk bar like I'd expected. "Is this TBI?" I was itching to get a gun on me, but while this seemed like it might be a government building, it didn't seem like the squat, blocky law enforcement offices I'd gotten used to in my travels.

"Ah, this is City Hall," Chandler said, hanging a right into an underground parking garage. Once he'd pulled into a space marked RESERVED, I joined him in getting out of the car and followed him right into the building. He led me through a staircase and up a few floors to an office where a receptionist on the phone greeted us with a smile and let us pass without comment through a door marked MAYOR.

"Oh, man," I said under my breath as Chandler held the door open into the Mayor's office for me. Politicians. Hadn't I had enough of these people for one lifetime? If not, my upcoming move to DC would certainly fill the quotient.

"Mayor Clea Brandt," Chandler said, indicating a

woman who was striding purposefully across the red-carpeted office toward me. "This is Sienna Nealon, as requested."

Mayor Clea Brandt was probably 5' 1", maybe 5' 2" if you pushed, which meant she was shorter than me. She was African-American, wearing a broad smile, and her greying hair was fastened back tightly. Her suit was pure white, almost glowing, and she was on me in seconds, shaking my hand quickly but warmly with both of hers. "Ms. Nealon," she said in the kindest voice I'd heard since...uh...probably since before I'd come to New York, at least. "Such a genuine pleasure to meet you."

"Nice to meet you, too," I said, a little flabbergasted. It had been a while since anyone had professed pleasure in meeting me. Basically since before Friday's San Francisco debacle had wrecked my reputation and made me toxic for any public figures to stand close to. "Are you sure you should be meeting with me? I'm not, uh...popular right now." I paused, eyes flitting as I considered that statement. "Again."

She made a psh-awing noise with her lips, waving a hand dismissively at me. "I read about what happened. You didn't even post anything."

"Where did you read that?" I asked, genuinely curious.

"In the twentieth paragraph of a twenty-one-paragraph article," she said with a knowing smile. "Having been on the receiving end of a political hit or two in my time, I've learned to take the reportage of the professional press with a grain of salt. Maybe a pillar, actually." She brushed my hoodie sleeve reassuringly.

"Well, thank goodness somebody does," I said. I looked around the office briefly and realized I'd been thoroughly disarmed by her charm. "Ah...I'll be honest, I didn't know I was coming here or I would have dressed..."

I looked down at my FDNY hoodie. "Well, more for the occasion."

"Don't you worry your head about it, sugar," she said, retreating for her desk and beckoning me to follow. "We're just so pleased to have you down here visiting us. Have you been to Nashville before?"

"Ahhh..." I racked my memory, but came up with very little. "Maybe on a layover a few years ago? I think we might have stopped during a flight to drop off a...friend." Her office was tasteful, but not over the top.

"A 'friend'?" Mayor Brandt's eyes sparkled.

I froze halfway to lowering myself in my seat and glanced back. Chandler had left the room and closed the door without even a word of goodbye. Hopefully he was waiting for me outside. "I, uh...during the war I knew someone who lived in Nashville and—"

"You wouldn't be talking about Senator Robb Foreman, would you?" Mayor Brandt's smile had turned mischievous.

I settled in my chair uncomfortably. "I hate to name drop, but yeah."

"You should drop that man's name every chance you get," Brandt said, still smiling. "He is an absolute delight. I saw him just last week at a fundraiser for the Baptist Children's Home. His party is trying to get him to run for President again, and I'll be honest—if he runs, he has my vote. He's a good man."

"That was my experience with him as well," I said, feeling a little more at ease. "But I hate to say I know him because...well, not everyone wants to admit they know me these days. Again." I felt a goofy smile spread across my face. "Because of the Socialite thing."

"Is it causing you a lot of friction back home?" Brandt settled in, resting her face on her hand like we were old friends. I felt weirdly at ease, and a distinct lack of alarm. Brandt's assistant opened the door and wheeled in a tray with tea and coffee that smelled fragrant and lovely, stopping at my elbow and indicating with a sweep of her hand that the world was my oyster here.

"Coffee, black," I said, and turned my attention back to Brandt as the assistant bustled at pouring me a cup. "Uhm, yes. It has made things...uncomfortable for me in New York City. Not every time I walk down the street, but probably at least once a week someone shouts something...rude...at me."

"That is genuinely unfortunate," Brandt said. "I hope —and I doubt—that you'll be subject to that sort of behavior here in Nashville, though I don't control the minds of all our citizens." She gave me a knowing sort of smirk that, given my history with politicians who did the mind control thing, should have had me either screaming with laughter or screaming for the hills.

Instead, I sort of laughed uncomfortably, which seemed like a genuine reaction. "I won't hold it against you if anyone's a dipshit."

"I appreciate that," she said. "We want your visit to be as pleasant as possible. Nashville prides itself on the being the kind of place where anyone can come and just let their hair down."

"You must be popular with the Medusas."

"Hm?"

"Never mind." I brushed a messy, frizzed hank of hair out of my eyes again. "My hair is definitely down. A choice I am currently regretting, but...it's down. Going in a ponytail as soon as I find a binder, though." A cup of coffee was steaming at my side and I lifted it to my lips. It smelled wonderful, a couple notes of chocolate buried in the smooth, mellow scent.

Brandt laughed. "Oh, that's nothing, sweetheart. The humidity here in the summer will have you looking like you just stepped out of the shower in the middle of the day." She sipped her own coffee. "It's worth it for this time of year, though. Did you see the cherry blossoms on your way in?"

"I did," I said, nodding. "Very pretty."

"New York's not exactly in bloom right now, is it?" She was still smiling, steam rising off the coffee cup under her chin.

"No, but the cold keeps the smell of garbage down, so it has its pluses," I said, and she laughed again. "I'm, uh...about to be transferred to DC, though, so...I won't be worrying about New York much longer." I watched the assistant roll the tray out the door and wondered when it would be considered polite to make my own retreat. Not that the conversation was lacking, I just wasn't sure what the point of it was.

"I had heard that," Mayor Brandt said, nodding along.

I frowned. "You already knew?"

"Politicians gossip among themselves constantly," she said, waving a hand. "Why, I was talking with the governor just this morning about your coming trip, in fact—"

"It's so nice to be talked about."

"All good things, sweetie," she said. "But we were discussing you in glowing terms—I mean, I look at what you've provided to New York...and I'm just green with envy."

I waited for her to snap a smartass quip on the end of that statement. It didn't come. "Excuse me?" I finally asked, wondering if I'd missed some sarcasm. "How is that?"

"Do you know how much your presence has cut down on street crime in New York?" Mayor Brandt looked at me over her coffee cup. "I mean, we can't attribute it solely to you. Gravity and that knucklehead with the ice powers are probably of some use, too, but my chief of police showed me the numbers just last night and...mmm!" She made a sound like she'd just eaten something wonderful. "Down seventy-five percent since last summer when you got there." She watched my eyes. "Did you know that?"

"Uh, no," I said. "Nobody tells me anything. And, I mean, the NYPD does good work—"

"Oh, without doubt," she said, nodding along. "But they haven't changed their policing." There was a gleam in her eye. "They are benefitting from what I like to the call the 'superheroine peace dividend.' And in City Hall, they know it." She winked at me. "And are already sick about you leaving."

"Wow." I put my coffee cup down. I felt...weird, actually. Welch had never told me I had a tangible effect on the crime rate. He'd never even suggested me being available did anything but cause property damage. I mean, he thanked me and all, but I'd certainly never met the mayor of New York, or the police chief. They'd wanted to get together, but I'd put them off, and after San Francisco those invites mysteriously dried up.

Now it suddenly made sense why they kept calling me to help.

"That's unfortunate for New York's crime rate, I guess," I said, coffee cup and saucer in hand. "I doubt I'd be allowed to intervene in DC as much either, which—"

"Do you ever get tired of the games they're playing with you?" Brandt's eye twinkle had just grown brighter.

I froze, feeling a lot like a deer squarely in the middle of headlights. "Yes," I answered, because why lie? "Why do I have the sense you're about to blindside me with something? Because I gotta warn you—I've already been hit by a train once in the last twenty-four hours—"

"Because you're not stupid, and the last time you met with a governor he ended up jumping out a window a few days later," Brandt said with a grin. "I'm going to guess most politicians are avoiding you like plague rats lately. But I parade you right in the minute you get to town. And you're not stupid, so you see I'm cooking something up."

"Yeah," I said. "What is it?"

Brandt set her coffee cup down and leaned forward on her desk. "Like I said, I talked with the Governor of Tennessee this morning, and we came up with this—

"How would you like to be the official superheroine of Nashville, Tennessee?"

Chapter 16

Reed

"Mr. Mills?" Shirt and Tie's quiet voice spoke into the dimly lit office. There was no admin assistant out here, or secretary, just an empty desk before an old, poorly maintained door that read LOGAL MILLS with CEO stenciled underneath it.

Shirt and Tie had the CEO's door open and his face poked in. I had a feeling he was the one who usually manned the desk out here. I took a glance at it, and sure enough, a golden nameplate on it read BEN KELLY. Now I knew Shirt and Tie's name. I filed that away for later.

"What happened?" a deeper voice came from inside, presumably the CEO's voice.

"Ah, Reed Treston has arrived, sir?" Kelly made it sound like a question rather than a thing that had definitely happened. "From Minneapolis?"

"Is that Sienna Nealon's brother?" Mills asked, causing me to sigh with impatience. But quietly. I was so sick of being ID'd that way. But I buried my Ringo Starr feelings quickly and moved on.

"Uh, yes, sir," Kelly almost whispered. Like he could sense my annoyance, though he didn't look back.

"What's he doing here?" Mills asked. I'd yet to catch a glimpse of him, though I remembered what he looked like from the article Harry had given me. Maybe thirty, thick dark hair, a strong chin, piercing eyes focused on the future. Like you'd expect a young and hungry CEO to look.

"Uhm," Kelly said, shooting me a quick glance. "He's—"

I strode up to the door and yanked it wide, so Kelly didn't have to speak through a little crack. "I heard you were having a hell of a time," I said, looking into the darkened office. There were no lights on, but there was a bank of old-timey windows, each pane no larger than 2' by 1'. Half the panes had been painted over so that you could see the lines left by the paint brush in the daylight where the sun shone through the thinner coverage. This was pure old factory décor, leftover from decades past, and evidence that Lotsostuff's HQ and warehouse had been something else in its previous life, long before their CEO had even been born. "Thought I'd come stick my nose into your troubles."

"Did you now?" Logan Mills was standing behind his desk, which was a beaten, battered old thing that looked like it was in such terrible condition that he wouldn't have even sold it on his website. And the man himself wasn't much better. He looked nothing like his photo; he'd easily put on thirty pounds since it had been taken, had dark circles under his eyes. His hair was thinning, and the office held a stale aroma, hints of booze and coffee, neither fresh, that seemed to fit the man I was looking at. He wore a shirt that was buttoned almost to the top, but the sleeves were rolled up, and a sport coat rested on the back of his chair. "Well," Mills said, "I've certainly got plenty of those, though I'm not sure what a man of your skills would want to do here."

I suppressed my surprise at how rough Mills looked. He seemed like he hadn't shaved in a few days either, and when he spoke, the wafting scent from his words told me teeth-brushing and showering had maybe gone by the wayside, too, in this current crisis. "I always seem to find a way to do some good," I said, "wherever I go."

Mills let out a soft, mirthless chuckle. "Do you? I suppose that's useful." He looked out one of the unpainted windows. "To someone, anyway."

"Are you not on the side of good here, Mr. Mills?" I asked, figuring I might as well go at him a little since he was being fairly uncooperative.

That caused a shroud of indifference to blanket his face. "I do what I can."

It was an interesting reaction to my question. "Well, I'm just here to keep your dispute from turning ugly," I said, figuring I'd trodden on his toes hard enough already with my probing question. His reactions, his very manner, were telling me a lot about how he saw himself.

"Good," Mills said, seeming to snap out of a short reverie. "We could use that. Though I'm not sure how much good it'll do, since it's already turned sorta ugly."

"But it hasn't turned violent yet," I said, fishing.

"No," Mills said quietly, looking down at his desk. "Thankfully not."

"Well, let's just do what we can to keep it that way, shall we?" I asked, smiling tightly. I gave Ben Kelly a nod. "I'll see myself out. Keep an eye on that line outside."

"Mr. Treston," Mills called after me, when I was

halfway across his outer office. "I don't suppose you might consider trying to figure out who flooded my warehouse?" I looked back, and the man was standing in the shadow cast by those painted windows. "They ruined a lot of merchandise, some of which was already sold and not shipped."

"That's not why I'm here," I said to the man in shadow. "I'm here to keep this from turning violent."

"Hm," Mills said, and I saw his head bob. "Of course." With a wave of his hand to Kelly, he said, "That'll be all then, Ben."

And with that, Kelly shut the door, frowning all the while. "That was...unusual," Kelly muttered. "He's generally a lot more talkative. Friendly. Charismatic, even."

"Interesting," I said, continuing my path toward the door. Here for five minutes and already the CEO of this company was freezing me out. I had a feeling I knew how this was going to go from here, and it was nowhere good.

Chapter 17

Sienna

The words "Official Superheroine of Nashville, Tennessee" were bouncing around in my head as I looked Mayor Clea Brandt in her warm, twinkling brown eyes. Her desk was crowded with papers all organized into neat piles, but from the top of one stack she pulled up a single page and slid it across to me, still smiling to beat the band.

I pulled the paper from the desk's edge and looked at it. It bore the seal of the State of Tennessee as well as that of Nashville city, that official look that documents have when government entities desperately want to impress upon you the officialness of something. I imagined angry letters from the EPA looked much the same.

Skimming the contents I found the points, very quickly:

First, a salary almost twice what I was making in the FBI.

Second, the ability to be cross-deputized by the state agencies so I could work anywhere in Tennessee, with a proviso that any other states that recognized my authority could solicit my help, either for money or charity.

Third...hell, what did I even need anything third for? The first two were good enough.

"Uhhh..." I stared at the page, blinking. No one had offered me anything like this since...well, ever.

Hell, no one had even acted like they wanted me around almost ever, with the exception of Heather Chalke and her blackmailing self.

"Say yes," Brandt whispered, "and DC will never be a worry for you."

For a moment I thought about it, and got caught up in the idea that I could hang out in a place that had cherry trees blossoming beautifully in February. That I could work in a place where, yes, they actually wanted me to fight crime. All the crime, in fact, not just the particular crimes that they fed me.

I could be far from the crazy bustle and insanity of New York City with its billion-population paparazzi, and maybe leave behind all the dirty looks from people who believed something about me that was widely reported but flatly untrue.

All these thoughts and more came rushing around me, whirling, really, because...damn. Sometimes I forgot how long it had been since someone had given me the simple act of kindness involved in saying, "You do good work. We want you to do it for *us*."

But...

"I...can't," I said, pushing the paper back across the table toward her.

"You sure?" She took the paper but dangled it enticingly. "This is flexible, all right? We're willing to let you work with other states as well. I know you're a problem-solver. A crime-stopper. You don't like to let injustice just go by. With this, you don't have to. If California calls and they've got a problem? You go. But you hang your hat here at the end of the day, and..." She smiled. "You might find some other benefits. We're centrally located in the country. The weather is pleasant most of the year. Gets a little hot in the summer, and our winters are nothing like what a Minnesotan would be used to—"

"It's all...so appealing," I said, unable to meet her gaze. "But I can't leave the FBI in the lurch right now. I hope you understand."

"Of course." She nodded. "The offer is open." She smiled, clearly disappointed but not bitterly. "If you change your mind."

I nodded. "Thank you." I rose, drinking down the last of my coffee. It really was good. A lot better than the store-bought swill I'd been drinking lately. "No one has wanted me to be...well, anywhere, for a while. So thank you."

"You are welcome here," Mayor Brandt said, circling around her desk and shaking my hand warmly, with both hands, again. She didn't act like she was rushing, but I was guessing if I hadn't been a succubus, she would have held on a lot longer. "Let me know if you need anything during your stay, all right? Anything. The governor also wanted me to let you know that he is at your disposal if you need to contact him." She looked me right in the eye. "While here, you will have the full cooperation of Nashville and the State of Tennessee."

"Thanks," I said. "I'll try to keep the destruction to a minimum."

"I know you always do," she said, and it was fully sincere, again in a way I wasn't used to. "Take care."

With that, I turned to leave, almost regretting that I had to. I'd known Mayor Clea Brandt for all of ten minutes, and already I wanted to work with her way more than Heather Chalke or Willis Shaw.

But that wasn't the path I was on.

Chandler was waiting for me, sitting on Brandt's assistant's desk, both of them chuckling at something as I walked out. He hopped up instantly, said, "Nice to meet you," to the assistant, and fell in beside me. "How'd it go?"

"Your mayor makes a hell of an offer," I said.

"You would make a hell of an asset to state law enforcement," Chandler said with his slight accent, keeping right up.

I gave him a sidelong look. "Are you going to be my tour guide, then? Selling me on why I should take the job?"

Chandler just grinned. "I don't think I'll have to do much selling. I'm just chauffeuring. Where to now? The scene?"

I nodded. "Take me to the scene." I ignored that faint, distant voice in my head that loved the sense of warm approval I'd gotten in the mayor's office. I'd almost forgotten how nice it was to be...wanted. Made me just a little sad to be walking away from it, but I had things to do. "Let's get this thing solved."

Chapter 18

Jules Sharpe

The loud sound of guitars wailing out of strained old speakers was not the soundtrack Jules Sharpe would have preferred for reading his morning paper. *The Tennesseean* was laid out neatly on the scarred tabletop in front of him, neon purple lights pulsating as focused beams swept the stage to his right. He sat in an aging booth, studying an article about the rise of tourism numbers in Williamson County, a substandard cup of coffee that had long ago lost its steam sitting next to his right hand, a stale grocery-store croissant hard as a rock to the left of his paper.

This wasn't how he envisioned his morning routine would go. Jules Sharpe imagined a more pleasant setting—the back garden of a Victorian estate in Brentwood, just outside Nashville proper. The rolling green hills would provide a lovely backdrop as he ate fresh croissants and pastries made by an in-house chef and drank freshly ground coffee of the highest caliber, poured from a hot

French press by a personal butler as he started his day in a leisurely manner, the birds chirping in the suburban quiet.

Not like this. Here he read his paper by the glow of the purple lights refracting off the stage as a naked dancer gyrated on a pole while idiot customers threw dollar bills at her. He wanted a country estate; all he had was this slumhole titty bar on the edge of Nashville, and barely that. He still owed a bunch of money on it, so he couldn't even properly call it his.

Yet.

Bones was the name of the place. Inside joke. Also not his. It referred to the side business that had typically been done in the back rooms of the establishment, before the Metro Nashville PD had gotten quite serious about eliminating prostitution and very wise to the fact that "private" dances at Bones involved actual privates touching each other quite a lot. That had been the downfall of the previous owner.

Jules Sharpe was a man who liked to live on the edge, but preferred to keep his criminal activities back from it a bit. There was no enjoying an estate in the rolling hills of Brentwood if you were sentenced to twenty up in Brushy Mountain, after all.

Gil Wallis was a mook, classic tough guy, and unfortunately the best that Jules had on his small but slowly growing team. The fact that one of his eyes was slightly larger than the other drove Jules just about nuts, which was how Gil looked. Gil slid into the booth next to him, broad chin so wide he might have had trouble getting a bicycle helmet with a strap big enough to fit. This was another part of the morning routine that Jules wasn't a fan of. Another reason he wanted his estate, his peace, his quiet.

"What's up, boss?" Gil asked, in a distinctly non-

Southern accent. He sounded like he was from Jersey. Because he was.

Jules did not answer at first. He liked to make Gil wait in the mornings. When he had to, Sharpe could be forceful. He'd busted a head or two in his time. Done a little worse once or twice. He preferred not to; what was the purpose of having flunkies like Gil if you had to do your own incriminating dirty work, after all?

Still, he made Gil wait a full thirty count before answering. Gil was wise to this by now, didn't seem to care. He chewed a fingernail while killing the time, finger looking tiny against the backdrop of his oversized chin.

"Something interesting," Jules said, sliding the paper over to Gil, shutting it so he could see the front page article.

Gil skimmed it. He was not a big reader in Sharpe's estimation. "So?" He looked up, blank-eyed, chin just sitting there waiting to be broken in five so it could be normal-sized. There had to be a surgery for that.

"Did you read it?" Jules asked calmly. Of course he had. Or parts of it, at least.

"Yeah, the thing on Broadway yesterday." Gil shrugged. "Saw it on the news. What about it?"

"*The Tennesseean* suggests it's a metahuman," Jules said, sliding the paper back and pretending not to give Wallis any attention while doing so. Looking him in the eye only encouraged him to talk more. Being pensive kept him off guard.

"And?"

Sharpe was tired of these conversations. Why was Gil the best right-hand man he could find? There had to be better, smarter criminals in this town. Still, he worked with what he had, so he spelled it out. "If one had a metahuman like this—" he tapped the black and white picture of the destruction in the honky-tonk with his fingertip "—on one's team, why...what do you suppose we could do with him?"

Gil shrugged. "I don't know. Break a lot of glass?"

Sharpe contained his annoyance. He was quite used to it. "The answer is, 'We could run this town,'" he said quietly. "This would be a game changer."

Gil just blinked. "Whaddya mean? How is this—whatever—better than a gun?"

Sharpe held in a sigh. "Think about a protection racket. About how you have to go and collect."

The slow light dawned in Gil's eyes. He was slow, but getting it. "Ohhh. You're saying a guy like this could wreck a non-paying customer—"

"In seconds." Sharpe folded the newspaper closed. "Without a gun. Without a bat. Without arousing suspicion by carrying those things around. Without leaving any evidence behind. And that's but one application of so many." He inclined his head.

"That's a good idea, boss," Gil said, nodding in respect. "What do you want us to do about this?"

"I should like it very much if you put some feelers out for this guy," Sharpe said crisply, tapping the photo of the wrecked bar again. "If we could find him before the police do." He eyed the headline: *Sienna Nealon is coming to Nashville!* "Before she does...well..." Sharpe smiled, and once more, he was envisioning himself on the estate he didn't own quite yet, living a life he hadn't gotten his hands on yet. "I think it could it be the start of something very profitable for all of us."

Chapter 19

Sienna

We parked about a block away from the crime scene, according to Chandler, leaving the government SUV in a tight lot next to a brick building. When I asked him why we couldn't just park on the street out front, he only smiled and said, "You'll see," before leading me off down a pretty average-looking city street.

My first impression of Nashville was that it was cute. It had a few skyscrapers that looked a little older, a lot that looked new, and quite a few construction cranes over the skyline that indicated more were coming. The tallest, most obvious building in town caught my attention for its strange architecture, and I pointed it out to Chandler.

"That's the AT&T building," he said, leading me down the somewhat aged brick street. "Everyone here calls it the Batman building, though."

I stared up; it did fit. There were two points at the top, separated by a gully between them, making it look like Batman's cowl. Another, geekier parallel came to mind and

I voiced it before I could stop myself: "It looks like a skyscraper version of the Eye of Sauron."

"You're not the first to point that out," Chandler said with a chuckle. "We're almost there." He pointed ahead.

I followed him to the next intersection, which was just a hell of a thing. The cross street in front of us was four lanes, but the intersection was just monstrous somehow. There were the standard crosswalks that squared it in, but also diagonal ones that cut through the middle of the square. Music was wafting through the air even though it was before eleven in the morning on a weekday.

"What in the magical shores of Asgard...?" I muttered as we approached. There was already a crowd on either sidewalk, moving up and down the street.

"Welcome to Broadway," Chandler said with a little hint of pride.

Each of the four corners of the intersection was taken up by a big, neon-lit bar, the signs glowing faintly even in the bright sunlight. Maybe they were just catching the sun, but they seemed to be shining, as though intended to draw people in. I saw signs that blared Luke's 32, Ole Red, another proclaiming BOOTS. The biggest eye-catcher was Kid Rock's Big Ass Honky-Tonk Rock & Roll Steakhouse. All the windows and doors on that one were open to the street for four floors, and music was pouring out into the street, along with the pleasant aroma of beer and something fried.

The pavement was old and worn, and we hooked a right on Broadway, me following Chandler a little dazed as I tried to take in the sights. "This is like a cross between the Strip in Vegas and Bourbon Street in New Orleans," I said, finally finding a way to put into words what I was thinking.

"One of the city's nicknames is Nashvegas," Chandler

said, now just full-on blooming with pride. "We are the nation's number one destination for bachelorette parties."

"I guess that makes you like a target-rich haven for single dudes looking to get laid," I said. The street went on for quite a ways in front of us. Looking back, I saw it ended in a couple blocks, a river shining brightly with sparkles of sunlight somewhere just beyond its terminus. A stadium sat just across it, a big one, with NISSAN written on its side.

Chandler laughed at my observation. "I think there are actually more women than men in Nashville, so maybe?"

"No wonder they call it Music City," I said. "I've never seen this much country music...uh, stuff—"

"Honky-tonks?"

"Yeah, that," I said. "And apparel, and...everything." I shook my head. Guitar music flooded my senses from a dozen sources. There was a lot playing on this street.

"Not a fan?" he asked.

I shrugged. "My mom liked some older stuff. Johnny Cash and whatnot. Then she went through a Garth phase when I was a kid and I got dragged along, but other than that, not particularly."

"Well, here we are," Chandler said, nodding at a bar to our left. It took up half the block, and the sign—busted out, but the glass already swept up off the street—said Screamin' Demons.

I chuckled under my breath at the ironic name. Next door, someone was playing an electric guitar and the opening riff of Metallica's "Enter Sandman" washed out through an open window. I paused, listening for just a second as the drum beats kicked in, and found myself tapping my steel-toed boots as Chandler held up the crime scene tape and I ducked into the ruin of the bar.

"Not a lot to see here," Chandler said. "The house

cameras were destroyed in the incident. We've got some witness accounts you can read over. They're mostly concurrent, a little variance here and there. No one lying in my estimation—"

"Just the normal dissonance you find when trying to get large numbers of people to agree on anything," I observed, looking behind the bar. Every single bottle had shattered, and the place stunk to high heaven of blended alcohols. I tried to hold my breath, feeling like I might be in danger of breaking sobriety if I even breathed too deeply. "Anything stand out?"

"We have a sketch artist rendition from three people, including the bartender," Chandler said, stepping over a table that had been knocked asunder at some point. "He had the most contact with the suspect."

I paused, looking up and examining a speaker that hung from the ceiling. It had completely blown out, the guts of it suspended by wire a few inches from the mount. "The guy did all this with his voice?"

"So they say." Chandler nudged a shattered beer bottle with the toe of his dress shoe. "He got up and was singing —it was karaoke night—and all of the sudden his voice just...changed."

"What kind of human collateral?" I asked. There was a small pool of what could only be dried blood at the table nearest the stage.

"A couple people had their eardrums popped," Chandler said. "Some migraines. Blurry vision."

I frowned. "Because of the fluid in the eyes being disrupted?"

"That's what the doctors suggested. Same with inner ears. Nausea. Vomiting—after the fact."

"I could do with some stomach acid to cover up the booze. It smells like a frat carpet the morning after a kegger in here," I said, taking another sniff of the rich smell of gin, whiskey, vodka—everything.

Chandler paused next to the bar, eyeing a cell phone that looked like the screen had exploded. "Have you ever seen anything like this before?"

"Not that I recall," I said, taking the step up to the stage. The mic stand was melted, like someone had taken a blowtorch to it from the top to about halfway down. Whatever had happened to the mass at the top, I had no idea. Similarly, the remains of a microphone rested nearby next to one of those numbered evidence placards with a *1* on it.

I made a slow turn to look out over the wreckage of Screamin' Demons. The sheer volume of destruction this guy had caused was pretty epic. It looked like a full-on bar fight had broken out, though obviously no such fight was in evidence. "How is there no video?" I asked, standing on the stage like I was the queen of this ruined kingdom.

Chandler shook his head. "Cameras were destroyed during the performance. And get this—somehow whatever he did traveled along the wires to the recording unit hard drive. Shattered it."

I let out a low whistle. "Got anything from street cameras, maybe?"

"Yeah, we have some footage. He's got his head down, though. Really shuffling. And of course it's mostly low-res, grainy. It's back at headquarters; we can take a peek when we get you armed up."

"I like that arming me is a priority for you," I said with a smile. I stood there on that stage, my steel-toed boot crunching in broken glass from the shattered lights.

He laughed. "Welcome to the South."

"Thanks. You keep pushing guns and swell job offers at me, I might end up liking it here. Nice contrast to..." My voice trailed off as I listened. Something in the background had caught my attention.

There was a guitar riff starting, slowly building next door. It had a twanging, morose quality, and I stepped off the stage to follow it without really thinking about it.

"What?" Chandler asked as I drifted past him.

It was really picking up steam now. I recognized it. A classic.

It was "House of the Rising Sun," by the Animals. But someone had slowed the tempo just a touch. I threaded my way around the fallen tables and broken beer glasses toward the busted panel windows that looked out onto the street. I didn't even bother with the door, I just hopped right out into the open air, the cool breeze rustling my hair as the notes became louder now that I was outside and there were no walls to muffle it.

The lead singer broke into the opening verse, and I blinked. It was a cover version, live, being done next door where they'd been playing "Enter Sandman" when I'd come in. I cocked my head; the bar had open windows, casement type, cranked open so that people passing by could enjoy the music.

I stood there on the sidewalk, the music washing over me. The lead singer's voice was powerful, bold, and yet somehow soothing. I found myself closing my eyes as they launched into the chorus. The band was on a corner stage, facing into the bar, but the music washed out the open window just fine and I swayed for a moment, the smell of the spring air filling my nose, the crowd on Broadway churning under the sound of this song.

"You like this one?" Chandler's raised voice came from beside me. I opened my eyes and found him swaying next to me.

"Yeah, I like the classics of rock," I said. "They were

what my mom grew up listening to, so she kinda passed that on to me, I guess. Didn't expect to hear it here, in Countrytown."

"It's not all about country here," Chandler said. "It's Music City. We have all kinds. I bought a CD from a guy on a corner the other day that was a rap debut."

I took a long breath as the singer in the bar, a tall guy who looked like a biker, really lit into the finish. "How was it?"

Chandler made a face. "A little heavy on the 'money and hoes' themes for my taste, but y'know, I like to support struggling artists."

"'Struggling artists'?" I chuckled. "You know, sometimes artists struggle for a reason."

"Because their art is not that good?"

"Harsh," I said, "but yeah, maybe sometimes. What I was actually talking about is how sometimes people need to learn hard lessons as they forge their craft." Here I was thinking of Friday's first intended single, "Droppin' Deuces," which was awful. His actual first single, which he'd recorded after he'd ditched being a hugenormous, muscle-begotten jackass, had charted into the Billboard Top 50, and was actually quite good. "How you don't just start out a natural and launch right to the top. For every overnight success, you miss five, ten years of work behind the scenes."

"Good point," Chandler said. "You read that in a biography?"

"I've read a few in my time, yeah," I said, and took one last look at the singer. He was really good. Surprisingly so. And he was playing in a dive bar here on the main-ish street in Nashville.

I looked up and down it. How many others like him, as

good as him, were playing here? How many others who were better maybe didn't make it as a star at all?

Probably a lot.

"We got a name on this guy?" I asked. "Our suspect?" I beckoned to Chandler, and he got the cue, started walking me back to the car.

"Sort of," Chandler said, as we headed back the way we'd come. "One name, like Elvis: *Brance*."

Chapter 20

Brance

When Brance woke up the next morning, the previous night had felt like a nightmare.

The taste of death was in his mouth, like he'd dumped a stale ashtray down there. He smacked his lips together. They were dry. So was his tongue, that nasty taste just malingering. He blotted at his face with his thick, dark arm hair. His eyes were slightly wet; allergies were kicking in with all these green shoots popping out of the trees. This was the downside of Nashville; allergies.

Brance got to his feet and stumbled to the bathroom. His apartment was a one-bedroom shoebox in Germantown. The neighborhood was gentrifying, which just meant it was getting expensive. And new. He'd gotten an old place, but it still cost a fortune compared to what he'd been paying for a one-bedroom apartment back in Wyoming.

He turned on the tap and filled the cup sitting by his toothbrush caddy. Cheap plastic from Walmart, both of them. All he could afford. He'd brought them from home.

Brance drained the cup, then looked at his face in the spotted mirror. It looked like it had been installed before World War II. Or maybe shortly after. His eyes were a little bloodshot, which was funny since he'd only had one beer.

Had it really gone like that? Was he misremembering?

He looked down at his hand. A fleck of metal was stuck to his wrist. Must have come from his melting of the microphone stand. Or the mic itself.

Brance shook his head, not daring to look at himself in the mirror. "No. No."

This had been his shot. How could it have gone wrong?

It couldn't have gone wrong. Not that way.

He belted out a few notes in the mirror. Looked at himself. Everything was fine. The mirror was still there. He looked out earnestly at the youthful face therein.

"*I know my feeeeelinnnnnns'*—" he started on one of his own compositions.

"*I need your healinnnn*

But I know that you won't shoowwwwww

Cuz you left me long agooooooo—"

Someone thumped the ceiling above him and Brance stopped. That happened sometimes. A look over his shoulder at the clock in the bedroom told him it was midday. The guy upstairs was a CNA or nurse or something, worked nights. Crabby bastard.

So what had happened last night? There was no way he did all that damage in Screamin' Demons. Not with his voice. He'd been singing for years. People back home had told him he needed to come here.

He needed to be heard.

"Something else was going on last night," Brance said, shaking his head. "That wasn't me. I didn't do that. Their sound system messed up. Something...something else happened. That wasn't me."

He looked at the lightly freckled face in the mirror, eyes yearning. "I wouldn't have done that. Couldn't have."

Still, it had happened. Bad luck, but it had happened. And Screamin' Demons' open mic night was now closed mic, for a long time he was guessing.

So...what next?

He thought back to Wyoming. To what he'd always do when something would go wrong. His dad had told him before he'd left that this was going to be hard. Stared at him with those empty eyes. Told him he'd probably fail in that hollow voice. That he'd have to dig deep in order to live the dream.

Well, it was time to dig deep, then.

"I'll do it again," he said, and that was that. Decision made. Someone had said once that you needed to go out there and introduce yourself to the world until you needed no introduction. That was what he had to do. With that, he took a breath, and thought about Broadway. So much careful strategy and planning, and it had blown up like the windows and speakers at Screamin' Demons.

Well, there was always another shot. There were other bars where they did open mics. Mercy's Faithless had one tonight, in fact. He'd hoped it'd be his triumphant second outing.

But instead, it was going to be his shot at redemption. Because this time...

This time he wouldn't fail.

Chapter 21

Sienna

T he TBI main office was a modern, boxy office complex made of glass and brick just north of Nashville. It had a weird little pop-out dome lobby that stretched a couple floors up from the ground level. A triad of tall radio antennas rose just before the lobby. Chandler had caught me staring at them, and I made the offhand comment, "I guess you guys must get awesome reception."

He just laughed and led me on, through the security checkpoints and into a warren of corridors.

First stop was the armory, where the rough-looking dude behind the counter gave me some options. Instead of going with the predictable, FBI-standard Glock, I decided to spice things up. He slapped a block of 9mm ammo and some choices down on the counter, and I tried a new Sig Sauer P320, the civilian version of the military's new standard-issue sidearm, as well as a Walther PPQ, then a Heckler and Koch VP9. All of them were striker-fired, like my FBI Glock, which meant no hammer to get snagged on clothing as I drew. All of them were 9mm, same cartridge and bullet size as my normal sidearm.

And I liked them all.

"Which you want?" the armorer asked, rough craggy face showing a hint of a smile, possibly from my own reflected enjoyment. I did enjoy shooting, just as I enjoyed almost all aspects of my training. Something about having an explosive chemical reaction flinging chunks of metal from my hand was oddly relaxing.

"I'll take the HK VP9," I said, and he slid me a holster and a couple spare magazines, already loaded. I looked for spare mags for the other two guns, but I didn't see them. "How'd you know I'd pick this one?"

"Same gun my wife uses," he said with a smirk. "Fits the hand well, right?"

I clipped the holster to my belt and pulled my hoodie down to hide it. "It really does. What about—"

"9mm, right?" He was already pulling out some smaller guns, clacking them on the counter surface. I ran my eyes over them—a Sig Sauer P365, a Glock 43, and a Smith and Wesson M&P Shield M2.0. He'd already pulled a selection of backup guns for me to consider.

"Yeah, I wouldn't want to step down to .380," I said, looking them over. I glanced up at his hardened face. "What do you think?"

He only took a second to slide his choice across to me. It was the Sig Sauer P365. "Extended magazine gives you twelve rounds."

I dipped my head lower, eyes bulging a little. "Uh, wow. I'd heard they had ten. Didn't know they had an extended mag. How big is—" He pushed the magazine toward me, and it had a little extra length, like a spare pinkie-hold, at the bottom. "For two extra rounds, I'll take."

He smiled again with that craggy face and slid me a

couple filled magazines plus a holster. I snapped it into place behind my back, and with a wave, I was off.

I found Chandler waiting outside the armory, focused on his phone. He picked up talking as soon as I walked out as though we'd never even parted. "I've got the security footage queued and waiting upstairs."

"Sounds good," I said, following him to the elevator. "I'm impressed with your operation here. I mean, a lot of it has to do with your armorer, who is clearly the greatest at his job, ever, and knows how to show a girl a good time—"

"Well, he knows how to show *you* a good time, at least," Chandler said. "I should have figured you for the type to be super impressed by weapons."

"What can I say?" I fiddled with my hoodie to make sure I wasn't imprinting all over the place. "I'm very into making sure I have the best means at my disposal to get out of the shit I always seem to land myself in."

The main bullpen was stunningly like every cop bullpen I'd ever been in. I was getting to the point where I really just wanted to walk into an investigative bureau and find myself in some sort of primitive forest with moss hanging from the ceilings and maybe a rock troll in the corner throwing out riddles. Anything to break the monotony of cubicle walls, guys in suits carrying cups of coffee, and LCD computer screens with open files. The boring hum needed to be replaced by something interesting, like maybe one of the performers from a bar on Broadway. The biker guy doing a fine rendition of the Animals would have been a good start, really.

But it was a bullpen, like any other. A white board with pending cases on one wall, a cork board with all sorts of mandatory memos pinned to it on another, and a variety of cop-like dudes lingering and working, not necessarily in that order.

At least they knew how to arm a girl around here. Diamonds may have been some girls' best friends, but mine tended to have dirty-sounding German names like Heckler and Koch, Sig Sauer and Glock (yes, I know the last one is Austrian. They border each other, they're so close. Spare me.).

"Prepare me for this video," I said. "Am I going to be seeing anything awesome?"

"No. Like I said before, he keeps his head down during most of it," Chandler said, waving me through to his desk. "We'll take a look and you can see for yourself."

Chandler's cubicle was decorated lightly, a couple motivational sayings printed and tacked to the walls, but otherwise nothing. No family pictures, no indicators of hobbies hung around him. Just the job, and one lone paper that had what looked like a playlist written on it.

"What's that?" I asked, pointing, because I'm never one to shy away from questions.

"Oh." Chandler put his head down, typing at his computer. "Well. My, uh, favorite playlist got deleted a few times so I, uh...printed it out so I can reconstitute it at will. For doing paperwork, you know."

I stared at the playlist, squinting to make sure I was reading this right. "Uh...I don't recognize most of these, but the ones I do—"

"Are country music, yes," Chandler said, sighing as though unveiling a great burden. "You gotta keep in mind, I grew up in East Tennessee in the 90s, okay? Country music was in a renaissance then. Not like it is now. I hate some of this modern country, but 90s country? It was epic. There was so much feeling, some great lyricists and singers. I mean, now a lot of it's like electronica or something, I can't even listen to it, but back then..." His eyes got a faraway look. "It was magic."

"Okay," I said, fighting the urge to back away slowly, mostly for comedic effect.

"Pfft, whatever, music snob," Chandler said, pulling up the surveillance video. "What was your golden age of music, then?"

"I dunno," I said. "I'm a classicist. But if you come at me with country and it's not Johnny Cash, I don't really know what to do with you."

"How about Big & Rich?" Chandler asked, swiveling in his chair to peer at me, all serious and intense. "'Save a Horse, Ride a Cowboy'—"

"Heard it. It's all right."

"'Holy Water'? 'Deadwood Mountain'? 'Big Time'?" He just kept rattling them off. "This is all from their debut album, which I loved. It's not even counting their follow-up, which had—"

"Please, can we just watch the video?"

"'8th of November,'" Chandler said. "One of the greatest songs of all time."

"Video now, preach the gospel of country music later."

Chandler just shook his head, but he did start the video.

It played out exactly like he said. There was a several-angle edit of a guy walking into Screamin' Demons, then staggering out afterward. I frowned as I watched, trying to glean anything I could from the footage. "He looks disoriented," was the only thing I could come up with.

"I noticed that too," Chandler said. "What do you reckon? Did his powers hurt him?"

"Maybe," I said, making a face. I didn't really buy that explanation. "Or he could have just been traumatized after finding out he almost knocked the audience dead in a literal way?"

"You don't think it was an intentional attack?"

"I mean, I haven't read the witness statements, but it seems to me if he'd meant to attack, he'd have pressed it until they were dead," I said. "Looks like he had the power for it."

"Unless the reason he was stumbling out was because he was drained by his own power?"

"Now you're just fishing."

"In the dark...?" Chandler grinned. "Nitty Gritty Dirt Band, 1987. You have to have heard of it."

I rolled my eyes. "Stop."

"Do your powers, like, leave you exhausted when you use them?" Chandler asked, mirth gone and his seriousness returned.

"Well," I said, "they do have an effect, I guess. It is a little like using a muscle to exhaustion if you overdo it, at least with things like fire and light nets and whatnot. So maybe there's some validity to your theory, if he wasn't used to using his powers."

Chandler nodded along. "Okay. Well, what I take away from this is we really don't know what Brance is up to, if he hit his limits and wanted to press on hurting people or just pulled back because he didn't realize he was."

"Witness statements don't say?"

"The witnesses were extremely confused," Chandler said. "And disoriented. Bleeding like crazy from the ears in some cases." He elbowed a stack of files on his desk. "I was going to sift them."

"I'll help," I said, starting to reach for the stack.

"No, it's fine," Chandler said, shaking his head and rising. "I've got help for this; it's scut work."

I blinked in surprise. "It's the work. It's what I'm here for."

Chandler shook his head. "Bosses don't want you doing scut work. Directive came down from on high: the mayor and the governor. They've got something else for you." He nodded toward the door and off he went. I followed, cautiously, wondering what the mayor and governor could possibly have in store for me.

If experience was any guide, though, I had a feeling I wasn't going to like it.

Chapter 22

"Do you like it?" Chandler asked, grinning broadly.

We were standing out in the parking lot outside the TBI offices, sun gleaming down from overhead and shining off the beautiful BMW 740i, a stunning black sedan.

"It's...very nice," I said cautiously, not sure why we were out here, admiring this very pretty and presumably very luxurious car.

"This is a $120,000 car," Chandler said, his grin almost infectious. "We seized it from a mobster six months ago, and now we use it for sting operations and whatnot." He strolled around the back. "The stereo is amazing. Leather seats with heat and AC. It's got all the bells and whistles."

"And now you get to use it...?" I asked, trying to figure out what the purpose of this display was.

"Uh, no," he said, chuckling. "This is for you."

I stared at him. Then at the car. "Huh?" He nodded at it, somewhat emphatically. I still stared blankly. "Wait, you're not giving this to me...?"

"It's for you to use while you're here," he said,

thrusting both hands at the vehicle like he was a *Price is Right* model showing me the awesomeness of what I beheld. He lifted one hand and a keyfob dangled there. He tossed it to me and I caught it easily. "Just be gentle with her."

I stared at the fob in my hand. "Wha...what am I supposed to do with this?"

"Drive."

I just stared at the fob. I wasn't used to driving myself...well, anywhere. Especially lately. "Huh."

"Take her for a spin," Chandler said. "See how she feels." He closed his eyes as though savoring something tasty. "I'll text you the details for your hotel. You can go check in. Maybe make a spa appointment or something—"

"My last massage left me scarred," I said, still frowning at the fob. "Literally, on the feet, for like a day. So...just because I'm dense...you are cool with me taking this car and driving it around your city unsupervised?"

"Yeah-huh." It was Chandler's turn to blankly stare. "Those were my orders, in fact. Give you the car, let you run loose and get the lay of the land."

"While you sift through witness statements." I just stared at him.

Chandler nodded. "That's right." His smile evaporated. "Why? Is something wrong?"

I took a deep breath, unable to shake the frown on my face. "This is...very unlike what I'm used to. Usually people pick me up, the FBI and the locals drive me around, supervise me like a hawk the entire time, and I really seldom get to drive. And never a car as nice as this."

Chandler let out a rumbling chuckle. "Sounds like your job really sucks if your bosses don't even trust you enough to drive a car. I mean, you've got superhuman reflexes."

"Yeah." I stared at the fob, and a sudden itching desire

to see how it drove washed over me. "Yeah. Yeah, they do oversupervise me." I said it, but not quite with a straight face. I had a near-legendary propensity for getting into trouble, after all, so me being supervised was not an idea entirely without merit.

Still, I hadn't realized how suffocating it had been. And taking New York transit meant that the last time I remembered driving myself anywhere had been in New Orleans, when Holloway had been too drunk to drive us back from a restaurant.

"Okay, I'm going to go get this mythical lay of the land," I said, shoving the fob into my hoodie pocket. My leather jacket was in my luggage, unfortunately. "Check into the hotel. See what I see."

"That's the spirit," Chandler said. "Get after it."

I got in the car and started her up as my phone buzzed. Message from Chandler with an address. I punched it into the car's nav, and a gentle, slightly robotic female voice started giving me guidance.

I set the seats to the right distances, admiring the smooth feel of the leather. I applied a foot to the pedal—slowly—and felt the subtle purr of the engine as I took the car through a gentle slalom around the parking lot. She handled well, and I remembered how to drive pretty quickly, though I'd never felt super comfortable with it.

The BMW, though, made it feel easier than it maybe was. Pretty soon I found myself on the freeway and hit the windows. They rolled down, and my hair whipped around me in the breeze, strays finding their way loose from my ponytail.

This was the life, I had to concede as I headed south toward downtown Nashville. The tall buildings were rising in the distance, and I could see the Eye of Sauron building over there, across a river. The BMW breezed along like a leaf carried on the wind. I slid in and out of the lanes of a mostly-empty freeway, passing the slower cars like they were standing still.

I'd forgotten the freedom that driving brought, that singular feeling of possibility that came from being on the open road with the wind whipping all around you. I settled back in the comfortable seat and pressed the pedal down a little harder as I headed toward Nashville, feeling strangely happier than I'd been in a long time.

Chapter 23

Reed

I shuffled out of the warehouse with only a few words exchanged with Ben Kelly. The admin assistant was muted, surprised, like the wind had been taken out of his sails from my little talk with his boss. He muttered a few platitudes about hoping I'd see my way through this, and I departed without any promise of future action or appointment to do anything else for them. Which was certainly more comfortable for me than committing to any specific action.

The crowd outside was just about where I'd left them, standing off from the cops at a reasonable distance. I guess I'd defused the tension with my wind-blowing tactic, because the separation between them remained. There was definitely some grumbling on the labor side, and the cops remained plenty tentative. They were doing their jobs, protecting property, but I couldn't see this going any kind of well if the crowd made the decision to storm the warehouse and start burning shit down. Not that I thought it had come to that point, yet.

"Hey," someone called as I stepped through the fence. I caught sight of a woman at the fore of the crowd, dressed like the rest in Lotsostuff company overalls. She was a little past her prime, wrinkles around her eyes combined with the leathery look of her skin telling me she'd some mileage. She looked serious, though, waving me over. "C'mere!"

I glanced around at the cops, who said nothing and kept their eyes straight ahead, save for one slightly over-weight cop who gave me a wide-eyed, "Wouldn't do that if I were you," kind of look.

Which I ignored. I'm not really the listen-and-obey type. I headed straight for Lady Overalls, taking note of the guys flanking her on either side like personal security. One was a big black dude, had to be 6' 5" or so, bald, arms folded forbiddingly across his Lotsostuff jumpsuit. The other guy was like a study in contrasts. Probably 5'9", white, nervous, twitchy, watching everything going on around him like someone was going to come thundering out of the crowd and smash him across the face with a fish or something.

I walked right up to the older lady, my own hands planted firmly on my hips to indicate I wasn't opposed to listening, and I stared right at her before smiling. "Yes, ma'am?" I even remembered my manners.

She didn't scowl at me calling her ma'am, which I took to be a good sign. "You just flew in here like you came off a cloud." She rolled her tongue around in her mouth as she looked me over. "What's your plan here, Angel Boy?"

I cocked an eyebrow at her. "I'm no angel."

"Well, you got the face of one," she said, and a wicked grin split her lips. "And the rest of you ain't doing a bad job representing, either. So...what do you want here, Angel Boy? You playing with Mr. Mills up there? You hired security?"

That got me bristling. "No. I work for myself."

She raised her eyebrows, which were two heavily painted lines. "Oh, lookie here. We got ourselves a concerned citizen." She made to offer a round of applause, which the crowd immediately joined in on. I guess I'd found their fearless leader. "What concerns you enough to fly on down to our little corner of the country? Plight of the working man? And woman?" She added the second as almost an afterthought.

"Sure," I said, trying to stay noncommittal. The crowd was back to shouting stuff at the cops, even though I caught enough eyes that I knew they were watching her for cues. "I'm always concerned about the plight of the working-class."

"Maybe you are an angel, then," she said, but the cynicism in her eyes said she didn't buy that, not for a minute. She slid on up to me, though, and reached up to pat me on the shoulder. Her flanking bodyguards hung back, watching me, especially the big black dude. "But if I were you, I'd watch which side of this thing you sit down on, if you know what I mean." Her hand slid down to my pocket, slipping something into it as she patted me again. A little familiar. "You might end up the wrong kind of angel." And with a wink, she slid back to her bodyguards.

I had a feeling by the way she'd moved, the way she acted, she'd commanded the attention of men aplenty in her day. I shook off the interaction, and turned my back on the crowd to walk away. I waited until I was far enough from the crowd before I reached into my pocket to see what she'd put there.

It was a piece of paper with a note written on it. Pretty simple:

Puckett's. Murfreesboro. 7 o'clock.

Guess I had a dinner date.

Chapter 24

Sienna

I really don't know what to do with myself when I'm not on the job.

Especially when I'm in a strange town, separated from my Netflix account, without even any luggage to call my own. I'd checked in with the airline (my luggage had somehow caught a non-stop flight to Seattle; *Such a mystery how that happened, Ms. Nealon, we are so sorry and will definitely fix it ASAP!*), checked into my hotel, and now I was just sitting with my charging cable plugged into my phone, on my hotel bed, scrolling to the ends of the internet.

Sure, I could have downloaded Netflix onto my phone and watched something, but bleh. My screen was tiny, because I had to carry the damned thing in my pocket since I wasn't a purse girl.

So...scrolling the internet. Yeah.

I'd had enough of my criminology audiobook. I pondered loading up my reading app and doing a little of the eyeball-style reading. Aaron Mendelsohn had recommended a book to me on the history of assassination as a policy tool in the Middle East. It was pretty good, what I'd read of it, but not exactly light.

My hotel had a great view of the city. I stared out, flat on my back, looking across downtown Nashville.

There was Broadway, already teeming with activity, though twilight was still a ways off. I'd read about it; you could literally hear live music any hour of the day there. Which I thought was kinda awesome.

But it was all in the bars, which for me, the recovering alcoholic, was less awesome. Testing my will to stay sober against my will to have a whiskey? Not a thing I tried to do. Not because I feared losing control again—much. But it was always a danger in the back of my mind, which was why I avoided the drink. And the bars.

This was not a year where I could afford to lose control or crack under the pressure. The stakes were too high, the margin for error too low. Getting drunk would not help me thread this particular needle.

I pushed off the bed and made my way to the window. Drummed my fingers against the glass as I looked out. One of the buildings downtown looked old and had a dome atop it, like one of those seventies classics where they put a restaurant up there that slowly turns to take in the whole city. A glance to my left revealed a massive construction project ongoing, blocks and blocks of it. North of that was what looked like an old federal building or railroad station, complete with a clock tower. That must have been old downtown.

The Eye of Sauron looked across the intervening buildings at me. Who had designed that? It must have predated the *Lord of the Rings* movies at least by a little, because there was no way some company would have approved that sucker to be built knowing it would draw those comparisons.

When my phone rang, I almost leapt to answer it just so I could have something to do. The 615 area code would have given away the game even if I didn't already have Chandler's info programmed into my contact list.

"Hey," Chandler said when I answered. "How are you liking it so far?"

I froze. He must have been talking about the car. "Very smooth ride," I said.

"Ah, good. And the hotel? Are you finding some time to relax?"

Tell him you're sitting on your ass doing nothing, and it's stressing you out.

I did not say that. "Yep," is what I went with instead. Seemed more diplomatic.

"Good, good," Chandler said.

"So...what's up?" I asked. "Making any headway?" I might have sounded a little eager. I tried to tamp down on that enthusiasm. Sienna Nealon was supposed to be cool, after all, and fearsome. She wasn't supposed to sound like she was waiting for some cute guy to call and ask her to prom.

So sad that, for me, getting called to go fight a bad guy was as appealing or more so than getting asked to prom.

"Hey, before I forget, I meant to tell you there's an AR-15 and a Mossberg shotgun in the trunk of your car," Chandler said.

"You are such a sweet-talker," I said. "And I really love the gift horses you guys bring, because...you get me. You guys really get me. But seriously...anything on the search?"

"Eh, not really," Chandler said. "We've got eight guys on it, and we've watched all the angles, but there's really no clear shot at a face, so we're left with a generic description.

White male, twenties or thirties, brownish blonde hair, a shade under six feet, we think."

"Is that from the footage or witness statements?"

"Both. We had one lady do a composite sketch with an artist because she said she thought the guy was handsome until he started singing and blew out her eardrums. Took the artist a while because the witness isn't hearing so good right now."

I cringed. How much would it suck to go for a night on the town and get your eardrums blown out? "At least you've got something."

"Not much, though. We'll have Metro PD disperse the sketches. They've got units on Broadway now, keeping an eye and an ear out, but so far...all is business as usual. The only eardrums hurting are from amplifier feedback and people who actually can't sing but belt it out at the top of their lungs as they walk down the street drunk."

"That's...peaceful," I said, channeling my disappointment and trying not to be too obvious about it. Having people get hurt was a bad thing, Sienna. "Maybe this guy realized the error of his ways and he's not going to cause any more trouble."

"Is that the way it usually works for you?"

"No," I said. "Usually once a meta gets powers, they escalate things a little at a time in using those powers. Rob a convenience store. Then a bank. Their aims get grander and they get bolder as they realize the laws that applied to them before don't really do so anymore. It's like a modified version of any perp as they climb the criminal ladder and get more and more comfortable on the other side of the law."

"That's interesting," Chandler said. "We haven't had much in the way of meta incidents in Tennessee. This is a real learning experience for me."

"So glad I can be an educator," I said, checking my watch. My stomach let out a growl. "What's the plan for tonight? You going to Broadway to see if this guy makes another appearance?"

"I think I'm going to hunker down with the crew and keep churning through the tapes, but...you know what? You should hit Broadway tonight." His voice rose, like he was excited for me. "You could pull up a chair and chillax at a bar, take in some live music." He was animated, like this was his kind of idea of a fun night. "If we need you, or something happens, we can call you up. Or if you want to check in with Metro PD, let them know where you are, they could just send in a uniform and pull you out if things go down. They'll have a heavy presence on Broadway tonight. Cops on every corner."

Relax and listen to music while waiting for a perp to make his move? I frowned. This was the weirdest assignment.

But...that actually sounded kind of...

Good?

"Yeah, maybe I'll grab something to eat and head on over to Broadway," I said, coming around to the idea. And the strangeness of being relaxed and not tense and crazy while waiting for terrible things to happen.

"Awesome," he said. "Hope you have a quiet night, but it's good to have you around in case it's not. Later." He hung up.

I pulled the phone from my ear slowly, holding it as though I didn't know whether I should pocket it or hang it up or just drop it like a mic. This was such new territory for me. I was hungry, and I was going to go get dinner—on my own. Not an unusual turn of events for life in New York lately, but it was extremely strange for when I was on assignment.

Still, I couldn't knock the freedom of it. I could go anywhere, eat anything. It was all up to me, no partner or sidekick or random jabroni to push me into a decision. "Hmm," I said, feeling a little at loose ends. "Well."

How weird was it that I wasn't used to being on assignments and having the freedom to do what I wanted?

Chapter 25

The neighborhood I was staying in was called The Gulch. I found this out from the hotel's friendly desk clerk whose life story I caught as I was asking for her advice on a place to eat (Jenny moved from Boston two years earlier because Boston was, "like, so terrible in the winter, and here's it *amazeballs*. Did you see the cherry blossoms?!"). Her enthusiasm was infectious, and she sounded a little like a tourist ad in much the same way as Chandler.

I walked out the hotel's front door knowing that I was going to Saint Añejo, a Mexican place only a few blocks from my hotel. I made it in about fifteen minutes, walking the hills of downtown with a relaxed ease borne of my complete lack of anywhere to be right now. The sun was starting to set somewhere beyond the tall buildings and occasional construction cranes that made up the Nashville skyline. Shadows greeted me like an old friend, and cars with their headlights on slid by on the streets.

No one said anything, no one honked. Unlike New York, Nashville was a surprisingly quiet city. There was little trash littering the sidewalks, and I only saw a couple homeless people on the entire walk. Maybe this was the nice part of town. It certainly seemed to be filled with brand new condo buildings that stretched toward the darkening sky.

Saint Añejo was a charming little place in a brick building, tucked away in the middle of a city block and surrounded by other restaurants. I saw signs for Moto, Virago and Whiskey Kitchen, along with a rather opulent place at the end of the block that had no sign. A couple of BMWs pulled around the corner, telling me that whatever that place was, it was probably a little too upscale for someone dining on a government paycheck.

There was a valet booth right across the street from the restaurant that looked like it might serve the whole block. Behind me, the entirety of Nashville was visible across a huge train yard with a dozen tracks. The building that looked like an old train station sat across the tracks and a parking lot, looming over it all with its huge clock tower. That looked like old Nashville; everything else beyond it seemed fairly new.

I got a table in the bar area and didn't spend much time lingering over the menu. I ordered tacos, and not the kind you get from a truck or an old-school Mexican restaurant. These were upscale tacos. Not fancy BMWs upscale, like that place around the corner, but definitely nouveau cuisine, the type of thing you see in the trendy restaurants. One of them was Korean barbecue, the other a Nashville Hot chicken, whatever that was. The server asked me if I wanted a margarita. I actually hesitated for a second, then remembered I was sober almost a year now. "No, thanks," I said, trying to shake off that momentary feeling of utter relaxation of all my standards. I was on the job, too. This was no time for bad decisions to creep in.

The front of the bar was garage-door-style windows,

and they were all open to the street. The breeze was coming in, starting to get a little of the night chill but not too much. People were eating outside on a terrace, and I wondered if this was unusual weather for February here. I couldn't complain; I'd been through enough bitter Minnesota Februarys at this point that this seventies weather was like a blessing from heaven.

The tacos were great. The Korean barbecue was sweet and tangy, perfect with the kimchi. The Nashville Hot chicken was hot, but also a little vinegar-y, making my mouth burn in just the right way. I didn't exactly go screaming for a glass of milk, but it was a pleasant heat. I wondered if, given the name, hot chicken was a thing around here. If so, I wanted to try more, because the flavor was top notch.

By the time I had some tres leches and paid my bill, the sun was down and the lights of Nashville were gleaming. I glanced at my phone, which I'd had on the table the entire dinner but tried not to fiddle with. That had been an exercise in patience. No one was texting, no one was calling. My new bosses were presumably into whatever the hell was going on in DC on an ordinary February night, and Shaw was done with me. I wasn't close friends with the agents I worked with (my choice, mostly), and so I didn't get texts from them.

My actual friends were at a distance because of my choices, because of what I had to do, so they were radio silent.

It made for a quiet dinner as I resisted the urge to just browse the internet. By the time I stepped out on the sidewalk, I found myself enjoying the silence.

But also eager for a little more noise. I didn't want to just sit around my hotel all night.

So I flipped open my map app and found that the part

of Broadway with the bars was a fifteen-minute walk away. I debated—just for a moment—whether I should go back and get my car.

Nah. I'd check in with Metro PD when I got there. If I needed to get into a chase, better I go with them. I did a quick retention touch; all my guns were still there. I flexed my feet inside my steel-toed boots. They were surprisingly comfortable, and I was ready for a walk.

Course set, I headed east along McGavock to the corner, then took a left. One turn ahead was Broadway and a bridge that would take me into downtown. With a wary eye out, watching around me carefully, I started that way, wondering if the night's peace would continue.

And if so, for how long?

Chapter 26

Brance

"You're going to be waiting a while," the lady behind the bar said with a shrug. "Should have been here an hour ago. Open mics and karaoke nights always fill up fast around here." She didn't sound the least bit apologetic, but that was fine with Brance. He knew this, which was why he'd taken a month to work up the courage to try the open mic at Screamin' Demons.

"That's okay," Brance said, casting his eyes to the stage. Of everyone in here, probably ninety percent of them were here for the open mic. Still, that meant ten percent were tourists or eager listeners.

The bar lady cleared her throat, and when Brance looked over at her, she was pointing at a sign: *Two Drink Minimum.*

"Oh, uh," Brance said, fumbling for his wallet. It was light, but surely he could afford a couple beers. "Just give me a Michelob Golden Light for now."

She didn't put aside her suspicious look, but she did

grab him a glass, which he slid some cash across the bar for, then threw the change in the tip jar. That didn't buy him any goodwill from the bartender. It was tough to buy much goodwill with a buck thirty.

That done, Brance settled in. Here, he planned to do something a little different, song-wise, than what he'd done at Screamin' Demons. Which was fine with him, too. He'd have changed everything in his act to avoid a repeat of last night. He was going to go with whatever they had available. No original song tonight.

Totally fine. He'd make it work.

Passing back through, the bartender slapped a big three-ring binder in front of him with SONGS in a printed page shoved under the plastic cover holder. Brance took a long pull of his cold beer as someone belted out the Chris Stapleton cover version of "Tennessee Whiskey"—that one was getting a lot of play these days—his voice cracking as he tried to hold the notes and failed.

Brance just grimaced. It wasn't going to be hard to stand out in this crowd. He just needed the right song, and for things to not go bad like they had last night. It had to be the equipment. Had to be.

Brance kept paging through, slowly, because he had a lot of time to kill before he'd be on, trying to figure out what the right choice was to make his mark.

Chapter 27

Sienna

"Y ou guys come get me in there if anything goes off, okay?" I looked Officer Sims of the Metro Nashville PD in the eyes. Broadway was swirling madly around me, the tourists, locals, drinkers, and song junkies apparently undeterred by what had happened at Screamin' Demons last night.

"Yes, ma'am," Sims said, nodding politely. He was parked right in front of Screamin' Demons, and I could see three other cruisers visible in spite of the thick-packed sidewalks. "We'll holler if anything happens."

"Great," I said, and slipped away, hands in my jacket pockets. I'd ditched the hoodie back at the hotel before dinner, done hiding my face and ready to look somewhat professional.

I walked into a bar called Old Burd's, just two doors down from the ruin of Screamin' Demons, which was still closed and covered in crime scene tape. The music coming out of Old Burd's had drawn me to it; there was a woman with a sweet voice lilting like honey out the open windows and into the street. I had to push through the clotted crowd on the sidewalk and a shoulder-to-shoulder entryway to get in, which told me I wasn't the only one that had stopped to listen off the street.

There was a less than zero chance of me recognizing a country song just walking along the street, I figured, given my limited repertory, but this one I knew, thanks to Mom: "New Way to Fly" by Garth Brooks. Mom had listened to Garth's *No Fences* album on repeat on our stereo for weeks, which meant I'd listened to it, too, though I'd complained bitterly to her that I did not like it.

But I did, a little. And I think she knew that.

Just another thing we'd never have a chance to really set straight between us. I ignored a feeling that crawled up from my guts into my chest, and elbowed my way—mostly gently—to the bar and took a stool at the end.

"Get you something?" the bartender asked. She was a twenty-something with powder blue hair cut in a bob and a nose ring. She raised her voice to make herself heard over the music.

"Sprite?" I asked.

She nodded. I guess they had it. "Want a maraschino cherry in it?"

I blinked a couple times. "Hell yeah."

She grinned and went off to get my drink as I turned on the stool to listen to the singer. She was winding her way to the close of the song. She finished with a flourish, and I actually liked her finish better than the original, to my surprise.

"Sprite," the bartender said, delivering a drink behind me. The sweet smell and the sound of the fizz over the sudden quiet now that the song was over preceded thunderous applause by a second as my ears caught the full power of a packed house smacking their hands together in wild approbation.

I managed my flinch from the noise as I handed the bartender some cash. I didn't need the calories from more than one Sprite, especially on a day when I hadn't done much but walk around a little. My meta metabolism was good and all, and certainly faster than a normal human's, but I'd proven it had limits for caloric intake a few years back and had been watching those limits ever since. Not quite as hawkish as a professional athlete or anything, but I wasn't all willy-nilly about it anymore either.

"Thank you, thank you," the lady singer called from the stage, flush with pleasure at her reception now that the applause had died down. "I'm Maesie May, and this is muh band, the Spotlighters." She nodded at the three guys behind her on bass, keyboard and steel guitar. "See that tip jar there?" She nodded to it, sitting at the front of the stage. "I take requests, so come on up here and be generous by supporting the arts. Thank you, darlin'," she said to a guy in a cowboy hat who put a twenty in the jar. "What do you want to hear? I've got three songs in the queue, and after that, you're up. What do you want?" He muttered something to her, and her smile never wavered. "That's a good one. All right. Next up—"

"She's good, isn't she?" I turned back to find the bartender looking past me to Maesie May on the stage.

"Oh," I said, a little surprised. "Yeah. I heard her from the street and wanted to hear, uh...more."

"Yeah," the bartender said, nodding. "She draws like that a lot." She smiled, then nodded to indicate the packed house. "She's going to be big, I think."

"That's...that's good," I said, not really sure what to make of that or what to say back. What did I know about music, after all?

The bartender must have taken my cue that the conversation was over, or maybe she just had work to do, because she went off to the other end of the bar as I turned my attention back to the stage. The Spotlighters were well into the opening licks of a song I didn't recognize, and Maesie May's eyes were closed in concentration, head swaying from side to side on her thin neck in time with the beat.

I stared around me for a moment, checking the crowd for danger, something I usually did a lot more often. There was no sign of any; everyone was focused on the stage, and there was not a malign-intent face to be seen. Everyone was as enthralled with Maesie May as I was. I settled back on my stool, sweat beading on my cold Sprite, and listened as she started to sing.

Chapter 28

Brance

"Hey. You're up."

Brance slipped off the bar stool and headed for the stage. There was a low hum around him, voices of the crowd all blurring together as he walked. Everything seemed a little louder these days than before, and he grimaced. Then again, though, Nashville was a bigger city than Cody, Wyoming, and the bars here were more crowded, the volume surely louder.

Every step his cowboy boots clicked, heel down, on the wood dance floor. Tables had been pulled over most of it to accommodate the throbbing crowd. Brance leapt up and took the microphone from the last guy, who seemed reluctant to let it go. He left a sheen of sweat on it, pure nerves given liquid form, and Brance tried not to make a show of wiping it against his pants. The last thing he needed was the mic slipping out of his hands before he could start.

"My name's Wayne," Brance said. No way was he using Brance right now. Not after last night. Disappointing, sure, but maybe he could go back to it someday, when he'd started to make his name and all this craziness was behind him.

But for now...he'd be Wayne. The dream was still the same for Brance, even though his name was not. "I'm going to be singing Keith Whitley's 'I'm No Stranger to the Rain,'" he said, and the bartender nodded to him as the first strains of the song started to leak out over the speakers. Brance closed his eyes, waiting for the moment to come when he'd open his mouth and sing.

Chapter 29

Sienna

"Thank you all," Maesie May said, waving to the crowd. "Thank you. I'm going to take a fifteen-minute break, but y'all stay right there. Keep your requests coming; just hand them to Bobby up here—" she nodded at her keyboard player "—and we'll get going again at 7:10. Trust me—y'all ain't going to want to miss this." She had a gleam in her eye, and with that, she hopped off stage, her drummer, a big dude in a leather jacket, escorting her through the crowd like a bodyguard.

"Wow," the guy next to me said to his date, "she's amazing. That voice—"

"Yeah," his date said, sounding a lot more jaded. "A voice like that in this town? Dime a dozen."

"But she's got, like...an X factor, don't you think?" The guy sounded utterly dumbstruck that his date couldn't get on board with his starry-eyed assessment.

"Sort of," she said, turning her attention to a vodka-based drink in front of her. The bartender had not been light on the pour, and I stuck a hand under my nose to blot out the smell until she drained it of some of the liquid and the scent, because it was making me want a drink.

I listened to the excited babble of the patrons as Old Burd's started to clear in the absence of Maesie May on the stage. Apparently they weren't going to heed her invocation to hang out, because soon enough you could actually see the exit, and the crowds moving past on the sidewalk again where before it had been too crowded with a slowdown and people lining the outside window to see the Broadway throngs moving by.

"Awesome work," the bartender said, and for a second I thought she was talking to me.

She wasn't. Maesie May was by my elbow, reaching out and taking up a drink that the bartender had put out for her. I took a long sniff; Cruzan rum, pineapple juice. Super sweet. I felt like I was getting cellulite on my thighs just smelling it.

"Thanks," Maesie May said, halfway into it. She took a look at me as she put her drink down, then did a double take. "Hey."

"Hey," I replied. "Nice work up there."

"Th—well—um—thanks," she finally managed to get out. She flushed, cheeks going pure red. "Sorry."

I raised an eyebrow at her. "For getting tongue-tied? You don't have to apologize to me. I wouldn't suggest doing it up on the stage, though."

She let out a weak laugh. "Yeah, that'd be hilarious. Also, the stuff of my nightmares."

"Really?" I glanced at the stage, where the keyboard player was taking a song request, presumably, from a girl who looked almost too drunk to stand. "Because getting up there at all? Would be my nightmare."

"It's really not that bad," Maesie May said. She stuck out her hand. "You are...her, right?"

"Depends on who you think I am," I said. "If you mean Trisha Yearwood, then I'm afraid you're outta luck."

She laughed again. "That's not who I thought you were. The lack of blonde gives that one away."

"Then I'm probably who you think I am," I said, taking a sip of my Sprite. I really wanted it to last the night, so I was taking it easy.

"Wow, a real superhero," Maesie said, still flushed, but this time with excitement instead of embarrassment. "In Nashville. That's so lit."

"Let's hope it doesn't get actually lit," I said. "I'm not really prepared to deal with fire anymore."

"Hah, you take my slang and turn it around into a literal thing," Maesie said. "That's something. Not really sure what."

"You're a hell of a singer," I said, trying to change the subject. "I was really impressed with what you were doing up there."

"That's high praise." Now she flushed again, back to embarrassment. It was kind of funny how easily she blushed. "I mean, coming from someone who actually does something worth singing about."

"Oh, I don't know about that," I said. "I don't think a song about me would be particularly...uh..." I searched for the right word. "Family-friendly?" That wasn't it. It was accurate, but not quite what I was looking for.

"I think it could be like one of the epic poems of old," Maesie said, sparkle in her eye. "Like a Homeric ode, you know? Poetry and song, united?"

"Probably wouldn't fit well into the current genres, though," I said. "I mean, where do you even classify that? Not exactly the 'Baby Baby' of modern pop, and unless you're turning it into a drinking song, I don't think it would fit well with country. I mean, I don't even have a pickup truck."

She sighed, as though feigning disappointment in me. "There's more to country than that."

"So people keep saying," I said, taking a sip of my Sprite. "And so I'm starting to maybe hear. A little."

"A little?" She angled her head low, eyes bright and locked on mine. "I'd take that. It's a start. How long are you in town?"

I shrugged. "'Til the job gets done."

"Oh, oh!" She straightened. "You're here because of the—" She pointed at the wall of the bar, and it took me a second to realize she was indicating Screamin' Demons, because she was pointing the wrong way.

I didn't correct her. "Yeah," I said. "Because of that. So when that's solved, I'm out."

"Cool, cool," she said breezily, picking up her drink. "Well...enjoy the show. You don't have anywhere you need to be?"

"Not unless something bad happens," I said.

Maesie favored me with a broad smile. "Let's hope for that, then. But definitely stick around for a minute. My next song's going out to you."

I felt my eyes widen without my intending them to. "Uh, okay. What is that supposed to mean...?"

She gave me a wink as she made her way back through the crowd. "You'll see."

Maesie took to the stage again in a quick jump up, her drummer trailing along behind her. "Heyyyyy," she announced once she was up there, waving to us all like it was a ten-thousand-person venue. "I'm back in like five minutes. I know that's a disappointment for you people who were hoping I'd come back as, like, Kacey Musgraves, but here I am." She glanced back at the bass player and he nodded, flipping his phone at her. "And wow, thanks for all your support. We've got a ton of requests coming up. But first!" She leaned over and whispered something to the bass player, then sat back on her stool, eyes all lit up with mischief that I found very uncomfortable. "I have a song for a very special someone in the audience..."

I felt a pre-emptive cringe coming on. What song could she possibly sing to me that wouldn't be absolutely terrible...?

The band struck up a tune, and I knew what it was in a second. Because people played it for me all the time in bars or on jukeboxes, in spite of the lyrics clearly referencing dudes.

"Holdin' Out for a Hero" by Bonnie Tyler.

And she sang it right at me, smiling, and seemingly on the verge of laughing the whole time.

Nice. At least it beat being called names.

Chapter 30

Brance

He was almost through the first chorus when his voice broke a little. He didn't mean for it to happen, but it did, and he tried to get back on track—

A wrenching squeal cut through the sound system, and a shriek came up through the audience. Brance heard it immediately, his eyes snapping open. He caught a host of people with hands at their ears, pushing, faces twisted in pain.

Brance froze, listening to the squeal of electronic feedback, feeling that slow, paralyzing sense of horror gripping him like icy hands on his heart.

It was happening again.

Chapter 31

Sienna

M aesie May was about halfway through her audio tribute to me when Officer Sims of the Metro PD burst into the door of Old Burd's, a wild look in his eyes and no time for what was going on onstage. He scanned the crowd just a level below panic, searching for me, presumably.

I put my Sprite down and leapt off my barstool quicker than a peal of thunder. I made it halfway to the door before he caught my rapid motion through the crowd. He stood there in the doorway as I finished my transit, shoving some poor sap out of the way to close the last meter.

He didn't have to speak. I asked first: "Where?"

Sims turned and led me outside, presumably holding his powder until I could hear him, the music fading as we hit the sidewalk and put a door between us and Maesie May's killer rendition of the song. Funnily enough, it looked like someone did, in fact, need a hero right now. "This way," Sims said, breaking into a run. I saw other

142

cops heading down the street, streaks of navy uniforms cutting through the plodding crowds. One cop had taken advantage of the street traffic's lack of movement with all Broadway's lights currently red, and he was sprinting between the cars. "Mercy's Faithless is the name of the place." He tossed a look over his shoulder as he stepped off the curb. "It's karaoke night."

I almost leapt past him, but paused mid-step. "How did you know that?"

Sims turned as red as a ripe tomato. "I, uh...go there sometimes on karaoke night when I have it off."

"Everyone's a singer but me in this town, I guess." I leapt ahead of him, coming down in the middle of the street, then leapt again. In this much foot traffic, no way was a traditional run going to be faster.

Neon nights spelled out Mercy's Faithless ahead, which I thought was a funny name for a honky-tonk in the Bible belt. Maybe that was part of the satire. A pronounced and horrific squealing was barely audible to my meta ears as I landed half a block from the front door and vaulted through an open pedal tavern sitting at a stoplight. A shit-load of bachelorettes were having a party and yelled approbation at me as I leapt sideways through them. I was surprised they had the wits about them to figure out who I was given the heavy smell of wafting beer coming off the pedal tavern, but maybe they thought I was a pigeon and were impressed by that.

Rolling off a Tesla SUV, I leapt up onto the sidewalk and over the heads of several pedestrians, clearing a spot on the sidewalk to land. "Move!" I shouted, commanding the attention of drunken pedestrians for an entire block with my serious-as-hell, foghorn voice. "Out of the way!" I was caught between needing to get to Mercy's Faithless in a reasonable window and not wanting to start an absolute panic and stampede that would kill and hurt many more people than this meta had thus far.

Luckily for me, most everyone just sort of turned and stared at me rather than losing it and heading for the hills. Unlike New York, almost no one pulled out a cell phone camera, and they responded very positively to my shoving them out of the way. One big guy in jeans and a cowboy hat that I shoved out of the way actually said, "Excuse me," and sounded like he really was sorry he'd had the temerity to occupy the space I was trying to transit through.

I vaulted one last person and I was there, the doorway to Mercy's Faithless. It was an old building, aged brick stained black by decades of pollution never once cleaned. It would have been a great headquarters for a villain if not for the glowing neon sign proclaiming it a honky-tonk. I paused for a second in my last steps to the door, shoving my hands deep in my pockets and coming out with a pair of earplugs I'd kept from the TBI range. I hastily pushed them into my ear canals.

That done, I stepped into Mercy's Faithless, past a couple cops that were paused just inside, faces racked with pain. A shrill screech was rolling through the air at a painful volume and octave. It made me flinch, even through the earplugs.

Steeling myself against the painful, shrill sound coming from within Mercy's Faithless, I readied myself, looked up at the stage...and opened my mouth to speak.

Chapter 32

Brance

It couldn't be happening again.
But it was.

Brance was squarely in the middle of a high note, taking it up louder because...

It couldn't be happening again.

It just couldn't.

He was locked in, though, had to prove to himself that no, it wasn't him. Couldn't be him. He'd never done this before last night. He couldn't even do this kind of thing!

People were screaming now, falling out of their chairs.

But Brance couldn't stop. Because it wasn't him. Couldn't be—

"BRANCE!"

The voice boomed over Mercy's Faithless, over the cries and screams and tinkling glass as bottles and glasses were knocked off the tables by the spasming patrons.

Brance's eyes swept in surprise to the door. He hadn't even used his real name. How could anyone know....?

Who could...?

Oh.

Oh, no.

Sienna Nealon stood framed in the doorway, a look on her face like thunderclouds on the distant horizon, a bellow that would have sent a whole herd stampeding. "Knock it off!" she shouted.

Brance stopped, trilling voice ceasing as though someone had stuck a sock in his mouth. He stood there and stared at her, and she stared right back before picking her way over a fallen figure in the doorway, then another, and another—

How many people had he...?

No! Brance shook it off. This wasn't him! It was the electronics in this place! It couldn't be him. He didn't...couldn't...

"Put down the microphone," Sienna Nealon said, slowly making her way toward him.

He looked down at the mic in his hand. The wire cage that wrapped the tip had been slagged off like it had just melted or blown away. The rest of it looked as though someone had given it a dozen hard taps, cracking the metal and making a mess of the thing.

"I didn't do this," Brance said, easing back from the edge of the stage.

"The evidence of my eyes disagrees with you," she said, not stopping her slow advance toward the stage.

"I couldn't have!" Brance shouted. "I don't have powers."

"I think you might be denying reality here. Unless this same scene didn't happen last night in Screamin' Demons?" She arched her eyebrows, giving him a look that made him feel like she thought he was stupid.

That burned him, sent a hot rush through his cheeks,

heat under his shirt collar. "I'm not stupid, okay? But I didn't do this. This ain't a thing I can do—"

"Maybe not—before. But this is a thing you can do now," Sienna said, taking a couple more easy steps toward the stage. "It's happened twice. It's not a coincidence anymore. This is you. This is a power, okay? I know some things about powers, and bringing people to their knees with your voice, bleeding from the ears? That's a super-power, not just you hitting some off notes."

"It can't—I can't—" Brance staggered another step back. He was sweating, and the mic slipped out of his hands. This had all happened so fast. Everything was ruined—again. This was supposed to be his shot at redemption, but it had all gone tits up—

"Brance," she said again, voice surprisingly soothing given that she was walking through a literal pile of people moaning and crying and bleeding. "I know you didn't mean to do this, but it is done. Twice now. We need to get you out of here and somewhere safe. Okay?"

"I needed them to hear me," he said, and his voice broke. Shoulders jerked, the sobs came out. "Everybody ought to hear me. I was going to be big, the biggest thing to hit this town since Garth—"

Sienna's eyes swept the carnage around Mercy's Faithless. "Well...you definitely hit the town hard, I'll give you that. Not sure you were going for doing it quite this way—"

How could she say that? Her little shot of misery was like a dagger straight to Brance's heart, and he felt it. Boy, did he feel it. He let out a sobbing cry, closing his eyes as he did so, and there was a spike of anguish that ran hot through him as he cried out—

His eyes sprung open and he watched Sienna Nealon get flung like she'd been hit by a motorcycle.

She smashed through the front windows and out into the street and Brance just watched her go, his jaw hanging open. How had she...?

Had he just...?

He flicked a look around. Nobody else in here was even moving, and he'd been looking at her when he'd let out that cry...

"Oh...no," he muttered, watching out the shattered front window. "No, no—this wasn't—I didn't do that—"

But he couldn't shake the feeling that no matter what he said, she wasn't going to hear him now.

Brance turned and ran off the stage, slamming off the wall as he ping-ponged down the hallway toward the bathrooms at the back of the bar. The emergency exit sign was broken, glass glinting in the dark beneath it, but he knew there was a way out here somewhere. He just had to find it and keep moving, keep running—

Before she could come after him.

Chapter 33

Sienna

Brance opened his mouth to let out a baby cry and it was like he vomited out a sonic semi-truck that slammed into me at full speed. My ass went flying out the front windows of Mercy's Faithless and I ended up crashing into a cop car out front, denting the hell out of the door before I landed on the pavement.

"Owwwwwwww," I let out a low moan as the full extent of my pain became apparent to me over the next few seconds. It felt like a giant had reached down and flicked me across the room.

But one hadn't. I'd just been battered by the voice of Brance, Mr. No-Last-Name-because-I'm-a-sensitive-artiste-in-denial-about-my-superpowers.

"Ms. Nealon, are you all right?"

I lifted my head, and through a curtain of blood running down my face I saw the guy in the cowboy hat I'd almost run over earlier. He of the supremely good manners and tight jeans.

"I'm a pretty damned far flight from all right," I said, taking his offered hand and pulling myself up while nearly ripping him down to me with my superhuman strength. He held on though, and I didn't yank as hard as I could, and pretty soon I was on my feet. I swept a hand over the top of my head and shards of glass came raining down on the sidewalk along with a fair few drops of blood. My hair felt like it really needed a washing now. Cowboy took a step back, surprise plastered all over his aged face, wrinkling around his eyes. "But I'm going to be all right once I punch the stuffing out of this human scream machine," I said, and leapt back through the shattered window into Mercy's Faithless.

My eyes adjusted to the bar's darkness in time to see quick motion in the hallway to the right of the stage. Everything else was slow movement, people like a pit of snakes on the floor in their pain. The glint of broken glass and blood glinted in the neon shining in from outside. I could smell traces of iron from the bleeding ears as I bolted through the bar, heading for that hallway in the back where I'd seen Brance disappear.

It felt like my chest had been hammered by a mule kick, which was, sadly, a common sensation to me. I didn't think the people in either of the previous bars had experienced the force projection I'd just got caught by. There was going to be a hell of a bruise on me within the next few minutes. Luckily, it'd be gone by tomorrow, but a normal person would have been nursing it until it faded in a few days. I would have liked to stop and massage myself, check the damage, but I didn't really have time to pause and strip down while my suspect was fleeing.

I plunged through the darkness, steering around fallen patrons and into the back hallway. An emergency exit had been blasted off its hinges by Brance's linebacker charge.

The man was operating on pure fear and adrenaline, his meta strength on clear display as I passed the metal door ripped asunder.

"Brance!" I shouted. He was sprinting down the alley at meta speed, footfalls pounding over the damage to my hearing. When he'd turned his voice on me I'd not only felt the hit, but a high frequency shriek had blasted its way through my ear plugs.

I suddenly felt very fortunate that the dumbass at the baggage counter in New York had sent my stuff to Seattle. Without them, I wouldn't have even needed a new gun, and thus wouldn't be carrying hearing protection.

Brance didn't answer my call. He reached the end of the alley and hung a left, sprinting out of my sight.

I cursed under my breath and drew my new HK VP9 pistol. No way was I taking a blind corner and walking into a possible ambush with nothing in my hand but hopes.

The alley was strewn with overflowing trash cans that smelled particularly ripe. A homeless guy in a flapped hat watched me go past with wide eyes, muttering to himself as I went by. Coming up to the corner, I let myself slow, putting my back against the corner before I planted the barrel on the side of the building. I angled my gun around, cutting the corner slowly, constantly covering as I turned the corner so I was perpetually behind cover until I'd ascertained that the alley was empty.

"Brance!" I shouted, catching sight of his back fleeing down the alley ahead. He hadn't slowed to ambush me. He hadn't slowed at all. Now he didn't look back but for a second.

I burst into a run. I couldn't recall having encountered his type of meta before, but he was awfully powerful, if completely out of control. Strength and speed usually corresponded to power level, and his running speed was impressive. He'd covered a hundred yards already, in a dead sprint toward the river. He crossed a road as I watched, hurrying to try and catch up. I cursed myself for not getting a radio so I could tie in with the Metro Nashville PD; it seemed unlikely I was going to be able to run him down on foot given his lead.

Coming up on the next intersection, a Metro Nashville cop car screeched to a halt just in front of me, as if in answer to my prayers. I did a slide across their hood and waved my hand to indicate the direction of the suspect's flight. As I bolted into the alley across the street, after Brance, I heard one of the cops radioing it in, complete with instructions on our heading.

Dodging past a garbage-filled dumpster, I again reflected that this was not the best-smelling part of Nashville. The tall buildings of downtown were to my left, and the river was glinting ahead. I had to wonder what Brance's plan was, because it certainly didn't seem like he had one.

"Brance, please!" I shouted, completely ineffectually. "You don't have to do this!" I wasn't in a close position to diagnose his problem, but by his behavior and everything I'd seen in Mercy's Faithless, I had a feeling this was a man in deeply over his head.

Ahead, I could see Brance pause, his broad shoulders and tight jeans coming to a slowdown. He didn't quite slump over and put his hands on his knees, but he certainly looked like he was struggling.

I stopped about a half block back, trying not to corner him too much. I had a bad feeling about this. Not because I thought he was plotting some sort of ambush. There was a different feel to Brance than I got with most suspects.

He turned, and I mentally confirmed my assessment. His eyes were wild, worried. He seemed about an inch from tears. "I...I didn't..." He couldn't even string a sentence together.

"It comes as a surprise sometimes," I said, letting my pistol fall to my side. If I had to, I could snap up and shoot in less than a second with lethal precision, but the event in the New York subway with Creeper was still freshly burned into my mind. On Brance's face I saw none of the crazed commitment. He had something different going on; a kind of helplessness that made me want to holster my gun.

I didn't, though. The weight of too much experience kept it in my hand, grip tight, ready to move if the situation changed.

"What does?" Brance asked, looking at me, that helpless sense wafting off him as he rolled his shoulders forward and put his hands on his knees. He was breathing hard from the run.

"Powers," I said. "Mine came as a surprise to me, anyway." I lifted my left hand and made a show of looking at my palm. "Never knew I could do...what I can do...until the day came that I used them to save my life."

He looked up, hard breaths coming one after another. "I'm not like you."

"No," I said. "You're not. Not exactly. But Brance...you've got a little meta something going on there in the vocal cords. Surely you must see that."

"I didn't," Brance said, shaking his head in pure denial. "That was the audio equipment—"

"In both bars?" I asked.

"Had to be." He was staring at the dirty floor of the alley.

"And the audio equipment kicked me out the window with an earsplitting burst of sound when you got mad?" I tossed that out as gently as I could.

153

"I...I..." Brance let a low breath of panic. He really didn't think he was responsible for this at all.

"Come on, man," I said. "You're not stupid. You have to see—"

A police siren in the distance made Brance jerk upright as he swiveled his head in the direction it had come from. The Metro Nashville PD was closing the net on him, and it would be obvious to even the most casual observer what was happening.

Brance tensed to run.

"Wait," I called after him. "This doesn't get any better if you run. So far, it's all been an accident. You discovered your powers in an unfortunate way. I can explain that. I'd testify for you. But if you run now...there's no explaining that away, Brance."

He stared at me across the distance, the dark shadows of the alley between us. His hands were balled into fists. "I just wanted people to hear me."

I think they heard you loud and clear. I did not say that. But I agreed with the sentiment. Instead, I said, "I know. Maybe you can learn to control it."

The sirens drew closer. He stayed tense, and I could tell he was still wanting to bolt like a rabbit staring down an eagle. "But I didn't do anything wrong," he said under his breath.

"I know you didn't mean to," I said, trying to head off that line of reasoning before it became a problem. "But you did."

"I—" He started to say something else, but the squealing of tires interrupted his thought as a black car came to a halt at the end of the alley behind him.

Someone was hanging out the passenger window, arm waving. "Hey, you! Come on!"

I stared, and so did Brance. My brain needed a

moment to process the fact that someone had driven a car into the middle of my chase scene and was now waving down my perp and offering him an escape.

"Brance, don't—" I started.

It was futile. When he had no viable way to outrun me, Brance was willing to listen. Willing to maybe face the consequences of his actions.

But he looked at that car like a starving man looks at their last crumb of bread. I watched the change go through his eyes. He went from looking at his opportunity for escape, open and wide-eyed, to throwing a glance at me, wavering.

I could see the decision being made. His glance slid back, deal done in his head, and he sprang for the car.

The back door was flung open as Brance sprinted for it. He threw himself in and the wheels spun madly. I caught the flash of a green and white Tennessee license place with DAVIDSON written in the county box across the bottom, along with the 73H 36J that marked it.

I made it to the road in time to see the car take the next turn as Brance disappeared with his new friends. The sirens grew louder around me as I stood there in the dark night and stared after them, wondering what the hell had just happened.

Chapter 34

Brance

"Woooooooooo!" the guy in the passenger seat howled like a wolf out the window as they hit the onramp for I-40 and headed east. They'd slipped out of the dragnet before the cops had managed to finish boxing him in, and Brance had watched the red and blue lights flash as they closed the loop six blocks behind him.

They'd escaped.

"Who are you guys?" Brance asked, settling back in his seat. The car was an older model Nissan Sentra, and from the backseat he could see it had close to a hundred thousand miles on it. His rescuers were in shadow, only visible in the lit instrument panels and occasional overhead lamp as they passed. Both wore suit jackets with collared shirts and jeans. The guy in the passenger seat was unshaven, working on a three- to four-day scruff across an extra-wide chin. One of his eyes looked bigger than the other, but maybe it was just the darkness. The one driving was bald and tall, a big slab of beef whose shoulder made it halfway through the margin between driver and passenger seat.

"I'm Gil," the passenger said, then pointed at the driver. "This is Leo. Say hi, Leo. He's a lion."

Leo grunted, nodding. A passing street light gleamed off Leo's shaved head.

"Why did you guys help me?" Brance asked.

"Leo and I have spent a little time at the unjust hands of the police, if you know what I mean," Gil said, looking back and tossing Brance a smile. "I wouldn't wish that on anyone, y'know?"

"I guess," Brance said. That was a thought on his mind, too. He'd done a very short stretch back in Wyoming for dealing weed. If he was being honest, it was at least half the reason he'd run. He frowned. "Where are you taking me?"

"Just figured you'd be happy to get out of there," Gil said.

"I...I am," Brance said. "But I still want to know where I'm going."

"We're taking you to meet someone real quick," Gil said.

Someone? That put a little fear in Brance's heart. "Who?"

"You'll see," Gil said. "Someone who can maybe help you with your problem." Gil turned around, conversation closed, Brance thought.

So he settled back in his seat, that feeling of unease doing nothing but growing as he waited and the miles started to pass.

Chapter 35

Sienna

"He responded to the name Brance, so I don't think it's an alias," I said to the officer taking down my statement. "Height was about six feet, maybe a little under, and the sketch artist's rendition was close, I'd say. Eyes were a little higher than in the drawing, nose was a little smaller." The cop wrote it all down dutifully.

I stood in the middle of a circle of flashing lights, cop cars all around me and more being added by the moment. An unmarked SUV came pulling up and disgorged Chandler and a woman, shorter than me, caramel-skinned, who looked to be in her late thirties or early forties. She wore a suit and struck me as someone who'd seen some shit in her time. The local cops parted and made way for her and Chandler. She led the way, right to me, and stuck her hand out when she got close. "Ms. Nealon. Ileona Marsh."

"Nice to meet you," I said, taking her hand. She was cool and professional. "Chandler." I nodded over her shoulder.

"Ileona is the Deputy Director of the TBI," Chandler said, almost apologetically. "My boss."

"Oh. Oh!" I pulled my hand back abruptly, keenly aware that I was not wearing gloves. "Nice to meet you, Chandler's boss."

"A pleasure, Ms. Nealon," she said with arched eyebrows at my reaction. "Glad to have you working on this."

"Yeah, well," I said, looking back at the Metro officer I'd been speaking to. He'd already moved off with his notepad. "Wish I had some better results to deliver thus far."

Marsh looked around the scene. "Seems to me you did all right."

I shook my head. "I could have pursued more aggressively. I could have—"

She shook her head. "You've been doing this a while. You know what we do in a car chase when the perp starts to endanger civilians?"

"Break off," I said. "Pursue as best you can, but break contact and don't endanger people."

She nodded crisply. "Seems to me you did that here. Trying to run down this getaway car on foot was a non-starter—unless you can do sixty on foot?" She glanced down at my boots.

"I'm not quite that fast, no," I said. "But I slowed to make sure I didn't get ambushed on a corner, even though I had a gut feeling he wasn't that kind of danger—"

"There's a whole lot of glass out on Broadway in the shape of what I imagine is your outline that disagrees." She frowned, a shadow falling across her face. "He throw you out a window like witnesses said?"

I flushed a little. "Yeah. I think that was an accident, though. He kinda screamed and I went flying like a shot."

"Accident or not, this Brance is dangerous," she said, eyes sweeping the scene again. "Our big mistake in my view was not having you mic'd with a radio wired to Metro units in the area. That would have saved time on fetching you out of the bar and allowed us to coordinate better. That's on us."

"I have a brain; I could have thought of it, too," I said. I couldn't remember a time when the people I was working with hadn't landed on me like a million tons of rock after a perp slipped away. At least not since I'd been working for the FBI.

Marsh smiled. "You don't get interfaced in with locals much, though, do you?"

I tried to think about it. I did usually tend to get stuck outside the chain of command in these sorts of situations. I'd gotten wired in during an assassination attempt in New Orleans, but otherwise... "Yeah, I'm usually out in the cold, but in fairness to them, I do tend to work alone."

"Well, you're not alone here," Marsh said. "The TBI is at your disposal. You've got way more experience in this kind of thing than we do. Let us know what you need. Metro Nashville is generally easy to work with, so if you think of something, say it. If it's within reason, we'll make it work." Her lips turned up slightly at the edge. "Mayor Brandt is very eager to keep you happy."

No jurisdictional squabble on this? I raised an eyebrow, because it was just a tad unusual, at least in my recent experience. The various Bay Area PDs on my last case had been only mildly helpful and generally suspicious of my efforts; the New Orleans PD on the case before had been kept at arm's length by my FBI badge or local politics. Probably more the latter. Cooperation wasn't utterly foreign, but this level of enthusiastic effort at it was...different.

"Well...thanks," I said, because I really couldn't come up with anything else, snark or otherwise. It was hard to be snarky to people who were offering you more than you expected or asked for.

She nodded. "Chandler will give you my number. Call if you need anything." She gave me a tip of the hat salute —minus the hat, because she didn't have one—and strode off through the scene toward a local cop, who nodded at her approach.

"I'm glad you're all right," Chandler said, easing in now that his boss was gone.

"I don't think I was in much danger, to be honest," I said, watching Marsh talk to the cop. "She good, your boss?"

"Oh, yeah, she's great," Chandler said. "The field guys love her because she came up through the ranks, not admin. Twenty-plus years of experience. Started as a beat cop in Memphis and worked her way up. They call her the 'Memphis Belle' because she was a Miss Tennessee finalist back in the day."

I raised an eyebrow. "Not to her face, though, right?"

Chandler laughed weakly. "I've never tried it, but I think she'd be okay with it. She doesn't strike me as the type to flinch from her past. This is a woman who's talked about her Officer-Involved Shootings in open meetings. Old school, Wild-West-type stuff. She's drilled some perps, man. Quick on the draw. Hell of a shot."

"Hmmm," I said, notching a little more respect in the column of the Memphis Belle. A beauty queen who could —and would—shoot? My kind of boss. I tried to imagine Heather Chalke drawing and firing a service weapon and it ended with her accidentally blowing a perfectly manicured finger off. She'd never even worn a gun that I'd seen.

"Got any new insights into the perp?" Chandler asked.

"Yeah, shared 'em with the locals," I said, nodding to one of the Metro uniforms passing by. "Witnesses basically had the description right. Told 'em a couple changes to make. Guy's name is definitely Brance. He turned when I shouted it at him."

"Yeah, but he might have turned if you yelled 'Bozo!' in a dark alley while chasing him down. Being chased by someone with a gun really focuses the mind on them and what they're saying."

"That's not a bad point, but he didn't deny his name."

"Well, we've got no record of him," Chandler said. "Every Brance with a Tennessee driver's license is accounted for. It's a thin crowd and no matches on the description."

I hung my fingers in my belt loops as I looked up and thought. The night sky was dark, the street lights giving it enough of a glow to blot out any stars even though there wasn't a cloud in sight. "So that means he's either new in town or he doesn't have a driver's license, right?"

Chandler nodded slowly. "Seems like. Lot of new people in town, though. Nashville's on a growth spurt."

"Ma'am." The Metro police officer who I'd given my info to crept up to us, as if afraid he was interrupting. "We ran that license plate you gave us."

"The one on the getaway car," I said, helpfully, to Chandler.

"Well, I didn't think you were running random plates," Chandler said. Oh, good, a smartass.

"It's registered to a Michael Markham in North Nashville," the officer said, "but was supposed to be for a 2018 Honda Odyssey. I ran the make/model of the Nissan Sentra, and it matches about a thousand cars in Tennessee alone. Assuming it wasn't registered in another state, which—"

"Given that it's bearing stolen plates, it could be," Chandler finished helpfully.

"Thank you, Officer," I said, and he nodded and dismissed himself from the conversation, leaving me alone with Chandler. "A car with stolen plates picks up our perp out of nowhere. That seem suspicious to you?"

"Little bit," Chandler said. "But not in a good way."

"So..." I said, coming to a conclusion, "basically...that leaves us with nothing to go on." I folded my arms in front of me, noticing Chandler's look of dissatisfaction. "We're back to zero."

Chapter 36

Reed

"So," I said, "what's up?"

There was a low roar of activity going on in Puckett's Murfreesboro location. Someone up on the stage was picking on a strange four-string instrument that wasn't a guitar but sort of looked like one. I felt like they were going to break into "The Ballad of Jayne Cobb" any second, based on the eclectic decor of the place.

Theresa Carson was the name of the older lady in the Lotsostuff overall that I'd been flagged down by in the crowd. She sat across from me now, a little smile curling the corners of her mouth, like she knew stuff—or probably lotsostuffs (terrible, but I couldn't avoid it)—that I didn't. Her two comrades sat on the other two compass points of the round table. The big black dude was Bert Wallace, and the squirrely white guy was Angelo Drake. I'd caught all their names—and a suspicious series of looks from Bert and Angelo when they'd introduced themselves before sitting down. The four strings were plucking along in the background, covering our conversation. Such as it was.

"Where do your sympathies lie in all in this?" Theresa asked, still giving me that small smile. Bert and Angelo glared on behind her, like I was going to jump her any second. Or jump her bones, maybe. Either way, they looked pissed off.

I looked sideways at the stage. I wasn't sure how to answer that. My sympathies tended toward working people, and my brief introduction to Logan Mills certainly hadn't engendered any great reason to change that up. "My sympathies lie in the direction of whoever's not committing violence."

"You're an agent of the status quo, then," Drake said, hyping himself up at my left. "Not a friend of the worker."

"Cool your jets there, Trotsky," I said, giving him a vaguely amused look. "This isn't a glorious revolution. You're fighting to move an $11-an-hour starting wage to $15 an hour. We're not talking starvation here." I looked Drake up and down. He was wiry, but hardly wire-thin. "Or, at least none of you look like you're starving."

"This isn't about starving," Theresa said, putting a wrinkled hand on Drake's arm before he piped off again. He looked like he wanted to. "It's about a company on the rise, one that we're helping to build. It's about getting our fair share."

I shrugged. "I'm not unsympathetic. But it looks to me like you were close to rioting before I showed up. The cops manning the perimeter at Lotsostuff? They're not management. Hell, I met management, and it looked to me like one guy—"

"It's not," Drake said. "There's more than just him."

"The company structure isn't the issue here," Theresa

said, again patting a soothing hand on Drake's arm and getting him to throttle back a little bit.

"What is?" I asked. "Because if you're really just fighting for a four-buck raise for new people starting—"

"It's about a fair wage for anyone who works at Lotsostuff," Theresa said, brow furrowing. "Logan Mills just did another round of funding a year ago. Private equity. Millions of dollars. And the company does millions in sales every year. We're the sole warehouse that fulfills those orders. Some of us have been here since the beginning."

"Okay," I said. "So you're unhappy with working conditions. With money. With—"

"With dignity," Drake said again, and I caught a nod from Wallace, who I was beginning to think of as Big Bert, versus Lil' Angelo. "Logan Mills won't even answer our demands personally."

"He hired a team of professional lawyers to negotiate," Theresa said. "So we did a little negotiating tactic of our own—we organized into a union." She put a wrinkled hand on her chest. "He didn't like that, oh no."

"So where does flooding the warehouse come into it?" I asked, doing a little frowning of my own. "Because, honestly? I'm with you up to there. Unionize? Sure. Collectively bargain on wages and working conditions. Right on, so long as you're not beating up scabs. But the flood—"

"That wasn't us," Theresa said, and it was like a cloud rolled over her face.

"But we're not exactly crying over it," Drake said, chuckling under his breath.

Something about what he said and the way he said it nettled me. It wasn't something that would have bothered me five years ago, three years ago, even. I wasn't an activist, but I didn't begrudge people a living or a chance to argue that their living wasn't enough.

But this... "Hey, numbnuts," I said before I could stop myself, "you realize that every dollar of merchandise that gets destroyed soaks up money that Logan Mills can't use to pay you guys more, right?"

"He's got plenty of money," Drake fired right back. "Look at the lists. The guy's a billionaire."

That was true. I'd seen him in Forbes. Something about that rankled me, too, a little dark surge of emotion that might maybe have had roots in my failing agency back home. Sucked that a douche like Logan Mills was a billionaire when I was wondering how to pay my employees next week. "Look, I just don't want to see people get hurt," I said, some of the wind leaving my sails. "Cops, workers, management—I'm here because I'm worried something bad is going to happen." I looked Theresa Carson in the eyes. "And it seems to me you might be getting close to exactly that."

"Our people feel disrespected by Logan's negotiation tactics," Theresa said. "Like I told you, some of us—a lot of us—have been here since the beginning. We've known Logan since long before he was a billionaire. He could have talked to us when this all came up. He chose not to. Handed it off to those lawyers." She looked like she was ready to spit on the floor. "That was an insult to us all. A thumb in our eyes. Well, we're not going to sit down and be quiet anymore. We're going to get our due. Logan Mills can spread his billion around as far as I'm concerned." She thumped the table lightly for emphasis.

"Damned right," Big Bert rumbled.

"Well, I think I see where you're coming from here," I said, pushing back from the table. "If there's nothing else..."

"You need to pick a side, wind boy," Drake said, causing me to raise an eyebrow. "You think you can stand between us and Mills, you're wrong. There's no middle ground—"

"Angelo," Theresa said, patting him again. "Mr. Treston, please. Take a look around. Talk to our people. You'll see what we mean. Logan's not negotiating this in good faith. He's worried about keeping his money—and not paying us fairly for what we're doing."

I brushed some of my long hair back. "I'll keep that in mind," I said. Pure boilerplate. With a nod to each of them, I turned to leave, because I damned sure wasn't going to sit around and drink with the three of them. Not when I was already having a bad feeling about what was going on here.

I hit the door and was out on the street a moment later, thoughts swirling in my head. What the hell had Harry Graves drawn me into? This just looked like a labor dispute of what I viewed as the normal variety—big rich versus little poor people, except someone had thrown a meta in.

"It's not as simple as it looks," came a voice from behind me, almost causing me a heart attack. I whirled—

And there stood Harry Graves, leaning against the front of Puckett's, an irritating smile on his face.

Chapter 37

Jules

"Here he is!" Jules said, throwing his arms wide as the dark car pulled into the warehouse and the door clanked down behind them. "Man of the hour, this guy." Gil hurried out of the passenger side and opened the rear door. Inside, Jules could see a scared guy. Twenty-something, good-looking kid, but scared shitless and looking miserable, like he'd sat on his balls the whole way here. "Here's our mystery singer. Why the long face, cowpoke?"

"Who are you?" the kid asked, taking Jules's hand, staring at it as Jules shook it heavily.

"Just an interested party who hates to see a good man take it on the chin," Jules said, putting an arm around the kid's shoulders and steering him away from the car. There was a naivete that whiffed off this kid like cheap cologne, so Jules prepared to pour it on thick. If this guy was older? No way. He'd have gone more reserved. Kids ate up the horseshit, though, especially this generation. They didn't know shit but thought they knew everything. This was going to be a pleasure. "I'm a guy who's been in your shoes, you know? Who's taken his hits. That's reason enough for me to help a man like yourself."

A strangely choked look ran across the kid's face, twisted into a frown. "Who are you?"

"Jules Sharpe." Jules placed one hand on his chest in a gesture of sincerity. "And you are...?"

"Brance," the kid said. And he really was a kid. Couldn't be more than twenty-two, twenty-five at most.

Jules split into a wide grin. "Brance. Good name. So, uh...what are you up to here, Brance? You trying to do the Nashville thing? Make your name?"

Brance's head sagged, eyes finding the concrete floor. Yeah, Jules had hit it. "Yeah," Brance mumbled. "Trying to. Or I was."

Jules put the arm back around his shoulder. "Hey, kid. Why the long face? It's a tough town. You had a couple rough nights."

Brance looked up at him with watery eyes. "I blew up the sound system in two bars. Hurt people with...I don't even know how I did it. And Sienna Nealon is after me now."

"That's a tough break." Jules nodded along, keeping his arm around Brance's shoulders. "Tough crowd, tough break. But look—did you do that on purpose?"

"No." Brance shook his head. "I was just singing. And it happened."

"Never happened before that?" Jules asked.

"No." The kid wasn't lying. Jules knew a liar when he saw one.

"Then it was an accident," Jules said. "Accidents happen. Believe me. My brother-in-law? He once plowed a car into a McDonald's. Almost killed a guy. You know what happened to him?" Brance looked up. "Nothing," Jules said. "I got him a good lawyer, and we took care of it. You have an accident in your car, it shouldn't be something you fear for the rest of your life, you know? It's not like you went into the bars and tried to blow people's heads up, you know?"

"No," Brance said, nodding along. "No, I didn't. It was an accident."

"Exactly," Jules said, pointing a finger at him. "Accidents happen. You just need a little help explaining your way out of it, you know?" He patted Brance on the shoulders a couple times. "I can help you with this. No problem."

Brance blinked. "You can?"

"Absolutely," Jules said. "You're new in town, right?"

"Yeah."

"How long you been here?"

"A couple months," Brance said.

"I've only been here a couple years myself," Jules said, smiling. "We out-of-towners got to stick together. I'll call my lawyer tomorrow, get him working on explaining this through." He walked a few more paces. "So, uh...you came to town to be a singer?" Brance nodded. Looked like the dream had stuck in his throat, he looked so stricken. "You mind favoring me with a verse or two?" Jules smiled. "You know, show me what you do? Nice and easy." He made a motion as if to cover his ears. "I don't need to start bleeding from the canals if you know what I mean."

Brance flushed, and it looked to Jules like his words had the exact effect he'd intended. "Yeah, no, I can—here." And he took a breath, then let out a small sigh before launching into some ballad that Jules had never heard. He did it a cappella through one verse and a chorus before sliding to a slow stop.

"That was great!" Jules clapped, looking behind him to

make sure that Gil and Leo did too. "Wasn't that great?" Nods, of course. "You got a real voice on you, kid." Here, he had to be a little careful, because he wanted to sample the goods, but not go deaf. "So, uh...how'd the thing happen? You know, in the bars."

"I don't know," Brance said, shaking his head slowly. "I just sang and it started to happen."

"Okay, okay," Jules said, nodding. Everything he did here was to be agreeable with Brance, to build the trust—but also get the kid to do what he wanted. By the time it was over, he wanted Brance eating out of his palm. So far, so good. The kid was in a tough place, and he was being plenty easy. Dangle his dream in front of him, feed the desires of Brance's heart, and Jules would have him. He could see it already. "About my lawyer—he's really good, by the way. Top lawyer in town. Here's what he's going to say: 'How did it happen if it was an accident? How are we going to keep it from happening in the future?'" Jules looked Brance in the eyes. "You know what I mean? Court's going to wonder. They can't have bars on Broadway getting blown up every night."

"Yeah," Brance said, sagging. "But I don't know how it happens."

"Okay, well, maybe we can work on that," Jules said. "Hey, Gil." He snapped his fingers. "You guys got any earplugs?"

"Yeah," Gil said, and tossed Jules a pair sealed in plastic. He grinned. "Got to have 'em if I go downtown. My ears are always killing me in those places on Broadway."

Nice. Jules had given him that line to put Brance at ease. He ripped them open and shoved a foam plug into each ear canal. "So here's what we do, Brance. You sing, see if you can hit that note or whatever it was that caused things to go off. I'll stand here, listen, and we'll narrow it down so when you go to the lawyer you can say, 'Here's how it happened, I got it under control, it'll never happen again.' Right? Right." Jules took a couple steps back. "Okay. Hit me."

Brance hesitated. "But...what if I..." He lowered his voice to a whisper. "...hurt you?"

"Just don't close your eyes and keep an eye on my face," Jules said. "You'll know. Just stop, right?" This kid. This kid didn't want to hurt a fly. This was the kind of naivete you couldn't buy. Jules had a fleeting moment of worry that this wasn't going to go so well, but then...he'd toughened up others in the past. Brought people into the lifestyle. That was toughening up, really. Making 'em coarse to decisions that would hurt others.

No big deal to Jules now, and it wouldn't be a big deal to Brance. Eventually. One step at a time, though.

"Come on, Brance," Jules said, prodding him. "You're going to have to learn to control that instrument if you're going to make it in this town as a singer. First things first: we find out where things went wrong. Then we work on making them right. Okay?"

Brance was just standing there, staring. "Why are you doing this? You've got no reason to help me."

Jules just smiled. He had a line for this, too. "Full disclosure: I'm kind of on the lookout for new talent. I'd like to break into managing. You know...if you might be open to taking on an...agent. Business manager."

A smile bloomed slowly, out of pure surprise, and spread dumbly across Brance's face. Jules would have staked his life on the fact that no one had said anything nice to this kid in a long time. Maybe ever. "Yeah," Brance said, grinning stupidly. "That's why I came to Nashville."

"Well, this worked out well for both of us then, didn't it?" Jules just grinned. "Come on, kid. I like your voice.

Let's hit it and figure out how things go wrong so we can start making them right."

That worked, too: Brance started singing, like the canary that found itself in warm crap, and Jules just listened, hands close to his ears in case he had to cover them, waiting to hear whatever note it was that destroyed things.

Because that note, that power? That was going to make Jules's dreams come true.

Chapter 38

Sienna

I was well familiar by this point with how it felt to find yourself back at zero. No leads except a drawing—slightly updated and more accurate—of Brance. A confirmation it was his name. No getaway car info, really, no idea who'd pulled his fat out of the fire. Just lots of threads, no tapestry.

Chandler and I were sitting across from each other at a conference table at TBI HQ. He'd brought me up here and we'd chewed over the same facts, limited as they were, over and over. We hashed them half a dozen different ways to come to the same conclusion:

We were nowhere with this investigation.

"So Metro's going to continue to canvas Broadway?" I already knew the answer, but I'd run out of other questions to ask.

"All night," Chandler said. "But you think he's unlikely to make another move, right?"

"I think he's unlikely to show his face on Broadway

again between now and Ragnarok," I said. "Unless he's thrice as dumb as the dumbest stump."

Chandler nodded, tapping a hand against the table. "Metro cops have shared his sketch with the local bartenders. They'll all be on the lookout for him now. He's not getting a spot on stage there."

"There's something to this," I said. "No way he should have tried again tonight. And when I talked to him, he really seemed like he didn't believe he was a meta."

"But he obviously is," Chandler said.

"Yeah, the massive bruise in the middle of my chest confirms that," I said, fingering the spot on my sternum where he'd belted me with his mule-kick of a voice. "But he apparently didn't know that until the last couple days. Really, until tonight." I remembered the terrified, disbelieving look on his face. "It was like I'd killed a puppy in front of him, Chandler, I swear." I shook my head. "This thing that happened to him? It hit him hard. Harder than it hit me, even." I massaged myself again, cringing as I found the worst of the bruise.

"Did your powers come as a surprise to you?" Chandler asked. He was probing, albeit delicately.

"Oh, yeah," I said, finding a particularly rough spot in my left pectoral just above my bra line. The underwire seemed to have bitten into my skin. Luckily it'd be gone by tomorrow, because ouch. "One minute I was heading down into my basement to sacrifice myself to an unstoppable monster threatening the cities of Minneapolis and St. Paul, the next I'm ripping his soul out through the touch of my hands. Came as a total surprise, especially when he started piping up in my brain."

Chandler's eyes danced in interest. "What is it like? Having someone else in your head?"

So fun. "It varies," I said. "I had one guy who was a

serial killer with terrible boundary issues, another who was a murderous lech...and who also had boundary issues. Another was a tough former soldier, another was an ex, and still another was a charming sociopath...they ran the gamut, really."

"This is all so very fascinating to me," Chandler said. "You must get tired of answering questions about all this."

I thought about it for a moment. "Uh...no, not really." I screwed up my face in concentration as I thought about it. "I don't get asked about myself much anymore."

Chandler cocked his head in curiosity. "What? Why not?"

"Well, I'm not allowed to talk to the media, and I don't really have great opportunities to talk to people outside of work, so..." I shrugged.

"But your co-workers must be forever asking you all sorts of things," he said. "You've been responsible for bringing down almost all the meta criminals imprisoned in the United States. I mean, like seventy percent of captures are you or your friends." He just stared at me blankly, as if waiting for me to say something. "How can they not be asking you constantly about this stuff?"

I gave it a moment's thought and shrugged broadly. "Well, one of them doesn't like me much and the other is a peeing puppy, she's so new. So the guy who doesn't like me—Holloway—doesn't really go out of his way to talk to me unless he has to, and the peeing puppy—Hilton—is always trying to weirdly ingratiate herself to me in a very millennial kind of way, by oversharing what she's done." I shuddered, recalling a memory of her telling me about some guy she'd met at a club and brought home recently, ending with hilariously bad sex and humiliation for all involved. I had silently wished for the ability to turn invisible during her entire telling of the story, wondering why she would feel comfortable enough with me to inflict it upon me.

"Oh," Chandler said, taking it all in. "That sucks. But I mean, your bosses have to at least be interested in your wealth of experience."

"Mmm, my bosses hate me."

Chandler blinked like that didn't compute. "What?"

"Yeah," I said. "In their defense, I'm kind of a pain in the ass, especially to authority figures. It's a personality quirk. Besides, I only have one boss now, and it's the FBI Director, apparently."

"I thought you worked in the New York office?"

"Just got transferred before I came down here." I smiled tightly. "I think they might have decided no one but the Director could properly put a leash on me. Not sure exactly how that will work, but I'm moving to DC when I get back."

"New York, DC; you really are kind of jet-setting," Chandler said, readjusting back to enthused now that he'd taken in my news. "I'm a little envious."

"Don't be," I said, shaking my head. "I don't want to be 'jet-setting' or whatever. I don't want to be in DC. Or New York, really."

Chandler just stared at me, brow furrowing. "Then...why are you?"

I forced a smile. "Because that's where the job is." I looked back down at the new sketch of Brance. "So...do you guys have access to a downtown camera web? Somewhere we could run facial recognition and see if we can pick this guy up?"

"I don't think we're quite that sophisticated," Chandler said, looking down at the picture. "We've got a BOLO out statewide and to neighboring states, but it seems to me this guy is probably a transplant, given that he's, y'know, 'Runnin' Down a Dream,' to quote Bruce Springsteen. Depending on how recently he moved here, I don't know how much contact he's had in the local area, which may make finding him more difficult."

"So far he's a nuisance," I said, sliding his picture around. "Hard to say whether it'll stay that way."

"What do you mean?" Chandler asked. Genuine interest. So nice.

"Well, there's a tendency among the newly empowered to get a little taste of godhood and like it a little too much," I said. "Usually there's a spiral effect where the crimes get progressively worse." I looked at the wide-eyed innocence displayed on the artist's rendering of Brance's face. "But this guy didn't start out doing criminal things. He ran because he was scared. I'm not sure what that means for his future in this investigation. If we're lucky—" I picked up the rendering and stared into the eyes "—maybe it'll end with a whimper. I think it would have, if not for his rescuers." I put the picture back down. "Whoever they are."

"That concerns me a little bit," Chandler said, nodding along. "I mean, who just randomly saves someone from...well, you?"

I raised an eyebrow to that. "Anyone with a decent heart, I would guess. I'm not exactly low-impact or merciful in my encounters. I believe 'police brutality' is the number one tag associated with my name on YouTube."

Chandler shook his head, looking at the sketch. "Maybe, but I don't know if I buy the premise that you'd pick up some random stranger being stared down by the world's first superhero." He shook his head again. "No, I think this is worse. I think whoever picked him up, they were looking for him." Chandler glanced up at me. "I think it's someone who has a plan for this guy. Maybe

one that Brance doesn't even know he's signing up for
—yet."

"If so," I said, staring at the sad eyes in the artist's new
rendering of Brance, "I hope we can get to him. Before it's
too late."

Chapter 39

Brance

"That's good, that's good," Jules said, arms folded in front of him as Brance hit the first high note on "Between the Devil and Me," the often overlooked Alan Jackson classic. The older man was tall, with big arms, like he worked out, and a belly that suggested maybe he didn't. Brance had a hard time getting a good read on Jules, other than that he seemed nice and had bailed him out of a real tight spot.

Brance had felt the ground fall from beneath him back at Mercy's Faithless when his voice started causing all that chaos again. It had been like he'd dropped out of his dream and into a nightmare, complete with the night sweats that came when you woke up out of one of those hellish dreams.

But now that he was standing here in front of Jules, singing his heart out...

Well, it felt like he was back on steady ground again. At

least for the moment, the older man had given him a measure of...what?

Reassurance. That was it. Standing there on the stage in Mercy's Faithless, with Sienna Nealon staring him down, it had been like his dream—all his dreams, every last one he'd wanted and worked for, from leaving Wyoming to moving to Nashville to getting himself on a stage singing here—had all died at once.

Watching Jules nod his head in time with the music— okay, maybe a little off time, but still—was like watching his dream get life breathed back into it. Dream CPR.

And it felt damned good. Like telling his dad he'd been wrong after all.

Brance took a breath through the nose, taking in the stale air in the cool warehouse. His skin tingled as he launched into the chorus, hitting those notes and knocking them down one by one until—

"Oh! Whoa!" Jules's eyes were squinted shut and he had a hand held up. His back was slightly bowed, and he started to wave the hand in front of Brance like a bull-fighter flinging a cape.

Brance stopped. He'd felt it. A quiver in his vocal chords that had resonated through the roof of his mouth, tickled his uvula like an itch in the back of his throat. His whole head had vibrated just a little, actually. Weird. It had felt a lot more pronounced without the electronic bass notes blasting from speakers surrounding him like they did in Screamin' Demons and Mercy's Faithless.

Jules stood up straight again, his broad shoulders pulling back slowly to stick out his broad chest. He had a slightly pained look, nodding as he opened his eyes fully once more. "I think we found it."

Brance put a hand over his mouth, then scanned over to the car, where Gil and Leo were both bent nearly double, looking at him tentatively. They had earplugs in, too, but didn't look half as pained as Jules. "I think you were too close," Brance said, feeling the flush in his cheeks. "I should have—"

"You're fine, kid," Jules said. "This is good."

Brance blinked. He'd half expected Jules to yell at him, scream at him, tell him he was worthless.

"You sounded great up until you hit that note," Jules said, nodding as he spoke, looking away like he was replaying the songs. "So I think our plan is this—we figure why it happens, and get you learning to control it. Because if you can figure out the trigger, you can stop pulling it. Right?"

"Right," Brance said, nodding a little less certainly. "But...how do we do that?"

Jules broke into a broad grin. "How do you get to Radio City Music Hall, kid?"

Brance stood there, thinking. "Uh...I don't know."

"Practice," Jules said, grinning. "Practice. Come on. Hit it again. We'll do this all night if we have to. For weeks. We're going to get you ready to be a star, okay? Whatever it takes."

Chapter 40

Reed

"Well, well, well," I said, moseying over to Harry Graves, who leaned against the front of Puckett's like he owned the place, "if it isn't my wayward benefactor." I cocked my head, feigning pensiveness. "Or is it malefactor?"

Harry didn't register an iota of surprise, but then, he wouldn't. The bastard could read my every word out of the probabilities before I even spoke them. "'Malefactor' would suggest I've got bad intentions for you, Reed. I don't." He smiled a little wider, probably because he knew how grating I found it.

"You know what I find interesting about you?" I gave him what I hoped was an aggravating smile of my own. "You know exactly how I'm going to react to everything you say, but you give no damns about ingratiating yourself to me."

"I've only got so many hours in a day, and you're a naturally suspicious individual, Reed, so..." Harry shrugged, as if any of that was supposed to mean something to me.

Wait, what was that supposed to mean? I asked him, affixing a few crude words to the question.

Harry's smiled moved from annoying to infuriating, and now I could tell he was trying to get my goat just for the hell of it. "It means regardless of what I say, you're going to choose to be annoyed at me and question everything about this entire endeavor."

"If I'm annoyed at you, Harry," I said, glaring him down, "maybe it's because you've got me running blind into some labor dispute without telling me a damned thing about what's actually going on here beyond vague warnings about calamity." I paused, thinking about it. "Actually, I don't even know if it's calamitous. Someone could be poised to lose a toe based on the vagueness of your warnings, and I'm down here working it anyway." I steamed for a second and he let me. "Are you jerking me around for shits and giggles?"

Harry gave a one-shoulder half-shrug. "I guess you won't know until you see where it goes."

That just about launched me off the ground. "Are you freaking kidding me?"

"Not really." He fixed me with a solid, if slightly lazy gaze. "There's trouble about to happen here, whether you want to believe me or not. I've seen it. The probabilities for clearing it without you here...well, you could do some good. If you wanted to"

I just glared at him. "You got anything else for me? Like maybe some actual idea of what's going on, where to look? You know. Useful stuff when you're on a case where mayhem is apparently in the offing."

Harry just broke into a wider smile. "Nah. I'm only here to listen to you complain for a few minutes before dropping an enigmatic hint and disappearing, so you can flounder on your own and curse my name for a while longer."

"You sonofa—"

"Oh," Harry said, holding up a finger to pre-empt my tirade. "You know how people say, 'It's not about you'? Well, this is totally about you, Reed."

I was about to tear off a piece of my mind and give it to him good when a horn honked behind me so loudly that I turned, afraid a car was about to run me over.

It wasn't. Some guy was parked up the street, and got out of his car to motion to a girl who was walking with a gentle, drunken sway as she made her way out of Puckett's. The music wafted out onto the street behind her as the door slowly swung closed.

I turned back to give Harry that piece of my mind—

But the bastard was gone.

"Figures," I said under my breath as I swept my gaze along the street, looking for him. Disappeared, just like he said.

Chapter 41

Sienna

"So what time do you want me at the office tomorrow?" I asked Chandler as we rolled along I-24 toward my hotel. I'd hitched a ride up to TBI Headquarters with him from the scene on Broadway, and now he was dropping me back on his way home for the night.

"Mm," he mouthed a noise, keeping his eyes on the darkened highway ahead. Overhead lights seemed to blink on and then off for long stretches as we passed them, the car ceiling cutting us off from one and casting Chandler in darkness again. "Whenever you feel like it."

"You're just so damned reasonable," I said. "Come on, man. Our perp just got picked up by unknown subjects. This could be building to a crisis."

"It could, you're right," Chandler said. "But it's still building, and we're pretty much clueless, in the most literal sense, until something breaks." He sent me a friendly glance. "That's all the grunt work, shaking the bushes. You can leave that to us. You're the superhero, after all. Let us little people do our part."

I didn't know quite what to say to that, so I lapsed into a silence as he took the downtown exit. "So...I guess I can just wander around downtown, then. Maybe hit Broadway and do some inquiries of my own."

"Sure, whatever you want," he said in a noncommittal way that left me wondering if he actually cared what I got up to.

"Okay," I said. We slid through the downtown area. I caught a street sign that read "Deaderick" as we funneled toward a courthouse. We turned at a T intersection beneath the high building with its immense columns, and kept going, passing a Roman-style building that had to be the state capitol, seated high on a hill. Some modern government office complex stood nearby, then we passed a giant crater of a building site where something was being constructed out of the earth. Ahead I could see that train station building, and then we took a left turn, giving me a clear view of a domed arena.

My phone buzzed and I looked down. I had a text message, one long wall of words from Director Chalke that caused me to frown. I unlocked my phone and started to skim it as Chandler piped up again. I didn't entirely hear him because my heart had started to thunder and my pulse was quickening.

"You don't have to do anything you don't want to here," Chandler said, keeping his hands loosely on the wheel. "We know we called you in on something that looks a lot less dire than your usual business. So, you know, you can just take this as a break between now and when you head to DC." He glanced over at me as he pulled the car to the curb next to my hotel. I must have been making a face, because he frowned. "What?"

I debated on whether to say anything, but ultimately, I'm not that good at bottling up my feelings, especially when they're raw anger. I held up my phone, stopping myself just short of violently throwing it out the window. "The FBI has unlocked my apartment in New York and let movers in without my permission. They're packing the rest of my shit and bringing it to DC for me." I pursed my lips tightly. "When I leave here, I'm to report straight to Washington." I squeezed the sides of my phone, feeling like crushing it in my grip so as to ignore this particular missive.

"They...they just opened your apartment and took your stuff?" Chandler asked, his mouth slightly agape. "Without even asking first?"

"Yep," I said, every muscle tensing, a seething sensation blanketing me. "And that's just paragraph one."

"How many paragraphs are there?" Chandler asked, looking at my phone as though it were about to explode. Or maybe he thought I was, which was not far off the truth.

I looked back at the message. "I don't know." I skimmed the missive again. "Paragraph two highlights a very direct order: I am not to work with the DC Police like I did the NYPD, to help them with any non-federal crimes—"

"Oh, did you like doing that?" Chandler asked.

"Hell yes," I said, closing my eyes for a moment. "Stupid as it sounds, I like policing. I like stopping bad guys and even not-so-bad guys like Brance who are making some bad choices before they become 'bad guys.' So, needless to say, there will be no more of that, because I'll be working on FBI assignments only from here on out." I sighed. "Which is a real shame, because I like being in the middle of whatever the biggest trouble is at the moment. Sitting back at the office doing nothing? Kills me."

Chandler nodded along. "Interesting."

"Yeah, it's super fascinating," I said, shutting off my phone. "The rest of this is just more of the same, and I'm sorry I've dumped this on you, and I'm sure you're sorry you asked—" I fumbled for the door release.

"I find it all very interesting, actually," Chandler said, brushing my arm as I tried to flee the car with my emotions—rage, basically—before he could tell me I was being stupid or boring. Which he didn't. "I'm sorry they did that to you."

"Yeah," I said, paused in the open door, my hotel's lights shining down from under their entry portico. "I doubt they are, though, so I wish they were you."

"Does it say anything else interesting?" Chandler asked.

"You don't have to worry about this, Chandler—Chandrasekhar," I said, amending it.

"No, really, Chandler's fine," Chandler said. "Though you totally nailed the pronunciation. Well done. But seriously—I know this probably sucks for you. You're in a strange city, bad things are happening back home—hell, you don't even have a 'back home' right now. Your bags got waylaid—"

I'd forgotten about that. Guess I'd be wearing the same clothes and underwear tomorrow. Good thing I didn't have to show up to the office early. Or I suppose I could do a Walmart run in my borrowed BMW.

"So anyway," Chandler said, "if you want to talk...you can give me a call." He nodded at my phone. "I'm sure you've got other people you could talk to and all, but still—offer is open." He smiled sincerely.

"Thanks," I said, and meant it. "But you've done

enough." I got out and closed the door carefully. Chandler gave me a little wave and drove off as I turned to head into my hotel.

The lobby was a sprawling, expansive affair, lots of couches and seats where people were talking, even at this hour. I headed for the elevator bank, which was just past the seating area and the hotel bar, giving only a cursory glance to the crowd inside in the name of my personal security. I was always on the lookout for people who were on the lookout for me, and as soon as I stepped in I caught a pair of eyes that caught mine and wouldn't let go.

I slowed my pace, then snuck a glance, wanting to see dead on, clearly, who was watching me. It could be just a tourist who was staring at my famous face, or someone who wanted me dead, and I needed to at least look at them to be sure—

It was neither.

"Sienna!" Mayor Clea Brandt lifted her hand, waving me over to a table that contained her and two other people. One was an older man, tanned, with greying hair. He looked vaguely familiar, and I thought I recognized him as Tennessee Governor Henry Boggs.

The other...I knew immediately and familiarly.

I took a slow walk across the lobby and found them all already standing to greet me. Mayor Brandt, Governor Boggs...

And former Senator Robb Foreman, who met my gaze with cool amusement and a dash of—was that pleasure?—at seeing me again.

My former boss.

Chapter 42

"Sit, sit," Mayor Brandt said, scooting over so I could plop down next to her, Governor Boggs and former Senator Foreman sitting across from us in the hotel lobby bar.

"Can I get you something to drink, Ms. Nealon?" Governor Henry Boggs asked in a pleasant Southern drawl. He wore a wide smile under perfectly styled grey hair with the occasional dark-rooted strand blended in. "Whatever you'd like."

"Uh, water," I said, as Robb Foreman extended a hand to me. I took it and let him shake it for a second as he continued to smile while the Governor of Tennessee bustled off to the bar to get me a water.

What the hell was happening here?

"How was your first day in Nashville?" Mayor Brandt asked, the perfect image of a sweet grandmother as Governor Boggs came back and set a tall glass of ice water in front of me. With a straw. Perfect.

"I hope our state is treating you right so far," Governor Boggs hastened to add.

"Uh, yeah, everything is just great so far," I said, trying to get my brain to keep up with what was going on here. Which, if I wasn't mistaken, was a charm offensive by the mayor of Nashville, the governor of Tennessee, and a former US senator of my acquaintance. "We had a little snafu earlier—"

"Heard about that." Mayor Brandt nodded. I found it interesting she was taking the lead on this, with Governor Boggs seemingly deferring to her. He appeared quite content to sip on his old fashioned while nodding sagely and hanging on her every word. "Seemed to me based on the Metro PD and TBI reports you did everything you could."

"Well," I said, "I could have maybe ended it if I'd overstepped my bounds a little more."

"I, for one," Robb Foreman rumbled, low and amused, "am pleased that you didn't shoot a man down in the street like a dog for hitting a few bad notes."

Mayor Brandt let out a cackle of glee. "If that was the criteria for shooting people, Broadway would be like the Wild West, people getting gunned down every which way!" That set the Governor off, too. Foreman just smiled.

"Still," I said, "I'd liked to have wrapped it up for you a little more neatly than what we have. Which is no clear line on the suspect, no idea who helped him, and no clue what their next move is."

"But you'll dig all that out; you always do," Brandt said. She started to reach across the table to pat me on the hand, but apparently thought the better of it. I caught her pausing the motion, and she grinned, very disarmingly. "I guess I shouldn't do that, since politicians already have to fight against the belief that we're soulless."

That got Governor Boggs roaring again, and it was hard for me to avoid smiling, because to my surprise...none of these people seemed to be faking that they were enjoying each other's company. Even Foreman, who was watching me quite cannily while the others talked.

"Now, Sienna," the governor said, once he'd finished his round of guffaws, "lest you think we're just whistling Dixie here, I feel like we should tell you—Agent Chandrasekhar has informed us that the FBI hasn't been real kind to you lately."

I blinked. "When? In the ten seconds it took me to leave him in the car and walk into the lobby?"

"He did send me a rather interesting text message as you were walking in, yes," Mayor Brandt said, lifting her reading glasses, which were on a chain around her neck, up to eye level as she lifted her phone. "Here—they're moving you to DC immediately. Entered your apartment without even asking in order to pack up your belongings." She made a mildly offended clucking noise. "I'm no lawyer, but that sounds like an invasion of privacy to me. What do you think, Senator Foreman?"

"It is indeed," Foreman said quietly.

"I'd have to check with the TBI, but I don't think I have ever heard of a state agency doing such a thing to one of its employees without a warrant, or without them even being under investigation." Governor Boggs shook his head sadly. This seemed to me just a hint less sincere than the laughter; I had no doubt that they were right, that the FBI under Director Chalke was doing some shady shit and treating me like chattel. But these folks were also playing it up somewhat.

And I couldn't say it wasn't working, but only because I'd already been pissed about it before I'd even walked in.

"A forced move to DC," Mayor Brandt went on, shaking her head sadly.

"A den of iniquity." Governor Boggs just shook his head like I'd been sentenced to the seventh circle of hell.

"And they won't let you interface with local law enforcement," Mayor Brandt finished, looking up. "Well, let me tell you something, Ms. Nealon—you can hang out with the Metro PD anytime. You can do it all day tomorrow if you want."

"You might want to check with your insurance carrier first," I said with a tight smile. "They might not appreciate having to cash the check you write with that offer."

"I think we're all familiar with your handiwork in the property destruction realm," Governor Boggs said, keeping a careful smile on his face, but shooting a sideways look at Mayor Brandt, then Foreman. "And we also have a general consensus that absent your intervention, the world would be in a much worse place if not for your efforts, including those that occasionally cause a mess."

I cringed, because clearly he had not seen my work firsthand. "You might be looking at this through slightly rose-colored glasses."

"I think we're looking at this in a very realistic way," Mayor Brandt said. "The world is always changing, but the revelation about metahumans has moved things in a very different direction. So many communities are approaching their policing situation in exactly the same way, as though nothing is different." She leaned forward. "We don't want to be caught in that trap."

"I know a lot of people think of Tennessee in the old way: backward rednecks," Governor Boggs said, and now he was leaning forward. "But Tennessee is always changing, too. We're trying to make things as good as we can without losing the things that made us distinct. For example, we have a program here which pays for the first two years of college if qualified students go to a community college or a tech school. We're trying to educate our population to meet the challenges of the twenty-first century job market. That philosophy to drive things forward—it extends to policing, too."

"Which is why you made that lovely offer," I said, sitting back. It was so strange to have someone pitch a job offer at me that was actually good and didn't involve threats. It was also the first time, in my memory, that it had happened since I'd joined the Directorate after leaving my house. Subsequent job offers had included Senator Foreman coercing me to re-form the Directorate under the government's aegis for purposes of stopping Sovereign, and Director Chalke threatening me to get me to join the FBI. Between the two, I suppose, I'd taken my job under the independent agency Reed now ran, but I didn't count that since it was really me offering myself a job through a lawyer so I could hide the source of the funds behind said agency. I wanted to take a sip of my water but I didn't want to uncross my arms and let them think they were getting through to me. "I appreciate that you want to get ahead of the curve here on metahuman policing or whatever—"

"Tennessee is one of the top states in terms of budget stability and financial solvency," Governor Boggs said, making me wonder if I'd walked into a campaign commercial. "We view this as a critical responsibility right up there with education. Protecting our citizens is job one."

"A very responsible view," I said. "But I'm employed with the FBI, and I'm afraid my agreement with them precludes the possibility of me leaving them right now."

"I understand completely," Mayor Brandt said, nodding again. "Personally, I like to work where I'm wanted and with people who appreciate me—"

I laughed under my breath. "I think Senator Foreman

could tell you that I'm no peach to work with once we get past the polite introductory phase."

"I thought you were fine to work with," Foreman chimed in. "Very straightforward. You kept the carnage to a relative minimum given what you were up against."

"You need to spend more time on the internet," I said. "There are videos. Sienna brutality and all that."

"I like to think you've learned a thing or two since you did some of those things," Foreman said.

"Maybe it's just me, but I didn't see anything wrong with burning that mad bomber alive given just what he did and what he was planning to do," Governor Boggs said. "I think smacking that handcuffed fella around in New York might have been a bit beyond the pale, legally, but once the video came out showing what he said to the waitress, most of us with an ounce of gentlemanly disposition came around to your side on it. At least around here." He settled back, crossing his legs. "Plus, as I recall, he was the one who destroyed the U.S.S. *Enterprise* in its dock, wasn't he?"

"He was," I said.

"That was a damned tragedy," Boggs said.

"Well, you've heard what we had to say," Mayor Brandt said, taking hold of the governor's arm and tugging gently to suggest they wrap it up. "You've had a long day between travel and everything else. Why don't we leave you to it?" She looked right at Senator Foreman. "Maybe let you catch up with your old buddy here."

I looked at Foreman blankly. He looked right back at me. I wondered if he was messing with my emotions given his empathic abilities, but since I didn't really feel anything other than burning rage toward Heather Chalke, which I'd had before I even walked in the door, I didn't think he was.

"Nice to meet you, Ms. Nealon," Governor Boggs said, finishing his old fashioned in one good gulp.

"Likewise," I said with a tight smile, and waved at Mayor Brandt as the two of them wended their way out of the hotel. I caught a glimpse of them getting into Chandler's SUV, which was still waiting there, before it pulled off into the night.

As soon as they were gone, I turned back to look at (former) Senator Foreman to find him staring at me, eyes narrowed, almost inscrutable in his concentration. I let him stare for a moment before I let out a deep sigh. "What? You getting the lay of the land in my brain?"

"Just wondering what's going on in there," Foreman said, eyes still narrowed in concentration, "because it's been a while...and things are mighty different."

"Life has a way of changing you," I said, a little guardedly.

"I should say so," Foreman said, finally easing up on his concentrating look. He settled back in his seat, let out a sigh of his own. "You have definitely changed." He shook his head in a way that reminded me of a disappointed father, slowly, patiently, and asked, "What have you let them do to you, Sienna?"

Chapter 43

Brance

"That's good, that's solid," Jules said as Brance brought another song to an end. This time it was "Outbound Plane," originally by Suzy Bogguss. He'd nailed it.

Or he thought he had. Jules wore a slightly pained expression, hands hovering, cupped, over his ears. Leo and Gil each had their fingers plugged into their ears and were across the warehouse, against the farthest wall.

"Did I...again?" Brance asked, heart falling in his chest.

"Just a little bit," Jules said, forcing a smile.

Brance felt like he was going to melt right there. He'd tried, really he had—

"Hey," Jules said, "it's fine. We'll get there, okay?" He sauntered over and planted a hand on Brance's shoulder, massaging Brance's trapezius muscle under the web of his meaty hand. There was a real tautness there, and Brance almost flinched away. "You're tense, kid." Jules gave it another couple squeezes. "We'll get you booked for a massage. I think part of your problem is you're expecting things to go bad at this point."

"Maybe," Brance said. He wasn't convinced. He didn't know enough about this—any of this, really—to know whether it had to do with tension, with bad luck. Hell, it could be an ancient curse for all he knew. It sure felt like a curse. He bowed his head. "I just...I can't believe this happened now. Of all times. I felt like I was so close."

"That's tough," Jules said. "Taking a hit to the dream like that." He brought his hand back up to Brance's shoulder. "Men live in their dreams, you know. We scrape along, work, but our head's in our dreams. At least, that's the way it is with those of us who have a vision for our lives." He wagged a finger in Brance's face. "And you, Brance—I can tell you're a man with a dream, with a vision."

Brance nodded. "Yeah. I had one."

"Tell me about it." Jules had the look of sincerity.

"I just wanted to sing," Brance said, letting it all fall out. "To be up on that stage, have people hear me. Like, really hear me." He looked back at his feet. "It's hard to explain, I guess. My parents were just kinda...I was the middle kid, so they didn't have time to listen to me. My brother and sister were rodeo riders since they were kids. Family business, because we had a ranch." He felt a little smile play over his face. "I wasn't into any of that. My brother is deep in the business at this point. My sister's heading toward a professional riding career. My parents were into all of that, running them everywhere, too busy for me." He let out a low breath. "But when I'd sing...they would hear me."

"You can make the world hear you, Brance," Jules said. "*We're* going to make the world hear you."

Brance looked up. That same sincerity was in Jules's eyes. It was weird, but he felt like Jules understood more than anyone else, maybe. Like he had a dream of his own. That was something Brance felt on a deep level. Sure, his brother had dreamed—if you could call it that—about running the ranch, taking it over. His sister had focused on her riding, on trophies, awards, all that.

But those weren't dreams, really. Not big ones, anyway. Not like...

"I want to sing on the stage of the Opry," Brance said. "Have a concert at the Ryman."

Jules nodded. "The Mother Church of Country Music? That's a fine dream."

"I've wanted it since I first listened to the Opry when I was a kid," Brance said, staring off into the distance. "My brother and sister were off somewhere, and I was at my grandparents' house and they were watching it...I just wanted to be on that stage."

"Maybe we can do a little something about that," Jules said, and the older man seemed deep in the middle of his own thought. Brance would have asked what it was, but he didn't want to push his new benefactor.

Besides, he was back in his own vision, thanks to Jules. For a moment, singing in this empty, decrepit warehouse, he felt like he was already on the Opry stage. If the real thing felt only a little better...

Well, maybe he would see his dream after all—with Jules's help.

Chapter 44

Sienna

"I didn't let anyone do anything to me," I said, hackles raised, my anger at Director Chalke for invading my privacy by breaking into my apartment now pointed at the nearest convenient target.

"You did," Foreman said, shaking his head. "I wouldn't have believed it until now. You let them get you—"

"I didn't let anyone *get* anything," I whispered, warring against the desire to let my voice rise in anger.

"How'd they do it?" Foreman asked, unflinching as he stared into my eyes. "You walked through the fire to get pardoned twice. You were free and clear after Revelen." He leaned in a little closer. "What could they possibly have on you that would make you work for these people?"

"Maybe I just like the job."

Foreman shook his head. "There's a limit to how much shit you'll put up with, and in my experience, it's really low. If anyone without leverage on you pulled half the crap I've heard Director Chalke has, you'd have killed them by now."

I broke into a thin smile. "See, the thing about getting pardoned twice? You're probably not going to get a third bite at the apple. Which means I have to learn to play nice, at least with people on the right side of the law."

"Humph." Foreman sat back, letting out that low grunt as he continued to stare into my eyes, trying to read the secrets written in my feelings. There wasn't much there, I thought, other than exhaustion, discontentment and a flaring rage I was trying really hard to tamp down. "I'm not quite sure I believe that, but let's say for the sake of the argument that I did. Why stick with these people when they keep jerking you around?"

Looking into Robb Foreman's eyes, I saw a glimmer of warmth that had been absent from most of my interactions these last few months. It was disarming in a way that Willis Shaw, my now-former boss, couldn't be, and that Heather Chalke, my new boss, never was. "I just...the work is important," I said lamely.

"Your brother does similar work," Foreman said. "He's down in Murfreesboro right now. Less than an hour from here. He doesn't have a boss like Chalke." He leaned in again, and I realized his voice was so low no one in the bar could hope to hear it without a listening device. "I know what she is. The type of person. I dealt with her for years when I was in the Senate. The mayor here, the governor— they're decent in a way she's not. Politicians, sure. But fair."

"Life's not fair," I said.

Foreman stared smokily into my eyes. "That's for sure."

"I can't," I said, pulling an unsteady hand back to rest on my chin. "I just...I can't take the job here."

Foreman nodded. "Mayor Brandt is determined to

show you a good time anyway." He reached into his coat pocket and pulled out a card. "They're going to drop off a Metro PD radio for you later tonight that will be delivered to your room first thing tomorrow. You've got your own designator here—" he waved the card "—and you're welcome to join them on any call you'd like to. Or you can just keep it on hand in case you need to call in next time you cross paths with your perp. Your choice."

I took the outstretched card, not entirely out of politeness. There might have been a slight hunger on my part to do something worthwhile with my time. "This...isn't going to convince me."

"No, I can see now you won't be convinced," Foreman said. "I also see that you've lost some of the travelers in your mind. You've got a harder edge now. A...colder disposition, shall we say." He smiled.

"Everyone knows I lost my souls," I said, looking down at my hands folded in my lap. "It was on the internet, so it must be true."

"It must be." Foreman nodded slowly. "I realized I haven't seen you since that business in Atlanta a few years back. It would have been interesting for me to...communicate with the passenger you picked up after that."

That made me raise an eyebrow. It was a clear reference to President Harmon. "I'm sure I don't know what—"

"He was a telepath, wasn't he?" Foreman asked, peering at me, weighing my words. "I thought he might be. The evidence fit, especially after I whipped him at the first debate like a lame mule."

I nodded slowly. "Those serums that unlock meta powers? He was working with Edward Cavanagh and others to create one to boost his powers." I licked my lips. "So he could go 'omnipath,' in his words. Be everywhere at once, put us all in alignment as a species. Create a hive mind."

Foreman's eyes went wide. "With him as the queen. I'd heard the rumors. Back channel stuff." He sat back, and he looked as close to shaken as I'd seen him since the war against Sovereign. Not that I'd seen him much since then. "But you and your friends stopped him."

I shrugged. "Not before he exacted a hell of a toll. One I'm still working my way out of."

Foreman nodded slowly, then lowered his voice to depths where only a meta could hear him. "There are some long knives out for you, Sienna. Even after Harmon. I hear the whispers. People talk, even to a has-been like me. Powerful people have you in their crosshairs for all sorts of reasons."

"They've got me in more than that," I replied, matching him at meta-low.

He looked at me evenly, as if trying to decide what sort of emotional feedback he was getting from me and what it meant. "You got it under control?"

I felt that same cold, clammy feeling in my stomach and on my skin that I'd felt for months. Since I'd walked out of that interrogation room and into a White House press conference where the President had announced me as his new solution to the metahuman policing problem. "I don't know."

Foreman just nodded slowly. "How bad are these people?"

"TBD." I forced a smile. "But not good."

Foreman nodded slowly. "I know what it's like to have enemies that you can't entirely see." He looked around us slowly. "Do you know any of their names?"

"A few," I said, keeping my voice at a level where not even a dog could have heard it.

He nodded. "I've got another for you, then: Russ Bilson."

I gave him a slow nod in return. "I know."

Foreman leaned back again, clutching his ankle where it folded over his other knee. "How are you going to handle it when you do get to the...heart of the matter...with these folks?"

"I'm open to suggestions." I drew a slow breath. "This is unlike any enemy I've ever faced. There are so many of them, hiding in the shadows. And it's not like Sovereign, who would have destroyed the planet, or Harmon, trying to kill us all, or Hades with his nukes. Hell, it's not even like the Clary family trying to kill me or that Scottish bitch who wrecked my life." I shook my head. "They're spiders in a web that I'm tangled in, and I don't know if they're violent, if they've got evil intent. All I know is they're applying pressure to me, pushing me, trying to wrap me up, control me. And I don't entirely know what to do about it. What the *right* thing to do is."

Foreman did not answer me, giving me a long moment where he stared down at the place where his pants leg didn't quite meet his fine leather loafer, giving me a view of his socks. They had a Tennessee Titans logo printed on them, tiny, about the size of my fingertip, dozens and dozens of them forming a pattern. He seemed to be studying it. "They pushed you into this job?"

"With a little less grace than when you did it." I tried not to smile. I failed.

"I did it to save the world," Foreman said, not looking up. "And all I did was put the government behind you for a mission you were already on. I like to think there's a difference between what I did then and what's happening to you now."

"There is," I said.

A flash of relief greeted me as he looked up. "Then I'll say it plain—these people seem to intend to enslave you outside the law on these matters. Put you to work on their will. Coercion via blackmail is still slavery by a kinder name, and I know what I'd do if someone said they were going to do that to me." There was a hint of anger in his eyes as he stood and put a hand on my shoulder. "You're a clever lady, Sienna. You know where the lines are, and you know your profession. I think you'll do just fine—so long as you go slow...and keep it quiet."

With that, he turned and walked out of the hotel lobby. I watched him go and wondered if I'd misunderstood him, or if he'd really just suggested I handle them like I did almost every other villain.

Lethally.

Chapter 45

I woke up the next morning to a bright, sunny blue sky hanging over the glass and steel skyline of Nashville. After I blinked the sleep out of my eyes, I took a long shower and started to get ready for my day. It didn't take too long, fortunately, because I woke up ravenous.

On my way out to grab breakfast, I picked up the police radio Mayor Brandt had Metro leave at the front desk. It was a handheld unit, able to be clipped to my belt, but with an extension I could mount on my car to extend the range.

The extender was easy to install. Simple suction cup on top of the car roof, plug in the outlet, and I was done. I noticed, not for the first time, that they'd put windshield-mounted flashing lights and a siren up front, and a quick inspection of the trunk found that, indeed, they had equipped the car with an AR-15 and a Mossberg 930 semi-automatic shotgun with ten rounds. I checked the loads because I was curious: double ought buck with a couple rifled slugs at the end of the magazine. I also found an ammo belt with extra magazines for the AR and more shells of each kind for the shotgun. Digging a little deeper I found still another gem Chandler hadn't mentioned—Remington's new V3 Tac-13 shotgun, a five-round semi-auto model that was just a little bigger than a pistol. Perfect for close quarters, it even had a sling harness so I could carry it on my back if things got heated.

I didn't know what the TBI and Metro police thought I'd get up to while I was in town, but I did appreciate that unlike the FBI, they'd loaded me up like John Wick for worst-case scenarios. It was a vote of confidence I certainly didn't feel at my job lately. I mean, I'd practically had to offer sexual favors to the armorer in New York to get a Gatling gun in order to face off with Grendel on my last misadventure, and my boss—unknowing—hadn't been real happy with that.

Here in Tennessee, they were handing me some major tools of destruction, and the case thus far hadn't required me to even fire a shot. It was a sea change, attitudinally, over what I'd become used to since taking the job. And a mark in their favor that, at least before we'd had a major chaos (AKA Sienna) incident, they truly seemed dedicated to letting me run wild and free. That was not common. Not anymore.

Once I'd finished all that, I sat in the driver's seat for a few minutes and let the car run, the darkness of the hotel garage shrouding me as I checked my messages. I glanced at my mirrors every few minutes to make sure someone wasn't sneaking up on me (even though I'd parked with my trunk almost against the concrete wall of the garage) until done. Nothing new from the office, no further notes from Chalke, nothing but a text from Hilton blathering her excitement at how great our next step was going to be and how she was already in the process of her move to DC. Holloway, I assumed, was sour about it, as he was about nearly everything. That was a man who bought his Corn Flakes with urine already in them.

Yay. My shit was presumably in transit, and the FBI hadn't sent me so much as a tracking number. Good thing I had very few possessions in my apartment and almost nothing I cared about. It took the sting out of the privacy violation. Also my lost luggage had shown up on my door sometime between midnight and three AM, looking like it had been transshipped via Syria.

I got breakfast at an artisanal, make-your-own-pancakes place south of downtown. It was pleasant, and gimmicky in a cute way. I stared at the complete lack of notifications on my phone, waiting for something to happen. I had the police radio turned way down, and all the action was quiet stuff, like traffic stops and paramedic calls.

It'd probably be like this most of the day, I figured, for a mid-sized city like Nashville. It wasn't a hardcore murder capital, like St. Louis or Baltimore, or big enough to have a massive number of shootings and gang violence, like Chicago.

Still, I listened as I chewed down syrupy goodness. It went on quietly up until I'd just paid my check.

"All units, officer needs assistance," the radio crackled. "Vicinity of 8th and Bradford."

I pulled up my phone, meta-speed, and tapped in the address as I walked out of the pancake place, leaving behind the luscious smell of syrup and the sizzle of pancake batter. It only took a second for the result to come up: it was six blocks away.

Hopping into the BMW, I started it up and hit the lights and siren. I sped through the next three intersections before having to slow down and let a semi through before running the next light. A couple turns later and I was on Bradford, houses blurring past in sequence. Some were old, some looked brand new, as though the neighborhood was in the middle of turning over.

There was already one Metro PD car parked on the corner, lights flashing. I slowed as I rolled up, no sign of cops anywhere nearby. I put the window down and listened, hoping to hear the sounds of a foot pursuit.

I did. Feet slapping in the distance, breaking through the sleepy morning. Someone yelled, "Stop! Stop right there!"

It was at least a couple blocks over, buildings between me and the foot chase.

Flooring the gas, I took the next corner with squealing tires, using my meta reflexes and a couple tricks I'd observed from Angel Gutierrez to drift and accelerate out of the turn. The BMW handled my maneuver beautifully, tires catching just when I needed them to.

I could see a cop running a couple blocks down. I pressed the pedal down and the BMW's engine roared. Sirens in the distance told me that backup was on the way.

I'd have this wrapped up before they got here.

The police officer was running after the perp but was easily half a block back. The sidewalks were uncrowded, the neighborhood of single-family homes giving way to two-story apartment buildings and shopfronts. The perp was running past one now, a Mexican grocery in what had once been a house. He had brown hair and wore a black shirt, and when he threw a look back over his shoulder, he was grinning at the cop he was leaving in the dust.

Then he saw me, BMW bearing down on him with flashing lights, and his smile vanished.

"That's right, dipshit," I said, mounting the curb and

listening to the BMW's chassis squeal in protest at the bump. "You're not getting away."

I rode the empty sidewalk until I was only twenty feet behind them, then jerked the BMW's wheel as I let out a blast on the horn. I popped the emergency brake and sent the car into a sideways skid. When it had slowed down enough, I threw it into park and flung myself out the door, hitting the ground at a run without missing a step.

"Ahhh!" the perp yelled, surprised at my sudden appearance a couple feet behind him. He'd had to look forward to dodge a cafe table sitting in the middle of the sidewalk, and when he'd looked back, I'd been there where a BMW had been bearing down on him a moment earlier.

I hit him in the kidney. Not hard enough to rupture anything, but hard enough to make him jerk like I'd applied an electrical current to his lower back. He let out a cry, and as soon as he'd relaxed, gripping where I'd struck him, I kneed him in the gut and he folded like origami. I slammed him over the cafe table and cuffed him in about two seconds flat. Then I pushed his legs out and gave him a quick pat down, discovering a pistol secreted in his waistband. "What have we here?" I asked.

"What...the hell...?" he groaned, trying to touch himself at that spot on his back where I'd made him hurt. "It's...that's not...mine."

"That means it's stolen, right?" I held it delicately between my thumb and forefinger so as not to mess with any fingerprints on the weapon. "Carrying a stolen pistol? So naughty."

"I..." He sagged on the table, giving in to his pain.

"You have the right to remain silent," I said. "Really suggest you employ that now, because anything you say can and will be used against you in a court of law and might annoy me. You have the right to an attorney. If you cannot afford one, one will be provided for you, but you should really question why you're out committing crimes instead of trying to procure the kind of work that would allow you to afford an attorney. Okay?" I patted him on the back, somewhat gently. It might have come off as a little bit of a slap between the shoulder blades that caused him to jerk involuntarily in pain, but hey, when the adrenaline is pumping, sometimes I don't know my own strength.

"Where'd you come from?" The cop in pursuit came huffing up. His brass name plate read *Collins*. He stopped a couple yards away, trying to catch his breath.

I shrugged. "I was eating breakfast a few blocks away. Figured I'd give you a hand." I placed the pistol I'd recovered from the suspect on the table, far from his reach. "Found this in my search of him."

"Thanks," he said, looking at the perp. "I was just talking to this guy and he bitch-slapped me and ran."

"You were going to search me, man," our perp mumbled, sounding pained.

"Yeah, and now we've done that," I said. "It's just that now you have a backache and stomachache to go along with being busted for possession of a stolen weapon. Next time just let it happen and you can avoid the pain."

"This isn't fair," he mumbled. "I was getting away."

"Yeah, life's a real bitch like that," I said, nodding to Collins to take over. He did, and I heard him start the familiar refrain of reading the guy his Miranda rights— again. Sirens were getting closer now, as I sauntered back to my BMW, pulling the radio off my belt. "Situation contained. Perp is in custody." I glanced at the street sign, then scanned the address, reporting it in to dispatch.

Dispatch came back a moment later, but it was fuzzed and crackling. "Who is this?"

"Oh, right," I said, remembering the designator they'd

assigned me. "This is Echo One...on scene." I felt a little thrill run through me, one which was magnified when the dispatcher answered back.

"10-4, Echo One," the dispatcher came back a moment later. "Good work."

Chapter 46

Jules

This was the idea.

"In here, come on." Jules waved a hand, beckoning Brance forward into the building and out of the blazing sunlight. He'd gotten the kid a pair of dark glasses and a cowboy hat. The combo was helping to hide his face, which wasn't famous yet but still had the Metro PD out in force looking for him. To Jules's eyes, Brance was a good-looking enough kid, fit enough to look nice in jeans, but of a type that was a dime a dozen in this town.

"What is this place?" Brance asked, crow's feet forming around his eyes as he squinted behind the glasses. "Can I take these off yet?"

"Not yet," Jules said, stepping inside. Once they were in, he let Gil close the door behind them, then waved a hand in a flourish like a magician. "You see this?"

Brance continued to squint. "These glasses are really dark. Can I—"

"Yeah, take 'em off, go ahead," Jules said. He waited.

Brance looked around once he had the dark glasses in his hand, blinking a few times against the faded light as he took in the wood overtones of the room. He look around with a furrowed brow for a few seconds, then his forehead started to loosen, the lines slackening as he realized where he was. "Is this a recording studio?"

Jules stepped behind one of the microphones, grinning broadly. "That's right, kid." He made a show of pretending to speak into it, though it wasn't turned on yet. "I got you...studio time."

Brance's jaw fell open, and he looked like he might seize up right there. Eyes crinkling...was the kid going to cry? Jules felt a faint shimmer of panic at this idea, a not-so-vague distaste at the idea of having to manage more of this kid's uncomfortable emotions. What was it about these millennials, always pissing their feelings out everywhere like a dog who couldn't control his bladder? "I...I..."

"It's okay, kid," Jules said, trying to remember he was fluffing this delicate little pussy until he got what he wanted. Whoever had raised this pitiful bitch had really done a number on him, Jules was starting to realize. But maybe that would make him easier to control in the long run.

Maybe.

But it would be easier still if Jules could just record this kid's voice going all high and painful, then employ it whenever he felt of a mind to do so. That'd be a lot simpler than attending to the care and feeding of Brance's stupid feelings and his stupid self.

Jules said none of this, though. He just held his arms wide and smiled, fueling the fires of the little bastard's stupid dreams a bit further. "What do you think? You ready?"

"I...I've dreamed of this moment for so long," Brance

said, about two steps from sputtering. "But..." His eyes welled, and Jules fought the urge to take a step back from the teary little pisspot. "I only have a song or two of my own."

"That's fine," Jules said. "Albums take months to assemble. This is just preliminary. Get your voice on some tracks, get a feel for things here, explore the studio space." He maintained his grin, even though he was cribbing from Christopher Walken on *Saturday Night Live* in what he was saying. What the hell did an organized crime guy know about making albums?

"Okay." Brance nodded, a little smile starting to form. "Yeah. Yeah, this is just a start. But...cool." Now he was grinning.

Perfect. "Let's get a song recorded, huh?" Jules was grinning, too, because if he could get a good, painful, screechy, murderous recording from this little shit, he could be rid of him by sundown, the body distributed throughout the city in a way that the cops would never find. "Let's start your career off right."

Chapter 47

Sienna

"This looks like some mighty fine work right here," Captain Barry Parsons said as Collins shoved our perp in the back seat of a Metro squad car. The sun was shining and a pleasant breeze stirred my hair. The smell of burgers cooking in the distance would have been a pleasant scent if I wasn't still gorged on pancakes.

"Thanks," I said, trying to keep it humble. "Just doing the job."

Parsons was a longtime vet, and not one of the chair jockeys I so often saw in Captain positions. You could tell it just by looking at him; he looked like a man who'd done his time on the beat. "And you did it well." He checked his watch. "We got a couple things cooking today you'd maybe like a piece of."

I raised an eyebrow even as I checked my phone. No messages from Chandler—or anyone else. "What did you have in mind?" I asked. "Because it looks like my schedule is open..."

Chapter 48

Jules

Sitting in the booth wasn't the most comfortable place to be. Gil was behind him, hovering, like a fly buzzing your head that you couldn't quite lay a hand on, no matter how hard you swung. "How long do these things take?"

"Months," said Dan, the sound guy in charge of the studio space. He had long grey hair and a goatee, and he was hunched over his sound board messing with the slider panel like tweaking it properly held the secrets of life itself. Jules had so little interest in the minutia here he felt he might keel over of boredom if not for the commanding possibilities in front of him if this plan worked.

"You're recording all this, right?" Jules asked, looking at the sound tech with jaded irritation.

"It's running," Dan said, not looking up from his slider panel. "But your boy's going to have to sing."

"He ain't my boy," Jules muttered, settling back in his seat to listen. Gil offered him earplugs, and Jules took 'em while Dan put on electronic headphones that were hooked to the mics in the studio. Jules eyed him as he got set up; this would be interesting to watch.

"You want one of these, too?" Dan turned to offer him a set of headphones plugged into the sound board.

"Nah, I'll listen to it on playback," Jules said, trying to suppress a smile and failing. He didn't mind watching the misery of others unfold. He spared an idle, musing thought about how Dan was going to take it when shit went sideways here and ended up chuckling heartily to himself. It'd be fun to see if it lived up to his vision when it played out.

"Yo, boss." Gil leaned down, whispering in his ear before he got that left earplug in. "What if he don't...you know. Go off." Gil twerked his eyebrows significantly, like an idiot. As if Jules wouldn't know what he was talking about.

"I don't think that's going to be a problem," Jules said, rolling the earplug between his thumb and forefinger, ready to put this conversation behind him and get on with his day. Such exciting possibilities.

"He made it through a few songs last night without it happening," Gil said. "Maybe he really is learning to control it."

Jules didn't bother fighting to hold in a smile that twisted his lips. "Don't fret. Let's see what plays out."

"All right, you ready in there?" Dan asked, his voice seeping through Jules's earplugs, muffled.

Brance was nodding, and he said something. Whatever it was, Dan seemed to think it indicated go time, because he hit a couple buttons on the panel and said, "Let's roll!"

Jules watched, chin resting on his hand, finger stretched along the side of his jaw as he waited. How long would this take? You couldn't rush greatness, but it'd be nice if he could get this ironed out quickly and get back to Bones. He hadn't read the paper yet, and he already had some ideas on how he was going to use the recording once he had it.

"You want to warm up a little?" Dan asked, responding to something Brance had said.

Brance nodded through the soundproof glass.

Jules tried to contain himself. This was going to be great. And, hopefully, work.

Chapter 49

Sienna

I rolled my BMW to a stop outside a police perimeter in a slightly older neighborhood apartment block. It was brick and aged, stains along the sides. I'd followed a couple of Metro squad cars to this location, and we all popped out to gather behind a building on a nearby street corner. Five local blues were already waiting, guns drawn, one officer— a black lady—looking around the corner every few seconds and providing an update, which I caught the latest of as I hopped up the curb and joined them.

"...selling to kids," she said, her eyes narrowed and her mouth returning to a stiff line when she finished speaking. I got the gist.

"What's the merchandise?" I asked, stepping into the circle and getting a few looks from the cops present. They all knew me, so it was mostly double takes that I would deign to step down and talk to them out here, I guessed.

"Heroin or fentanyl," she said. "Vice detectives were supposed to be quarterbacking this, but somehow we got handed the job of picking these guys up. I thought it was a little funny at the time, but..." She gave me a very jaded look. "I guess we know why, now."

"I'm plainclothes; how about I go in and take the heat," I said, stealing a look around the corner. Sure enough, there was a guy standing on the corner, well above legal age. That was interesting; lots of times they stuck minors out there holding because the penalties were much less harsh if you got busted. This guy, though? He was doing it for himself, and I had to respect that kind of brassy stupidity. "You guys work your way around behind him, then we pop him in one good move."

"He's got a partner doing lookout and holding behind him," the lady cop said. Her name plate read Smythwick.

"You guys circle and grab him, I'll take care of this guy," I said. "Maybe even get him to sell me something first."

Smythwick gave me a look. "How you going to do that?"

I glanced at the BMW parked behind me. "Well...you said he's selling to kids...and I've been told I can still pass for a teenager if I wear my makeup right..."

Chapter 50

Jules

The first hint that something was wrong wasn't something Jules heard, but rather something he felt.

It was a tremble in his chair, a warble that ran through the metal armrest, vibrated through the seat, quivered in his bones. He'd been almost dozing, ignoring Dan's entreaties to—well, whatever the hell he was telling Brance to do. The relative quiet was enough for Jules to feel the sleepy drain of not getting his forty winks last night. Time was, he remembered being able to stay up all night.

But that hadn't been true for years, and pushing it had him dozing in the chair when shit started to go off.

When his eyes snapped open, the soundproof window between the studio and the booth was shaking, the lights wavering in it like the fixtures were shaking. They weren't; it was the window itself that was flexing, bowing as though the room were being pressurized and depressurized in turn.

Jules sat up straight in his seat, looking over at Dan,

who was staring at the window as though something alien were happening. He didn't register a hint of pain, which was also interesting in its own way, Jules thought dimly—

Brance was inside, eyes closed, mouth open, letting it rip with everything in him. He didn't seem to realize what was happening, had no clue what he was causing until—

The window shattered. Jules threw himself backward and upended the chair, almost taking out Gil as he fell. He thumped to the ground and felt the pebbled sound-proof glass rain upon him. It felt more like plastic than shards, and he brushed it off, frowning as he picked himself up.

Brance was standing in the middle of the studio next to a half-melted microphone that looked like an ice cream cone that someone had left in the sun. No ice cream, all cone, it ended just above where the stand clamped around it. The singer was just looking at the broken window stupidly, as though he couldn't wrap his pea brain around what had happened.

"Did you hear anything?" Jules looked down at Dan, who had not been so quick to move as Jules, and now had shiny pieces of the broken glass sprinkled in his grey hair for additional sheen.

Dan blinked and looked up, pulling off his head-phones. "What?"

Jules repeated himself, keeping his voice under control. Barely. Maybe the dumbass was deaf now.

Dan shook his head once he'd got it. "No. I didn't hear anything but him singing. And some feedback." He stared blankly. "How the hell...?" He looked back at the sound-board. "Whatever it was, I think it fried the recording!" He slid over to another console, where something was smok-ing. "It did!"

Jules looked up. Brance was watching him, eyes all

teary—again. He contained himself—barely—in time. He looked over his shoulder at Gil. "Let's move."

Dan stirred. "Hey, man, there's a lot of damage here—"

"I'm not responsible for your equipment failure," Jules said as he stood, stopping himself from belting the sound tech for being a dumbass. He snapped a finger at Brance. "Session's over. We're out of here." When Brance didn't move, he raised his voice to jar the idiot out of his stupor. "Come onnnnn!" Clapping his hands once, loudly, he beckoned for the door.

Brance stirred, nodded once, and followed Jules, who was already chafing under this failure. On the plus side, he had an idea for what to do next.

On the downside, he reflected as he held open the door to the alley out back for Brance, the moron, he wasn't going to be able to just dump this idiot and be done with it.

Chapter 51

Sienna

My hair was in a braided ponytail, put there by Smythwick, who'd glared at me sullenly the whole time she worked on it. I felt it was some nice work, personally, and went well with the halter top I'd picked up at a nearby Goodwill. I was as close to teenager as I could make myself look, and I pulled the BMW up to the curb next to the dealer on the corner and rolled down the window. We'd removed the dash lights and radio antenna, of course. "What's up?" I called out to him.

He looked at me suspiciously, but sauntered up to the window. "Yo. Whassup with you?"

"I need to lay my hands on something fun," I said, smiling. If he knew my face, the makeup and braided hair weren't going to fool him for long. "Someone told me I needed to come down here for that."

He looked up and down the street, probably searching for cops. They weren't obviously in evidence, though, so his gaze tracked back to me. "Maybe, maybe. If you got some green, you can make your dreams come true."

"Look at my car, baby," I said, leaning over the center console. "You think I don't have any money?"

He looked around again, making a decision. "All right, I got you. Whatchoo looking for?"

"I got friends who have been around the block, y'know?" I made eye contact and didn't shy away. "We've done everything, almost. So I need something...exciting. Nothing boring. Not the shit you sell the tourists looking to have an easy high, you know?"

He rubbed grubby fingers over the scattered facial hair that surrounded his mouth and chin. This guy was in his twenties, probably the early side, but the wear and tear on him suggested he had been using his own product at least lightly for a while. "I feel you. I have something you might like. If you're strong enough."

"Baby," I said, still smiling, "you won't find many stronger than me."

He nodded and stood up, looking around one last time. He stuck a single finger up, telling me to wait one minute, I assumed, then turned and hustled back down the alley.

Dutifully, I waited, looking around like somebody might spot me at any time. Because, really, they could. I was sitting in a BMW looking like a teen with more of daddy's money than brains of my own, for all the world to see. It was my good luck that this drug dealer hadn't noticed I was the world's most well-known superhero. That happened sometimes. Hell, it was the reason I'd been able to evade the cops for two years while on the run. People just couldn't reconcile that I was Sienna Nealon when I wasn't dressed in my signature way, or in the places where I would normally be seen.

My phone buzzed with a text and I pulled it out because a teenage girl would totally do that.

It was Smythwick: *In position.*

Wait for my signal, I sent back, and then put my phone down when I saw my quarry returning with his hands shoved deep in his pockets. I had my HK VP9 pistol wedged in the crack between my seat and the center console, hidden from the dealer's view but ready to draw in case things got hostile. I watched him walk back with that same eager smile, and added a sniff, wiping my nose with my left hand for effect. "What you got for me, baby?" I asked as he leaned down into my window.

He checked the street one more time and then reached deeper into his pocket. I watched him very carefully in case he decided to pull a gun, but a moment later he came out with a plastic sandwich bag filled with a tiny corner of...something. Fentanyl, I was guessing, based on the proportion.

"I don't care how strong you are," he said, holding up the baggy, "this shit will kill your ass if you ain't careful. Go light, y'hear? Real light."

"Mmmmm," I sighed, trying to make it as luscious and lusty as possible, like I really was a strung-out idiot in need of a fix. "I like the sound of that. How much?"

"Two grams for a hundred," he said, and once more he was sweeping the street with his eyes, and completely ignoring the much more real danger staring at him like a hungry shark from inside my car. "That's the discount price."

"Awesome," I said, and reached out, snapping a hand around his wrist. He looked down, curiously, for a second before trying to pull it back.

That did not work.

"Yo, whatchoo doing?" he asked, voice a little higher but well below the panic threshold.

"You're under arrest," I said.

"What?! Bitch, let me go or I'ma—"

I yanked his wrist so hard it would have dislocated his elbow and shoulder if he had mounted any resistance whatsoever. As it was, he was unprepared to fight back, and that saved his joints—at a cost.

The cost was he got jerked forward and rammed his head on my car. It was loud, it sounded painful, concussive, even, and he immediately sagged to his knees, dropping the Fentanyl on my passenger seat.

He lost interest in the fight after that, and Metro PD officers stormed in all around him. They had him cuffed on the hood of my car thirty seconds later, eyes still struggling to focus as they searched him, legs spread and unable to hold his own weight.

"You're coming with us!" Smythwick's voice came from the alleyway. I hopped out of the BMW and jogged over to lend a hand. Four officers were warring with a guy about twice the size of the one currently being felt up on my hood. "Stop resisting!"

I walked down the alley as the big guy threw his weight against one of the cops and sent the whole pack of them staggering in one direction. The officer behind him—a smaller lady named Munoz—crunched between him and the wall and I saw her lose her grip on him as she slid down, clutching the back of her head.

"Y'all ain't taking me in!" the big guy said. Apparently we'd paired off in teams of big versus little, and the Metro PD cops were on the "little" side today. Whoops. If I'd been running this—really running it—I might have gone with a more even distribution of muscle to this group, because as I made my way toward them, the big guy reached over and grabbed hold of one of the smaller cops, a guy named Braddock, and physically shoved him back down the alley. Braddock hit the ground and rolled, but he looked like he might have landed on something uncomfortable, like a bottle, because I saw blood on his hands.

"Hey, big fella," I said, calmly walking toward him. He snapped his attention to me, his eyes all on fire like he was looking for his next target.

He needed a new target, too, because he elbowed Smythwick and sent her staggering, her vest unable to do much more than muffle the impact of his elbow to her midsection.

"Why don't you pick on someone your own size?" I asked, looking up at him as I kept coming.

"Ain't no one my size, girl," he said, giving me a savage smile. He slapped a fist into his other, meaty hand, and took a couple steps toward me. He swung a fist toward my face—

Except my face wasn't there. My hand was waiting, and caught his fist in my grip.

"I've met bigger men," I said, holding his fist in mine like it was nothing. Really, it was, thanks to my super strength. "Taller ones. Braver ones. Ones that don't scream like a bitch when you break their hand."

He stopped struggling to get his hand back—with no luck—when I said that. "Wha...?"

I flexed my grip and shattered half the bones in his hand like I was Superman squeezing coal into a diamond. It sounded like I'd stepped on a cockroach, at least until he let out a scream that drowned out the sound of the tiny bones breaking.

With a quick yank, I brought him closer, pulling him to me and down as I raised my knee to greet his face. The snap of his nose breaking was like sweet music, and his eyes fluttered as he swung back and I caught him before he hit the ground, gently lowering him to his face.

Smythwick, still recovering from his attack, scooted over and cuffed the big bastard, then looked up at me with hints of pain and recrimination in her eyes. "Why didn't you just take him to begin with?"

"What? I was busy out on the street, soliciting drugs," I said with an impish smile. "I only came back here when I heard your honor needed avenging."

Munoz let out a dry laugh that sounded like it hurt, because she stopped immediately and clutched her ribs.

"Call it in," Smythwick said, settling back against the wall of the alley.

"Will do," I said, and hoofed it back to my car to grab my radio. When I had it in hand, I depressed the button again. "Echo One to dispatch. Officer-involved ass-whooping, situation resolved." I couldn't hide my smile, because...dammit, it felt good to be doing something useful.

Chapter 52

Jules

"I can't believe it happened again," Brance whined, sitting in the back of Jules's car. His head was leaned against the window, a perfect picture of despair.

It made Jules sick just looking at the waste of flesh, waste of talent. Somehow he'd ended up with the power to make people hurt from across a room, and this little whiner was sad about it. Jules held that in, though. Instead, he said, "Every dream has its setbacks, kid. We need to practice a little more, that's all." He waved a hand to Gil. "Take us back to the warehouse."

"Again?" Brance sounded like he was just a little short of crying. "Jules, it's not working." The sad sack looked down at his lap, and his voice broke. "Maybe we should just give up—"

"Oh, I'm sorry," Jules said, letting fly with the sarcasm. Less than a day and he was already sick of coddling this weakling. It was time to put some screws to this little bitch. "I thought you wanted to be a star, but if you want to be a loser and just tuck your little tail between your legs and mosey home to your mommy and daddy back at the ranch, we can do that. Lemme get you a bus ticket."

Brance's mouth fell open and hung there as thoughts spun behind his eyes, most of which were obvious to Jules. The kid wanted to argue, because he had hurt feelings. Ooh, hurt feelings! Jules didn't care; he waited for that shit to pass.

"I don't want to give up," Brance said, finally, and softly. "This is my dream."

"You think any of your so-called heroes that sang on that stage you're so obsessed with—you think they didn't have setbacks?" Jules kept his eyes forward. "You think people didn't tell them *no*? Didn't kick them out of bars? Reject them—"

"That's a little different than having a voice that hurts people—" Brance started to say.

"Lots of voices hurt people, kid," Jules said. A flash of his own father came back to him, yelling at the top of his lungs at Jules and his ma. "What you need to figure out how to do is get tougher. Learn some control. Because ninety-five percent of the time, your voice is fine. Something's happening in that other five percent that's messing everything up." Jules simmered for a second, let Brance stew on that. "What are you thinking about when it all goes to hell?"

Brance hesitated. "I...I don't know."

"Is it a note you're hitting?"

"No." Brance shook his head. "No, definitely not. It's happened on songs that are radically different. It's not a common note, or even a common range."

Jules had an idea. "Is it a feeling?" He looked over at the kid, who was staring back at him with his face all screwed up. "Something you're thinking about when it happens?"

"N-no," Brance said, too shakily.

There it was. Jules had it. Something was going on there. Something—or someone—that cropped up in the kid's head, that was the trigger..

But for now, Jules would let it rest. At least until he figured out what *it* was. He had a suspicion. He'd need to confirm it.

Then he could pull the trigger anytime he wanted.

Chapter 53

Sienna

"You seem to have a knack for this policing thing," Captain Parsons said, giving me a coy smile. "It's almost like you've been doing it for a while, that teeny-bopper look notwithstanding."

"I am clearly but a spoiled trust fund baby with no one's money to spend," I said mockingly. "Just a girl making her way in the world with but her fists to lead the way."

Parsons chuckled. "I don't quite think I believe that. Might have missed that part of your bio."

"Oh, well, you know those things are always completely accurate," I deadpanned.

Parsons's look turned sober. "Seriously, though. These two have been dealing to kids—teens, I guess. They're frequent flyers. This time maybe we'll be able to keep 'em for a while. The big guy had a lot of Fentanyl on him."

"Good, good," I said. "I'm not a fan of the hard stuff, especially not when it's being sold to kids."

Parsons had a gleam in his eye. "So you want join us to bust people for pot possession later?"

I cocked an eyebrow at him. "Uh, no."

He grinned, clearly enjoying having pushed my buttons a little, but it faded quickly. "How about for something a lot more serious? Something with a real impact."

"I'm listening."

"We're getting a warrant right now for a house not far from here," Parsons said, watching his cops clean up the scene. The two cruisers with the dealers were already pulling away from the curb, taking our boys to jail. Parsons watched them go for a moment before turning back to me. "We have a guy on the inside who's turned state's witness. Sex trafficking and hard drugs combined to keep the girls compliant." He pursed his lips in extreme distaste. "They're moving minors up from Alabama, Georgia and Mississippi. Maybe even points beyond. Catch the runaways, get 'em strung out and addicted, then—"

"Yeah, I know how it works," I said, looking away. Down the block, spectators were watching from beyond the police perimeter. No one was looking particularly at me, which was...new. Maybe I was unrecognizable like this. Or maybe they just didn't think Sienna Nealon would be talking to Metro PD on a street corner in this neighborhood dressed like a tweener.

"We could use someone to either be primary or go in through the back, cut off the retreat," Parsons said. I could tell he was fishing. He was using good bait, too, because anyone who'd ever read about the nasty things sex traffickers did would have been hard pressed not to leap all over it with a fury and fervor. It wasn't the type of reaction I evinced when thinking about the street-level prostitutes, addicts feeding their own habits, which was unpleasant, nor the high-class escorts, who mostly knew exactly what they were getting into.

Sex traffickers preyed on teenage girls, got them hooked on the hard drugs, forming the type of habits that were nearly impossible to kick on your own, like heroin. Then they strung them along, selling them to men with promises of their next hit. I'd read the FBI reports in my ample downtime, and they'd turned my stomach.

I looked back at Parsons. Yeah, I was well familiar with the horrors of what sex traffickers did. "Hell yes, I'm in for kicking down that door. Just say when."

Parsons didn't even blink. "When." He angled his head toward my car. "Let's go."

Chapter 54

I followed Parsons to a staging area a couple blocks from the house in question. I wasn't sure where we were going to end up, but my question was answered when he stopped in a neighborhood north of the city filled with brand new townhouses mingled with the occasional old commercial strip or old house.

"This is Germantown," he said, leading me to a command unit, which was like a SWAT team truck parked in the middle of an abandoned parking lot. "Older neighborhood that's really hot right now, turning over like crazy."

I frowned, casting one last look out at the neighborhood. "Is it my imagination or are all the old neighborhoods in your town being demolished for gentrification purposes?"

Parsons let a thin smile slip out. "You're not imagining it. A hundred people a day are moving to Nashville right now."

"Hm," I said, mildly impressed. "You're like the Austin of the Southeast."

He made a face at that. "I guess," he said, and ducked into the command unit.

There were a bunch of guys in SWAT attire, already geared up for the assault. I counted an even dozen, and they acknowledged me with polite nods but not a whole lot else. I understood that; when it came to kicking in doors, respect was earned, and even though my reputation might have preceded me just about everywhere, cops and military guys generally operated from a "trust but verify" operational footing. As in they'd see how I handled things before warming up to me.

"I think you all know who this is," Parsons said, strolling over to a small table in the back of the van with a house blueprint on it. "She's here to try and make your job easier."

"Somebody ought to," a grizzled older guy said under his breath.

"This is Lewis Spencer," Parsons said, nodding at the team lead, a dark-skinned man who caught my eye and gave me a quick nod.

Spencer had a bearing that reminded me instantly of Roberto Bastian: no bullshit was allowed within ten meters of this guy. "Ma'am," he said, with a hint of deference, and that was about all the indulgence I expected he allowed. He was leaning over like we'd caught him in the middle of a briefing when we walked in.

"Don't let me interrupt," I said. "What are we up against?"

Spencer turned back to the blueprint. "Our informant says there are girls kept here, here, here and here." He pointed to each of the various bedrooms on the blueprint, all toward the back of the house, plus two larger rooms, one at the front and one at the back. "Mattresses stacked almost one on top of another, curtains tacked to the ceiling between them. High-ups of the organization are brought in for visitations to the site, but it's mostly a holding location for them, not a brothel." His lip curled in disgust.

"Not exactly *The Best Little Whorehouse in Texas*, is it?" one of the other cops observed. No one laughed. Everyone in the van had seen what sex trafficking looked like, then. Thinking about it sapped most of my desire to make a good joke.

"Two entry points," Spencer said, running a finger over the impromptu map. "Door here—" he pointed to the side of the house "—enters through the attached garage. The other is the front door." He looked up, surveyed his team. "There are going to be girls everywhere. The potential for civilian casualties is high, especially because of some of the other details." He straightened up, looking intently at the blueprint.

"Because we needed more bad news," that same grizzled jokester put in. Again, no one laughed, not even him.

"Our informant suggests that these thugs are heavily armed," Spencer said, looking about as serious as I'd ever seen a cop look. Which was pretty serious. "They've had some trouble before—some local rivals came around and hit their bank roll a few weeks ago—so now there's firepower at the front door and it's reinforced. Same drill with the rear door, which is not actually a rear door. It leads into the attached garage, and you can enter the house from there. Both are steel, with reinforced door stops. Same goes with the front door."

Someone groaned; I couldn't blame them. Kicking it down would make a hell of a lot of noise, and not be quite as easy as a normal wooden door.

"I can get in the front myself," I said, looking down at the blueprint. "That'll distract them. Then you guys hit them in the back and extract the girls while I keep them occupied up front."

"What about the bad guys?" Spencer asked. His eyes were still searching me.

I glanced over at Captain Parsons, who'd been watching all along. He just shrugged, like it was of no consequence.

"Well," I said, making a show of looking down at the blueprint, "I guess that depends on how they play this." And I tried not to smile.

Chapter 55

Reed

I stood around and watched a protest edge gradually toward becoming a riot, and I was *bored*.

The crowd was doing its roiling/raging thing, the small flood of people in Lotsostuff overalls rolling like a tide. I watched them from the side, keeping an eye on them with one eye and the wary Murfreesboro cops lingering next to the gate every once in a while just for variety. At the head of the crowd I could see Theresa Carson, raging harder than any of them, her grey hair flashing under the sunny sky.

The cops, again, didn't seem too pleased to be here. Occasionally I'd float up into the air to remind the crowd of who I was in case they decided to get out of control and to take a glance at what was going on over the fence at the Lotsostuff warehouse.

Nothing. Nothing was going on at the warehouse. At least on the side I could see.

I had a clear view into the executive suite, such as it

was, when I flew up into the air. It appeared utterly abandoned every time I looked, leaving me to wonder if Logan
Mills was on the premises today or if he'd decided to take a
day off. I wouldn't blame him if he did; this crowd
certainly did a fine job of maintaining their enthusiastic
irritation for him on day two of this spectacle that I'd
witnessed.

The crowd of protesters was in the middle of an
interminable chant of, "Mills! Mills! He's a shill!" I'd
settled back on the ground a moment before, questioning
why I was here and why my various life choices had led
me to watch a damned labor dispute (curse Harry Graves
right to hell) when I saw someone not in a Lotsostuff
overall snaking his way slowly through the crowd
toward me.

There was a camera phone in his hand, and the guy
was wearing jeans and a trucker cap with a mesh back that
had *Boise Noisy* written on it. He was snapping pictures as
though he was a real photographer, or as real as you could
make yourself look using an iPhone as your equipment. He
was trying to play it casual, talking to people as he wended
his way through the crowd. Theresa nodded at him and he
gave her a short wave, then took a picture as she got back
to chanting.

He broke free of the crowd, and I gauged his intent
was to come over to me. He didn't disappoint, taking a
couple pictures of me from a distance and then making a
slow approach, hands by his sides and clearly visible, as
though I were the type always looking for threats from
every direction. With him now looking right at me, I recognized him.

"Hey," he said, coming closer. "I'm—"

"Alan Kwon," I said, peering at him. He had a thinly
traced goatee, and he smiled when I said his name.

"You know me?" he asked, sidling over, pace quickening just a little.

"I've followed your work," I said as he closed on me. "You're one of those new breed of independent reporters that crowdsources your funding."

He pocketed his iPhone, nodding. "Yeah. I kinda have the best gig ever for someone like me. People pay me on Patreon and I just go out and cover whatever story interests me."

I nodded along. "I saw your reporting from Yemen. Not to go fanboy on you, but you're braver than me."

"Yemen wasn't even the craziest thing I've seen this year," Alan said, offering a hand for me to shake, which I did.

"Well, this has to be a bit of a come-down after covering foreign wars," I said, turning my attention back to the crowd. They'd switched chants again, Theresa leading them in a repetition that had, at its core, the words, "Hell no! We won't go!" paired with something else I didn't want to waste the time trying to decipher.

"I think it's an interesting story," Alan said. He had his phone out again, fiddling with the settings as he brought it up, recording a video of the crowd while we talked. "You've got a right-to-work state here, a non-union shop— at its root, it seems like a typical story of a big start-up corporation against the plucky work force that's put them in the position they're in, disrupting the e-commerce market with rock bottom prices."

He stopped talking, and I waited a second for him to finish the thought before prodding him. "But?"

Alan paused, finishing his video and hitting the stop button before turning back to me. "I feel like there's more going on here than just that typical setup, though. I mean, the company won't even make a statement. At all. Usually a PR flak would at least issue a press release. Boilerplate, you know, when asked for comment?"

"I guess," I said, not really knowing...anything about these types of situations other than some basic, surface-level stuff I'd read in the papers in the past.

"So, why are you here?" Alan asked, flipping his phone around in his hand so that the bottom was facing up. "Oh, do you mind if I record this?"

"I'm not giving an interview," I said, waving him off. "I was just talking."

"Damn," he said, smiling as he shut off his phone. "Worth a try. My patrons would love to hear from you if you ever change your mind." He pocketed the phone. "But I'm cool with just talking, too, since you and I are some of the only people here not to rage against the corporate machine."

I frowned. "You're a journalist. Don't you, y'know...have some sympathies toward these guys raging against said machine?"

"Hey, I'm all for a living wage," Alan said, throwing up his hands like I'd attacked his orthodoxy. "But I'm here to cover this as a reporter. That means I go where the facts are. So far, what we've got is a dispute over worker pay in which someone has destroyed part of the warehouse, rendering—well, I don't have a number for the damage, at least not from Lotsostuff. The police put the losses in the millions." He shrugged. "It's not violent—yet—but my sympathies aside, I'm interested to see where this goes."

"I don't love the direction it's going myself," I said, focusing back on the crowd, and Theresa, with her chant-ing. They'd switched to another one, but I was tuning it out. "I just wonder why Mills isn't at least coming to the table to talk. It seems like it'd be a decent way to calm things down."

"You think he's playing hardball?" Alan asked.

"Hell if I know," I said, then I lifted a couple feet off the ground. Beyond the crowd, I could see another car pulling in, and a young lady got out, a blond ponytail visibly flashing in the sunlight.

Alan craned his neck, but I doubted he could see as well as I could, so I gave him a little boost with a tornado under his feet. "Whoa!" He looked like he almost shit himself before realizing he was walking on air. It took a second of him high stepping like the ground beneath him was on fire before he composed himself and looked up at me. "Cool trick." His voice shook a little, but he managed to get himself together enough to look across the crowd where I was. He frowned. "Oh, great."

"What?" I asked. The blond lady was making her way through the crowd, taking pictures with an actual camera.

"I'm not the only reporter on the scene anymore," Alan said with a sigh. "That's Yolanda Biddle." His lips twisted in distaste. "She's a reporter. One of the few *actual* reporters employed by Flashforce.net."

Chapter 56

Sienna

I had a Kevlar vest strapped on under my flannel shirt, which was loose and allowed the spaghetti straps of the tank top I'd worn during my fentanyl buy to display a little of my cleavage. That was not a normal look for me, but since I was heading up to a sex trafficker house at a slow stagger, I was willing to make some compromises. For the job, you know.

I strolled up to the door, acting like the drunk I'd once been and giving it a good hammering with my palm. Slung under my overshirt was the Remington V3 Tac-13, a shotgun that was only about the length of my arm from elbow to fingertips. It was paired with the HK VP9 on my hip (sixteen rounds) and the little Sig Sauer P365 in the holster on my ankle (thirteen rounds).

Hopefully I wasn't about to have to use any of them, but since when did things in my life ever go to plan?

I swayed gently out in front of the door and hammered it with my palm again. For effect, I called out, modulating my voice so I sounded drunk, "Karen! Kaaaaaaren!"

"Echo One, this is Oscar Five-Five," Spencer's voice came over the radio bud in my ear. "We are approaching the back door."

"Understood," I muttered under my breath, swaying away from the door so they couldn't see me through the peephole. "I am wired for sound and good to go in a minute." Footsteps echoed behind the door, so faint I could only hear them because of my meta senses. The door was thick, too, probably reinforced steel. I clicked my send mic. "Front door is super heavy duty, Oscar Five-Five. Be advised."

I reached out and gave the door another hard thumping, flashing irritation across my face now that I knew someone was watching me. "Karen! Karen, open up! It's me. Meeeeeeeeee."

A guy unfastened the bolt and swung the door open. I blinked in at them, standing there in the darkness of the interior hallway, the sun over my shoulder causing the guy to blink. He blanched against the brightness, revealing some teeth that were so stained from tobacco and coffee they looked like they were almost green. I immediately designated him Grimy Teeth, and tried to withhold my internal revulsion.

"I need to talk to Karen," I managed to slur out, getting uncomfortably comfortable with my new (old) role as a drunk. "Go get her."

Grimy Teeth stared at me through slitted eyes. "There is no Karen here," he said with hints of an Eastern European accent. "Go away."

"Hey, is that Russian?" I said, looking in at him. "Are you Russian?"

"Go away," he said, more firmly this time.

"Not until I talk to Karen," I slurred.

He stared at me with rising irritation. "There is no Karen here."

"She's totally here, dude," I said. "Karen!" I called past him, then looked him in the eye. "Karen. You know, Karen? Punching bag of the entire internet. That Karen."

Grimy Teeth looked me over one more time in evident disgust and started to swing the door closed.

I planted my foot on the door, interrupting his attempt to close it. Giving it a meta-hard shove, I launched Grimy Teeth staggering back into the house as I pushed my way in. "Karennnn!" I shouted, "Where are you?" This I said into the mic, so that Spencer and the others could hear me clearly, because it was the signal to start the party.

Once I was inside, I got a quick lay of the land. To my left hung a curtain separating me from the living room, where some of the girls were supposedly kept and where some traffickers might be lurking. Through all that was another curtain that separated it from the dining room. Straight ahead lay Grimy Teeth, hurting from my blow, and a shadowy hallway that led past every bedroom in the house. One of those was to my immediate right, but the door was padlocked shut. I'd need to leave it that way for now, to avoid risking the lives of the girls who were in there while I went to work freeing them.

Grimy Teeth was picking himself up from his knees. He was radiating fury. "There is no Karen here, I told you. Now..." He slid a hand behind him to a strap across his shoulder and started to lay a hand on the rifle across his back. "You cannot leave."

"Wasn't planning on it, Grimy," I said, dropping the slurring. He cocked his head in surprise and I threw a fast sidekick that caught him beneath the chin and changed his nickname from Grimy Teeth to No Teeth in about two seconds flat. He was going to be healing a severely busted jaw in the jailhouse hospital, but that was more his problem than mine.

Plus, when he got dental implants, they'd hopefully be a lot more resistant than his real teeth to whatever corrosive business he was perpetrating upon those green meanies. Ew.

"What is going on up there?" came a voice from down the hall straight ahead. Grimy-No-Teeth was already out, so I quickly ripped his AR-15 from his insensate body and checked it. It was a Rock River Arms gun, but looked pretty standard to the platform. I put the strap over my shoulder and checked the chamber. It had a round in it, so I adjusted the stock and then let it sag to my side while I drew my HK pistol. No point using the rifle and its highly penetrating rounds in a civilian area unless things went really sour in here.

"I'm looking for Karen!" I called, playing the part of the drunk again. "I need to talk to her. Why won't any of you just take me to Karen?"

I ducked to the left, through the curtain into the living room as I heard footsteps thunder into the hallway. They were a second or two from finding Grimy-No-Teeth, at which point I was guessing things were going to get realllll-llly interesting.

Behind the curtain was a maze of more curtains. These were no sheer, lacy fabrics that were easy to see through. This was heavy curtaining, industrial strength, the kind you use when you're a vampire and seeing a hint of sun meant guaranteed death. They were tacked to the ceilings with nails, cordoning the room. Anyone or anything could be lurking behind them, and I could tell they were set up to turn the house's living room into a curtained ward.

There was some chatter in the hallway behind me in a

non-English tongue, loud and growing in alarm by the second. I was about to get some action, so I ducked through into the first curtain to my left—

The smell was what hit me first. It was rank; disgusting didn't begin to describe it.

I found myself in a space that couldn't have been any bigger than ten feet by ten feet. The curtains cordoned three sides of it, from where they hung, ceiling to floor. They'd been taken from somewhere else and repurposed to this.

In the middle of the wall of curtains was a stained mattress without a sheet to cover it. Based on the level of grime upon its once-white surface, it had been in continuous, hard use for a period of years, and under operating conditions that were never intended in the factory where it had been made. If I looked hard, I could see hints of what might have been close to its original white or off-white color, but they were buried under layers of yellowy grime and stains of all kinds, most related to the sort of bodily functions that would have made any mattress I owned an immediate write-off.

Not this mattress, though. Its owners were cool with letting it just keep on trucking. I stared at it for a good two seconds, mostly because I didn't want to consider what was *on* it.

But with the voices behind me rising as the men in the hallway found Grimy-No-Teeth and started to panic, realizing I was somewhere in the house...I really didn't have any choice but to come to grips with what I was looking at.

She was maybe...*maybe*...fourteen. She might not even have been that old, because the wealth of track marks in her arm suggested opioid use that would have aged even my meta-perfect skin. She'd been on the shit for a while, and her eyes were fixed on the ceiling in a way that told me she was in la-la land and would be for a while.

I tried not to look at her for more than a second before I whirled and yanked down the curtain separating me from the next "room," and away from the angry voices behind me. It tore from the ceiling easily and I stepped through, finding myself looking at another barely teenage girl-who-wasn't-there, eyes fixed a thousand miles past the ceiling. She didn't register my presence, nor my violently pulling the curtain down or stepping over her and ripping down the next one to reveal the final "room" in that line.

Here I found something just a little different. Still another drugged out almost-below-teenager, but here the girl in question was being crouched over by a thirty-something man with big ears who was partially upright, looking around with wide, surprised eyes. He was reaching for an AK-47 when I tore down the curtain. His ears were big enough that I immediately tagged him Dumbo, and his hand was far enough from the AK that I could have kicked his teeth in before he got within an inch of it.

He was hunched down, on top of the girl. I looked at her vacant eyes for a flash while he stared at me, fingers frozen a foot from the AK's pistol grip.

She was pale, dazed, green eyes faded and dark in the low light of the hellish room. Her hair was clean, wet, as though she'd just been bathed, her skin free of the accumulated oil and grime of neglect I'd seen on the others. Still, the smell of bodily fluids and murk from the room was rank in my enhanced meta senses, making the place smell like some combination of a sewer and a nursing home, with a little brothel thrown in.

"Okay," he said, in that same Eastern European accent as the others. He started to slide his hand away from the

AK. "Okay," he said again, shooting me a nervous smile as he looked at my hand...

Which was holding my HK pistol.

Aimed at him.

I looked at the girl one more time, then slid my gaze back to him. His friends were shouting behind me, about a second from ripping down the first curtain and discovering my handiwork. They'd shoot over these girls to get at me, and I'd need to be ready for it.

"Okay?" He smiled and held his hands up. "Police, right? Okay. We make it easy."

"Yes," I said. "We make it easy."

And I shot him right in the face. He toppled onto the girl he'd been abusing.

She didn't even notice.

I spun to the shouts of the men behind me, so many more bullets to use...

And I just felt cold.

How many of them were there?

I didn't know.

A hot flush of anger came flooding over me as I aimed over the two girls I'd stepped over to get this far.

These were just the ones I could *see*.

The rage burned in my veins, my own personal drug of choice.

I knew what I wanted to do, and it was going to be so easy.

Kill them. Every.

Last.

One.

Yep.

Chapter 57

I ripped the curtains down as I dodged sideways, trying to clear the open field of fire between me and the front door. One of the bad guys popped a head—and a gun—around the hallway edge, sweeping clumsily to find whoever it was that had busted down their door and started shit in their sex trafficking house.

"He's got a gun!" I shouted, loud enough for them to hear me in the back of the house as I dropped to one knee. The shout was to cover my ass, so the team kicking in the back door would know I was up against someone who was armed. Hitting a knee wasn't because I was worried about the guy coming around the corner shooting me; he'd be dead before he fully cleared it. It was to make sure that my shots didn't tear through the wall behind him and rip into the girls held captive in the bedroom back there.

Lining up my HK VP9's sight picture on the sex trafficker's head and squeezing the trigger was a cold, clear feeling. A pink mist puffed toward the ceiling and he dropped like a puppet whose strings had just been sliced clean.

The next wouldn't come so easily, I knew. A thump echoed to my left, and I tore through the aisle of curtains and plunged ahead into the next row of little divided "rooms." I leapt over a mattress with yet another insensate girl on it, this one so filthy it took me a moment to register her natural hair color was blond.

I ripped through the curtain and through an archway, going by memory of the house blueprints. This would have been the intended dining room, and Spencer and his team were due to bust down the door to my left at any moment. It looked to still be closed, which meant they were probably still gaining access to the garage through its reinforced back door. A muffled thump in that direction suggested I was right, and I veered right, my pistol pointing everywhere my eyes did.

The dining room opened on my right into the kitchen, a small room centered on a folding table in the middle. It looked like it had been abandoned swiftly, three out of the four chairs overturned, one with a fresh bowl of cereal poured and waiting in front of it.

I ignored the snap, crackle and pop as I slipped around it, keying in on the sound of grunts and whispers ahead and to my right. Around that corner were the guys who'd been eating here recently, all lined up at the front door where I'd come in. They'd be expecting me in the living room, but I'd just circled around and now I was coming at them from behind.

Using my meta speed, I hurried forward, turned the corner at an angle with my pistol barrel braced against it for cover, and came around slowly.

Three of them huddled in the hallway, stacking up like they were about to come around it. Looking for me, surely. Two bodies were on the ground already, one dead—the one I'd just shot—the other Grimy-No-Teeth, who was clearly out.

They were talking amongst themselves, making ready to storm the living room where I'd just been. The tension in their muscles was plain, their weapons the ubiquitous AR-15.

I checked behind me; Spencer and company still hadn't crashed through the interior door, but the first sound of a crack came a second after I turned back.

All three men heard it. All three jerked in surprise at the sudden, unexplained noise.

And all three started to turn toward me, guns in their hands.

I stayed behind the cover of the wall and started firing. I drew a bead on the first and stroked the trigger gently, bullets ripping up and through his chest. Switching targets, I moved to the next, peppering his chest. One sliced through his neck, making a mess that would only get worse with time and blood loss.

The last guy threw his gun aside violently and put his hands up as his two colleagues dropped. He sputtered and shook, falling to his knees like I'd shot him even though I was pretty sure I hadn't.

Yet.

"Please," he said. "Please!"

I kicked the guns away from his fallen comrades as I approached. "How many more men in the house?" I asked, keeping my pistol leveled at him.

"None, none," he said, shaking, hands just above his head, fingers curled in fear like he was arthritic. He pointed into the living room without lowering his hands, a strange tableau. "He dead there. All others, here." He indicated the three dead bodies and Grimy-No-Teeth all fallen here in the hallway. "No other men. Just the..." His voice trailed off and he looked like he'd swallowed a frog.

"The girls?" I asked coldly.

He nodded, face twitching like he'd just had to admit something terrible. As if it wasn't already blatantly obvious what this place was. What he was doing.

"Spencer, front of house is clear," I said, clicking my mic. I heard the door crash in behind me. "I am in the hallway with three tangos down, one injured and one captive."

"Understood," Spencer's tight voice came back over the mic. I could hear the team's footfalls sweeping through the back of the house. "Moving through."

Something thumped against the door beside me. It was the master bedroom, and it had a padlock keeping it closed.

I swept my weapon off Mr. Cooperative, toward the noise. "That the girls?"

He nodded, swallowing visibly as he did so.

"Cross your ankles, fold your hands behind your head," I said, and he did so. I cuffed him and put him flat on his face. Not gently. Then I did the same to Grimy-No-Teeth, as the thumping from the bedroom door continued. "Stand back!" I called, checking up and down the hallway again. There was motion to my left, and I saw Spencer all the way at the end of it, at the back of the house, sidle up to a door there and prepare to breach it.

I didn't have the patience to wait, so I rammed my shoulder into the bedroom door and it crashed open. I kept my pistol up, just in case Mr. Cooperative had been lying to me and there were men waiting inside.

There weren't.

The scene inside the master bedroom was the picture

of squalor and despair. Where there should have been one big bed in the middle of the room, furniture arranged around it, there were instead a dozen military-style cots. My eyes swept the room, and I counted a girl for every cot.

Not one of them looked as though they'd bathed this week.

Some were in the same drugged-out state as the girls in the open living room. I passed them quickly, confirming chests were still moving up and down. The girl who'd knocked her hand against the door was looking at me like I was an invader from outer space as I swept through into the small bathroom beyond where I found two more girls sleeping in the bathtub, one with her head at each end. The once-white tub was stained a brownish color through long use and zero maid service.

"Master bedroom clear," I said, taking a ragged breath and trying not to let what I was feeling right now bleed out into my voice.

"Clearing last bedroom now," Spencer's voice came back to me. "No sign of tangos." A muffled thump echoed through the house, and a faint scream came through the wall next to me. I left the bathroom and paused next to a closet, hit with a vague suspicion.

I threw it open and found a girl huddled there in a stupor, curled up in a sleeping bag, hair as matted and filthy as any of the others.

Leaving the closet open in disgust, I walked back to the only girl standing in the room, holstering my pistol as I did so. "What's your name?"

She blinked at me. She'd watched me the entire time, never said a word.

Nor did she start now, exactly, because whatever she said, I didn't understand.

"Spencer...we're going to need a translator," I said.

"Copy that," Spencer's voice came back, both over the radio and faintly, in the distance. I could hear him and the others arguing with the girls to get moving. They were getting everybody out of the house, I guess. Probably for medical treatment. I thought that was kind of a lost cause, given the state of some of these girls.

Movement out in the hallway caught my attention, and I stepped out, hand hovering over my weapon.

It was Grimy-No-Teeth, coming back to wakefulness. Or at least semi-consciousness.

He moved only slightly, stirring as he lifted his head. Blood dripped from between his lips, a tooth stuck in the flow, perched on his chin like an unchewed kernel of corn. He'd have a lot of those now, at least until he got some dental implants.

"Whuh...happn...?" He looked up at me with bleary eyes, not fully conscious.

I looked down at him. He looked up at me, uncomprehending. He didn't know what or who he was looking at, he might not even have known where he was. "You got about a tenth of what you deserve," I said, lifting him to his feet. He staggered, but I held him up, then pulled up Mr. Cooperative with the other hand. He wasn't adding anything to this conversation; by the look on his red face, I could have kneed him in the kidney and he would have done his best not to make a sound.

Part of me hoped some unseen friend of theirs would come leaping out of a closet, try to shoot me. I'd throw one of them in the path of the bullets, then the other one, draw and dust the shooter.

But it didn't work out that way. The house was quiet, except for the rattling breathing of one of the girls in the living room to my right and the sounds of Spencer's team at the back of the house. Metro PD squad cars were already rolling up, and I grabbed my prisoners and started walking them out, eager to rid myself of them before I did something to them that I probably wouldn't regret.

Chapter 58

Jules

The warehouse, again. Jules was pretty tired of this place. But he wasn't tired of the dream of having a superpowered person at his disposal to make Nashville his town. Even if it was this little weenie, Brance.

"I just don't think this is going to work," Brance whined. Jules resisted the urge to slap him. For now. He had a look on his face like he already might cry. Jules didn't have kids of his own, but he suspected he could have raised one better than this. Kids these days were giant crybabies because their mommies and daddies blasted through every legitimate issue they could have ever faced, leaving them nothing to deal with but low-grade emotional problems.

Jules chafed at that. He'd grown up hardscrabble, in Jersey, to a mother who'd given no shits about him and a dad that thought spoiling the rod meant you were a wuss, and any kid who didn't snap-to at the sound of his father's voice just needed a beating. He hadn't spared the rod, and Jules had the scars on his bare ass to prove it. His definition of a problem diverged from Brance's by a pretty fair margin, he guessed.

"Listen, kid," Jules said, keeping his patience on a thin thread so as not to scream at the kid, "I'm not going to lie —you got a problem." He held his hands out, trying to get the dumbass to see reason.

He didn't, but he didn't speak, either. Just stood there like he was going to cry. Jules shuddered inside. What the hell had happened to country music? Once upon a time, even their luminaries knew what real shit was like. Some of them even did time. This kid was so weak he'd walk out bowlegged after an hour in jail, just because the other detainees could smell how ripe he was for plucking.

"But this ain't an insurmountable problem," Jules said, trying to bring his thoughts back around. The dumb shit wanted to be a star, singing for crowds. Well, whatever Jules put in front of his ass right now was going to end up with bleeding ears—

Heeeyyy.

Jules paused, thinking that one through. "And you might even say it's got its own sort of possibilities attached," he said, once he was sure, yep, that was an idea.

Brance just squinted at him. "What...how has this got any possibilities?" He touched his throat. "I can't control this."

"Sure you can," Jules said, eyeing him. "There's some-thing specific you're thinking about whenever this goes off. Right?"

"No," Brance answered, way too quickly.

Yeah. This little shit had daddy issues, because of course he did. Jules could see it a mile off. But he shook his head. "I'm going to set up a small concert for you."

Brance's eyes went wide. "But—I just—I blew up that

studio!" His voice lowered. "People could get hurt. Really hurt."

Jules was counting on that, actually, but he wasn't going to say it to this knucklehead. "We're going to work on this. Train your mind to avoid the thing that's causing you to break into this, uh...killer frequency or whatever. And the best way to solve a problem is plunge right through the fear and do something amazing." He arched his eyebrows. "Hey, Gil. Check on whether we can rent the Ryman for a small event. Tonight, if possible. Otherwise, as soon as we can."

Brance looked like he'd swallowed a truck tire.

Jules was smiling, though. It was like a coming out party for him, and all he had to do was get some influential assholes in the organized crime world there, then get dumbass Brance to do that thing he did so well—screw up.

Yeah. This one was in the bag.

Chapter 59

Sienna

"That should have been a lot harder," Spencer said, sauntering up to me amid the sea of police cars and flashing lights that swamped the once-calm city street.

"It was plenty hard," I said. I longed for something to do with my hands as I sat on the hood of my BMW, watching paramedics escort dirty, heroin-addled teenage sex slaves out of the house one at a time to waiting vans. For the first time in my life, I wished I smoked, some combination of antsy-ness and self-loathing combo-ing up. I could imagine taking a deep breath of that toxic air, letting it fill my lungs like the poison it was, feeling it choke my super sense of smell and grip my lungs like the hands of death.

Yeah. That'd be better than how I felt right now.

"You ever seen anything like this before?" Spencer asked. He had his arms folded and was leaned against the BMW next to me.

"You got a cigarette?" I asked, looking over at him. He gave me a subtle shake of the head. "No, I've never seen a sex trafficking house before. Only read about them." My hand twitched. "I generally stick to the metahuman side of the business, unless the NYPD asks for my help in an emergency. Which is usually bank robberies, assaults—the stuff you get 911 calls for, you know?"

Spencer nodded. "There are places like this in all fifty states now."

"So I've heard."

"Ugly business," he said as the paramedics led another girl out covered in a blanket. A lot of them didn't have even a single outfit to call their own. Whatever possessions they'd come into this with had been sifted by the guys who took them. Valuables were sold. Extraneous clothing was tossed. As near as we could tell, this was a passing stage of their new lives, the one where they got to experience the joys of opioid addiction before being handed off to the establishments and pimps where they'd fully begin their working lives in the underground, underage sex trade.

Another was led out just then, shaking like she had a palsy, the paramedics having to hold her up. Whether it was from the drugs or from what she'd experienced in the house, it was hard to say. It wasn't hard to imagine what she'd dealt with in there, given the living conditions.

And what I'd caught Dumbo up to before I painted the wall with his brains.

"They're going to be on methadone the rest of their lives, aren't they?" I asked. My hand was shaking. No one had taken my HK yet for evidence, though one of the officers had gotten the AR-15 I'd picked up from Grimy-No-Teeth and bagged it after unloading it.

"Some of them, maybe," Spencer said flatly. "But at least we got them out before—"

"Before they got to experience the soul-crushing life of a drug-addicted career prostitute?" I balled my hand into a hard fist. My nails dug into my palm. "I guess that's something, but it would have been nice to get them before they even got to this house."

Spencer nodded in my peripheral vision. "It would have. But we were lucky to even find out about this. Most of the time these places are kept pretty tight secrets by whatever organized crime group runs them. The fact that one of our confidential informants managed to get a tour..." He shook his head. "Well, let's just say that kind of break doesn't happen every day."

"They were runaways, weren't they?" I asked.

"Probably." Spencer gave a half-shrug. "Hard to say without getting their stories. Some of them might have been sold by their parents or guardians. Some could have been kidnapped."

God, I wanted a drink. "Figures," I muttered. "What's next?"

"Someone'll be by to get your statement," Spencer said. "You know, because of the shooting."

I nodded. "And then?"

He shrugged. "Nothing, probably. Every one of them had a gun in their hand or damned near to it. We had the intel that said they were armed going in. We all knew it could get messy. Personally, I consider us damned lucky to have had you." He cast a look over his head at the front door, where yet another girl was being brought out, this one on a stretcher. "If it had been down to me and my men having to try and bust down both entrances while neutralizing the suspects?" He shook his head. "I don't see how there aren't casualties." He cocked his head at me and I looked him in the eye. "The guys in there were ex-military, weren't they?"

I nodded. "They knew their way around their rifles and had basic tactical knowledge. Eastern European accents. I'd say they served in their home country before joining the local mafia and coming to America for the sweet, sweet opportunity to traffic young women at prices far above what they'd get in their home countries."

"That was my guess, too," Spencer said with a curt nod. "Yeah, if we'd tried to rush that door ourselves, without you? The place would have turned into a shooting gallery. Your reflexes, the way you lulled them..." He shook his head. "It was a hell of a fine job." He stuck out his hand.

I stared at it for a second before I shook it.

He must have caught me making a face. "What?"

I shook my head. "Why is everyone so nice to me here? I just killed people. Several people. My boss is currently pissed at me for killing one guy who'd taken a famous hostage. You didn't even blink when I ripped down an entire squad of sex traffickers. Not to mention the brutality I perpetrated earlier on a couple drug dealers."

Spencer looked like he was trying to hide a smile behind his caramel lips. "You're a little jaded, aren't you?"

"Just a bit."

It was Spencer's turn to shake his head, I guess. "They were trafficking little girls. The oldest was maybe seventeen, the youngest...I don't even want to think about it. It wouldn't have troubled my conscience if none of them had walked out of there alive, so the fact you saved two for interrogation, we saved all the girls, and suffered no team casualties?" He just smiled. "This day was nothing but a win to me."

My phone started buzzing in my pocket, and when I pulled it out, the caller ID read HEATHER CHALKE.

"Let's hope my boss feels that way, too," I said, nodding that I was going to take it.

"Good luck," Spencer said, "ma'am." And with a slight smile that seemed like respect, he walked off as I hit the button to take the call.

Chapter 60

Reed

I felt a visceral twist in my stomach at the mention of Flashforce.net. If there was any purported news organization that had done more to rile up humanity into a mob and then point it at my sister, I couldn't think of one.

And they'd sent a reporter here, to this already simmering labor dispute where I was seemingly stuck against my will.

Yay.

It didn't take too long for Yolanda Biddle to make her way over to me and Alan Kwon where we stood at the sidelines of the Lotsostuff worker protest. She was tall and blond, and her face had a very blank, plain look to it, the make-up she wore just enough to convince me that even if she applied the level volume that a hooker did, she'd still be just about the plainest-faced Jane I'd ever seen.

"Hey," she said, smiling, and I couldn't get the image out of my head of a clown face with a smile painted on, it was that damned hollow. "I'm Yolanda Biddle, with Flash-force.net."

"Hey," Alan said without an ounce of enthusiasm.

She gave him an unpleasant look, telling me she knew him, too. Then she switched back to smiling at me, ignoring Alan entirely. "Can I ask what you're doing here?"

I kept my voice level and out of the realm of loathing, but only through pure control. "You can ask. My answer is 'no comment.'"

"Oh, come on," she said, brandishing a phone in front of her like a reporter of old carrying a microphone. Because she was recording our entire exchange. After I didn't say anything for a few seconds, she switched tack. "How long have you been here?"

I just stared at her. She stared back, smiling, in patient expectation.

"I've been here an hour or two," Alan said. Clearly he couldn't handle the stony lack of response I was inflicting on her. I got that. It wasn't easy for me, usually affable, conversational, to completely ignore someone. It was almost painful, in a way, but I managed it because I hated the hell out of Flashforce.douchenozzles.net.

"Do you have any comment on—" she started.

"No," I said. "No comment. On anything. Ever."

"Wow." She made a sort of faux-pained, contrite face. "Look, I don't know what you've heard about me—"

"Nothing," I said.

That took her aback. Her shoulders drooped. "Nothing...? Then why—"

"I didn't know who you were until Alan here told me, and I don't really care who you are, per se." I stared her down. It was really a drain to project this much unrelenting hostility to a person who was trying to be nice, but I had a lot of inner fire to work with thanks to Flashforce's prior actions. "But I know who you work for, and I'd rather fling myself off a cliff than ever talk to someone associated with your rat-fucking website."

Yolanda's jaw dropped, presumably at the boldness of my word choice. "I—ah. Flashforce isn't what you think—"

"It's the news outlet that literally led the shit-hot-takes charge against my sister when she was wrongly accused of —well, everything," I said, just glaring at her. "You guys had a listicle of reasons why Sienna was 'worse than Hitler,' which doesn't just offend me on the basis of being crappy, histrionic, historically illiterate and hideously inaccurate with regards to my sister. It also annoys me that you went full Godwin's Law. You never go full Godwin's Law." I paused. "Well, *you* do, but that's a perfect argument for me not to ever do anything related to your site."

Yolanda took that one on board, processing, her blankish face moving a little as she considered her reply. "Wow, that's like...wow." She went through the full range of emoting that I suspected she was capable of. "I can see how you'd feel that way. But—"

"Everything before the 'but' is bullshit," I said. "Spare me the rest." Alan Kwon was trying hard not to laugh, barely holding it in.

"But you're, like, a legend," she said, and I could feel the flattery oozing out of her. It triggered a reaction of pure disgust; this was hardly the first time someone had tried honeyed words to get past my guard, especially since I'd become quasi-famous. It was actually one of the reasons I liked—no, loved—Isabella. She had no patience for flattering me. She just told me how it was.

"I'm, like, bored of you," I said, and pushed wind beneath my feet, flying up over the crowd again. They were definitely raucous, but every time I took to the air they seemed to simmer down while watching me. Theresa Carson threw me a little wave. I guess she still wanted my sympathies, or my help, though what she was leading her people toward here was anybody's guess. Especially since Logan Mills didn't even seem to be showing his face.

I turned toward the Lotsostuff warehouse, figuring I'd do a quick flyover. It looked as it always seemed to, a big warehouse in the middle of a big, empty country, just a little steam rising out of the heating system—

No.

Wait.

It was black smoke that poured out of the far side of the building, at the distant tip of the sprawling warehouse, and I realized what I was looking at a moment later—

Fire.

Chapter 61

Sienna

"Hello," I said, bracing myself before Chalke had even gotten out a salutation. I paced away from my BMW, preparing myself for whatever ass-chewing my boss could throw out.

"What the hell are you doing down there?" Chalke spat out, surprising me only a little in that she was straight to pisseder-than-pissed, no warm-up needed.

"Cooperating with the local authorities," I said, keeping as neutral as I could. No point pouring gasoline on the fire. "Isn't that what you sent me to do?"

"I sent you to deal with the stupid meta who effed up a bar with his voice," Chalke fired back. "Because I thought maybe a few days out working on something inconsequential would remind you that your job is dealing with the important things, not screwing around in the kiddie pool with the locals."

I cast a long look back at the sex trafficking house, where another girl was being brought out on a gurney. She had an IV hooked up to her arm and was covered in a blanket. "I think you and I have a very different idea of what constitutes important things."

"Yes, and mine is paramount," Chalke said with a voice like hardened iron. "This case is almost insignificant. It should have been an easy lay-up. Listen, you—"

I killed the conversation by hitting the end button. Staring at the screen for a moment, I let the phone fall from between my fingers. It hit the ground and bounced once, then lay there, on the street.

I turned and walked away from it without another thought. There was no point arguing with Chalke, no point yelling at her, nor listening to her yell.

My give-a-damn tank was empty. Months of this, isolated, alone, yelled at, ordered around. Cut off from my friends.

I headed for the BMW and started it up without bothering to wait and give my statement. Metro PD could catch up with me later. Or maybe never.

I threw the car in gear and executed a three-point turn, then burned off down the road, looking for the nearest freeway that would take me to Murfreesboro.

I was done. With all of this shit.

I was going to find the nearest road to Murfreesboro, and there I was going to find Reed.

And then...

I was going home.

Chapter 62

Somehow, in the age of GPS and completely lacking one, I found the nearest freeway. Interstate 40, the sign read, offering me two choices: East to Knoxville, West to Memphis.

I picked east, since that was the direction of Murfrees-boro, and smoothly accelerated up the entry ramp, joining the steady but light flow of traffic on the Nashville roads. They weren't empty, a dozen or so cars in the hundred yards in front of and behind me, glaring in the sunlight. But neither were they as full as the streets of New York I'd become accustomed to in the last few months.

My hands cemented on the wheel, I thought about Reed. I hadn't actually seen my brother in the flesh since Revelen. Since he'd fallen out of the sky to save me from an army of angry, killer mercenaries that were advancing on me with the illest intentions I could imagine.

Sure, I'd talked to him since. In my dreams, at least.

But I hadn't seen him, hadn't hugged him, since Revelen.

Hell, I hadn't hugged anyone since Revelen, I didn't think. That probably sounded like a silly thing coming from a succubus, especially me, but the lack of caring human contact had been wearing on me. Almost two years on the run, the better part of another year now with the FBI...

Yeah. I was done.

The interstate was splitting ahead, and I blinked, trying to figure out which to take. The choices offered were I-65 South to Huntsville or I-40 and I-24 East to Knoxville. I realized I'd probably missed the earlier signs, because hell if I could recall if I'd seen one while I was in my reverie, thinking about Reed and how great it'd be to actually see my brother—

I squealed tires moving over two lanes to the right in time to get on the ramp to I-65 South. Murfreesboro was definitely south of Nashville, so I was going with my best guess here. A quick glance at my speedometer revealed that I was going 85.

Oops.

I backed off that a little as I drove down the ramp and joined the steady traffic flow heading south. There was a lot of greenery here, and the freeways seemed to be cut into rocky hills, dynamited right through the terrain leaving the most curious strata of the rock bare on either side of the overpass above as I raced south.

For a few minutes, I zoned out thinking of the near future. The last few months had been a strange routine, alien to me. Living in an unfamiliar city packed with people who alternately loved me and then disliked me was not an altogether pleasant experience.

When I came out of my dazed thoughts, urban development had given way to tracts of seemingly wild woods on either side of the road. The occasional house peeked out from between trees as I-65 moved south over rolling hills. Ahead, I could see a mighty radio tower of some sort, taller and somehow fatter than any I could recall seeing before. It was distinctive in its diamond shape. It stood the better part of a thousand feet tall, but the oblong nature of it made it look like two mirror towers, stacked one atop each other with their squatter bases meeting in the middle. Heavy metal support wires hung off it in every direction, securing it against the winds in the area.

I gave the tower only a little more thought as I drove south, scanning for signs of Murfreesboro. I passed a lot of local road exits in sequence: Concord, Moores Lane, Cool Springs, McEwen—

Then I saw it.

Murfreesboro Road.

I let out a breath I didn't even know I was holding as I changed lanes. The exit was still two miles away, but I was ready. If it was Murfreesboro Road, surely it went to Murfreesboro, right?

Passing under a huge overpass with hundred-foot retaining walls on either side of the freeway to keep the Tennessee hillsides from sliding down onto the interstate, I caught sight of a panhandler standing on the side of the road ahead. He was just close enough to my lane to make me wary, but not enough that he was in danger of being hit.

He had a big poster board sign that said PANAMA CITY BEACH—his destination, I assumed—written in big, black letters on one side. As I looked at him, though, he flipped it over.

DON'T DO IT, the sign read.

I stared at it for a second, then looked at his face.

Harry.

I almost slammed on the brakes, but caught myself just in time.

Don't do it, he'd said.

I was past him before I could stop, looking over my shoulder at his figure as he receded, disappearing into my blind spot and then visible in my rear view mirror.

DON'T DO IT.

I took the exit ramp to Murfreesboro Road because I was trapped into it by this point. A glance back in the rear view revealed that Harry was still standing there, though it looked like he'd rolled up his sign. He looked like he might have been turned toward me, watching what I was doing.

Coasting, I looked forward. At the top of the exit ramp, there were two signs, two directions to go.

To the left, and most obvious, the sign read MURFREESBORO.

The right hand?

FRANKLIN. Whatever the hell that was.

The traffic light at the top of the ramp was red, a few cars in front of me stopped. I pulled into the center left lane, which was for the turn to Murfreesboro.

Years. I'd spent years isolated, with only the occasional contact with my friends, barely any time with my newly discovered grandmother and great-grandmother. And it had been months since I'd had anything more than a dreamwalked conversation with a human being who gave anything other than a passing damn about me.

Harry's sign came back to me once again: DON'T DO IT.

Ah, Harry. Harry and his warnings.

Harry and his plan.

My knuckles had turned white on the steering wheel. The light flipped from red to green. Cars started to move.

"Dammit," I whispered. "Damn...all of you."

I flipped my turn signal to the right and changed lanes, toward Franklin, leaving my ideas of going to Murfreesboro—of seeing my brother—behind.

Chapter 63

Reed

The fire was visible from the windows, smoke beginning to billow out of the warehouse structure. I wondered, dimly, if this was the section of the building that had suffered from the flooding a few days prior, and doubted it, though it was possible. Given how many prongs, wings, whatever this building had, it was entirely possible this was a new section of the building that was under the torch.

Distantly I heard the crowd shout something through my enhanced senses. They'd caught sight of the fire, but I had no time to deal with their reaction. Not now.

I swooped down, dropping with the wind beneath me, reducing the swirl. I plummeted, pillowing my fall about twenty feet from the roof of the warehouse. The fire was starting to break through, but it wasn't burning up the roof structure—yet. I wondered how the fire alarms hadn't activated, because I heard no ringing of klaxons over the roar of the flames below.

"Shoulda brought Scott with me," I mumbled as I dipped closer, trying to gauge the trouble I was facing. It wasn't good; there was no clear source of water nearby. The building's sprinkler system—if they even had one— was not engaged. Or at least it wasn't making any difference, and there was no sound of water, which was hardly conclusive given the crackling roar of the flames.

The rooftop was insulating me against what was surely a raging inferno inside. I didn't want to dip any closer to the roof, though, if I could avoid it. A clear view of what was going on inside would help, but—

I was hardly reliant on my vision to develop a clear picture of what was going on inside.

Funny little quirk that had happened to me since President Harmon had overclocked my Aeolus powers: I could feel air at great distances. The bigger the disturbance, the greater distance at which I could feel it. I could feel a hurricane brewing across the planet. I could feel a storm system that could produce an F3 tornado from across the country.

And from twenty feet above the warehouse, I could feel the dry, scorching, hot air inside as the temperature rose.

Air was my domain. My control was absolute in this arena, like a god of old.

I drew a short, sharp breath—

Then I blew the air out of that sector of the warehouse.

Windows blasted free, residual glass showering the ragged weeds and scraggly grass that ringed the warehouse walls. The flames rushed out in a vortex as I excised the oxygen from the building, driving the fire out with it.

I brought it up in a flaming tornado, beads of sweat breaking out on my forehead in the cool air. Not from the temp but rather the exertion. The fiery vortex flamed up, rising past me. It warmed the air around me, conducting heat as I launched it up, up—

It ran out of fuel as I carried it as far as I wanted it to go, letting it settle like a flaming thunderhead above me some hundred feet. The waves of heat coming off it radiated down to me as I strained, keeping oxygen from rushing back in to the warehouse below. I'd created a zone as airless as outer space in a section of the warehouse where the fires had been lit. I needed to maintain that for about a minute, but my control was straining as I fought to keep the residual fires above me.

The flames overhead petered out as my vision started to darken around the edges like I'd been pushed underwater. My brain slowed, fixated on the course of action. I had one job—keep the air out, keep the air out—

There was a silent countdown proceeding in my head, and when it ticked past sixty I let the air in—slowly—to the blackout sector I'd created in the Lotsostuff warehouse. I funneled myself down to the window, peering inside.

Blackened crates and cardboard boxes filled the space within, the concrete block exterior scorched from the fire. In the building's rafters I could see the sprinkler system's bones exposed, but not a hint of water dripping down.

No sign of fire, either. I'd succeeded in starving it out. I took a long, slow breath, and—

A blast of flame shot at me from within, a ragged gasp and a scream following it—

I dodged down, trying to ignore the blurriness in my vision. I'd just exerted myself—madly—to put out this fire before it had consumed the whole warehouse. I didn't think I had much left, huddled there under the warehouse window, trying to catch my breath, get my mind around me. My thoughts were slow, chugging along toward an inevitable conclusion.

Someone—the metahuman who'd started the damned fire, I guessed—had just heaved a ball of deadly flame at me.

Chapter 64

Sienna

F ranklin, Tennessee was not what I expected.

Picture a small American town. If you've ever been to one, you know what I mean—the classic Main Street ideal, but faded in modern times. Half the store fronts surrendered to time's slow march. The other half filled with stores that were fighting against the slow wasting away of the good old days. I'd been to a hundred small towns like that, faded from glory.

That wasn't Franklin. At all.

Franklin was that Main Street ideal with new life breathed into it. There was a sweet shop, a theater, a Starbucks and a bunch of local restaurants all sharing the same strip. It was like one of the touristy towns of the Oregon Coast but minus the draw of the coast.

I'd parked my car in a garage a couple blocks off the square and just...walked. Because I had nowhere else to go, nothing else to do, and no damned cell phone to buzz and give me someone else's bullshit directives and guidance.

I went into the sweet shop and got a little cake lollipop. Paid cash so Chalke couldn't get a hit off my credit card and find me. Because screw the Director of the FBI, that's why.

When I got done eating my cake lollipop, I was still hungry. I ignored it and walked down the street under a big sign that said GRAY'S ON MAIN with neon lights unlit in the shining sunlight.

This town could have been pulled out of the fifties, but the cars were all modern. There was a weird feeling of nostalgia surrounding me as I walked the streets, listening to the conversations of the tourists and fellow shoppers. Moms in yoga pants pushing strollers. Bearded hipster guys walking with their piercing-laden girlfriends.

Small-town Tennessee did not look like I thought it would, at least not in Franklin.

I paused to look at the historical marker in front of the church opposite Starbucks. I'd reached the clear end of walkable Main Street, with the pedestrian sidewalks giving way here to roads that looked like they were more meant for serious traffic. The end of downtown, then. Looking behind me, I could see the town square at the opposite end, with a statue atop an obelisk in the middle of it all.

With a sigh, I started back the way I came. I still had no idea what I was going to do when I got back to my car. Maybe walk in the opposite direction for a while—

The honk of a car's horn startled me. A car with a LYFT emblem in the front window pulled to the curb on the opposite side of the street and—to my rather extreme surprise—Chandler popped out, waving at me. He waited until there was a break in the traffic and jogged across. Someone slowed to a near stop for him without honking, something that would not have happened in New York City. Hell, he'd have been lucky if they'd stopped at all instead of turning him into a hood ornament in their hurry to get on with their life.

"How the hell did you find me?" I asked, frowning as he hopped up the curb. He was smiling, only a little winded from his hurry to cross the street.

"We have a GPS tracker in your BMW," Chandler said. "I mean, BMW put it in; it's not we like we're sinisterly going, 'Hahaha, let's track her.' But when you disappeared from the, uh—"

"Sex trafficking house," I said, unabashed by what it was.

Chandler's eyes flitted around like he was seeking escape. "Uh, yeah, that. Anyway, I was pulling up and I saw you leave. When I called you, your phone buzzed from the ground nearby." He patted his coat pockets until he came out with my phone. "Once I realized you'd lost it, the Memphis Belle authorized a trace, and I followed you out here to get it back to you." He finished with a smile. "Also, we have a very tiny break in the case to discuss." He offered my cell phone back to me.

I stared at the cell phone. The screen was cracked across the front, probably from my dropping it like a mic. I hesitated before taking it, reluctance playing across my face.

"What?" he asked, looking at the phone as though it might be a bomb.

"Nothing," I said, taking it from him and pocketing it. I wanted to take it and throw it over my shoulder, hit the garbage can on the corner behind me in a beautiful three-pointer.

I didn't, though.

Chandler was staring at me in serious concentration, his perfect, slicked-back black hair ruffled by the gentle breeze blowing through Franklin. "I know a place near here that's really good." He chucked a thumb over his shoulder. "You want to get some lunch?" He eyed my pocket for a second. "We could drop off your phone at the car first, if you'd like?"

I pursed my lips. I was hungry. "Yeah," I said. "Let's do that."

Chapter 65

"What the hell is a brisket nacho?" I asked, looking at the menu.

We were at a place called Puckett's, right in the middle of downtown Franklin, and the menu was interesting if somewhat close to indecipherable for a northerner like me. It included items like Fried Green Tomatoes, which sounded good, as well as Nashville Hot Chicken (which after my experience with the Hot Chicken tacos also sounded good).

"You've never had brisket?" Chandler's eyebrows almost touched that wave of black hair that sat crested above his forehead. He waved down the server. "Brisket nachos, stat." The server just smiled and disappeared to put that order in. "Brisket is the chest muscle of the cow." Chandler pointed at his pectoral, hidden beneath his blue dress shirt. "They use it every time they get up or lie down, so it's really tough. Cook it too quick, you end up with a chunk of shoe leather. But if you cook it low and slow on a barbecue or a smoker, it comes out melt-in-your-mouth tender."

My mouth watered from his description. "Mmmkay. I would like some of that."

He reached over to the condiment holder in the middle of the table and pulled out a squirt bottle of barbecue sauce with the restaurant logo and signage that further read, *Memphis Style: Sweet, No Heat.* "This. This is the perfect accessory."

"For nachos?" I took my eyes off the menu long enough to sear him with a skeptical look.

"Trust me," he said, and planted the bottle between us like a flag. "If you like a little more spice, there's a Texas Style sauce, too."

I shook my head and turned back to the menu, trying to narrow down my entree. I was puzzling what a "Meat and Three" was when Chandler spoke up.

"So, uh...you want to talk about it?" He had already put his menu aside. Home field advantage.

I let my eyes continue to play over the menu. I decided not to bother with playing coy. "Kinda sorta not really."

"I hear that," Chandler said, and apparently took my cue, falling silent.

The server dropped off sweet tea, a drink I was well acquainted with from my occasional previous cases in places like Atlanta. I counted myself lucky that metahumans didn't suffer from ailments like diabetes, because Southern sweet tea was an almost certain trigger for Type 2.

"So...country music," I said, giving Chandler an experimental glance.

Chandler just looked at me like I was about to slap him. "What about it?"

"Dude, you're Indian," I said. "I don't mean to racially stereotype, but I think the Venn diagram for overlap between 'people from India' and 'Those Who Like Country Music' might be you and no one else. Explain, please."

"Hey, country music has more broad-based appeal than you think," Chandler said, making a show of reading the menu that he hadn't had an iota of interest in a moment before. "But like I told you, I grew up in small-town Tennessee. Country music was big there in the nineties. I mean, I listened to other stuff. Rap, alternative-"

I frowned. "Did alternative die? Because it doesn't really seem like an active category these days."

"It's taking a rest. Like grunge, I assume," Chandler said. "I was an awkward kid. Fitting in was not super easy. I was into *Star Trek* and video games and whatnot. Things that were too geeky for the cool kids. But the geeky kids were all into whatever was mainstream popular, music-wise. But I don't know—I really *liked* country music. It had a different sound. Anyway, my group turned out to be a bunch of working-class kids, with working-class parents, and they turned me on to their music." He shrugged. "It's strange, I guess."

"I know a little of what it's like to feel like an outsider," I said. "And I get developing a contrarian interest to avoid being sucked into the conformist whatever of that...elite class, I guess?"

"But that's the thing," Chandler said. "I didn't do it just to differentiate myself from the elite kids. I was already differentiated just by who I was. I really liked the songs about men who worked hard and got screwed by life or their loves and had bad shit happen. I got that, I could feel it, you know, even though I actually had a really calm upbringing, overall. I could empathize with someone, like in 'Workin' Man Blues,' who's just working his life away trying to get by." He tapped the center of his chest. "It made sense to me here. And even though I knew I wasn't exactly the target demographic for those songs, they really felt like they were being sung to me. That's probably weird, I dunno." He shook his head.

"Speaking as someone who had a very, very unconventional upbringing...that doesn't sound all that weird to me," I said. "And I know exactly what you mean about not fitting in."

"Your, uh...current FBI situation?" Chandler asked. "That what you're talking about?"

"I definitely don't fit in there, either," I said, "but no, I meant how when I first came out of my house, I got picked up by a group called the Directorate. There were...socialization issues, let's put it that way. I don't play well with others."

"I did hear something about body bags coming out of that sex trafficking house," Chandler said with a muted smile.

"I like how casually everyone takes my killing around here," I deadpanned.

"I have a hard time working up moral outrage about you capping sex traffickers," Chandler said. "If you drowned a bag of kittens, I'd be pissed. But those guys...?" He made a face, rolling his hand left to right on a horizontal plane. "I mean, I know on a basic level they were human...ish...but it's hard to read much humanity into someone whose job is renting the bodies of teenagers they've enslaved with drugs."

"Their job is to dehumanize and trade the girls, yeah," I said. "But that's not what I'm talking about. I mean, look —I have a hair trigger, personally. I used to really beat myself up over it. Then my bosses stepped in to beat me up over it. Now I'm just sort of over it. I kill people. Bad people. Like you, I have no attack of conscience over planting those guys in the ground. I'm not bloodthirsty; I don't regret not killing the two that survived or anything, I'm just..." I shrugged. "Jaded's a good word for it. I've seen enough of what the evil people do to cast life in black and white terms. I've developed the oddest moral line, and it just...doesn't even bother me anymore. It's stark; you do this much harm to others, present this much threat— Sienna kills you. And it has nothing to do with their humanity. I do see them as human, weirdly. I just...they crossed the line."

"I think everyone's got that line, somewhere," Chandler said. "That doesn't make you an outsider. You're not strange—at least not in that regard."

"My willingness to kill and my body suggests otherwise."

"You have a little more power to maybe exercise that will," Chandler said. "Plus the threats you generally come up against are either superhuman or—"

"Mercenaries," I said. "I've killed a lot of soldiers for hire."

"I have a hard time getting upset about that for some reason," Chandler said, frowning. "I mean, I should be, right? You're casually admitting to killing people—"

"Yes, you should be."

"Yeah, I don't know." Chandler shrugged. "Doesn't bother me for some reason. Maybe because I'm not a soldier of fortune...?" He tapped his fingers on the table. "So let me ask you this—what would it take for a guy like me to get on the bad side of Sienna? Cross that line you're talking about."

"Point a gun at an innocent, unarmed person," I said.

"That easy?" Chandler nodded, thinking. "What about if they were a meta, with powers that were threatening—"

"You just undermined your premise. You said 'innocent' and 'unarmed.' That would be 'hostile' and 'superpowered,' and thus it changes the scenario, so your actions are totes valid in Sienna world."

"Oh, fair enough, I guess," Chandler said. "Is there a line for redeemable people?"

I blinked. The server was heading our way with a plate of nachos stacked with all manner of excellence and I didn't have my meal picked out yet. "How do you mean?"

"Like, if someone's done something really bad," he said, "but then they want to give up—"

"I accept their surrender. Duh. I'm not an executioner." I thought about that guy trying to surrender to me in the trafficker house. "I mean...up to a point, probably. If they're looking to surrender because they're trying to play me—you know what? I don't actually know. My rules of engagement are probably more fluid than I'd like to admit."

Chandler raised an eyebrow as the brisket nachos were set in front of us. He kept his peace while we ordered. He got the Nashville Hot Chicken Sandwich, and I got the Redneck Burrito. Pulled pork, baked beans and coleslaw wrapped up in a burrito shell. I could already feel my mouth watering thinking about it, but first—nachos.

As soon the server was gone, I hit the nachos like I'd hit that sex trafficker house—viciously and without mercy.

"Okay, another hypothetical," Chandler said, mouth full of delectable nachos. There were black beans in there, sour cream, jalapenos—plus the brisket and a healthy dab of barbecue sauce. It was heaven, and I loved him for recommending them. "What if the person is genuinely sorry for what they've done? Because I get the feeling what you're talking about in the last example—correct me if I'm wrong—but they've done such wretched shit you can't find it in your heart to believe they're redeemable, basically."

"Almost everyone has the capacity for redemption," I said, trying not spatter nachos everywhere as I chewed with the enthusiasm I usually (these days) retained for getting a new gun to play with, "but most people—perps, I mean—don't exercise it. How many times have you caught a criminal and they're genuinely remorseful?" I arched my eyebrows at him. "Go on. I'll wait. Because I can count the number of times it's happened to me on one hand."

"Does that count you, though?" Chandler asked. "Like, the things you did you got pardoned for?"

He was watching me carefully on that one.

I almost choked on a tortilla chip. Or maybe the question. "Some of the things I've done I regret," I said, after catching my breath and washing down nacho detritus with some sweet tea. "Some of the people I killed and was pardoned for—yeah. I wish I hadn't done that. Others?" I pondered it, but had a hard time mustering much remorse for killing Roberto Bastian as he tried to turn into a dragon and kill me, or Eve Kappler, even though technically I'd stalked both of them.

Glen Parks, though...him I felt remorse for killing. I even felt a little for drowning Clyde Clary, right at the end of that. Sometimes I'd wake up and hear his piteous cries right before the gurgling started.

"Others...I think they had it coming," I said, and suddenly the nachos were no longer of interest as my appetite faded. "Or maybe I just justify it to myself that way, because I know that I never killed a person who hadn't either killed people themselves or ordered it. So I justify that, neatly, to me. That's how I started to live with it. Like we're all players in a grand game, and once you're on the board, these are the rules. It applied to metas trying to take over the world with Sovereign, it applied to mercenaries hired to protect bad people, like cartel members doing murder, or on garrison duty in Revelen." I pressed my lips against each other. "I guess it even extended to those sex traffickers. I don't know if they ever killed anyone, but they were sure armed to, and they were clearly doing plenty of non-lethal harm. They were in the game, all of them." I stared at the nachos. "And I took 'em off the board, some of them before they could do the same to me, some of them before they could do it to someone more innocent than me. Or after they did." My voice felt suddenly hoarse and scratchy.

"I didn't mean to make you justify yourself," Chandler said, clearing his throat. "You don't have to do that to me."

"Kinda felt like I had to," I said, with a bittersweet smile. "But this is the problem I run into, right? My FBI bosses? They've seen the practical side of this. Never asked the questions you have, about my own special rules of engagement, but they've seen the reports, watched the body bags come in. Everyone in the world knows who I am and a good portion of what I've done, for good and ill. And they don't—mostly—see me in the shades of grey that denote the nuance that is my life. They see either black or white. The 'Holy shit, she's a murderer,' or 'Damn, she's a hero who will do whatever it takes to protect us!' Not a lot of in between." I thought back to this morning, and the rage I'd felt boil over at what I'd seen in that house. "And I think there's a fair amount of 'in between.'"

"That's something people don't like to talk about," Chandler said quietly, lowering his head. "How order has costs. You can't have zero punishment or lawful consequences for crimes like robbery or stealing or murder, or you'll get a lot more of it." He shook his head. "The flip side—and boy, do the boys in blue hate talking about this

—is that if you get too crazy with your imposition of order, you get cops who act like they have godlike powers and no accountability. Some of them won't abuse it, I guess, but most men—"

"Enough men are weak that they would," I agreed. "I heard a story about cops in Minnesota dragging this mouthy kid into his garage and beating him so hard he never walked again. He was a little douchebag, for sure, but did he deserve not to walk again for being a prick?" I shook my head. "You're right. This isn't an argument anyone wants to have. It puts too many noses out of joint. And it's something I think about a lot, as pertains to me. To my behavior."

"I like that you can see it, though," Chandler said, pointing a finger at me. "You said you didn't have to justify yourself to me, and that's true. But not going to lie, I'd be terrified of you if you did the things you'd done and weren't as self-aware as you are of the lines you cross. Because that's power without any accountability. Or humility, really. And that's...frightening."

"I've seen that," I said. "Worse than me. So much worse than me. I think a lot of people who criticize me see that as my endgame, maybe. 'Sure, she's killing sex traffickers today, but what if her moral line shifts and suddenly little old lady shoplifters are fair game?'"

"'Then the thievin' old bitches clearly had it coming,' your staunchest defenders would say." Chandler wore a ridiculous grin.

I broke out laughing, then cut it off suddenly. "That...shouldn't be funny. But it is."

He had dancing laughter in his eyes. "It really is." He gestured to the nachos. "Come on. Let's talk about something better and happier, huh?"

"I like that plan," I said, scooping up a nacho full of

brisket and cheese and sour cream and sauce and—hell, everything—and shoving it in my mouth. I couldn't entirely put aside the feeling of malaise that had come over me in the wake of my conversation with Chalke, but I damned sure tried as I chowed down at that table in Puckett's.

Chapter 66

Brance

"I don't know if I can do this," Brance said, following Jules down the sidewalk in downtown Nashville. He was looking around worriedly, sure someone was going to see him.

They were on 5th Avenue downtown, between Broadway and Commerce Street. The construction site across the street took up the whole block, but the brick building next to them seemed surprisingly small for the outsize importance it carried.

"You need to relax, kid," Jules said. The older man almost seemed to let it out in a growl. He was probably tired, which Brance understood totally.

"I just don't see how I can do this," Brance said. He fumbled with his hands, wiping them on his jeans as he looked up at the arched windows. "I don't—"

"Yeah, yeah," Jules said.

Brance paused. He'd known where they were going, but...

Now that he saw it...

The Ryman Auditorium.

The former home of the Grand Ole Opry. The Mother Church of Country Music.

Brance felt his mouth gape open, jaw flapping uselessly as he attempted to shut it. No good.

Jules cast him a look. "Oh, that's what quieted you down? I would have brought you here earlier if I thought that was the thing that'd make you stop protesting like a girl who's all fussed about her modesty."

Brance frowned. What the hell did that mean? Jules didn't explain it, instead just stepping up and opening the front door. Brance followed because...well, because following was apparently what he did now.

The Ryman. It really was the Ryman. He'd driven past a few times, but he'd never actually been in here. The brick facade gave it an aged look, white highlights brightening it. The doors and signage looked old, but some new digital additions made it a little more modern. Regardless, a breathless feeling settled in on him, like he'd exhaled everything out of his lungs and couldn't get it back.

He blinked, trying to take it all in, make time slow down somehow.

Here he was, though. At the Ryman.

If only his granddaddy and grandmaw could see him now. How many times had he watched the Opry with them? Every Saturday night he'd been at their house when he was a kid, which was plenty. Sure, it had moved on to its own theater by then, but still...this place had real significance. It was a part of tradition that wove into his own past.

"Impressive," Jules said, beckoning him forward, through the door, which was held open by Gil. Down the aisle they went, Brance unable to say anything. The seating was pews, like a church. The stage was curtained, but Brance had a brief vision of himself standing there...

Jules was nodding his head. "Yeah, this'll work."

"I..." Brance started to say.

How many legends had performed on that stage? How many had launched their career trajectories upward from here?

He covered his mouth, unable to hold back his awe at the sight of this place.

Jules turned around to favor him with a look of pure amusement. "I don't know, kid, what do you think?" He shot a long look at that stage, that legendary stage. "You think you want to do some singing from up there? Or nah?"

"Tonight?" Brance asked, those reservations about hurting others fading in the sight of his dream.

"Tonight," Jules said. "I've got a very special guest list in mind, and Leo is already working on it." He checked his phone. "Oh. Looks like it'll be very well attended."

Brance could sing from *that* stage. To real, live people.

What the hell else had he ever wanted as badly as this?

All he had to do...was keep this...other thing...under control.

How hard could that be?

"Tonight," Brance said, and saw Jules smile out of the corner of his eye. Tonight.

Chapter 67

Sienna

"You know what really bothers me about all this?" I kept my hands firmly on the wheel as I steered the car on I-65 North, heading back toward Nashville. "I went up to the door of that sex trafficker house and knocked, playing all drunk, and the jerkoff that answered?" I paused for comedic effect. "He didn't even try and sex traffic me." I swept a hand over my tank-topped and braided self. "I mean, look at me. Do I not look like a ripe, Gen Z runaway to you?"

Chandler, poised and waiting for what he must have thought was going to be a deep, profound, case-related clue, took a second to realize what I'd done. He cocked his head, then his mouth went slightly agape, and finally he let out a snort and broke out in a laugh. He shoved his hand in front of his face and cut it off a moment later. "That...uhm...that shouldn't have been funny." After he got control of himself, he let out a low whistle. "You like the dark humor, don't you?"

I didn't quite hold in a smile of my own. "I live in the darkness, Chandler. If I didn't laugh there, I wouldn't laugh at all. Especially lately."

We cruised along the green-lined freeway, trees blurring by on either side. To our right, that bizarre, pyramidal radio antenna came back into view, and I pointed at it. "What's that, Mr. Tourist Guide?"

"What, you expect me to know every random object on the side of the road around here?" Chandler asked, sounding vaguely offended. After a short pause, he chuckled. "Actually, I do know what it is. That is the broadcast antenna for WSM 650 AM radio, which is the original home—and still to this day broadcasts—the Grand Ole Opry. It has a historical landmark sign on it and everything."

I made a noise to indicate how impressed I was. "Anything else I should be aware of on this road?"

"There's historical markers all through here," Chandler said. "Back where we had lunch? That town is loaded with them, because it was the sight of the Battle of Franklin, during the Civil War. This whole area's been settled for so long, though, practically everything's got a historical marker."

"Hm," I said. "That's kind of interesting. If you're into that sort of thing. Which I kinda am."

Chandler looked down his phone. "Uhm...have you looked at your messages since I gave you back your phone?"

I felt myself deflate slightly. "No."

"You probably should," he said. "Mayor Brandt wants to meet with you."

It took everything I had not to slump my head against the steering wheel while driving. "Tell me she's not pissed at me, too."

Chandler shrugged. "I don't know. I can't imagine she's highly enthusiastic that you left the scene of the raid, though, without giving the police a statement or any of the other procedural things."

"I wasn't highly enthusiastic about it," I said, now white-knuckling the wheel.

"Is it my imagination or is your job stress really taking a toll on you?"

"What, do I not still look like a teenager?" I asked as lightly as I could, trying to loosen my grip so I didn't destroy the BMW by wrecking my ability to steer it while traveling at seventy-five miles per hour. I thumped the wheel with the palm of my hand. "It's probably not your imagination. I shouldn't have left the Metro PD holding the bag while I went to...cry in my total lack of beer. Brandt should be pissed at me. She certainly has every right to be."

"I'll tell her office that you're driving and that you'll call her back," he said, texting.

I smiled. "Why not just have me call her back now?"

Chandler cringed. "Tennessee has a law against cell phone use while driving unless it's hands-free."

"Oh, fine," I said. "Let's just stick with practicing safe driving, shall we?"

"Good call," he said, and we settled into the quiet, the hum of the tires on the freeway a soothing melody all its own.

Chapter 68

Reed

Another fireball shot over my head as the blackened blurring around my vision persisted. This happened sometimes when I exerted myself too hard, pushed myself to dispel a hurricane or push it off course, keep a tornado from touching down—something of that sort. I expected it was like a normal person running ten miles and then engaging in the heaviest weightlifting protocol they could, or running an ultra-marathon.

I was already exhausted when I dodged the first fireball. The fact that more were following, that whoever was shooting them sounded like a wounded animal, well—

It was a bad sign for a guy who was ready for a nap.

I kept deathly quiet, huddled under the burned-out window, back against the warehouse's concrete block wall. Sirens were blaring in the distance, the sound of fire engines already on their way a hint that help, too, might be on its way.

On the other hand—no. Pitting the Murfreesboro PD

against a pissed-off Gavrikov-type was a formula for disaster. A Gavrikov could blow up their cars with them standing right next to them. Could burn down this whole warehouse—

Which begged the question—why hadn't they?

Another, weaker fireball flew out the window. It was aimed randomly, and petered out almost as soon as it went over my head.

The Gavrikov was weak. A probable explanation formed in my head: I'd caught the bastard in my vacuum of airlessness when I'd put out the fire. Without any air, the Gavrikov had been choked to either brief unconsciousness or as near to it as you can get without passing out. Being a metahuman, it hadn't killed them, and they'd woken up reallllllly mad. Anger was fueling them, but their strength was now fading.

I could relate. My strength was definitely on the faded side of things. I huddled, waiting for the Gavrikov to finish their little tantrum, which was achieving absolutely nothing except to showcase their weakness.

While another fireball flew overhead, this one smaller than the last two, I tried to decide my course of action. If they got wise, they could still cause a hell of a mess in the warehouse by starting another fire or two. In a way, I'd been lucky they'd woken up mad; it had made them forget their original "Burn it all down!" plan. Which I'd have been hard-pressed to stop in my current condition. My right hand rested, knuckles down, in the dirt beneath the window, in the shadow of the warehouse. My skin was pale from exertion, and I didn't even feel like standing right now, let alone leaping inside to face off with this guy. Or gal.

So...negotiation, then.

"Hey, look, the cops are on their way," I called out.

"Not sure what you're trying to accomplish here, but if you make me, I'll snuff your flames out again."

No answer.

"I don't want to choke you out—again—but I will, if I have to," I said. No fire answered me, and I couldn't hear them creeping around inside. "No one's been hurt yet. But if you keep doing this, it's going to go really badly for you. You've already figured out what life on Mars is like once today, right? Don't make me suck all the air out of there again." A total bluff. There was zero chance I could do that a second time. It was one thing to send down an F5 tornado, which was just pushing on elements of nature that existed to begin with.

Creating a vacuum zone of airless space where there was damned sure supposed to be air? Talk about doing the impossible. I was so tapped out a well-aimed cricket might have been able to knock me out right then.

"Come on," I called, leaning against the brick. "Do the right thing." I deemed there was a better than even chance that this firebug was already making their escape through some other sector of the cavernous Lotsostuff warehouse. There were certainly no shortage of windows and fire exits that were not proximal to me. I could hardly cover them all, especially since I could barely stand. "Dammit," I whispered when there was no answer.

I flew up, carefully and gingerly, which, surprisingly, was easier than standing. Peering in the window, I found—

Nothing. Scorched boxes, burnt pillars. The remains of a fire and nothing more, a few embers burning weakly among the ashes.

No sign of a Gavrikov. No sign of anybody—

The crunch of a foot made me spin. Someone had stepped on something inside, and I blew myself through the window in stupid haste. Maybe the Gavrikov was as wiped out as I was. Maybe they were almost as powerless to resist as me—

I swept toward the noise on a tornado, hoping my speed and initiative would allow me to take them by surprise, dimly aware that they knew I was here. But haste, haste might be my friend. It certainly beat the hell out of standing outside and letting them fire, uh...fire over my head over and over.

Another crinkle of a footstep sounded, and I blew toward it. They were behind a shelf, and I flew overhead, cutting out the wind as I shot overhead then pushed my hands down toward them and brought with it a gale-wind—

I pushed the shadowy figure down, catching myself only a foot above them. They were trapped in a small vortex, pinned against the warehouse floor, a windy barrier erected around them. I doubted it'd entirely stop a fireball, but it might keep it contained for a few seconds until...well, I didn't know what. This was not my greatest plan ever, and I chalked it up to the fatigue.

"I've got you," I said, hovering over them. It was a man, that much was clear. In a sweated-through dress shirt and jeans. I'd pinned his body face down against the ground. I stared down at him, then used the wind to give him a gentle flip.

That caused me to raise an eyebrow.

Because I was looking into the contorted, angry face of Logan Mills, the owner of Lotsostuff.

Chapter 69

Sienna

"Anything else?" I asked the Metro Nashville PD investigator, a lady named Quint. She shook her head, then shook my hand, and off she went, leaving me alone just outside the scene of the trafficker house.

The police cordon was still up, the Metro PD was still working to clear the place of evidence and whatnot, working the scene. No one had seemed all that upset I'd left and come back, probably because I wasn't really in their jurisdiction. I had a feeling there were some surly voicemails waiting on my phone, but I didn't dare check that until I'd cleared this mess, which...

Hey, I'd cleared this mess. Lucky me.

The first voicemail was an acidic one from Chalke, which I listened to two seconds of before deleting. I could already tell where it was going, and it was nowhere good. "To hell with this," I muttered, once again dropping my problems for a later time. Instead, I went looking for Chandler.

I found him chatting in the garage of the sex trafficker house with Captain Parsons, surrounded by cardboard boxes that had been broken open to reveal extra sleeping bags and mass-produced cheap clothes for teenage girls. I suppressed a pang of revulsion and anger as I wandered in. Chandler was deep in a story.

"So he says to me—" Chandler's tone was animated "—he says—"

"Chandler."

He turned to face me. "Oh, hey. All done?"

"All done," I said. "You want a ride back to your car? Or the TBI office?" I shrugged. "Whichever."

"Yep, Marsh took my car back to the office," he said, and exchanged a quick handshake with Captain Parsons. "See you soon."

Once we were in the BMW, Chandler opened his mouth to ask me something, but I cut him off. "Hey, do you have your playlist on your phone?" After hashing over my statement about what happened in the trafficking house—complete with graphic detail about what I saw, all emotion carefully stripped out—I really didn't feel like talking. But I still felt strangely obligated to get Chandler back to his car, especially since he'd waited for me. Which was weird since I hadn't made him abandon his ride for a Lyft out to Franklin.

"Oh, sure," Chandler said, fumbling with his phone, then screwing around with the screen in the middle of the dash between us. A couple minutes later, and the first chords of a ballad started piping through the BMW speakers.

I frowned, screwing my nose up in concentration. "Hey, I know this one." I took a finger off the wheel and snapped it. "This is 'Wolves,' by Garth Brooks."

"Yes!" Chandler seemed pleased I'd gotten it. "You know it from your mom's Garth Brooks phase?"

"Yeah." I listened as Garth's silky smooth vocals launched into the first verse. "Also...I always liked this one."

"Well, it's about the weak getting picked out of the herd by wolves," Chandler said. "It sounds right up your alley." He must have caught a look from me, because he backpedaled. "Because you're strong, I mean. Not because you're a wolf."

"I am kind of a wolf," I said, turning my attention back to the road. The sun was already descending toward the western horizon. "I don't generally prey on the weak, though."

"I think you're more of a sheepdog," he said, then his lips tightened into a tight pucker. "Maybe I should just stop with the dog analogies."

I couldn't keep the amusement out of my voice, nor the slight smile from breaking through on my face. "Are you saying I'm a bad bitch?"

"Yeah, no, that's not what I—"

"Chill, Chandler. I'm just messing with you. I'm not easily offended. Easily annoyed, yes. Offended, no."

We settled back as Garth launched into the first chorus. I was pulling onto the freeway, heading around the ring that girded Nashville. Older buildings were passing, and I listened to the music without the benefit/drawback of Chandler talking for a few minutes, and was a little surprised when it wended to its close.

"You know what I like best about that song?" I asked. "It's reflective of the brutal reality of nature."

"Do I want to know what you mean by that?" Chandler asked cautiously.

"Probably not, but I'll tell you anyway—I like that it

doesn't sugarcoat the fact that we don't all make it through." I kept my hands settled on the steering wheel as we came to the first split that would take us around to the TBI HQ. The Nashville skyline was visible just to my left, the sun reflecting off some of the glass and steel buildings as it sunk lower and lower in the winter sky.

"Well, that's glum," Chandler said.

"But accurate."

"But...glum. And kind of in opposition to our job. We're supposed to protect people, after all."

I chuckled. "No. We're supposed to do our best to protect people. But you know as well as I do that most of the time—for the serious stuff, anyway—we don't even get called until the first body has already reached room temp. And that's if we're lucky. Lots of times we don't find out about these things until years later. Don't get me wrong, I'll always bust my ass and risk my life to protect people from harm. But reality doesn't allow it. We don't watch them every second of their day, for good reason. They're on their own until some triggering event brings us into their lives. The smarter among them realize that, and ready themselves."

Chandler's eyes were wide, and he hesitated. I could tell he was wondering whether he should ask the natural question. Of course he did. "What do the dumber among them think?"

"That there's such a thing as 'safety,'" I said. "That they're entitled somehow to make it through life without getting—I dunno, murdered. Which, hey, that'd be sweet. I am in favor of that concept, but it's so utopian as to defy reality. There isn't a guarantee that we or anyone else can make. I kill all the wolves I can, but there are still wolves out there. Still trying to get into the herd. Some see it, some don't. I wish more did."

"Wouldn't that steal the joy out of their lives?" Chandler asked, a little quietly. I guess I'd gotten to him.

"Not many people ask why cops tend to get super grim after years of service," I said, musing off tangent from what he'd asked. "You know what I mean? The veterans with the dark sense of humor like mine. The ones that have seen, oh, everything?"

"Yeah, I know the type," he said, keeping his eyes off me.

"You can't see what we see on days like today and not be awake to the dangers around you," I said. "I'm not talking about pushers on the corner, or even the addict who needs a fix, lurking in the parking lot watching as you wheel your groceries to your car. I'm talking about the worst of us, the ones that have always preyed on humanity, from the days when we lived in caves until now. They'll never change, no matter how much we try. In some ways, they only get meaner as we get weaker."

"I'm really sure I don't want to know what you mean by us getting 'weaker.'"

"Our society has snowplowed the biggest problems of humanity out of our way, Chandler," I said. "Come on. We've destroyed so many fundamental challenges of our survival we don't even remember they were challenges. Our ancestors of fifty years ago wouldn't be able to believe the world we live in. All the collected knowledge of humanity can be accessed through a piece of plastic and metal in my pocket. If I'm hungry, I can stop at a corner gas station and get a meal that would have been better than anything King Henry VIII ever supped on—"

"I think it might be pushing it to say you can get that at a gas station. Maybe Arby's." He looked up at me. "And we still deal with stuff. Loss. Death. Pain. It's not all sunshine and roses. We have our struggles. Some of us have larger ones than others."

"On the plus side, nature isn't as effective at killing us as she used to be," I said. "But you're right. My point is just that...whatever. I'm a cranky old lady who's seen too much shit and listened to too many people complain about things that seem so trivial by comparison. So lacking in a real world understanding like the kind afforded the girls that came out of that house earlier today." I shook my head. "They're going to struggle to trust another human being in our so-called civilized society. And they should, after what they've been through, which is what I'd quantify as 'real shit.' As opposed to—I don't know, whatever people are whining about on the internet today."

"Yeah, I think you got that crabby old lady thing down," Chandler said, looking down at his phone. "No more Garth Brooks for you, ma'am."

"Johnny Cash?" I asked.

He snorted. "How about 'When the Man Comes Around'? Or is that too on the nose?"

I chuckled. "Maybe something a little brighter. Got anything with a little more...I dunno, kick?"

Chandler thought about it for a moment. "Yeah. I know just the thing."

The blazing tear of a fiddle opened up over the BMW's speakers, and I listened, sure I'd heard this but not sure what it was exactly.

"'The Devil Went Down to Georgia,'" Chandler said by way of explanation.

"Talk about on the nose," I said, as Chandler gave me a funny look. "Going by the opinion of my boss, you're only one state off."

Chapter 70

Jules

E verything was nearly ready.

The Ryman looked perfect. Jules had been a little hesitant to hire out this place, specifically, because of the price tag, because the size of the group was going to be small—but hey, he'd leaped out in faith.

And it looked like it was going to pay off.

He'd gotten a surprising level response back from the local criminal underworld. He figured they'd all have taken the invite as him—a low-tier player—trying to aspire beyond his station.

Nope. Apparently the news that Sienna Nealon was hitting criminal hotspots all over Nashville had them worried. The Russians, the Triads, the Eastern European types, the local Mafia, Dixie mafia, the bikers—hell, everyone had fallen over themselves to RSVP to his little soiree. They were scared already, which was good for him. Most of them had even said yes before he'd put down the security deposit. Which was also good, because he didn't know if he was going to get that back.

Low-profile would have been the conventional way to do this. Keep it quiet, announce it slow. Inflict Brance on a few people at a time. Roll them up, consolidate them in fear, let them know he was the new power in town.

But Jules was tired of the slow-march bullshit, and Brance was enough of a pussy that he'd probably bitch out after busting the eardrums of a couple people.

The Nashville underworld needed a visionary leader.

Jules was the guy. This was going to show them all.

Sure, it was a big bet. But you didn't get to the winner's circle on penny ante bets. He needed to open in a big way, and this was it. This was going to get all their attention.

He'd make his play tonight, in front of every mafioso of consequence in this town. The organized crime in this burg seriously needed someone to organize it.

That was going to be Jules. All he needed was a display of power, and he was convinced he could make the moves necessary to solidify it from there. Play one against another, convince them of his supremacy...

Yeah, it'd be tough. But he'd pull 'em together, one way or another.

And failing that, he'd just let Brance kill 'em all tonight and step into the power vacuum that resulted.

The best part? If Brance did it, no one could even blame it on him.

Chapter 71

Reed

Logan Mills struggled under the force I was applying to him beneath the tornado. He didn't say anything, just looked up at me as he tried to push through the curtain of wind that was holding him down.

"That's not going to do you any good," I said, staring at him in concentration. "Question: what are you doing here?"

Mills looked up at me without bothering to insert any credulity into his expression. "This is my warehouse!"

"Which you tried to burn down?" I asked, watching him for a hint that he was about to burst into flames.

"No!" He sure seemed insulted, but he stopped struggling a moment. "I came as soon as I figured out what was going on with the black smoke." He paused, looking around. "Why aren't the fire alarms going off?"

"Because someone disabled them and the sprinklers before starting the fire, I assume." I looked him right in the eyes. "Who'd have the ability to do that?"

"I don't know," Mills said, hackles rising as he looked in my eyes. "Did you?"

"I don't know my way around any fire suppression system, let alone yours," I said. "I did catch the firebug in the process—after I put out the flames. When I came after them, I found you. Coincidence?"

"Yeah, it's a coincidence." Mills started struggling again. "Why the hell would I burn my own warehouse?"

I surveyed the torched debris. There was no one in here, no hint that anyone had been for a while. Even in the distance, only sunlight flooding in through the aging windows provided light, suggesting either the fire had devastated the building's electricals, at least in this area—

Or they were just turned off. Maybe because there was no one in here.

"Are you accepting orders right now?" I asked, not letting him up. The sirens were close now, and I could hear doors slamming outside through the broken window. The cops and firefighters weren't far off.

"Yeah," Mills said, looking me squarely in the eye, quite angrily, again. "Backorders. For when we get everyone back to work."

"You collecting any money for those?" I asked.

Mills stopped struggling, then hung his head. "No. Without a line of sight to the end of this...no. I wouldn't take their money until we can fulfill the orders."

"So," I came back to my feet, lifting him up, "I'm just spitballing here, but—insurance fraud."

"What?" He just stared at me.

"You asked why you'd burn your own warehouse? Insurance fraud." I shrugged. "The merchandise isn't doing you any good just sitting here during the strike, so..."

Mills just stared at me in dumb disbelief. "I did not burn my own warehouse." He made an effort to break out of my wind trap and failed, again. Holding him in wasn't that taxing of an effort at this point. He was definitely human, and had the strength to prove it. "I just came to see what was happening." He tried one last futile time. "Will you please let me go? You're trespassing, the cops are almost here, and I'm not going anywhere."

"Yeah, okay," I said. Somebody hammered on a door in the distance, presumably the nearest one to the outside. I could hear someone running to it, then opening it. Words were exchanged, then a whole lot of footsteps came pounding toward us.

The firemen came first, followed by the cops, followed by Ben Kelly, his tie askew, flapped over his shoulder. It took a few minutes for me to tell my story to the officer in charge, then Mills to say his bit.

The cop in charge was a plainclothes detective named Houghton. He seemed to be straight-up handling it, and was a career man, hard-nosed and suspicious-eyed. This was the first I'd seen him, but he looked like he'd been around the block a time or twelve.

"So you didn't see who was throwing the balls of fire at you?" he asked.

"Nope," I said. "I was pretty worn out after sucking all the oxygen out of here. Had to keep my head down."

He nodded. Mills had been separated for the purposes of the interview, and was a little farther away, explaining his part—very mutedly for a guy whose life's work had been both burned and flooded the last couple days. "What do you make of this?" Houghton asked.

"I don't know," I said, watching Mills. "My gut runs to insurance fraud. Catching this guy in the area of the fire? Convenient, at least for me. But he could be telling the truth about running in the direction of the fire." I shrugged. "I guess it's in your hands, but—"

"Nope," Houghton said. "Not mine."

I waited. "Uh, okay. Then whose—"

"Tennessee Bureau of Investigation," came the voice from behind me. I'd never even heard anyone approach, but there stood a black woman with knockout, model-good looks in a suit, gun revealed where she held her suit jacket back to park a hand on her hip next to it. She was wearing a grin that crinkled all the way to the corners of her eyes. "Ileona Marsh. And this must be my lucky week."

I cocked an eyebrow. "Oh yeah? Why's that?"

"Because yesterday I met your sister for the first time, and now I've got you," she said, clearly far too jolly about this. "I'm collecting the whole metahuman family set here."

Chapter 72

"I'm just getting all the metahuman business this week, I swear," Ileona Marsh of the Tennessee Bureau of Investigation said, still bearing a winning smile. It was hard to take offense at what she was saying when it sounded like she was pretty amused about the whole thing.

"You don't get metahuman 'business' on a regular basis now?" I asked, trying to keep calm about the fact that Sienna was somewhere in the same state—and that I almost certainly wouldn't see her.

"It's still pretty rare for us here," Marsh said. "That big blowout case your sister had in Atlanta a few years back, that was the biggest and closest thing we've had around here. Everything TBI has touched has been minor stuff, the kind of thing that we haven't had to call you in on."

"Lucky you," I said. "Lots of states haven't been so fortunate."

She nodded. "Yeah. Hard to miss some of the incidents in the news." She perked. "So...flooding a couple days ago, and I'm assured this location isn't in a flood plain. That one seemed suspect. Now we've got arson. Is this a metahuman incident?"

I nodded. "Yep. I spied with my little eye what we call a 'Gavrikov type.' Threw some flames at me, then...possibly escaped." I eyed Logan Mills with great significance.

Marsh caught my inference. "I see. You got any proof to go with that?"

"Circumstantial at best. Caught him in the vicinity. He says he came running when he figured out the building was on fire. It could be. It's a big place; the firebug could have run in the opposite direction." I nodded that way; the building extended for four or five more football fields of length in that direction.

"I appreciate your honesty," Marsh said, pulling out a pad and making some brief notes.

While she scrawled, I figured I could play it cool and get some info. "So...you met my sister. How's she doing?"

Marsh looked up. "Why don't you call her and find out?"

I made the motions of an uncomfortable reaction, letting out a grunt and kicking a foot at the concrete floor. "We, uh...don't really talk anymore." When I looked up, she had the perfect inquisitive look of a cop. "We had a falling out."

"Oh?"

"Yeah, I'm not a fan of her current job," I said, hoping that would be explanation enough for her.

It was. "Oh," she said. "Well, she's...alive and kicking, at least. By which I mean she kicked in the door of a sex trafficker and saved about forty underage girls from a hellish life in the trade this morning. And killed a few traffickers." She kept a thin smile. "A couple survived, which...honestly, is kind of a shame."

I didn't know quite how to take that. It certainly wasn't the sort of thing TBI would have said in a press release. I hoped. "How'd she get on that?" I asked. "Was it a metahuman operation?"

Marsh shook her head. "Nah. The mayor and governor are trying to get her to take a position with my agency and figured letting her run with our local law enforcement on some cases would sweeten the pot for her after what the FBI just did to her in New York—"

"What did the FBI just do to her in New York?" I asked. I hadn't heard this.

"Ahhh, maybe I shouldn't say." Marsh debated for about two seconds before apparently deciding, whatever, I was cool. Or at least that was how I saw it. "They yanked her from duty in the field office and moved her to DC, effective when her assignment here ends. Landed on her for assisting the NYPD outside of formal FBI requests and channels."

I frowned. Keeping my sister's nose out of trouble was an impossible task, but it sounded like the FBI was about to give it a try. "Whatever," I said under my breath, all part of the act. In reality, I wanted to talk to her ASAP, and tried to do the mental arithmetic around when the last time we spoke was. It had been a few days, which meant I was probably due for a visit in my dreams soon.

"So, this case," Marsh said, tapping her pad against her black suit pants. "A metahuman kink in the nozzle of what otherwise looks like a labor dispute. You came down here on your own accord or what?"

I froze. "Yeah, kinda. I got a tip it might be getting out of control, so I've been watching the demonstrations the last couple days."

Marsh wrote that down, too. "Interesting," she said

without looking up. "Very interesting. See anything of note?"

"A damned near untenable situation," I cracked. "The CEO doesn't seem to want to talk, and the demonstrators are getting...well, restless. Speaking of..." I paused, trying to listen over the sound of the crime scene. "I wonder if they're still going?"

"Oh, they're still going," Marsh said. "Loud and proud when I drove through a few minutes ago. Looks like a real handful for local PD."

Ugh. I let out a long sigh. "I should probably get back out there. I have this fear that if I'm away for too long, it's going to turn into a riot."

She quirked an eyebrow up while smiling at me. "Why is that?" she asked innocently. "Do you sense the desire for violence among these poor, oppressed workers, who make considerably above the minimum wage?" Her words were just drenched in irony.

I tried not to dignify that with a guffaw, but I failed. "They have a point, you know," I said, trying to make up for my chortle. "Especially about the working conditions here."

"Yeah, apparently it's a real fire trap," Marsh, turning back to her notepad. "I think I'd be a lot more receptive to their protest if someone wasn't using it as a cover to cause a lot of property damage." She looked up at me, that same knowing smile plastered on her face. "I wish someone would look into that. Someone with some real expertise in dealing with metahumans. I feel confident saying that the State of Tennessee would pay handsomely for someone to take this burden off our hands. Some expert, maybe."

It was my turn to raise an eyebrow. "Is that so?"

"That's so," she said.

"I'll see what I can do," I said, with a tight smile. I

mentally wrote off her offer immediately, given we were already beyond broke and state governments didn't exactly pay with haste. But with that, I hurdled out the window and flew off on the wind, heading back to make sure the protest didn't get out of hand.

Chapter 73

Jules

"Open the house," Jules said. He'd always wanted to say that.

Of course, he was saying it to Gil and Leo only, because he'd refused the typical compliment of ushers and staff the Ryman recommended for his event, but still. He said it.

And Gil and Leo stepped to it. They propped open the doors, and mob bosses from across Nashville started to flow in.

Jules set himself up to greet them all, just inside the main aisles into the theater proper. He was ready with a smile and a handshake. "Larry. Good to see you."

Larry Philmont took his hand and gave him a firm shake, gripping Jules's elbow. "Interested to hear what you have to say here. No one's ever summoned us together before. I assume this has something to do with that miserable superhero bitch tearing up our town?"

"I felt like there were some things that needed to be

addressed," Jules said, still grinning. Subtle was the way to go. "Someone needs to take the lead here, given current events."

Larry nodded at that. "Someone does indeed." And he walked off, a couple bodyguards in tow.

The inference was obvious: no way in hell did Larry feel that Jules was the man to lead, but he'd shown up anyway to see what was going on. That was smart on his part, and Jules could respect that, even if he didn't care for the blatant disrespect shown by Larry's lack of enthusiasm to him taking up the crown.

But Jules did understand it. When it came to operators in this town, he was small-time. Little fish in a medium-sized pond. Better than Jersey, where he'd been a minnow in an ocean, though.

Still, how did a fish get bigger? It had to eat. And summoning the bigger fish here, well, he was about to take a big bite. He had it in his head how it was going to go, and even if he only made it happen to 50%, he was still going to make a big splash.

"Hey, Billy," Jules said, grinning as he glad-handed the next guest. "Long time no see."

Billy just grunted. Taciturn bastard. Disagreeable, too, but this was what he was dealing with. Jules just smiled and got on with it. Once they got everyone greeted and seated, then they could begin.

Chapter 74

Brance

The dressing room was a little smaller than he might have thought, but still—this was the freaking Ryman Auditorium. Brance just stared at himself in the mirror.

Gil had gone out and gotten him a new pair of blue jeans and a shirt, had picked up his guitar from his apartment up in Germantown. His boots were the same ol', but they were okay. Had a layer of wear on them that came from Wyoming.

"Keep it cool, keep it cool," Brance whispered under his breath. He needed to stay level for this. That was going to be the key to not...

Well, to not having an...incident.

A knock sounded at the door, and Brance almost shat himself. "Come in," he said, voice all wobbly.

"Hey, kid," Jules said, grinning wide as he came in. "The house is open, almost everybody's here...you about ready?"

Brance stared at himself in the mirror. Was he? "I

don't know," he said, suddenly unsure. Was this stage fright?

"I think I can confidently say you're ready," Jules said, meandering over to him.

"But what if it goes wrong?" Brance bubbled over. All his fears seemed to be coming out now. "What if the same thing that happened at the recording studio, at Screamin' Demons, at Mercy's Faithless—what if it happens here?"

There was a slight waver in Jules's demeanor that looked—for a second—like amusement. Then he shook it off and smiled, warm and engaged. "You'll be fine," Jules said, clapping that heavy hand on Brance's shoulder. "You're going to do just great, kid. I have faith in you."

Brance didn't argue, but the thought popped up nonetheless: *How can you have faith in me when I keep messing up?* He did not give voice to this thought. Instead: "Thank you."

"You're welcome," Jules said. "And I have something for you. To help." He produced a tiny earpiece from his hand, holding it out for Brance.

Brance took it, staring at it. It was no larger than a hearing aid. "What is this for?"

"Stage direction. All the big stars use them for their concerts." Jules grinned. "I'll be right there, ready to talk you through any problems. I'll be watching the whole time."

Brance nodded, trying to get command of himself. "Okay. Right." He looked up, filled with a steely determination. "All right. I'm ready."

"Good, good," Jules said, heading for the door. "I'll send Gil for you when we're ready. I'm going to go say a few words, warm up the audience, y'know."

"I can go wait in the wings—" Brance started.

"No, no," Jules said, gently but firmly. "Meditate. Soothe yourself." He smiled. "I'll warm them up, get them

all set for you, and you come on out and knock 'em dead."
He winked. "You've got this."

Brance felt a curious chill in his blood as Jules shut the door.

He did have this...didn't he?

Chapter 75

Reed

"So." Yolanda Biddle had sidled up to me as soon as I was back to watching the protest unfolding at the gates next to the Lotsostuff entry. "Why did you stop it?"

A cool breeze blew across me, rattling the nearby chainlink fence, barely audible over the protests. I wasn't sure how they'd been chanting all day without their voices getting tired and scratchy, but they were still shouting, somehow. I looked at Yolanda, tempted to just blast myself into the air away from her again, but instead I asked, "What are you talking about?"

"Logan Mills built this place on the backs of his workers," Yolanda said, cradling her phone in front of her. Yep, this was an interview, and one I'd not given consent for. "Letting it get burned down would be justice. Why'd you stop it?"

"How does burning it down help these people keep their jobs?" I asked, eyes slitted. "How does it get them what they want?"

Yolanda shrugged like it didn't matter. "Burning it down sends a message to Logan Mills that he can't roll over people. He'd be forced to negotiate in good faith, finally."

"I don't know if he's negotiated in good faith up to now or not," I said with a shrug. Something about this woman annoyed me to the point I was willing to defend Mills, who I found grating at best. "And it's awfully presumptuous of you to say he built this place on their backs. It's not like he didn't pay them while they worked for him."

"Logan Mills is worth billions," Yolanda said, looking at me like I was dumb. "You don't see that money trickling down here, do you? And the wages he paid them? Theft. He treated them like dirt."

Every word she said was like needles in my skin, and again, I felt stirred to offer a defense of Logan Mills. Why? "They didn't have to take the jobs," I said. "And they actually pay better than any company around here for a starting wage, so there's that."

"A lot of the employees actually like Mills personally," Alan Kwon said, wandering over. He'd been taking pictures of the crowd, recording their latest chant. "Even some of the ones here. They just, y'know...want more money."

"Don't we all," I muttered.

"Seems to me seeing part of this place burn would have been a nice strike for the workers," Yolanda said, so haughtily. I looked her over; I doubted she'd done any warehouse work in her life. Her hands were perfectly manicured, lacking any calluses save for those caused by a pen and a keyboard.

Why did that annoy me? Was it her bearing? The fact

that she was lecturing, hectoring, and she didn't have a clue what it was like to run a business?

My eyelid fluttered in a twitch. Since when did I take up the cause of billionaire CEOs against their workers? I shook off the feeling, trying to get my concentration back on the protests. Ignoring Yolanda felt key to that.

"Would you not want the cops and firefighters to show up if someone burned your apartment?" Alan asked. Good. Maybe if he and Yolanda got into it, I could stay out of it.

"I didn't steal my stuff," Yolanda said.

"No," I said, launching myself in as a hot, red flare of anger welled up in me, "you make your living the honest reporter way—writing hack jobs against people like my sister that know are composed of absolute bullshit. I see you over there, Yolanda, thinking you're all righteous. Do you know how much damage you did to my family two thousand words at a time?" I let it all flow out. "Let me remind you: '*Sienna Nealon is a Deadly Threat to Our Way of Life, and the Cops Should Shoot Her On Sight.*' June of last year, I believe, is when you published it."

Yolanda looked like I'd planted a fist right in her face, though I would never do any such thing (but Sienna totally would). "It was...right at the time."

"It was a lie at the time," I said. "The evidence was out there. You weren't looking for it. Why is that?"

"I only have so much time and resources," Yolanda sputtered.

"Ahhh, so that's the reason for your absolute career malpractice," I said. "I noticed a lot of hot takes like that while Sienna was on the run." I smiled, a little viciously. "In about five or ten years, so-called 'reporters' like you, you clickbait farmers who do nothing but sit around a newsroom and dick around on the internet while you try to generate outrage to get eyeballs on your sites and stories? You're all going to be unemployed, because none of your insipid little websites or magazines or newspapers do anything but lose money. And I'm going to be sad, because it's unfortunate to witness the death of a once-vital profession like journalism due to the narcissistic shit-mongering of low-grade crapweasels like you. Learn to code, asshole, because you're going to be out of a job."

Alan made a little gasping noise, and his mouth was all sucked in itself. "Burn," he whispered. "Like a super ghost pepper burn, wowza."

"Well, whatever," Yolanda said, her heavily made-up face showing blush through the plaster of concealer. "We've been on her side lately, in case you missed it."

"How many articles did you guys write blasting her after that stupid thing went viral on Socialite?" I asked. "That she didn't even write?"

Yolanda flushed. "That's just business. Everyone online was dragging her for that. We couldn't stay out of it—"

"Yeah, you wouldn't want to go against the herd or anything," I said. "Show moral courage and swim against the consensus? Heaven forfend. That might mean you didn't get as many clicks that day!"

"What do you even care?" Yolanda asked, still clutching her phone in front of her. "Aren't you two fallen out, or whatever?"

"There's a difference between having a big side of beef between me and my sister," I said, "and not caring when the collective ADHD opinion columnist circle jerk takes aim at her."

And with that, I flew back up into the air, stewing. Yolanda shouted a question below me, but I ignored her, focusing on the overall clad protesters, floating in the weak February sunlight and letting the pleasant breeze lull me as I tuned out the dull roar of the crowd.

Chapter 76

Jules

"Don't let the kid out of his dressing room until I call for him," Jules said, brushing past Gil on his path toward the stage. The dressing room was close, but not too close to the wings.

"You got it, boss," Gil said. "Knock 'em dead."

"Maybe." All the smiles faded for a moment as Jules walked along the dim corridors of backstage, listening for the sound of his gathering out front. He could hear them, dimly. A peal of laughter here, someone's loud comment there. Backstage was a warren of corridors, a miniature labyrinth. Not too complicated, fortunately. He found the stage in moments, and strode out like he owned the place. Because for tonight, at least, he did.

"Welcome, welcome," Jules said, throwing his arms expansively wide. "So glad you all could attend our little event here. I know it's short notice, but I think it's past time we all had a little sit down."

"Why here, Jules?" Charlie Xiong called out. Charlie

was from the Triads. He had a reputation for not messing around. Evidence of his reputation had washed up in the Cumberland from time to time, which was a little bit messier than how most of them in the biz preferred to do things. For his part, Jules liked it when the people he wanted dead never turned up anywhere again. Not even a piece of them. "Kinda showy," Charlie said. There was a hoot of laughter from one of his minions.

"We all know it's 'First Class with No Class' for you, Charlie," Jules called back, grinning. "Naw, just kidding. Nothing but the best for you guys, that's how I'm playing this." He clapped his hands together, a little trick to get their attention. "I think you all know the general idea about why we're here. A little confabulation among those of us in the biz who might concerned about current events in Nashville. There's some desire, springing from this, I think, to unify in the face of a new challenge from out of town. We're all businessmen and women. All trying to capture our particular markets. Expand our revenues."

Jules looked out over his crowd. They were listening politely enough, but he had a little boundary to push here. Make himself understood to be a visionary. "We all deal with the same problems. The law sticking their nose in our business. Us, fighting back with lawyers. Putting the noses of their confidential informants out of joint—or in the river, in Charlie's case." Everyone laughed at that one but Charlie, and he just nodded.

"I want to submit an idea to you," Jules said, adopting a pensive pose. "What stops us—we few, we visionaries, we masters of our respective domains—from taking over the world?" He paused for effect. "Or at least Nashville?"

"The cops," someone called, prompting a hoot of agreement. What the hell, was there an owl in attendance?

"You're not wrong," Jules said, pointing out in the

direction the call had come from. He couldn't see who had said it, but it didn't matter. "See, in our respective busi-nesses, sometimes you got to get tough with people. Most of us like to keep that under cover, right? Quiet like. Except Charlie." Another hoot, definitely one of Charlie's people this time. "Society is a little tender for some of our purposes. That's an opportunity, right? They're weak. Easily intimidated. But it's a challenge because the cops, the TBI, even the FBI sometimes, they're out there protecting the people from our honest efforts. How are you supposed to get a protection racket going in this town if the cops are always out there knocking down your door every time you establish a customer?"

Jules clenched his fist. "We could take over everything, extend our reach well beyond its current, minuscule levels. But the violence it would require? Well, we all flinch from that. Too loud, we'd say. Too much attention. Not quiet like. We'd be gophers sticking our heads up and waiting for the hunters—or Sienna Nealon, apparently—to pop it off, am I right?" Of course he was right.

"But what if there was a way to do the violence," Jules said, "where it was deniable?" He paused. No one inter-rupted. "Gunshots are loud. Beatings leave bruises and scars. Surveillance tapes show what we do, what our mooks do, at least. But what if there was a way to put the fear of God in these people we want to do business with...and it didn't leave those kind of marks? In fact, what if it took care of the surveillance video problem for us and left us with a kind of plausible deniability our lawyers love? Would that be of interest to you?"

"Yeah. A flying car would be nice, too," Larry shouted, and boy, did they laugh at that.

"All I'm saying—" Jules kept his smile even "—is if someone could unite us and deliver that kind of business growth...why, there'd be a big piece of pie for all of us. Expand our revenue picture, give us control of things we never dreamed of having control over."

"And you're going to do that, I suppose?" Larry called again. He waved a hand dismissively. "Come on, Jules. Back to the strip club. You're high on your own product. Or mine—" Larry grinned "—since we all know mine's the best stuff in town." That produced another laugh, slightly more uneasy. These were competitive folks.

"You guys just give it a thought for a minute," Jules said, keeping up that grin. "Consider it. I've got some entertainment for you while you think it over. Okay?" He looked sideways offstage, wondering if Gil had gotten the message.

A moment later, Brance appeared in the wings. He'd gotten the message and obeyed. Perfect.

The mobsters were talking among themselves. "Gentlemen, lady...I give you...Brance."

And Jules walked off the stage to tepid applause as Brance took his place. He didn't envy the kid at the start, because these guys probably thought Jules had brought some of his strippers, but that was okay. He'd win them over in the end.

One way or another.

Chapter 77

Brance

It was his warmest and yet coldest introduction, being really the only one he'd ever gotten. Still, Brance walked out onto the Ryman stage with none of the thunderous applause he might have hoped for, but, then, there were probably only forty or so people—almost all of them guys—out in the audience. In his nervousness, Brance hadn't even remembered who this audience was he was performing for. Probably some talent scouts or something, someone Jules was trying to impress.

On wobbly legs, Brance stood in front of the microphone stand. He knew Leo was working the sound and light board, and past the stage lights, which were rising as the theater lights dimmed, the audience faded out beyond his view. Their conversations were audible, though. And hardly flattering.

"I thought Jules's entertainment would be prettier. And leggier."

"I don't need to see him take anything off, thanks. Jules

doesn't need to be in charge of anything if this is his idea of a good time."

Brance sucked it up. He'd show them. "My name is Brance, and tonight I'm going to be performing 'Is It Cold In Here' by Joe Diffie."

Someone booed. That was okay. Brance took a breath, and the music started.

Leo knew at least a little of what he was doing. The track was the background music, steel guitar kicking in, but with the vocals turned down somehow. That was good. Perfect, in fact. They'd rehearsed—briefly—so he could hear what he'd be doing, but not long enough to make him too much more jittery than he already was.

Control. He just needed to control it.

Here it came. Brance launched into the first verse, and the chatter before the stage cut off like he'd silenced them personally. He suppressed a smile. His voice had done that. Not the screeching, wailing, inhuman voice, either, because he wasn't making that.

No, it was his natural voice. He'd shut them up by sheer virtue of his performance.

He could do this.

Launching into the run-up to the chorus, Brance closed his eyes.

And gave it everything he had.

Chapter 78

Jules

T he earplugs did a fine job of tuning out the singing, Jules reflected. He stood in the wings next to Gil, watching Brance as much as the audience. He had a little bud of a microphone in his hand that would pipe directly to Brance's earpiece when he needed to, but he'd have to step back a little farther from the stage, maybe all the way into the back, to keep the feedback from blowing up Brance's ears. Sensitive little bitch would whine about that, too.

"He's doing a pretty good job," Gil said. Jules lifted his headphones to hear the idiot.

Then Jules nodded, frowning. He'd give it a little more time before he did his thing.

The chorus gave way to the second verse, and a small burst of tepid applause broke, spontaneously, from some of the audience, surprising Jules. The kid did have a pretty good voice and all, but surely they didn't think this was the actual show?

They must have, though, because from his position at the side of the stage, Jules could see Charlie and his crew getting up, one of the bodyguards hesitating, like he wanted to stay. Charlie wanted to leave, clearly. Seen enough, he supposed.

Then it was time to give it hell.

Jogging back behind the stage, Jules flipped on the microphone. He huddled next to a potted fern, and said, "That's great, kid. You're really knocking them dead." A pause for effect. "Think about how proud your mom and *dad* would be, seeing you up here achieving your dream like this."

Then he flicked the switch off on the microphone and waited, straining to hear through his earplugs.

It didn't take very long.

Chapter 79

Brance

"Think about how proud your mom and *dad* would be, seeing you up here achieving your dream like this."

Jules's words cut through Brance's concentration like a bone saw starting up. He was deep in the second verse, running up to the chorus, letting loose with his voice——

He could feel that waver of uncertainty run through him. A little emotional tremor. He'd been so focused on the song, delivering the song, making the song sing. Why had Jules gone and brought up his parents?

Now he felt...off. He warbled a wrong note. Then another one, trying to bring himself back on track.

Something was wrong, though. He was on the right note, he could feel it.

There was something else, something beyond——

Screaming.

No, it couldn't be. It was in his head. He'd just hold this note and it'd be fine.

This was his dream, dammit. He had to hold this note.

All day, if need be. He'd show these talent agents or scouts or whoever they were what he could do.

Think of the dream. He tried to, but somehow the thought of his dad laughing at him when Brance told him he was moving to Nashville echoed in his ear, loud and high and cold and cruel, and terribly, terribly off key.

Chapter 80

Jules

Holding his hands over his ears, Jules still felt his eyes twitch a little. The plugs helped keep the worst effects of Brance's singing voice off of him, but they were hardly perfect, and it still rang in his head like a shrill bell going off ceaselessly.

Gil didn't look to be having much better of a time. He was holding his hands over his earmuffs, cringing. It was loud, it was agonizing.

It was perfect.

Jules looked out, past the stage lights, over the crowd. Some of them were writhing. Some were screaming, he was pretty sure, though it was hard to tell over Brance's caterwauling. No one was upright and walking. Charlie and his entourage were visible up the aisle. They'd almost made it to the door, but not quite, and now they were forced to stay, squirming in the aisle, regardless of what they'd wished.

He could just barely keep from rubbing his hands

together as Jules watched it all unfolding. He was trying to gauge how far he wanted to push this thing. He wanted to make his impression, but didn't want to kill anyone.

This was probably about enough. Jules stepped out onto the stage and made the gesture to cut it across his neck. Leo was supposed to be watching.

He was. The sound system died—not that it was transmitting the deathly sound—and the lights on stage went out, the audience lights rising instantly to full brightness.

The sudden shock of light caught Brance's attention, and he stopped singing, opening his eyes. Kid sang with his eyes closed a lot. He really got into the emotion of things. Jules might have found it admirable, if it had come from a singer who didn't put their audience in indescribable pain, seemingly at random.

But it wasn't random at all, and Jules had figured that out. And he found the eyes closed thing very useful.

"Okay, okay," he said, flipping on the microphone. Leo had routed it over the loudspeakers, so he piped in across the theater. "That's enough."

Brance was standing in the middle of the stage like he'd busted during the song. His mouth was slightly open, his eyes were fixed in place, starting to get a little red like he was holding back a good cry. He probably was, but Jules didn't have time for that now. He pushed the microphone tip into his shirt and said, "Brance—go wait for me backstage. I'll clean this up." He tried to make his smile reassuring rather than predatory, which was definitely how he was feeling right now.

"I—I just—" Brance started.

Jules wasn't in the mood to put up with his bullshit, and he couldn't show weakness now. "Brance. Backstage." He laid down that law like a parent of a mouthy teenager.

Brance buckled, because of course he did. Looking like

he'd just seen war—such a little bitch—he tottered off, passing Jules with a misty look in his eyes.

Jules waited, watching, making sure Gil got Brance the hell out of here. He turned the corner and Jules felt comfortable at least opening up his speech. His audience was definitely still captive; none of them were going anywhere anytime soon. None of them were even able to stand, by the looks of it. "Well. Let's hear it for my boy Brance. Wasn't he something?"

No clapping. Good. That meant everyone was picking up what he was laying down here. Or they were deaf. Hopefully not completely.

He waited a few more seconds. He didn't want to say too much where little bitch Brance could hear him. "I think you're all starting to get the point here." No answer from below. He could see them; some were bleeding from the ears, probably struggling to hear him. They wouldn't be walking out; he'd have to have them carried. The faces below him, usually so composed, so serious.

Yeah, there was fear there. These were men who'd been in gunfights. Men who'd fought the law, even sometimes. Done prison stints and faced all that entailed.

But they'd never had their eardrums blown out from one guy singing on a stage, and in spite of the fact metahumans had come crashing into reality out of the comic pages however many years ago, most of the people in this room had never even passed one on the street, let alone had one come close to blowing up their head in a concert performance.

"Here's how I see things," Jules said, starting to pace across the front of the stage. "Nashville is a big town. Big enough for all of us. Big enough we can do one of two things from here—one, get along. Increase the size of the pie, and we all take a bigger piece as a consequence." He shared a grin with them. "There are things we can do with this power at our disposal that none of us could do before. Things we can get away with, things we can solidify control with, things we can reach our hands out for, past the cops, that we never could have without it." He slapped his palm on his chest. "I can bring that to you. All you have to do...is unite under my banner. We'll be able to avoid the heat in a way we never could before. Go below their radar in ways they can't prove. Keep people afraid in ways they can't describe, that maybe aren't even against the law." He smiled. "Because the law, even after years of trying to prepare—they ain't ready for this. And if we move fast, they won't be ready for us. We will create a whole new market. A whole new world."

"What's the alternative?" someone—Charlie, he thought—called out from the audience.

"I'm glad you asked," Jules said, because hell if he would have advertised a second point if he didn't intend to use it. "Option two is that you don't get on board with this program. You decide...'Hey, that Jules, he's full of shit. Hell if I'm going to go along to get along, even for a bigger piece of the action.'"

Jules just waited a second, smiling like the shark he was. "Maybe you think...'I can whack Jules.' But lemme tell you something—I'm going to be a lot harder to get than you think. And when I come back at you?" He shook his head, still smiling. "What the cops find of you? You'll have died screaming—just like this." He waved a hand in front of the stage. "Hours will feel like days, am I right? Days will feel like years. I don't know how long you'll last, but I'll make it go for a long time. It's a little different than what Charlie does—" he waved out to Charlie in the audience "—but I promise...it'll be unique in how it feels for you."

"Boss," Leo's voice broke over the loudspeaker, "sirens coming from outside."

Shit. Jules hadn't anticipated that, but it had always been a possibility some annoying neighbor would dial 911 when they heard the screeching out on the street. "Gentle-men," Jules said, "I think you all should seriously consider my proposal. I'll expect your answer within...oh, a day." His expression darkened. "After that? Well..." He made a hand motion beside his ear. "You'll be *hearing* from me."

With that, he dropped the mic, and off the stage he went.

Chapter 81

Sienna

"Gunshot microphones in downtown Nashville picked up some sort of sonic anomaly from the Ryman Auditorium," Chandler said, voice crackling over my cell phone. "Metro is on the way, but I figured I'd give you a shout in case you wanted to run down there."

I sat on a stool, live music playing behind me. There was a band on the stage; I was down on Broadway. Again. The lights were low, some people were dancing out on the floor between me. The bartender was looking at me with stern disapproval for answering my cell phone in the middle of the show, I assumed. Like anyone could hear me in the middle of all this.

"Got it," I said, smacking my lips together. I'd kind of been enjoying the atmospherics of this place. It had been a long day, and boy, did I feel it. After dropping off Chandler and getting some dinner, I'd found myself drawn here like a moth to a big ol' bonfire. The stress had been eating me alive, and I was still ignoring stupid Chalke's calls. Not that she'd made one in the last couple hours. "I'll head that way," I said, coming to a decision.

Well. Two decisions, really.

"Heading that way myself," Chandler said. "Save some for me." And he hung up.

Save some of what, I wondered? With a slow exhalation, I stood up, leaving my stool behind. I gave one last, longing look at the shot of whiskey that was poured and waiting on the bar. The one I'd been contemplating, deeply, for the last twenty minutes.

And then I walked away, leaving that addiction behind in favor of my other—maybe slightly less healthy—one.

Chapter 82

Reed

I sensed that avoiding Yolanda's annoying ass was going to be a constant endeavor, so I stayed airborne for quite a while, riding the breezes across the clear blue Middle Tennessee sky for several hours as the sun started to move toward the horizon. The sky had picked up a pink cast, the clouds tingeing with its fading glare, giving me a hell of a view of the impending sunset.

Keeping the natural breeze down so that the falling temperatures didn't get to me wasn't difficult. My jacket kept the very slight chill at bay, and the waning sunlight kept things warm enough, around seventy degrees, that I didn't feel too cold.

Below me, it looked as though the protesters were feeling the prolonged exposure to coolness, especially as night started to fall. Jackets began to come out, heavy ones, too. I chuckled to myself, thinking none of them would have been prepared for a Minnesota winter. It had been twelve degrees when I'd left, and we were in the bitterest part of the season.

I caught a wave of motion beneath me, Theresa signaling to me from the edge of the crowd. I slowly drifted down, not wanting her to think I was at her instant disposal. When I got to about ten feet, I asked, "What's up?"

"Just wanted to talk," she said. Her bodyguards, Angelo and Big Bert, ever in attendance, were hanging back a bit, on the edge of the crowd. Both were watching me with their usual level of suspicion. I wondered if they'd appointed themselves her watchers, or if she'd somehow convinced them to do it. The whole thing reeked of a grandeur I didn't see in attendance here. Lotsostuff had maybe five hundred employees, and only a hundred were present at the protest at any given time. I'd yet to see any potential threat to Theresa other than the Murfreesboro cops, and they sure didn't seem dangerous. "About the fire, earlier."

I nodded. "Okay. Talk."

She twisted her lips a little. "What do you think happened there?"

I couldn't pass up the chance to be sarcastic. "Well, when an object becomes heated to its flash point, it catches fire—" It was a family trait.

"I know that much, smartass. But who do you think started it?"

I stared down at her, deciding how best to answer. Tired of being here, tired of floating endlessly in the air above a protest that was going nowhere, where almost nothing other than an attempt at arson had happened, I settled on leading with the brutal truth. Like a hatchet flung between the eyes. "Well, I'm about sixty/forty on it being Logan Mills or your people responsible."

When I said "Logan Mills," she'd brightened into a smile, but when I'd dropped the hammer by mentioning it could be her people, it had turned into a scowl immediately. "Why would you go and think something crazy like that?"

I chuckled. "You're leading a protest that's pushed up against the cops in an unfriendly way a few times. Not because your people hate cops, but because the cops are standing between you and your object of ire, the Lotsostuff warehouse. I don't need an active imagination to guess that if the cops weren't here, your people's intentions for the warehouse wouldn't involve giving it a nice cleaning and maybe some paint retouches."

All her good humor had vanished like the sun over the horizon. "I can't believe you think we'd do that."

I shrugged. "I'm sure Logan Mills would say much the same about my suspicions of him, and hey—I gave you the benefit of the doubt. You're the forty percent."

"We just want fair wages and fair working conditions," she said, still gazing up at me irefully. "Now, we got every right to protest—"

"No argument there." I tried not to be patronizing, but...I was so tired of hanging out overhead like some sort of avenging angel who wasn't actually doing any avenging. "But like I said, if the cops weren't here, or I wasn't, I don't believe for a minute it'd be a totally peaceful protest. Your people have some anger issues."

"We got good reason."

"Also known as 'motive,'" I said. "And people in crowds? Not known for their calm and measured approach to things."

"Well," she said, clearly trying to scale back the anger, "I think I know what you ought to be doing right now."

"This should be good," I muttered under my breath. "Please, do tell."

She licked her lips, then beckoned me closer. As though anyone could hear me over the dull roar of the protest. They didn't seem as loud as they had first thing in the morning. Maybe they were wearing out. Still, I flew a little closer, and she said, "I think you ought to fly up there and talk to Logan Mills."

"Oh?"

"Yep," she said. "I've known Logan a long time. He may seem all forbidding and implacable now, but I knew him when he was knee-high to a cricket. You can put the fear of God in that boy, and he'll probably tell you everything about what he did."

I frowned. "You mean...?"

She looked around. "I bet you give him a little wind blast or whatever, you could get him to confess to burning his own warehouse."

I nodded slowly, not bothering to explain that I'd had him pinned to the ground earlier and he hadn't exactly looked like he was breaking. "Tell me, because I'm curious —why do you think he'd burn his own business?"

"Ain't it obvious?" She favored me with a crooked smile. "The insurance money. We done shut him down. But he's still greedy, and he don't want to make a deal. He can't find enough scabs in this town to run the place without us, so he burns part of it down, collects the insurance. More money for him."

I raised an eyebrow at her, because she'd just reminded me of something. "One problem with that. The fire was started by a metahuman."

Theresa stared at me dully. "So?"

"So there's no insurance money," I said. "'Acts of gods.' Insurance companies don't pay for damages caused by metahumans." I shrugged. "So if he flooded and burned his own warehouse thinking he'd make a buck? He's probably not going to, at least if his insurance company takes my word for it on the meta with the fire, and draws the logical conclusion from the mysterious flood outside of the flood plain."

That clearly had not occurred to her, because she paused, thinking it over. "Well, that don't seem right."

"And yet it is," I said.

"Well, he must have thought he could get away with it, then," she said, and it was a little fun to watch her try to scramble to adjust her logic to fit with her preferred conclusion.

"Maybe," I said, "but honestly, I think my sixty/forty just switched to the other direction." I gave her a tight smile as I flew back up, because I sensed that conversation was going to go nowhere fast after I'd dropped that bomb on her.

Chapter 83

Jules

"That was a mic drop moment," Jules said to himself as he stepped into the wings. The sirens were blaring in the distance, and he had a little urgency in his step. Needed to get out of here, with Brance, before the cops showed up.

How had they found him? Hell if he knew. Maybe it wasn't so muffled in here as he might have hoped. Busybodies were gonna busybody, he figured. Concerning himself with how the cops had found him didn't concern him so much as making sure he was poised to survive their arrival.

Turning the corner into backstage, he almost plowed into Brance. "Hey," he said, not slowing down. They needed to move, after all. He reached out for the kid's arm, intent on snagging it like hooking a line—

And Brance pulled away from him.

Jules paused, stopped. The kid's eyes were red. Had this little bitch been crying? Of course he had. "What?"

Jules asked, trying to home in to what the kid's concerns were. Give him an opening to get his bitch-ness out.

"You did this on purpose," Brance said, and his voice was choked and hoarse.

Gil lingered behind the kid, shrugging. "He wouldn't go to his dressing room like I told him."

Jules kept from blowing up at Gil. *And you couldn't make him?* Who was the little bitch here, again? "Listen, kid—" Jules started.

Brance stepped away from him, making it quite obvious how he was feeling. "You used me."

"Kid, we all use each other," Jules said, holding up a hand to calm him, like warning off a dangerous animal. "I was going to do some good for you, you did something for me—it's a medium of exchange."

"You didn't tell me you wanted me for what my voice could do," Brance said softly. Oh, boy, did this kid sound betrayed. Like Jules had kicked him square in the balls and laughed while doing so. Which would be fun.

"I actually did," Jules said. "You got a hell of a voice, kid. You can make a lot of money with it."

"Your way?" Brance croaked. "By hurting people?"

There was a strain pushed onto Jules as the sirens closed in, got louder. "There's more than one way to skin a cat. And you gotta work with what you got. You? You got a hell of a voice. I mean that on multiple levels. You sing good, and you got that other thing you can do—"

"Hurt people," Brance said, and boy, was it obvious the little bitch was feeling it right in his soft little heart.

"Those are gangsters," Jules said, pointing back to the stage. "The roughest, the toughest. Nasty bastards. They know the game. You didn't hurt them worse than they've ever been hurt before. You just did it in a different way that shocked them because they weren't psychologically prepared for it. If you had to pick an audience to hurt, they were the ones, because they at least deserve it."

"I didn't want to hurt anyone," Brance whispered.

"But you did," Jules said. "You've hurt a lot of people, kid. Innocent people who just wanted to have a drink and listen to some music. You were holding so tight to your dreams, you didn't care who got hurt in the process. You're only mad now because you feel like I didn't tell you the whole truth. Which I didn't. For your own good, I might add."

"How is this good for me...?" Brance asked.

"This is a path," Jules said. "You want to be a singer? I can help make you a star." In the criminal underworld, anyway. "It's real simple. You scratch my back, I scratch yours. I get what I want, I have the money and the means to help you get what you want." Jules gave him that smile. "I mean, look...you already sang at the Ryman and you've known me two days, kid. Imagine where you could be in a year."

"Yeah," Brance said hoarsely. "I could be in jail."

What. A. Little. Bitch.

"You're being dramatic," Jules said. The sirens were getting closer. "Come on, we need to go." He reached for Brance's arm again.

Brance staggered back from him like Jules's hands were on fire and he feared getting burned. "I'm not going anywhere with you."

Jules's face was burning. He'd had it up to here with this kid's whiny bullshit. "Gil..."

Gil came in on Brance hard, snatching him into a headlock and anchoring that arm around the kid's throat. The kid struggled, jerking Gil around the hallway, fighting like a demon against him.

"Come on, kid, just go with it," Jules said. "Let us get

you out of here."

"I—don't—want to—go—anywhere—with you!" Brance said, ramming Gil into the wall and making a hell of a hole. That was going to come out of Jules's security deposit.

Jules watched for another second and then he just lost it. He swept in on the kid as Gil battled with him, riding him like a cowboy on a pissed-off horse, and Jules slipped in, raised his hand up—

He cracked Brance across his bitch face so hard that it popped loudly, echoing down the hallway. Brance's eyes bugged out from the impact, from shock that someone would have the audacity to smack his bitch ass. He stood there for a second, mouth moving up and down fruitlessly at Jules.

"Listen to me, you little shit," Jules said, keeping his hand raised, primed to deliver another slap. "I have done a lot of work getting your stupid self out of trouble. I'm not asking for much, but you owe me—"

Brance opened his mouth and something came shooting out that made it feel like Jules had stepped out in front of a bus. He went tumbling down the hall, legs flipping over his head, bending in ways he hadn't since he was a young man.

Jules came to rest on the hard floor, knees shellacked as they slammed into a small riser of stairs. Blood dripped down his forehead, and he rose—just for a second—in time to see Brance ram Gil into the wall again, then throw him off.

"Don't...kid...don't..." Jules managed to get out.

Brance looked at him for a second, then bolted down the hallway. In the distance, Jules could hear him bust through a door, but that was all before he succumbed to the raging pain in his head.

Chapter 84

Sienna

"Got a real interesting mess here," Captain Parsons said, walking me into the Ryman. I'd passed the cordon already thrown up after running the whole way to the auditorium. I had a feeling I wasn't going to get there in time to do any sort of car chase, and downtown Nashville was packed solid with rush hour traffic anyway, so I'd showed up sans car.

"Interesting how?" I asked, still idly thinking about that shot of whiskey I'd left back at the bar on Broadway. I'd come awfully close to kissing my sobriety goodbye after a solid year, and I wasn't entirely convinced that I'd made the right choice.

"This place was rented out for a private show tonight," Parsons said, trying to keep a smile off his face and failing. "Now, we just got here and finished sweeping the place, but here's what I can tell you: the audience?" The smile broke out. "Local mafiosos of every race, ethnicity and creed,

362

from La Cosa Nostra to the Russians to the Triads—and their bodyguards."

I frowned. Why the hell would the heads of the local underworld all meet at a historic auditorium where our perp had been hitting his high notes?

Parsons waved me on, and I followed. Paramedics were swarming down on the floor stage, tending to a whole mess of dudes, mostly. I saw one woman in the bunch, but that was it. The rest were burly guys who tended toward the ugly, not a pretty face in the bunch. What was it about ugly work that attracted ugly people, ugly souls?

"So these guys are frequent flyers for you?" I asked, making my way down the aisle.

"Yep," Parsons said. "We've arrested them all at some point, or connected them to something. Not an innocent one in the bunch." He waved me toward the stage. "This might be the most interesting thing of all, though. Follow me."

He climbed up on the stage and offered me a hand, but I hopped it before he even got it proffered, clearing it with a jump that made one of Lebron's dunks look like he was hopping over a stone in the road. I came out of it in a soft landing, too, and gestured toward the wings, indicating age should go before beauty.

"Have you considered the Olympics as an alternative career?" Parsons asked with a smirk. "Seems to me you'd walk away with the gold—and I do mean walk, because you don't look like you strained hard to do that."

"The IOC is really struggling on how to handle metas in the Olympics," I said. "I'd suggest we be banned, but no one wants to hear from me."

"Oh?"

"Yeah, unless you want to destroy the ability of normal humans to compete," I said, ducking behind the stage with him. "I'd like to see any of you non-powered people try to outrun me. I'd leave Usain Bolt in the dust without even breaking a sweat. And I'm not exactly a hard trainer, you know? I prefer the couch to my morning run by a factor of miles. Which is why I don't run that many."

"Interesting, interesting," he said. "You should be signed up for a billion endorsement deals by now."

We rounded a corner and found a guy sitting on the steps, a couple Metro PD officers for company. He was older, grey, running toward balding, but wrinkled and severe. He was watching everything, and caught sight of me immediately, though he played it cool, holding a bloody bandage to his forehead.

"Jules," Parsons said with quite a bit less enthusiasm than I'd imagine he'd have shown if he'd stepped in dog shit, "can I just say how surprised I am to find a lowlife like you in this gathering of esteemed shit piles?"

"You're really busting my balls here, Captain," Jules said, looking up from beneath the ice pack. He pulled it back to examine it, and there was a stain of red across his forehead that looked like he'd taken a hard landing on something, or maybe gotten neatly sliced by a knife. He pretended to notice me now, giving me a casual once-over.

I wasn't entirely sure, but in Jules, I thought I might have encountered one of those oh-so-rare smart criminals. So rare. Not genius, but a cut above your average moron who grabs a knife and waves it at unsuspecting victims for fun and profit.

"Better than busting your head," I said, giving Jules an excuse to look right at me, which he did. "What happened here?" I pointed at his forehead. "Cut yourself shaving? Those unibrows are a real hazard."

"Thing about getting older, you get stray hairs in the funniest places," Jules said. Cool customer.

"Speaking of, lemme draw your attention to your nostrils," I fired back.

"So much ball busting," Jules said with a sigh. "What do you people want from me? I'm clearly the victim here." He waved the bloody bandage in front of us.

Captain Parsons let out a light snort of derision. I just busted out laughing.

Jules didn't take it personally, but he acted like he did. "The sympathy. You see this?" He looked over his shoulder at the mook he'd gotten caught with. The guy looked like he'd been run through the ringer. Drywall dust on his suit jacket suggested that the indentations in the wall around us had been made by him being shoved into them, repeatedly, throughout the hallway. Looked like someone had a wrestling match in here, and this guy had lost.

"Where's the singer, Jules?" Parsons asked.

"We tried to stop him," Jules said, almost sincerely. Almost. "You see this? We were doing our Samaritanly duty—"

"That's not a word," I said.

"—and he just linebackers over us like one of the Titans," Jules said. "Hey, we tried."

"You get a good look at him?" Parsons asked.

Jules shrugged, made a face. "It's dark, I don't see so well these days. He was on the young side."

I stared at the guy over his shoulder, and the mook started to squirm just a bit. His profile looked familiar—like he might just have been the guy that had picked up Brance in that alley. He looked at me, looked like he wanted to say something.

Jules shot him a look and he clammed up before he even got started. I just smiled at him—my best predatory smile. I hope it made him shit his pants in worry. "How'd you happen to be here?" I asked. "At this time?"

365

"We rented the place for a corporate event," Jules said. "We're a growing company, and we were having a team building exercise."

I shared a look with Parsons, then looked back to Jules. "That's so interesting. What's the name of your company? 'Scumbag, Inc'?"

"Hah, very funny," Jules said. "I'm a legitimate businessman. I own a club here in town called Bones."

"It's very reputable," Parsons said. "You can get a lap dance, a martini and a sirloin there for all the money in your wallet plus a missing ATM card." He looked like he was suppressing a smile. "Allegedly."

"I'm glad you added that last word there," Jules said, "because otherwise my lawyer was going to put some teeth marks in your ass."

"Your lawyer is an ass-biter?" I asked. "Figures he'd be a pit bull. Like lawyer, like client and all that?"

Jules smiled, like I'd just paid him some great compliment. "I am a bit of a pit bull, now that you mention it."

"Really?" I faked a frown, surveying him. "You look more like an ankle-biter to me. Strictly small-time. A wannabe Tony Soprano whose aspirations of middling glory never quite came to pass." I let a slow smile spread across my face. "How'd you get hooked up with Brance?"

"I don't know no Brance," Jules said, and he was a reasonably convincing liar—if I hadn't already known he was lying. "I just tried to stop that singer after he assaulted us."

"And how'd he come to assault you?" I asked.

"He came busting in here during our meeting," Jules said. "Took to the stage like he was Aretha Franklin or something, flouncing like mad. Knocked the audience dead. Or close. I guess we were lucky."

"I don't know about that," I said. "He hasn't killed anyone—yet."

"Felt like he was going to kill me," Jules said. "He opened his mouth at me and it felt like a piston got driven into my chest." He slapped the stairs he was sitting on. "Knocked me over here."

"One sympathizes," I said, not really sympathetic but remembering the mule kick feeling when Brance had used his voice to pound me. "Say, you wouldn't know anything about the Nissan Sentra that picked this guy up last night?"

"Nope," Jules said. Liiiiiiiiar.

I looked over his shoulder at the mook. "I was actually talking to him. He looks more like the driver type."

"I don't know nothing about that," the minion said. He was less convincing than Jules.

"Okay," I said, smiling. "Well, this has been enlightening. Any idea where this Brance would go?"

"No idea," Jules said, shrugging broadly. "I'm just happy I got out with my life, personally. Hope I never meet this guy again."

I couldn't help but keep smiling. "I wonder how many people have said that after meeting you?"

"I don't want to talk to you no more," Jules said, waving me away.

"Thanks for your help, Jules," Parsons said as he steered me away. Once we were safely out of earshot, he asked, "What do you think?"

"He's in this up to his neck," I said.

"Yeah, that's the feeling I got, too. What's his play?"

I thought about it for a moment before answering. "Seems to me if you've got your entire criminal underworld pulled together and this is the guy doing the pulling, and then they get hit by Brance? This was a move. By your small-timer over there. Which would explain why he doesn't have blood coming out of his ears and why his muscle got run into every wall over there. They tried to wrangle Brance and somehow it went wrong after the fact. Brance skips out, leaving them stuck explaining what happened."

"You don't think this Brance could have run for it?" Parsons asked. "With Jules's approval?"

I shook my head. "That fight scene wasn't staged. Brance got mad at Jules and nailed him with his full singing voice. It hits like a meta punch, sent Jules flying. Then he tried to get that big bastard off his back, hence the man-sized indentations in the wall. After that, he busts through the emergency exit and voila, disappears into the city."

Parsons nodded along. "So what was Jules trying to orchestrate here? Just a power move? Assert dominance?"

"Maybe," I said. "Unite the underworld kind of play? Under his leadership?"

"If it was intimidation, they certainly looked intimidated."

I nodded. "Even for scary guys like these, metas are still a new ballgame. Having a guy disrupt your ability to hold a coherent thought while a sonic shredder disables your senses? That's gotta be disorienting even to the seemingly fearless and experienced mafioso. Yeah, I think he tried to intimidate them into something, put the power play on them for his purposes, and it backfired after the fact. The question is..." And this really was the kicker, the one I was going to need to figure out: "What happened to Brance?"

Chapter 85

Brance

Brance had headed back to his apartment, because where else was there to go?

That was the problem he was facing now. Same problem he'd faced after Mercy's Faithless, really, or, to a lesser extent, after that first night in Screamin' Demons. He was stuck out on a branch by his lonesome, hanging out here alone.

Jules had betrayed him. His voice had betrayed him.

His dad...hell, he'd just been the first to turn on him.

"I gotta get out of here," he muttered, throwing his stuff in a bag. He didn't have that much, didn't want that much, really. He was packing on rote instinct alone.

The dream had died. He'd sung on stage of the Ryman, the Mother Church of country music.

And he'd screwed it up.

Bag packed, he hit the door. Looked around one last time at his furniture, which was near ruin, worthless, like his life. At the small number of personal effects he had but couldn't carry in the bag. Nothing he'd miss. A family photo from a few years before he'd left. Brother and sister in riding gear, Brance in...

Well, no one cared what Brance was in, did they?

"I just wanted you to hear me," he whispered to the empty room, then shut the door without locking it. The police would probably be along soon.

Jules had used him. That stung. His voice had turned on him. That was worse.

Sienna frigging Nealon was after him. That was maybe *the* worst of all.

Time to go. To leave Nashville behind. He fumbled with his keys as he walked to his vehicle. His old truck hadn't been serviced in a while. He'd been deferring maintenance, thinking if he hit it big, he'd just buy something new.

Now he was never going to hit it big. But he was going to have to get out of here, that was for sure.

But where to? He shuddered as he contemplated going north. Anything in the vague direction of Wyoming was out, as far as he was concerned.

South, then. Key West, maybe? He'd heard people talk about the Florida Panhandle, too. Lots of people here liked to vacation on 30A.

Throwing his stuff in the passenger seat, Brance wiped the fatigue from his eyes. It had been a long day. Long couple days, actually, but he needed to get the hell out of Dodge now, not later.

So he started his truck, listened to the choking sound of the engine until it caught, and threw it into gear. "Southbound" by Sammy Kershaw came on the country classics station his dial was tuned to. How appropriate, Brance thought, as he turned his vehicle toward I-40. He'd catch 65 just south of the city and be in Florida by morning—if he could stay awake that long.

Chapter 86

Reed

Hanging out waiting for something to happen as the protest began to peter out felt like a losing endeavor. I actually had felt like a loser all day, and maybe part of yesterday, too, given how unlike a normal case this had been. Usually I chased a criminal, mostly serious ones, but here I was performing picket duty for protesters, and knowing I was around had taken some of the gusto out of them. They hadn't even edged up on the cops as aggressively as they had the day before.

No chases, no evidence, no obvious criminal other than the guy who'd set fire to a (mostly) unoccupied warehouse. I was having trouble mustering enthusiasm for being outraged, even though that Gavrikov had putatively done something violent. I mean, technically it could have endangered lives, if I took Logan Mills at his word that he wasn't the arsonist. He had, after all, run right toward the fire and into a section of warehouse where the sprinklers and alarm had been purposefully disabled. That could have resulted in his death.

Still, people running into raging fires was an abnormal set of actions. Most people stayed away from danger.

Then there was the flood, which had happened when the warehouse was closed, not a soul around for the night. The crimes that had been presented here were a hell of a lot closer to victimless than the usual sort, and despite Alan Kwon's fine defense of property rights earlier, I was seriously wishing I was somewhere else.

My mind kept drifting up to Nashville, and I wondered how Sienna was doing.

I was edging toward saying, "To hell with all this," and at least calling it a night if not abandoning the case altogether when I saw a familiar figure standing near the back of the crowd.

Harry.

That asshole.

As soon as he knew I'd spotted him, he sauntered away from the crowd. He crossed the highway and entered a small grove of trees out of sight of the protesters, suggesting to me that he wanted to have a conversation, but not be seen.

What the hell, I wasn't doing anything else. After giving him a couple minutes to disappear into the woods, I conjured up a wind and let it blow me in that direction. Not too fast, but fast enough Yolanda wasn't going to catch me.

Once I was out of sight of the protest, I dropped altitude into a gap in the woods. Unsurprisingly, I found Mr. Sees-the-Future waiting for me right there, leaning against a tree, arms crossed, examining his nails.

"All right, go ahead," he said as I fluttered to the ground.

That caught me off balance. "Go ahead with what?"

"Get all those bad feelings out, champ," Harry said, still studying his fingernails. "You might want to hurry, though. That annoying Flashforce reporter is heading this way, and if you yell for too long, she'll find us in about, oh...four and a half minutes, give or take. I'll have to take off before that, because I really don't need to be caught on film with you. It'd put a major kink in your sister's plans."

I clenched my teeth. "You want to know what I hate?"

"Besides people who don't use their blinkers?" Harry asked. "And ones who talk during movies? Oh, and let's not forget—people who play online shooters with their headset mic on but who don't actually talk to their team-mates? They just sort of sit there and have conversations with the people in their house, sharing all sorts of personal details you could easily live without—while their team loses from lack of coordination."

I blinked, taken aback. "Yes, okay, I dislike all those things."

Harry grinned, and I'm sure he knew I found it infuri-ating. "So we're in agreement there. But yes, I know what you were going to say—you're so very unhappy with me. If you were any less pleased with me right now, I'd be on your enemies list, somewhere between people who reach the front of a fast food line and still don't know what they want to order, and people who film themselves licking food and then put it back on grocery store shelves. For fame."

The fact that Harry was preying on my dislike of people who did...well, all those things...only added to my irritation with him. It almost felt like he was reading my mind, though really he was essentially just plucking them out of other realities where I'd vocalized my feelings about them. "Yeah. All that. But—"

"You're unhappy because you think I'm wasting your time here," Harry said. "To which I say—I am not."

Having my argument ripped away from me was more irritating still, even though he clearly understood my feelings on the matter. "I am hovering over a bunch of irate people incensed over their working conditions and dealing with the closest thing to a victimless crime that I could be without arresting teenagers for loitering outside a movie theater."

"It's a little more serious than that, Reed," Harry said. "If it wasn't, I wouldn't have pushed you to come here."

"Yeah, it's the push that's the problem," I said, a little heat boiling over.

"It really is, isn't it?" Harry asked, that smug grin splayed across his lips so damned infuriating. "You just don't like being out of control, do you?"

"I handled it fine when I was with Alpha," I lied.

"No, you didn't," Harry said.

"Oh, did I tell you that in one of the unused probabilities you just ran through in your head?"

"You don't have to," Harry said. "It's pretty simple, isn't it? You worked independently when you were with Alpha. Over here, in the wild lands of America, far from their European operations, which is where they were strong. I'm older than the average meta, Reed. I've been around. I knew the players, what they did back in the day. Mostly because I was trying to avoid them."

"Fine, I worked alone until Sienna came along," I said. "Until she had me working with her, then stuck me with...this." I shook my head. "I don't like dancing to your tune, especially when I don't see the point. This is—"

"Beneath you?" Harry offered.

I didn't like how that sounded, so I tried to take a

second and reframe it. "The lack of seriousness suggests...yeah. Maybe."

"You need to be here, Reed," Harry said. "Though you might not see it yet."

I shook my head, felt a stupid smile spread across my face. "Did you bring me here to put me in place to help Sienna?"

"Nope," Harry said. "In fact, you *can't* help her right now. To do so, or to have her come to you...it'd be the undoing of everything she wants to accomplish this year."

"When did you two plan this out?" I asked. "Did you know before Revelen—"

"I knew it all, always," Harry said. "If you're asking when *she* knew...it was after Revelen. Everything except one part, anyway."

"Which part?" I asked quietly, pretty sure I wasn't going to get an answer.

"I warned her to take the job when the FBI chief offered it," Harry said, now quiet himself. "Told her to take the next job offer that comes along, and said it in a way that guaranteed she'd remember it when it rolled up to her door. I told her that well before she went to Minnesota to help Angel. Before she was surrendering. I gave her that much. Everything else..." He shook his head. "Well, it's take it as it comes, almost. This is a tough hand. The cards she drew are not in her favor, and the enemies she's up against? They play meaner than it would appear from the outside. You should know that. You've talked to Andy, after all."

My cheeks burned at the name. Andy Custis had been one of the family of IT specialist metas that helped this group of enemies hide the evidence of Sienna's innocence for years. He was...indisposed at present, taken captive by us just before the Revelen incident. We'd kept him on ice ever since, but the trail to his family was cold, and they were missing, completely. "Is dealing with the Custis family part of Sienna's plan? Or your plan?"

"I told her some of the most probable ways it could unfold," Harry said. "But I'm as much at a distance in this as you are. New probabilities are becoming clearer because of choices made in the process. Some things I thought were certain fell by the wayside. When you try and predict too far out, there are too many paths, it starts to get hazy— except the big events, the ones that come from outside of Sienna's world. These people, this Network...they're not your traditional boss fight, to use a phrase you'd understand. They are not coming at her head on. They know better. They've studied her, and the only way to make sure that they don't act in haste—and before we're ready to deal with them—is to keep her where they think she's wholly under their control. That means you and me and all her other friends are out of the picture so far as they can see. They have her isolated and alone, surrounded by people who are at best indifferent and at worst actively working against her. That's the game, Reed. I know it sucks. It wouldn't have been my choice, sending her into this. But you should know what she's up against."

"Fine, she's in deep," I said. "Then why are you out here in the woods with me?"

Harry stared off into the distance over my shoulder. "Because she's not here to pick up the slack you're carrying...and someone needed to help."

"That is such shit, Harry," I said. "Why don't you just—"

"Time to go, Reed," Harry said, slipping behind a tree, calling back to me as he went. "Take flight. You gotta get back anyway. Oh, and wrap it up, bud. Talk to your girlfriend and move forward, will you?"

"What? I—" Footsteps crashed in the brush somewhere behind me, and I cursed. Harry was already gone, quietly disappearing under the shade of the trees. I swore under my breath and listened.

Yolanda. I could hear her heavy breathing as she came this way, drawn by the sound of my not-so-peaceful tones.

With that, I put the wind beneath my feet and lifted off, up above the canopy and back into the darkening sky.

Chapter 87

Sienna

"This is like 'Murder on Music Row,'" Chandler said as he joined me on the balcony of the Ryman, looking down on the paramedics doing their work on the mobsters. "Except Music Row is that way." He pointed, presumably in the direction of this mythical Music Row.

"I have no idea what you're talking about," I said. He started to explain, and I held up a hand to stop him. "Not a request for info, Chandler. Some other time, okay?"

"Anything to be had here?" Chandler asked, apparently not at all offended at being shushed. That was the mark of a good partner to me these days. Someone who didn't get all worked up about Sienna being Sienna.

"Our boy got recruited into a mobster's scheme—I think." I waved a hand over the remaining carnage. About half the mobsters had been taken away by ambulance. They were readying the rest to move 'em out, presumably so the janitors could come in and clean the place up for…whatever was coming next to the Ryman. "It didn't go quite like anyone planned."

"Any charges to be filed?"

"Against Brance, probably," I said. "If the mobsters want to press. I'm having trouble seeing how anyone else gets hit on this one, unless Brance gets caught and rolls, specifically implicating someone in the scheme." I shook my head. "I actually think I ran across a smart mobster on this one."

"Oh?"

"His execution was a little sloppy because Brance is a loose cannon—and probably not exactly a willing accomplice—but he did a solid move here." I leaned over the balcony, peering down at the mobsters. They were still discombobulated from Brance's aural assault. Some of them had lost eardrums. "But I think overall he might have hit on something, because how the hell do you prove an audio attack happened? There's no tape, no recordings thanks to Brance's power frying electronic recording devices. There's not a lot of provisions in the criminal code for assaults you can't see." I shook my head. "I mean, even fire blasts and meta punches are visible, they leave an obvious mark, there's defined laws against them, you can collect physical evidence to substantiate, but Brance…his attacks are nearly evidence-free."

"No surveillance footage survived?" Chandler asked. "Surely, in this place of all places, they have something, at least?"

"Fried like Nashville Hot chicken." I shrugged. "And I'm not sure what this location has to do with—"

"Oh, come on!" Chandler said. "The Ryman! This was the home of the Grand Ole Opry for decades! The—" He gave up. "Never mind. You're a philistine. Or too modern. One of those."

I chuckled. "One of those, for sure."

Chandler settled into a silence for a few minutes. "What, uh...what song did he sing?"

I blinked. That was a funny question. "To do this, you mean? The attack?"

"Yeah."

"I don't know." I looked around for anyone to answer that question, and finally just shouted down at one of the mobsters. "Hey! You!" A total mobster-mook guy, half as wide as he was tall, looked up at me, blinking in disorientation. "What song did this guy sing?"

Mobster Mook's face crumpled in concentration. "How the hell should I know?"

"It was an old one," one of the Asian bodyguards called up to me. "Joe Diffie tune. 'Is It Cold In Here.'"

"Oh, I love that song," Chandler said.

The bodyguard shrugged. "It's all right. Diffie had better ballads. Like 'Home.'"

"What does that mean?" I asked. "That he sang that song?"

"It's a fairly obscure tune," Chandler said. "It's from the 90s. Was a decent hit but mostly forgotten in today's country environment. Great song, though. This guy Brance...he's a student of country music. Like me." He glanced down at the bodyguard. "Like him, too, apparently."

"What was the, uh, provenance, of this place again?" I asked, looking around the Ryman. "Original home of the Opry? Which was, uh—"

"The longest-running show on radio," Chandler said, sounding a little like a fanatic praising his object of worship. He checked his watch. "It's actually about to start in a few minutes. I wonder who's on tonight...?"

"Where?" I asked, seizing him by the sleeve. "Where is this happening?"

"Oh, uh, they moved to a new theater over by Opry Mills Mall. East of the city."

I gave one last look around the Ryman. There was nothing else to be had here. "Take me there," I decided, heading for the exit. Maybe I'd find Brance, still chasing his dream. Maybe I'd find nothing.

Either way, it'd beat just standing around here, waiting for something to happen.

Chapter 88

Brance

He didn't make it very far before the last two days settled on him like a cloud, a fog that choked him out of consciousness. He passed the tall tower of WSM 650, unable to even muster a smile at that little piece of history.

Brance saw the Moores Lane exit moments later and took it, coasting up the ramp and looking for a place to park. He passed an Outback Steakhouse, a gas station glowing green, before turning into a Publix parking lot. He was already having to blink his eyes quite a bit, fighting to keep them open.

The street lights were already on, the sun having dipped below the horizon before he'd even stormed out the emergency exit of the Ryman. It was all the way down now, night settling in. The temperature was dropping; it'd probably hit the fifties tonight, maybe the high forties. Nothing compared to February in Wyoming, but cold.

Pulling into a spot at the back of the lot, he looked

around. The place was still relatively full, people still out doing their shopping. He put the truck in park and got out, not bothering to stretch his legs before crawling into the back seat of the King Cab.

He covered up with a blanket, drawing his legs close in, curling up. The truck had been his dad's, a hand-me-down that he'd never liked. Brance would have preferred a car, something smaller, but now he was appreciating the extra width and the long back seat.

Man, it would have been great if he could have made it, Brance thought weakly, his thoughts already starting to fade. He should have been wired, terror infusing his veins. But he was tired. He felt like he'd been running for weeks. The lack of sleep was catching up with him.

Closing his eyes, he faded out, leaving all the worries of Jules, of broken dreams, of Sienna Nealon—all of them behind him as he sunk into a deep slumber.

Chapter 89

Reed

When I got back to the gates of Lotsostuff, I found the crowd had died down, their enthusiasm sapped after a long day of yelling and chanting grievances. Alan Kwon was nearby, still tirelessly taking the occasional photo of the diminished crowd. I estimated about a quarter had trickled away, and more were pulling off, ready to call it a night and (presumably) return tomorrow.

Ben Kelly was waiting just inside the gate, looking up into the sky. The moment he saw me he waved me down, and so I dipped, cutting through the chill evening air to land just behind the fence inside the warehouse property. My shoes and the wind stirred up the dust as I came down, turning Ben's black suit a slightly lighter shade.

"Hey," I said.

Ben coughed, dusting himself off, one eye squinted closed like I'd blown some dust into it. "Been looking for you."

"Found me, you have. What's up?" I took a look over

my shoulder. The crowd was shrinking even now, people in overalls trudging back toward the parked cars that filled the nearby lot and lined the highway leading up to Lotsostuff.

"Um. Well." He was still squinting, but now it seemed to be in contemplation of what he wanted to say, not because I'd blow dirt granules in his eyes upon landing.

"Come on, spit it out. I don't have all night and I assume neither do you."

"I just, uhm," Ben said, really warring with himself, "I thought having you here...things would go differently."

I raised an eyebrow. "You mean you thought nobody would try and burn down the warehouse?"

"No. I don't know," he waffled. "I just thought...hero! Here in Murfreesboro!" He made some hand wave gestures that I interpreted to be magic. "All your problems are taken care of!"

"Yeah, I don't have godlike powers to change human nature," I said. "There are two sides who have a genuine conflict here. I can't move those entrenched positions with the wind."

"I just thought...a hero," he said again, enthusiasm flagging. "I thought you could..."

"Save you?" I asked.

"Yeah," Ben said quietly. "Now I realize it sounds kinda...stupid."

"Saving someone jumping from a building is easier than trying to untangle the problems of reality," I said. "Actually, no, sometimes it's not, because sometimes the person jumping? Genuinely wants to jump and will fight to keep you from saving them. Which is sort of analogous to this, I guess, in that it doesn't seem like your boss really wants the help. At least not like you do."

"Yeah," Ben said, "Mr. Mills is complicated, I guess."

I wanted to bemoan the day Facebook had introduced the "It's complicated" relationship status, because damn if it hadn't become the default for people trying to explain the tangled webs we humans got involved in. "It doesn't seem that complicated. He seems like he just doesn't give a shit about talking to his workers about their concerns."

"I don't think that's true," Ben said.

"Is that so?" I asked. "Or do you just not want to believe it's true?"

Ben thought that one over for a moment. "Maybe you're right."

"Maybe I'm wrong," I said. "I don't know what's going on here other than there's two groups of people who badly disagree about what needs to happen to make their lives work. Your boss says, 'No, you can't have more money or the improvements you want,' and meanwhile the workers say, 'You're killin' us. Let off, pay us better, give us our breaks,' or whatever the secondary complaint they have is. Time off, maternity leave—all that."

"It's...all that, yeah."

"This isn't clear-cut for me, either," I said. "Usually it's simpler. Someone's broken a law, usually the kind that involves lives being threatened, and I show up to help save the day. The line crosser is brought to justice, everyone rejoices. That's the heroing I do, and even when it gets into the shades of grey complexity, it usually doesn't get this complex." I shook my head. "I don't believe in everyday life that everybody falls purely into the 'hero' or 'villain' category. We do both."

Ben smiled faintly. "So...it actually is complicated?"

Damn you, Facebook. You ruin everything. "Yeah," I said. "It is complicated. And I can't fix it with a snap of my heroic fingers." A chill unrelated to the coming night fell over me. "There's a lot in my life I wish I could do that for.

A whole lot, especially lately. But I can't. It just doesn't work that way."

"I understand," Ben said, head sagging. "Mr. Mills said something similar when I talked to him about the flooding and the fire. How some things, once they're broken...you just can't fix them."

"Mills is right," I said. "Sorry, Ben."

"But you're going to keep trying, right?" he asked. He looked up at me with those wide, impressionable eyes that I'd probably had before I'd met Sienna and gotten embroiled in the thousand shitstorms that seemed to come along with life with my sister.

"Maybe," I said. "But you might want to reconcile yourself to the idea that this thing...this seemingly intractable thing...it might actually be unfixable."

"Yeah," Ben said, nodding slowly. "All right. I'll try and adjust my expectations, I guess." And he trudged off, back toward the building, nodding his head slowly as I watched him go.

Chapter 90

Sienna

I followed Chandler's official SUV out to the Grand Ole Opry, over a path of freeways and surface roads, past a huge mall (Opry Mills, I presumed) and up to a theater the size of a five- or six-story building. We parked, lights flashing, in the fire lane, and left them going as I followed Chandler up to the front of the theater.

"When they moved to this building," Chandler said, giving me another history lesson as we climbed up the brief sets of steps to the entry, "they took a circle of the stage from the old Ryman and put it where the singers, uh...sing. It's a little piece of tradition, you know?"

"I guess," I said, not quite sure how to feel about that, so I just sort of filed it away in the back of my mind. "What's the big deal about this? I mean, longest running, I get that, but—"

"The Opry is the heart of country music," Chandler said. "Like a weekly concert, a showcase for the music. Multiple performers per show. New breakout stars doing their modern hits. Classics of the past. Even some of the guys you might think of as one-hit wonders from days gone by make an appearance. And it's like an exclusive club. When you're invited to join the Opry—and there's only been a couple hundred members in the life of the thing, and they're part of a country music club, I guess, that has only the best. Anyway, it's great if you're into country music." He shivered, and it wasn't from the cold. "Which obviously I am. I come out here sometimes when I can, and there's acts I want to see. I haven't seen a bad show yet here."

"That's...cool," I said, flashing my badge at security. They had metal detectors set up like it was a stadium show. The guards waved us through with only a little curiosity, and on we went, presenting our badges to the ticket takers and passing on.

"Where's the security office?" Chandler asked the ticket taker, and got a hand point in the general direction for his trouble.

I followed him, taking it in as I went. The building was brick but modern, a mighty lobby that was filled with people. Giant doors opened into the theater beyond, and it was packed with people, crowded as any concert hall I'd ever been to. I frowned. If this show had been ongoing since 1930-whatever and was still this popular, there had to be something to it, even if I didn't quite get it.

Chandler must have walked on, because I halted as an announcer read off the text for a commercial, live, right there in front of me. I felt an absurd smile push onto my face; the guy had a perfect voice for radio, and as he read out his advert for kitten food, I couldn't help but feel I might not be the perfect target audience for it.

"Hey, Sienna," Chandler called, and I looked over. He was striding toward me with a guy in an official-looking uniform, security head all the way. I could tell by his bearing.

"Bob McKay," he said, thrusting out a hand. He had the suspicious bearing that a man in his role ought to carry like a second skin.

"Not to be a jerk, but you know my name, I'm guessing," I said. "We're looking into this singer who's causing problems around town. You up on this situation?"

McKay nodded. "Yeah. We've got extra security posted tonight in case he decides to make an appearance."

"Oh, good," Chandler said, and then he let out what I can only describe as almost the girliest scream I have ever heard anyone let out, his eyes fixed through the double doors into the auditorium and down to the stage. "That's *Travis Tritt!*" he squealed, very un-Chandler.

Rocking drums thudded and the strains of a guitar cut across as the crowd let out a small roar. The opening riff was pretty cool, I had to admit, and sounded a little more rock and roll than I would have expected.

"That's 'Put Some Drive in Your Country,'" Chandler said, almost cooing. "What a fantastic song."

"Do I need to get you a towel?" I asked, ready to take a step back. "Cleanup on aisle four."

"It's just so good, though," Chandler said, eyes closed. McKay was wearing a very slight smile at Chandler's childlike interest. "I mean, listen to that. The perfect synthesis of Southern rock and country. I love it!"

I wouldn't have admitted it in that moment, with Chandler tapping his toes gently and me exchanging an extremely cynically amused look with McKay, but...it was pretty good. My toe might have tapped, too.

"Do you have a specific reason to think this guy might be targeting us?" McKay asked with perfect Southern drawl.

"Just a suspicion," I said, letting Chandler get swept away by the music. "He's pretty into country music, and there was an incident at the Ryman earlier." I looked to the stage, and the long-haired guy singing. The crowd was really into it, and there was an energy in the room that I had felt—albeit a little more lightly—at Guy Friday's show a few weeks ago. It was really something, and I felt it pulsing in my veins. Electric, in a way, like I could feel the crowd. "We're just here playing a hunch. And you might want to issue some earplugs to your security team." I blinked, thinking of how that might be misinterpreted. "For the guy with the voice. Not because the music is bad or something."

McKay just smiled. "Yeah, most of us are fans. You're not, I take it?"

I started to say no, reflexively, but something about the music, and the performances I'd heard over the last couple days, made me pause before answering. I looked toward the stage, felt the rumble of this particular song, the excitement of the crowd, the nearby vibration of Chandler, who was letting out low moans of pure joy...

"I'm starting to see the appeal," I said, trying to shake it off so I could concentrate. I thrust a hand out and shook McKay's hand once, fast. "Thanks for taking it seriously. I don't think you have anything to worry about, but let us know if anything wicked this way comes?"

"You got it," he said, nodding once.

"Can we just stay until—" Chandler started.

"We need to go," I said, pulling him along. "This was a gamble. Brance can't be stupid enough to crash the Grand Ole Opry after what happened at the Ryman earlier. It'd be asking for the level of trouble he's been avoiding all this time." I shook my head. "No. We need to look in a different direction."

"Can we at least listen to it on the radio as we drive?" Chandler pleaded as I pulled him out of the Grand Ole Opry theater and into the cool night air. The mall was lit up like an airport runway across the parking lot, and our police lights were still flashing wildly down at the curb, attracting the attention of interested passersby.

"You can listen to whatever you want in your car."

Chandler nodded. "Good. Uh...where are we going?"

"I'm going to call Parsons," I said. "Find out where this Jules Sharpe hangs his hat." I squared my jaw as I headed down the steps toward my BMW. "Because I have a feeling that there's more to get out of him...and I mean to get it."

Chapter 91

Brance

Sleep had seemed like a far-off possibility after Brance had gotten in the fight at the Ryman. How could he have possibly slept after that, after clashing with Jules, with Gil, after damned near killing a whole auditorium of people? Again.

But he'd faded out in that Publix parking lot, sure as shooting, dropped off into that dreamless slumber that had finally turned into a dreaming sort of sleep over time.

Now he was imagining himself in the Ryman again, dreaming about that moment. It was an empty house now, though, the seats all clear as his voice sang out.

Not a noise punctuated that quiet theater, his own voice the only sound ringing out the notes to George Jones's 'Who's Gonna Fill Their Shoes?'

Something broke in through the music and lyrics, though, like a distant whisper.

"Yo, how about this one?"

"You see anything?"

"Bag on the seat."

"Okay, okay. Ain't no one looking. Smash it!"

Brance was in the middle of his song in the empty Ryman. Where was that talking come from?

Crash!

Glass shattered and Brance jarred out of his sleep. He was in the back of the truck, jolted awake in the middle of the damned night, it felt like, parking lot lights overhead shining down on the scene. Someone was in the front seat, unlocking it, opening the door—

"Oh, shit, there's a guy sleeping in here!" one of the shadowy figures said.

Brance opened his mouth and a scream came out, one infused with panic.

One that hit...*that* particular frequency...hard.

The guy at the door froze, then screamed, hands coming right up to his ears. Dark trickles of liquid came rushing down his cheeks, and he flew back like he'd gotten launched, slamming into the guy who'd been standing lookout behind him.

The other windows, the windshield, the back window glass of Brance's truck all shattered at once, pebbling safety glass rolling down over his blanket and showering the bed.

Scrabbling for the door handle, Brance tumbled out. Caught himself before he hit the parking lot blacktop.

He came around the truck and found the two guys rolling around. They were both holding their ears. Blood was just piping out, running harder than he'd seen out of any of the people he'd hit with his song previously.

"Shit," Brance whispered. One of them had dropped his bag.

It wasn't hard to figure out what had happened here. They'd decided to burgle his truck, steal his stuff where he'd left it in view on the front seat.

Brance looked at 'em for a moment, then felt sick. They were rolling, writhing. Weren't going to be getting up anytime soon, he reckoned. "I'm sorry," he said. No chance they heard him, not with that blood coming out of their ears.

Stumbling back to his truck, Brance hauled himself up into the driver's seat and jangled the keys. Once he had her started up, he threw it into gear and floored it. He throttled her up, headed for 65 South and raced down the on ramp. Traffic was sparse, dying down for the night.

He wiped the sleep out of his eyes. Felt the pulse, thudding, as the cold air blew in on him from the missing windshield and the windows all around. He hadn't meant to do that—any of it—but he wasn't sorry, nossir.

He was mad.

But he headed south with that anger, in the silence, feeling the cold wind blow and hoping that maybe by tomorrow he'd trade it for a warm Florida wind, and wouldn't feel so awful.

Chapter 92

The highway signs for Columbia and Spring Hill were close at hand, coming up at the next exit. Brance had driven in quiet for the last thirty minutes, maybe forty.

It was starting to wear on him, the lack of voices. The judging silence. His gaze fell on the radio, and he turned it on. Checked the time. Hell, the Opry was probably on.

It was. He caught them in the middle of an ad for fried chicken crust. That was well-targeted. Made him want to stop at a Popeye's.

"Well, folks," the announcer popped back on after the commercial wrapped up, "what we got for you next is a man who's been around since the age of the dinosaurs—awww, I'm just kidding, folks. But he was there at the founding of the Babylonian Empire. Might even have argued with ol' Nebuchadnezzar himself. I'm speaking of course of country legend—"

Brance felt a trace of sadness settle over him. He'd dreamed about being on the Opry someday.

For how long? Forever.

Hard to believe only a few hours ago he'd been

397

standing on the stage of the Ryman, about to perform. And it had all gone straight to hell, of course, because that was the direction of the last few days. All the years of hope, the forward movement, the minor setbacks, they'd all culminated in the last few days. Reached a crescendo. It had been like an accelerated curve of everything he'd hoped for out of a career, but so breathtakingly rapid and awful as to beggar belief.

Screamin' Demons.

Mercy's Faithless.

The recording studio.

And finally the Ryman.

Those last two had been Jules's fault. The bastard had been manipulating him from the beginning, hadn't he? Playing into his dreams. Filling him up. All this time, since it had come out, Brance had thought maybe he'd had the right of it after Mercy's Faithless, that just leaving town was the right thing to do.

"I wanted them to hear me," he whispered over the roar of cold blasting through the cab.

But no one would want to hear him now. That much was true after the last few days.

"But I wanted them to hear me," he whispered again, the cold, chilly wind blowing through the busted windows.

Those car-burgling bastards in the parking lot had sure heard him. He felt a smile of vicious satisfaction for that. But hadn't that kind of been the sum of his time in Nashville? The last couple months? Sure, he'd met a few nice people, but he'd met a few sonsofbitches like Jules who had absolutely outweighed the nice ones.

He'd just been trying to sing and people in Screamin' Demons had acted like he'd been trying to kill them. Well, he hadn't.

"I just want to be heard," he said, louder this time.

Bobby Osborne was singing "Rocky Top," and it was...it was good.

Why couldn't he have that?

How many people were listening to this right now that would have wanted to hear him, if given a chance? Hell, he didn't even care anymore. Jules had screwed him over hard. They were going to chase him to the ends of the earth now. There was no outrunning this in Florida, not a chance.

Now...it was a matter of how he was going to go out.

"I want 'em to hear me," he decided, and brought the truck to slow down before whipping her around in a turn-around in the freeway median.

How many people were listening to the Opry tonight? A whole hell of a lot, that was how many. Well, he knew a way he'd make them hear him.

And if it hurt 'em? Well, that was fine. Nobody liked him anyway, and he might as well go out on a note Brance himself chose.

"I'll make 'em hear me," he said. And that was decided.

Chapter 93

Sienna

Okay, the Grand Ole Opry was pretty good.

Yeah, I'd told Chandler he could listen to it in his car, without me, not intending to listen to it myself. But after a very brief phone call to Parsons that got me Jules Sharpe's whereabouts, I found myself driving in silence. As much fun as it was to be left alone with my own thoughts, after about two minutes of that shitshow—there was a reason I was contemplating drinking again earlier, after all —I turned on the radio to AM 650.

"Next up we have Collin Raye performing his classic, 'Little Rock.'"

It only took a couple minutes and I felt like I'd been singled out by it.

The tune that was playing was mournful, a male voice as smooth as that whiskey I'd passed up earlier, and talking about...well...not drinking. It seemed to be speaking to me, strangely enough, which was not a thought I figured I would have had with a country music tune. Yet here we were.

I dabbed at my eyes a couple times, because they were very definitely misting up due to the humidity and/or road conditions and not the song.

And soon enough, there we were, actually, pulling into the parking lot of Bones, which announced itself with a neon sign that had the N and S burned out, but the outline of a lady's form was still working perfectly. They were advertising what counted, I guessed. LIVE BEAUTIFUL LADIES was painted beneath it but unlit. Still mostly visible thanks to the ambient street lights in this part of town, which was a little more rundown than most parts of Nashville I'd been to.

I parked the BMW and Chandler rolled up next to me. He was still humming as he got out of the car. "Oh, man, you should have heard it," he said. "It was so perfect—"

"Collin Rayne," I said, heading for the door. "Yeah, it was something."

"Raye, like the sun but spelled different." Chandler scrambled to keep up with me. "And you were listening?" He came alongside, grinning. "We'll make a Nashville convert of you yet."

"Don't go counting your guitar strings before they get plucked." He gave me a weird look and I shrugged broadly. "I don't know music."

The doorman didn't seem impressed to see us, but a flip of our badges got him to move aside. He was of a kind with Jules's other minion and the countless other slabs of meat that had been hauled out of the Ryman by ambulances earlier. His squinted eyes bespoke of his suspicions regarding the law, but he kept it polite.

Bones was, unsurprisingly, a grubby sort of strip club. Not that I'd been in many, but it was definitely in the bottom of the barrel. Dancers circulated, one passing by me with a glazed, artificial come-hither look that she directed at me and then Chandler in turn, no more real than her breasts. Heavy amounts of makeup couldn't completely hide the telltale signs of methamphetamine use, and even if I'd been remotely disposed toward the fairer sex, it would have been a world of NO NO NO if she'd tried to give me a lap dance, along with an extensive spraying for pelvic lice and boiling or possibly burning my clothes afterward.

"This place is..." Chandler said, following in my wake, seemingly lost for words.

"Like a truck stop toilet where the janitor resigned six months before in protest over the filthy conditions," I said.

Chandler gave that a moment's contemplation. "That sounds right. I mean, I don't ever want to see that place, but...I have to imagine it's close to this."

"But look at all these struggling artists you could support with your patronage, Chandler. Apropos of nothing...are you up to date on all your vaccinations?" I asked.

"What? Why?" Chandler asked.

"Maybe don't sit down or touch...well, anything, really," I said.

I had clocked Jules the moment we walked in the door. He had a booth all to himself beside the stage and was studying a newspaper like he was having coffee in some sedate cafe by the Seine rather than in the neon glow of the crappiest nudie bar this side of *From Dusk Til Dawn*. But with more frightening dancers. He was informed of our approach by that same minion who'd gotten smashed into the Ryman's walls. The mook was lingering a reasonable distance from his boss, but scampered over to tell him, drawing Jules's nose out of his paper.

"Well, well," Jules said as we approached, not remotely

enthused at our appearance. "And here I was hoping my evening's entertainment was over." He had that bandage taped to his forehead now.

"There's really not that much entertaining about my visits," I said, pretending to cast an eye over the place. I raised my voice to make myself heard over the screech of whatever techno-garbage the DJ was filling the air with. A girl who was a little past her prime was gyrating on stage, spinning on a pole. She had some skill, I'd give her that, but she seemed to be going, quite unenthusiastically, through the motions, lifting her leg up to the—if possible—even less enthusiastic reaction of the two guys seated on stools beneath the stage, one of whom was diligently paying more attention to the taco salad on his plate than the girl flashing—uh, everything—at him from above. I wasn't sure if this was a good choice or not, unable to believe the food here was any better than the dancers.

"I've already told you everything I know," Jules said, putting his palms down on top of his paper.

"I have little difficulty believing that the sum total of your knowledge could be imparted in one conversation," I said, inviting myself to sit down across from him—and also very thankful my meta immune system protected me from such minor annoyances as syphilis, typhoid and the black plague. "But I can't help but feel that you might have, locked in that near-empty skull of yours, some small nugget of information that could help us catch Brance and end his reign of terror over the fine citizens of Nashville. Like yourself. Except not criminals."

Jules seemed caught between desire to reply to my baiting insults and one to tell me to take a flying leap. His response split the difference: "This seems like your problem and not so much mine anymore." He gingerly touched the bloody bandage that decorated his forehead. "Thankfully."

"How would you describe Brance's state of mind?" I asked, plowing right through his fruitless denial. Mostly so I could hammer home the point that denial was, in fact, going to produce utterly zero fruit for Jules.

"Crazy as hell," Jules said. "The guy went nuts and attacked my group, okay? How am I supposed to see him? As some kind of benevolent talent, punching me in the chest like that?" He massaged his chest a little to the right of his sternum, and I knew that pain well. Too bad for Jules he'd be feeling it long past the time I did.

"Did he say anything to you on his way out?" I asked. "Any sort of comment blurted aloud?"

Jules tried to give me a look like I was crazy. "What am I, your stenographer? I got hit, I stopped remembering the pleasantries of conversation. The guy wasn't exactly looking to discuss the ins and outs of Tennyson in any case, if you know what I mean." He feigned a punch. "He looked crazy, acted crazy, hit me, hit my boy here, and left. What else is there?"

"Crazy, huh?" I asked, trying to keep cool with this unintentional thing he'd just handed me. "You don't suppose he's crazy enough to...track you down here, do you?"

Jules's already narrowed eyes slitted farther. "I sure hope not. I'm unlikely to be caught by surprise in that particular way again. I see this guy coming...well, he better hope I don't see him coming."

"I'm sure he's trembling in his cowboy boots at the thought of you coming at him," I said, smiling. Infuriatingly, I hoped.

"Guy's out of control," Jules said. "What do you want from me?"

Something beeped behind me, and Chandler fumbled at his belt, coming up with his cell phone. "Sorry, just a sec," he said, stepping away. I could hear the conversation over the radio, but pretended I couldn't.

Mr. Mook shuffled toward Chandler, but I reached out and grabbed his arm, turning him back. "Give him a second," I said, "and a little breathing room. By which I mean take your stinking breath back a step."

"You can't come into my club and start bossing my employees around," Jules said, but not really putting a lot of oomph into it.

"You seem like a guy who understands power," I said, "and realpolitik. Earlier today I had to go into one of your...friend's? Competitor's? Hell, I don't even know. One of their trafficking houses—"

"Heard about that on the news," Jules said mildly. "Lot of body bags came out of there." He spat on the floor, which might have actually enhanced the cleanliness of his establishment. "I got no sympathies for sex traffickers."

"Where was that?" Chandler asked, muffled, behind me. "Brentwood?"

"An honorable criminal," I said. "Lemme just stand up and salute you. Anyway—that was a thing that happened. And it happened because...I could do it. So...what do you think I could do here?" I made a show of looking around.

Jules did a little survey of his own, then made a show of smiling at me, totally placatingly. "I'd like you off my property unless you've got a warrant."

"I'll leave in a second," I said, listening into Chandler as he wrapped up his talk.

"That's off Moores Lane?" Chandler asked. "And you're sure—bleeding ears? Broken glass? All right. Be right there." He slipped the cell phone back into his pocket and waved to me. "We need to go."

"See?" I asked. "No need to try and push, Jules. You might get pushed back on, and I'd hate to see you suffer from two solid mule kicks to the chest in one day. Because mine would crush your ribs, not just leave you wheezing a little."

"Yeah, yeah," Jules said, gesturing with his hand like it was a broom he could sweep me away with. "Don't come back without a lawyer unless you just want to enjoy the company of my girls—and you're willing to pay for it."

"Pretty sure I could do better than this while getting someone to pay *me* for it," I sniped back, then clammed up until Chandler and I were outside. "We got a Brance sighting?" I asked, once we were out of earshot of the meathead bouncer.

"Certainly sounds like it," he said. "South of the city, north of Franklin. Brentwood, Cool Springs area. Grocery store parking lot. Sounds like somebody might have caught him sleeping in his truck while they tried to burgle it. Didn't go the way they planned, and now they're bleeding from the ears and suffering concussions."

"Let's check it out," I said, hustling back to my car. "Lead the way."

Chapter 94

Jules

"Sounds like something happened down in Brentwood," Gil said. "The audio's a little scratchy, but...yeah. Brentwood. Cool Springs."

Jules stroked his chin thoughtfully. Wiring the parking lot with microphones and recording everything that happened out there had been an idea suggested by his security company to keep his girls safe. That it had produced a little blackmail video from the...outside work his ladies did...had been quite the boon. This was just the latest—and most unexpected—payoff. "And it's Brance?"

Gil shrugged. "Sounds like it. Bleeding ears."

That was all Jules needed to know. "Get Leo. The last thing we need is Sienna Nealon catching up to that pussy Brance and having him squeal his big flapping gums to her about what happened at the Ryman."

"So you want us to do some...pest control?" Gil asked, with a smile.

"Yeah," Jules said, rising and leaving his paper behind.

"I got no patience for a rat, especially when I'm this close to nailing down the throne of Nashville's underworld. Let's get it taken care of." He paused, and thought of something. "Oh, and Gil? Bring the police scanner, will ya? We might just need it."

Chapter 95

Reed

I t was always sad to see someone's hope take a hit, and this was no exception. I'd watched Ben Kelly trudge back up toward the Lotsostuff facility with his shoulders slumped, and felt bad. Ben seemed like a good kid—and he was a kid, really, no more than twenty-two—and having to deliver the news that whatever was happening here might just end up running its course without me able to do a damned thing about it seemed like being honest.

Still sucked to watch him take the hit.

My phone buzzed and I fished it out of my pocket. A small smile popped to my face when I saw the caller ID: *Isabella Perugini*.

"Hey, babe," I answered. "How are you doing?"

"It's cold up here," she said, and I could almost hear the slight chatter of her teeth sandwiched in her words. Was that for effect? I doubted it. Minnesota was a chilly place. "When are you coming home?"

"I don't know," I said, letting the waning enthusiasm

carry through my voice. "I don't half know what I'm even still doing here, to be honest."

"Was everything not as you expected?"

"Nothing was as I expected," I said. "Least of all the set-up. Harry promised violence when he handed me that article. The worst I've seen is destruction of property by a Gavrikov who then hurled some fireballs at me. Kind of halfheartedly, I think, or maybe they were just really new at it. Or mad—"

"You do make people mad sometimes."

"Mostly you, though, right?" I asked with a grin.

"You do not make me so mad anymore," Isabella said, accent flowing through. I really liked her accent. Loved it, even. "I didn't understand you, at first, when we got together. You are...so young, you know—"

"Yes, cradle-robber, I know this."

"—that I think sometimes our worlds are too different for me to see what you are thinking. But that faded over time. Now, I think I understand you well enough. Mostly. I will never understand the interest in *Pokémon*—"

"You gotta catch 'em all. It's just a thing."

"—but otherwise, you make sense to me," she said. "You are a good man. You do your best to make things right, even when it costs you."

I frowned lightly, almost amused. "Costs me? How?"

"I know it hasn't been easy for you lately," she said. "With the business. With it...failing." Boy, did she struggle with that word. "I know you have trouble sleeping with the worry. That you feel ashamed sometimes that things happened the way they did."

My cheeks burned, and it wasn't from the light, chilly breeze. "No. No. I know what I did, how I burned through the money—that I made mistakes. But it's fine. It's fine. I'm...fine," I finished lamely.

"Uh huh," she said, in that tone of voice that told me she knew I didn't believe my own bullshit. "It's okay if you don't want to talk about it, but that is what I mean when I say it costs you. Worry. Stress. You fear losing...everything. It makes you not act like yourself."

"What do you mean?" I asked quietly, kicking at a pebble in the parking lot. The protesters had melted away to about a fifth of their size during the day, and even now they were still shrinking, like an ice cube dropped in warm water.

"You're not yourself. Not as you used to be. Too much responsibility. Always trying to be the hero. You do too much. You've cut people you cared about. Looked them in the eye and said goodbye, yes? That is not an easy thing, especially to wait and dread it as long as you did. It was like letting the axe hang over your head for months before it finally fell."

"I didn't know you knew," I said. "You never mentioned it. Any of this."

"You have had enough on your mind already," she said. "I didn't need to add more to it, you know? And you weren't talking about it. Just a little, really. You needed someone to listen, not throw advice at you when you were already under pressure."

"Yeah, it's been a lot," I said. "For a while now. I didn't know you were worrying. And I definitely didn't mean to make you worry—"

"I'm not worried. Well, maybe a little. But not much. You are a big boy, Reed, even if you are young—"

"Cradle-robber, I say."

"—but you have a good head on your shoulders." I could hear the faint smile in her reply. "You will figure it out, and be back to yourself again."

Something clicked for me in all she'd just said. "I...gotta go," I said, blinking furiously.

"Of course. I love—"

I hung up, suddenly very cold. Could it be that easy? Was my head up my ass?

I turned toward the Lotsostuff building, and saw the light was still on in the office of Logan Mills. A brand new question open in my mind, I broke into a run, flight forgotten, as I hustled to get it answered.

Chapter 96

Sienna

"Next up, we have the amazing Miranda Lambert singing her chart-topping instant classic, 'Gunpowder and Lead.'"

The announcer's voice faded away as I took the slow curve of the onramp onto 65 South, following the flashing lights of Chandler's SUV ahead of me, my own flashers going like crazy in the front windshield. It was a little distracting, so I tried to focus on the darkened road ahead as the opening strains of a killer guitar riff started up and a woman's taut, forceful vocals broke into a song about how her man had beat her up, and how she was going to go and get her shotgun and lie in wait for his ass to come home.

"Oh, yeah," I muttered to myself. "I remember liking Miranda Lambert." In fact, she might have been my spirit animal.

Hauling ass down Interstate 65, I had a flash, and suddenly for a second I was back in that house this morning, unloading on some asshole abusive sex trafficker with Miranda Lambert playing me along.

"I gotta stop killing people so much," I muttered, meta-low, as the song came to a crashing close, hoping that the loudness of the radio would muffle my voiced thoughts, especially because I knew for a fact that the Network had bugged the shit out of my government phone. They were almost certainly listening even now. Which was why I so seldom liked carrying the damned thing. I knew they were spying on me almost every hour of the day. It grated on my nerves every time I thought about it.

If there was any word in the dictionary that was synonymous with Sienna Nealon, it was not 'passive.' Nor was 'willing to put up with abundances of crap.'

But all I did was take crap lately. All I did was deal with shit from Willis, from Chalke. From the people in Chalke's secret club who thought I didn't know about them.

The secrets I was keeping in isolation these days felt like enough to eat me alive, to make me want—so desperately—to take a drink.

A year ago, five years ago, if I'd walked into that sex trafficking den and seen what I saw this morning...I probably would have done the same thing I did.

But I might not have.

I could feel the fraying of my nerves in real time. This assignment, this decision, this thing I had been doing since I'd gotten back from Revelen last year...

It was killing me. Never a great team player, I'd still always had my friends. People I could rely on, talk to. And I did talk to them, still, at night, in the dreamwalk, where no one could see or record us.

Then I spent my waking hours in the company of agents of the FBI, surveilled by darker forces beyond who had spent years trying to destroy me before they figured out that I could be the ultimate accessory in their toolkit if they just pushed me the right way.

I felt the push. I was not the sort to be pushed without pushing back.

Yet I was not pushing back. I was waiting for a fantastical, far-off day when I could, by God, push back so hard they'd learn I was not to be manipulated or played with like a pet.

That day was definitely not here.

And it was draining my sanity every day I put up with this shit and it didn't arrive.

"I gotta do something different," I muttered, again below the volume I hoped the mic in my phone would pick up. I shouldn't haven't spoken at all. Or maybe I should have, to make them think I was losing it. I didn't even know what my best move was anymore, I'd gotten so lost in this fiction I was living.

But for now, I would do something different. I would.

Lights flashing, I followed Chandler through the night, the Grand Ole Opry playing in the background, the sounds of Miranda Lambert's vengeful anthem fading into the back of my mind as I tried to figure out what I could do differently to help me survive the slow chiseling away of my sanity by these circumstances.

Chapter 97

Reed

"What's up?" Ben Kelly asked, answering the door after I'd hammered on it for a good minute or so. I was surprised he'd come so quickly; I was about to fly up to his window and get his attention—assuming he was even still here.

I pushed past him into the warehouse, put a little pep in my step as I headed toward the stairs that led up to the offices. "I just had a thought, and I need to ask your boss about it right now."

"Uh, well, I was just about to lock up for the night, but sure," he said, struggling to catch up with me. I was leaving him in the dust and it was easy as pie. Clearly, he wasn't the meta saboteur, because he couldn't have moved that slow at a run if he was.

I blew right through the reception area where Ben's desk sat, knocking only once on Logan Mills's door before hearing, "Yes?" and taking it as my cue to *entrez-vous*.

"Hey," I said, leaving the door open for Ben as he

huffed his way into the reception area, finally. "I need to talk to you."

Mills looked away abruptly. "I'm...busy at the moment. Maybe you can schedule something tomorrow—"

"How long have you been broke?" I asked. Ben, now only a few steps behind me, physically gasped.

The reaction from Mills was not quite what I would have expected.

He chuckled. And looked me in the eye for the first time since I'd met him.

I stared at him, not flinching back a bit.

He stared back at me, and that little light of humor in his eyes died, blackening

"Ben..." Mills said, gaze falling back to the floor. "Would you mind closing that door and getting back to locking up? I need to talk to Mr..." He looked up at me again, and I realized he genuinely did not know my last name.

"Treston," I said.

"I need to talk to Mr. Treston for a moment," Mills said. He was quiet, still. He looked at Ben with patient expectation.

"Uh, Mr. Mills...?" Ben asked. I could tell he was struggling to figure out what he wanted to say there.

"In a few minutes, Ben," Mills said quietly. "Please. Go on."

Ben shut the door, face wild with curiosity as he did so, peering in until the lock softly clicked and the line of light coming from the reception area's lights faded into nothingness.

Mills remained quiet for only a moment more, then spoke with the gravity of a man who was tired in a way I fully understood. "How did you know?"

"I was talking to my girlfriend a few minutes ago," I

said, "and she was mentioning how I'd been sullen and withdrawn lately. Depressed, I guess you could say? My business is failing," I said, saying aloud to him something I'd been thinking but so damned afraid to vocalize. "Has failed. It's over, however much I haven't wanted to admit it to myself." I looked down at his carpet, which was ugly and secondhand, I guessed. None of the furniture in his office was particularly opulent, actually. "It's funny because I listened to your employees talk about you, and how you're not acting like yourself. At least not lately. And I thought..."

Mills nodded, not looking up. "You thought it sounded...familiar?"

It was my turn to nod. "Yeah."

Mills was quiet only a moment more. "Yes. I'm broke." He laughed mirthlessly, and it died just as quickly as it started. "Beyond broke, actually." He steered himself to one of the chairs in front of his desk and hauled it around, nearly collapsing into it as he sat. "Up to my eyeballs in debt, and Lotsostuff—by my accounting, anyway—is worth...zero."

"Your company was valued in the billions last year," I said. "With a freaking B, man."

He shook his head. "I never valued it like that. My accountants—the smart ones—never did. I mean, we hoped, right?" He tried to smile, but failed, his lips curving back down almost immediately. "Boy, did we hope. Investors hoped. Employees hoped—for a while, anyway. And I hoped. Hoped, and worked at it and kept the margins razor thin to nonexistent as we expanded our hold." He shook his head. "Too low, in fact. I burned through cash at an alarming rate. Every time we'd open a new round of funding, thinking, 'Yeah, this time we'll make it to profitability if we just do X.' And every time...we burned right through the money. So, yeah. I'm beyond broke."

"That's why you aren't negotiating with the workers," I said. "You actually can't afford to give them raises."

He shook his head. "No. I actually can't. I can't afford to pay them what I've been paying them, even, and my accountants told me that...years ago." He raised his eyes to me, and they were...teary. "But hell if I was going to cut their pay. They work—worked—so hard for me. Seeing this place succeed? They poured their lives into it like I did, some of them." His voice cracked. "You know what kills me?" He looked up at me.

"Wondering what they're going to do after you let them go," I said, knowing exactly what he meant. I knew those feelings well.

"Some of them have been with me for a decade," Mills said. "Since the beginning. Theresa, I mean? From the start. Employee number one. My mom recommended her to me. This business is...it's become who I am." He ran fingers through his hair. "I have poured everything into it these last ten years. Everything. My life. Every dime I had and then some. I made promises to investors that I was going to make this work." His voice cracked again. "I thought I could make it work."

"I know what you mean," I said. "When everything started to go wrong for me, it was like...like a tsunami behind me, a flood trying to catch me. I thought if I could just run faster—"

"You could get out from underneath it," Mills said.

"Yeah. But I couldn't." I drummed a hand against my thigh. "No matter how hard I worked, no matter how many contracts I accepted...the hole only got deeper."

Mills nodded along. "Same. Our profit margins have been screwed up since the beginning, but we had to cut some prices recently to stay competitive with the other big retailers. It killed us. Every order we fulfilled, trying to get people in the door by selling those at a loss, actually set us back because the other products didn't make enough to offset the loss. So..." He smiled wanly. "Yeah. A hole. A crater, I guess, in my case. Not to minimize your own suffering."

"We all have our own struggles," I said, "and none of them feel small to the person carrying them. Though...*billions* in stock value lost? Damn."

"Yeah," Mills said in a whisper. "I feel really bad for the people who believed in me enough to invest in my company, because they're the ones who are taking the hit. And I feel bad for my employees, because there's not another job in Murfreesboro that's going to pay them what I did."

I cringed. "Don't you think maybe you should...tell them?"

"I couldn't even really tell myself," Mills said. "Until just now. But you're right." He stood, his shoulders suddenly a little straighter. "Thank you."

I nodded. "Did you set that fire or flood that other part of the warehouse so you could try and get out from underneath this? I mean, I understand if you did—"

Mills's face got all screwed up. "Hell no. I was still working every hour of the day figuring out how I could get out from behind the eight ball. I mean, even after the flood, which—my insurance adjustor already said, I'm almost certainly not getting paid out on that, which means the fire is definitely not covered. I haven't even bothered to call them—"

"Someone's pissed at you, then," I said, my sixty/forty swing going to a ninety/ten, and definitely away from Mills.

Mills's shoulders slumped again. "Yeah, well, who can blame 'em?"

"It goes a little farther than that," came a muffled voice from outside the windows. I turned my head to look at the old, painted glass panes.

"Hey, take a step back," I said, trying to get to Mills.

Before I could, the glass shattered before me, blasting into his office and showering us both. Stinging shards cut my hand, one laced my scalp—

And suddenly there was a man on fire hovering in the middle of the room, blazing flames, the heat radiating off of him like a sun had lit in the middle of Mills's office.

Chapter 98

Brance

There it was.

The antenna was coming up ahead, just where he remembered it, off the Concord Road exit from I-65. Brance took the ramp slowly, then hung a right, pulling over next to the historical marker sign that denoted the history of this place.

WSM 650 AM's antenna looked unlike so many of the modern antennas that made up the skyline of America. The strange, bowed-out, stretched-diamond structure marked it as different, worthy of notice. Brance had read up on it beforehand, of course, but when he'd moved down to Nashville he'd seen it for himself after a trip to the battlefields in Franklin.

It reached up into the dark night, lit by navigational flashing strobes at the top and middle, and floodlights at the base. He could see the concrete slab anchoring it to the ground, and the dark steel cables securing it against the wind.

There was a house-like structure close to the road, a couple lights on inside. He'd heard they'd transmitted live from in there at one point, though he wasn't sure there was even anyone present now.

Slamming the door to his truck, Brance took it all in. What was he going to have to do here?

Well, he'd start at the house. Maybe there was some kind of override switch or something...

Chapter 99

Sienna

"So we basically just found 'em squirming around, bleeding right here on the asphalt," the Brentwood PD officer told us. He had the high and tight haircut that cops and military guys wore so commonly. "Sitting in a pile of shattered safety glass."

The suspects were getting treated by EMTs, and I hadn't talked to them yet. I wasn't sure I'd need to, either, even if I wanted to. Both of them had cotton balls tinged with blood hanging out of their ears. "You think they were breaking into his car, then?"

The cop nodded. "That's my guess. We got a lot of that around here. Car break-ins and retail thefts—shoplifting—are our biggest calls. We've had three break-ins reported tonight, and when we checked out the car these fellas drove..." He pointed to a Honda Accord about a hundred yards away that was swarming with officers. "Well, let's just say we found a couple items that have been reported stolen."

"Any idea what these guys heard?" Chandler asked, hands on his hips.

"They're not real receptive to questions at the moment," the officer said. "And I don't mean they lawyered up, either. They can't hear us, so unless you want to teach one of them sign language...?" He shrugged. "All we could get out of them was there was a guy sleeping in the car."

Chandler turned to me. "This is well south of Nashville. Not a normal destination for Brance I would think, unless he lives in Franklin or something."

"Are there many places he could be living?" I asked. "South of here, I mean?" I shook my head, working it through. "No. Why would he be sleeping in his car if he lived near here? He'd just go home."

"He's had a rough couple days," Chandler said. "Maybe he's tired. Overtired."

"I feel that," I said. "But here's what it suggests to me —he got clear of the dragnet back in town and he was so tired he needed a break before he did the next thing in his plan."

"Which is...?"

"Get out of town," I said. "He probably figured it was a long drive, so..."

"He took a nap first," Chandler said, nodding. "Well, if he's heading south, it's a straight shot to Birmingham. From there—Mississippi, Louisiana, the Florida panhandle...there's a lot of places he could go."

The cop's radio crackled: "Trespassing reported at WSM Tower on Concord."

Chandler and I exchanged a look. "Eureka," I said.

Chapter 100

Jules

The police scanner went off with the call about the WSM Tower, and Jules was left scratching his head. "What the hell is that?" he asked, directing his question almost as much to himself as Gil and Leo.

"Dunno, boss," Gil said. They were cruising down 65, heading for the shopping center after Nealon and her partner. "But I think it's right up ahead here. Next exit or two."

Jules pulled his phone out and typed "WSM Antenna" into the search bar. The result came up a moment later.

As soon as he saw the words "Grand Ole Opry," he changed his mind on what to do.

"Take us there."

Chapter 101

Brance

"How do I get on the air?" Brance asked the empty room. The "house" on the antenna property was abandoned, dusty, looked like it hadn't been occupied in forever. He didn't see a single soul in here, just a bunch of machinery and equipment that was too complex for him to decipher.

He stared at the combination of blinking and non-blinking lights on an instrument panel. Off to the side there seemed to be a recording studio, but the level of dust in that place made it seem unlikely it had been used since the Nashville flood.

"What the hell do I do here?" Brance asked, still staring at the lights. They were red and green and yellow—

And blue?

He saw blue, and stared, the color casting a strange shade over a set of LEDs. It took him a moment to realize, no, it wasn't the lights that were that color—

It was the lights of a police car pulling up in the driveway outside.

Brance didn't even think about it. He sprinted for the door, busting through and out onto the flat field that surrounded the tower for a hundred yards in every direction. With a look over his shoulder, he saw two cars pulling up with flashing lights in their front windows, another behind them with roof-mounted flashers.

"Brance!" a hard female voice shouted. He knew that voice. Had heard it before, in Mercy's Faithless.

Sienna Nealon.

She'd found him.

With nowhere else to run and nothing but open ground for a long ways in every direction, Brance sprinted all-out for the antenna.

Chapter 102

Sienna

"He's running for it," I said, breaking into a sprint to follow. "Chandler, grab the AR-15 out of my trunk and cover me, will you?" I tossed my keys at him.

Chandler fumbled the catch and the keys glittered in the headlamps of the cars. "Why would you do that?" he called as I ran into the darkness of the field surrounding the WSM antenna. "I hated cricket and baseball as a kid. You're giving me flashbacks here."

"Find the keys, get the gun!" I shouted.

"Yeah, yeah, warn me next time before you throw the sharp, sparkling, possibly blinding keys at my face with super strength? This is all I'm asking."

The house that sat on the antenna property looked like it had been built long, long ago, the door hanging open and the lights all off within. I didn't know what Brance had been doing inside, but I suspected it was trying to get on the air. Whether he'd figured out a way to do so before we'd pulled up was an open question, and one that was worrying me as I tried to run him down.

The grass reached to calf-height on me, slick and cool, wetting the bottom of my pants legs as I sprinted along. Brance was beelining straight for the antenna. Not the woods a few hundred yards beyond, not the fence to our right. Hell, he hadn't even tried to go for the freeway to our left.

He was going straight for the antenna, and that gave me a really bad feeling.

What if he had figured out a way to get on the air? What if he was just trying to make some final adjustment out on the tower and then he'd...I dunno...sing to half of North America, liquifying their brains in their heads. That seemed a long shot, but we really didn't entirely know how his powers worked.

I reached for my pocket as I ran, coming up with the earplugs I'd been carrying and squeezing them into my ears as I sprinted after him toward the antenna.

The tower rested on a solid, several-foot-high concrete base. The antenna was the shape of an extremely oblong diamond, like a classic diamond shape had gotten caught, pointy-end first, in a black hole and stretched for the better part of a thousand feet. I could see red and white high-lights on the metal in the shine of the spotlights that lit it against planes crashing into it in the dark.

Brance hit the concrete support and leapt up, grabbing hold of the antenna and leaping between the latticework supports with metahuman strength. A normal person could not have made those jumps; they'd have been consigned to using the ladder on the side of the antenna. Brance had no trouble, though, and jumped on up like a spider who'd felt a tug on his web.

"Stop, Brance!" I shouted over the muffling effect of

my earplugs. I drew my HK pistol, lining up my sight picture.

Brance leapt through the latticework of the antenna, disappearing—mostly—behind one of the big supports that gave the antenna its shape and structure. Safely covered by the metal beam from me shooting him, he continued to climb, and within a few seconds he'd made it a good fifty feet up.

"Dammit!" I tried to circle around, but Brance was keeping a good eye on me. Just as I came around, he swung and leapt through the center, taking up cover behind another corner beam and blocking my shot. Evasive little bastard, but then, that had been my problem with him all along.

I didn't have any other options, I realized, looking frantically for Chandler. He was nowhere to be seen, probably still scrabbling around in the grass looking for my keys. For all I knew, he wouldn't get the AR in time to stop Brance from doing...well, whatever he had in mind to do.

Out of options and pressed for time, I leapt up onto the concrete support, intending to start my climb after Brance.

Chapter 103

Jules

"This is it!" Jules said, pointing as Gil took the turn hard. There was a cop car with lights flashing in the driveway, another couple vehicles with flashers parked ahead of it. The antenna loomed over everything, and Jules licked his lips as they pulled in behind the Brentwood PD car.

"This don't look like the kind of thing we're going to be able to involve ourselves in, boss," Gil said. "There are cops here."

Jules stared at the parked car. "There's one cop here, yeah. And probably Nealon and her partner, that Indian guy."

Gil looked back at Jules. "Well...what are we supposed to do about that?"

Jules frowned. He'd been considering this real carefully. "We need to be a little cautious here. We—"

A cop came wandering up toward the window and Leo

432

rolled it down. "Hey, you guys can't park here," the cop said. "We have a situation, and—"

Leo opened the door, hard, hitting the cop right in the gut and doubling him over. Before the officer had a chance to respond, Leo was out, and slammed the man in the side of the head, knocking him out cold.

Jules just stared for a second, then sighed before sliding out of the back seat. "Okay, in for a penny, in for a pound, I guess. Leo, get his body cam and disarm him, then cuff him and toss him in his back seat. Watch out for the cameras on the cop car." He shook his head. "We need to play this careful and—" Distant shouting drew his attention.

Someone was climbing the big antenna out there in the field. Jules peered into the distance, then nodded, smiling. "Okay," he said, pointing, "there's our boy. Let's go deal with him before more of these cops show up."

Chapter 104

Reed

"Whoa." Logan Mills staggered back as the flaming man burst through the window into his office. "What the hell...?"

"I guess we've found the person who burned your warehouse," I said, readying the windows. The man on fire breaking all the spotted glass as he came in was helpful; now I could bring a full-fury tornado if I had to. I squeezed my hand into a fist, felt for the air...

And realized...damn, was I tired from creating a vacuum zone in the warehouse during the fire. I suppressed a yawn. Using meta powers at high volume was intense stuff, and making me wish I could take a nap before this confrontation.

Fire Man didn't look like he was waiting for anyone, though. He was burning, completely covered in flame, and glaring down Mills with...well, pitted eyes of black surrounded by crackling orange flames. "I heard you telling your lies."

"They're not lies," Mills said, eerily calm given that a man whose skin was living flames was hovering a few feet about his office floor. "I'm busted, uh...guy."

The fire man's flames receded from his head down his face, leaving us with a view of Angelo Drake's leering face. He looked a little different wreathed in flames. Also, not hanging around two inches from Theresa's shoulder.

"Figures," I muttered under my breath.

Angelo stared at me, eyes a little wild now that they weren't on fire anymore. "What figures?"

"That the super intense guy who was super invested in the cause would turn out to be the violent lunatic," I said.

"I want my people to get what we're due," Angelo said, thumping a flaming hand on his fiery chest. "We worked hard for you. You became a billionaire while paying us peanuts, and now you're saying you've got nothing?"

"Yeah," Mills said. "Just about. I mean, think about it, Angelo. I didn't do the normal CEO thing and sell my stock for gain or put it up as collateral for a loan. You've seen what I drive; it's a Ford Escape. You've been to my house. It's the same one I had when we started this thing; 1500 square feet on half an acre." His face darkened. "And I'll guess I'll probably lose it, too, along with the car."

Angelo's face darkened. "You can't fool me. We all saw the cover of Fortune. You're a billionaire. Like the Amazon guy, or the founder of Apple."

"Except those companies made money," Mills said, almost mournfully. "I was trying to compete with them and I cut the margins too thin. We've never made a dime. And my stock is worthless, which means I'm not a billionaire." He chuckled ruefully. "In fact, you're probably worth more than I am at this point."

"Liar," Angelo whispered. "You hearing this, Bert?"

"I'm hearing it," Big Bert said, vaulting into the

window with streams of water holding him aloft, spraying out of his hands.

I barely raised an eyebrow at his entrance. "Well, well, if it isn't Theresa's second bodyguard. Is she going to be showing up next?"

"She didn't know we were doing this," Big Bert said, looming over us all.

"Well," Mills said, "now you know why I wasn't coming to the negotiating table."

They were both quiet for a second, then Angelo spoke, with a dangerous, quiet malice. "Yeah...I don't believe you."

"You greedy guys are all the same," Bert agreed. "You're holding out because you want to keep us working people down."

"I really don't," Mills said. "I—"

Not really one for drawn-out conversations with the overly angry, I raised a hand and blew Angelo and Bert out the now-gaping hole where the windows had stood. It caught them by surprise and they both went tumbling out into the night as Mills stood there, blinking, at their sudden departure.

"This conversation was going nowhere good." I grabbed Mills by the arm and dragged him toward the door before he could react. "That's not going to keep them away for long. We need to get you out of here."

I could see the gears click into place for him. They weren't going to listen to a damned thing he said, they were so convinced he was lying and snowing them. "Yeah," he said, and I threw the door open so we could get the hell out of there.

Chapter 105

Brance

How the hell was he supposed to get out of this?
Brance was climbing like a fiend, unsure of what to do. Like a man backed into a corner by bad choices, he'd chosen to climb the wall. Well, the antenna, in this case.

The results were predictable.

"Brance, stop!" Sienna shouted up at him for about the fifth—tenth—who even knew how many times it was? Did she know any words other than, "Brance, stop!"? He wanted to keep climbing, but at the same time he needed to make sure she wasn't crossing over to get a clean angle to shoot him, so he looked down—

She wasn't.

His panic did not abate, however, because instead she'd moved right to the middle of the tower's structure and was bracing herself to climb.

His reaction was pure instinct. He leaned his head over,

looking down through the center of the diamond and let out a yelp—

The air distorted around the sonic blast he'd bellowed, just like the one he'd hit her with before, flying through the shaft in the center of the antenna—

Chapter 106

Sienna

I'd made up my mind to climb when I heard the bizarre yelp from above. It wasn't the first time I'd heard it, and the last time I had—

I'd ended up catching a donkey kick to the chest.

My fingers firmly clutching the antenna lattice, I swung out of the center of the antenna just as a wave of powerful sound rushed through—

It hit the concrete foundation of the antenna, that huge slab, and I heard something rattle fiercely as busted shards peppered me furiously.

I paused for only a moment until the chaos had subsided, then started to climb. I'd made it up ten, fifteen feet when the foundation beneath me, where the metal met the now-shattered concrete, let out an ominous squeal.

"Uh oh," I muttered. But I didn't stop climbing.

Chapter 107

Jules

"What do we do?" Gil asked into the quiet night. The police lights were flashing from all three cars, and Jules was staring up at the antenna in the distance. Now a second figure was starting to climb from the base, and unless he'd misinterpreted what he'd just seen, Brance had blasted the foundation of the radio tower. The dumbass.

"What the hell are you doing?" came a vaguely accented question from just ahead. Someone was shining a light toward them from the back of that BMW that fancy Nealon had been driving at the club.

"Hey, we're just concerned citizens out for a walk—" Jules started. Denial was in his blood.

Unfortunately his denial was cut off by Leo—that fucking idiot—opening up with his pistol.

Jules sprinted, his old legs not quite as good at this as they used to be, but his hands up in the air. He wasn't even really armed, unless you counted an old snubbie revolver in a shoulder holster. He damned sure wasn't going to draw it, and if he heard even one bullet whistle his way, he was stopping, dropping and rolling like he was on fire. "Idiots!" he shouted, mostly to himself, because the Indian TBI agent opened up with what sounded like a machine gun, and Jules gave no cares for what happened next, so long as he didn't catch a round.

He figured he'd run toward the antenna, seeing as it was the closest cover, but he wasn't exactly thinking deep or he would have hidden behind the cars. Still, something was better than nothing, so Jules puffed and huffed across the field, listening to the exchange of gunfire behind him and making sure that he was running perpendicular to where any shots might be coming.

About halfway across the field, Jules stopped as something loomed in the dark, casting a slight shadow across the yellow-green field grass. It stretched up in a diagonal toward the middle of the tower.

A support cable, anchored to a concrete piling, buried in the field.

The gunfire kept going behind him, and Jules stared at the cable support for a second, trying to decipher how it worked. There was a metal anchor in the middle, and Jules stooped, putting a hand on it. With a tug, he tried to free it.

It didn't move but a little. Still...

He gave it another tug. It moved a little more.

Jules grinned and ripped at it with all his strength.

The anchor popped free, and with a little kick to the mated support, the cable let loose of the support piling.

In the distance, the tower squeaked, then swayed. He looked where it joined the tower, squarely in the middle, and counted eight support cables. They were sunk around the antenna like compass points around it in the field.

With a grin to himself, Jules wiped the metal anchor for

fingerprints and tossed it. Plausible deniability was all he needed here. "I didn't have anything to do with the shooting, Your Honor," he muttered to himself, breaking into a jog toward the next support piling, "and I have no idea what happened to make the tower fall...with that singer guy or Ms. Nealon on it..."

Chapter 108

Reed

There was nothing like a brisk run when you were already physically exhausted. Especially when the obstacle course you'd chosen for your cardio was a cluttered warehouse office, then a set of steel stairs down an even more cluttered warehouse floor which would never have passed an OSHA inspection.

"Where's Ben?" I asked as Logan leapt down the stairs as though the fire was chasing behind him. He was a little aggressive, and I used some wind to cushion his fall so he didn't break an ankle and bring our little Logan's Run to an abrupt halt.

"Locking up," Logan said, also huffing. "Probably at the far end of the building. That's where he usually starts." He had a little bit of extra weight around his midsection, and I suspected—if he was anything like me—one of the things he'd sacrificed for his business was his physical fitness. Because I hadn't hit a gym in months, but luckily my meta metabolism and genes kept it off my waist, unlike Mills.

"Hopefully," I said, giving us both a wind at our backs to keep us moving along. I didn't hold out a lot of hope that we were going to be able to outrun them forever. But if I could get us to an exit and out, I could fly us clear of here—

The windows above shattered, and in came Big Bert riding a wave like he'd was in Malibu.

"Heads up!" I shouted, puffing air beneath Logan and myself and blowing us over the crashing waves, which swept in behind us and formed an instant breakwater, cutting off our escape in that direction.

I only gave it another quick look before deciding, nope, sticking around here was a bad idea. I readied myself to blow us both out the window where Big Bert had entered, but—

Angelo came crashing in through the windows in front of us, bringing a wall of flame with him.

We were trapped.

Chapter 109

Sienna

"Brance, why are you making me climb a freaking historic radio tower in the dead of the night in Tennessee?" I asked, wondering who the hell Chandler was unloading on below. Whoever it was, they were firing back, and he was pumping a hell of a lot of rounds at them. "I mean, really, who does that? Losers, that's who, Brance. Losers climb historic radio towers on a Saturday night. Everyone else has plans. Lives. Dates. Sex, even. That's not a suggestion, by the way. Your next stop is jail, so that's probably not going to be an option you want to pursue. Unless it is. I won't judge."

The tower was creaking quite angrily, which, I assumed, had a lot to do with what Brance had done when his voice shot down to the bottom. A fine sheen of concrete dust covered my clothing thanks to that, and it couldn't have been good for this multi-ton metal structure to get its support footings partially demolished.

"Leave me alone!" Brance called back piteously. He

was almost to the top, hanging up there at the point of the diamond. I was a little over halfway up and had slowed my advance in case he decided to voice blast me. With no real desire to be pancaked, I was exercising caution.

"I can't do that, Brance," I said. "You've done some wrong. But it doesn't have to be the end. What you've done so far? Assault, battery. I mean, quite a few of those, but still...you could do your time and get out and still have lots of ability to reform or whatever."

"I just wanted them to hear me," Brance sobbed into the cold night air.

"They still could," I said. "Metas live longer, man. Go do your time; it'll be like—like—uh—what's that Johnny Cash song inside the prison—?"

"'Folsom Prison Blues,'" Brance answered, instantly.

"Yeah," I said, "except you can get out. Really." I steadied myself as the tower swayed. I'd heard tall structures like this moved in the wind, but to feel it—wheeeeee, yikes. Disorienting. "This doesn't have to be the end."

The tower let out a moan of protest, as if to contradict me, and I looked down.

Something was happening below. The cable supports that held the tower in place? Two of them seemed to be just hanging there, all tautness gone.

With a creak, the tower shifted to my right, hard, lurching, and my feet went out from under me.

Chapter 110

Jules

"Heh." Jules watched the second cable fly free of the concrete support and didn't stop to admire his handiwork for long. The tower was already showing a pronounced list in the other direction.

"Two to go?" he wondered aloud. The gunfire continued behind him, without a break. Hopefully the boys would sort that out before he got back to the car, but if not? Ehh, he'd just walk to the freeway and get an Uber or something.

Chapter 111

Brance

"How could I possibly get out of this?" Brance asked. His cheeks were wet and cold, the heights of the tower swaying. He didn't feel afraid of them, for some reason. "All I wanted was to sing! To be heard!" His knuckles were a pale white, fingers chilled and numb. "How could I ever do that now? With what I am?"

"Uhm," Sienna's voice came, wind whipping over it, now only thirty yards down. "Well, I have an idea about that." She was easier to hear now that the gunfire had stopped echoing in the night.

"You've seen what I can do!" Brance called. His fingers were loosening, his grip fading with the cold and having to hold tight to the tower. Every moment he spent up here, the closer he came to dropping off. "How am I supposed to sing to people when I hurt them?"

"There's this thing called suppressant," Sienna said, deadpan. "Maybe you've heard of it?"

Brance stopped dead, stunned. "Wha...yeah." His

voice rose. "Yeah! Suppressant!" A smile pulled up the corners of his mouth. "Yes! Yes!"

"Yes, yes," Sienna said, leaping up another few rungs of the latticework. "We can get you suppressant. You're going to be on it for a while anyway, I'm guessing. But I'm sure we can work something out where after you do your time, given the nature of your powers and your, uh, tenuous control over them, you can have a supply of suppressant." She reached a hand up to him. "But Brance...we really need to get down from here. Okay?"

Brance nodded, warm relief streaming down his cheeks. "Okay. I—"

Something popped in the distance, and the tower groaned, then jerked again, hard to the side. Brance's fingers slipped, numbly, and—

Chapter 112

Jules

There was a certain level of satisfaction in working with your hands to solve your problems. Jules smiled as the cable snapped up. That was four, and the tower was rocking unsteadily. It was definitely going to go over soon.

"All my problems are about to vanish, suckers," Jules muttered. One last cable would do it for sure.

He broke into a jog, listening to the wind whip around him. It was really going tonight. Grist for the mill; the tower was already rocking madly, and the wind was only making it worse.

Jules made it to the next anchor and dropped to his knees, well familiar with the procedure by now. Just a quick tug...then another...the anchor would pop out of the support and...

"Stop right there!"

Jules turned, anchor gripped in hand. It was so close, almost ready to pop out.

It was that damned Indian TBI agent, and he was

holding an AR-15. "I killed your men," he said, business end pointed right at Jules. "Stop now, or you'll end up like them."

"Hey, I surrender," Jules said, taking his hand off the anchor. It was almost out. He rose slowly to his feet. If he gave it a little nudge it'd probably pop out on its own...

Ah, what the hell. He was so close to solving this particular problem.

He gave it a bump with his foot as he stood there, hands in the air and—

BOOM BOOM BOOM!

Jules felt like he got punched in the chest. Thrice. Sharper, more pointed than what Brance had done.

He tumbled back a staggering step, hit the dirt. Out of the corner of his eye he could see the Indian guy running for the anchor, trying to catch it before—

It plopped out and shot across the grass, cable jerking it toward the tower as another ominous groan filled the night.

Jules let out a gasp. Touched his fingers to his chest, felt the wetness between them.

The tower made a terrible noise, but Jules didn't enjoy the thrill of his "success."

This wasn't worth his life. His dreams.

He was going to get a house here in Brentwood. Drink tea in the luxurious green hills. Live a life of leisure.

"Not...worth it," Jules whispered, lips slick with blood as the darkness closed in around him for the last time.

Chapter 113

Reed

Trapped between a flood water and a raging fire, I stood with Logan Mills in the Lotsostuff warehouse, not sure of what to do next and definitely out of room to run.

The flames licked at us from in front, and the water rushed behind me. I wished, not for the first time this adventure, that Scott Byerly were here.

"Well," Mills said, "this sucks, but I guess my life's kind of over anyway."

"No, it's not," I said. "This isn't the end for us." The fire burned, moving forward a little bit. Angelo loomed above, grinning a black and soulless grin down at us. I touched Mills's arm. I knew how he felt, what he meant. "One failure doesn't end it all."

"You sure?" Mills asked, irony livening up his dead tone. "Mine's a pretty big failure. When your screwup results in the erasure of a billion dollars from the planet, I think I might qualify as life-ending."

"Your life is over," Angelo agreed.

"No, it's not," I whispered, my hand shaking. I reached out with the wind—

Chapter 114

Sienna

The tower shifted again, now in a pronounced lean to one side. I was hanging, my cold hands numbly fighting to hang on as I pulled myself up. "This," I muttered, "would be a prime time to have Gavrikov with me. Thanks, Rose, you—"

What I called her was lost to the wind.

"Ahhh—ahhhhh!" Brance was taking this turn of events about as well as he seemed to take everything else in his life lately. He was hanging on with one hand.

"Dude," I said, climbing up the side of the tower as it angled farther sideways, "you desperately need to do some reading on anti-fragility while you're doing your time."

"What?" Brance looked down at me, voice ripped through with terror.

"Never mind," I said, climbing the last bit between us. "But also, maybe read a book on problem-solving and coolness under pressure."

When I reached him, he was holding so tight to a red

piece of latticework that his fingers had indented the solid steel.

"How...how are we going to get out of here?" Brance asked, the tower tilting another degree every few seconds.

"Well, ideally, you would have climbed down to me rather than forcing me to go higher up to come save you," I said, bleeding irritation as my mind worked the problem, "but now that we're here—can you climb down?"

Brance looked down, and whether it was the fact that the once-stable tower was now tilting ever more dramatically to one side or that he hadn't worried about dying until I rejuvenated his hope in life, the stark-white terror that painted his face told me he wasn't climbing anywhere on his own.

"Okay, well, I'm going to have you climb on my back, then," I said, "and then we'll—"

A sickening groan of stressed metal put the kibosh on that plan as the tower listed wildly. Something buckled far, far below us, and I could feel the metal supports giving up as the tower began to fall.

Chapter 115

Reed

Fire and water, two elemental forces standing in opposition to me and Logan Mills.

The plan was clear, even though these two geniuses hadn't said anything: trap us with water, scourge us from the planet with fire. The warehouse walls boxed us in to right and left.

Fire to the front of me, water to behind...here I was, stuck in the middle with Mills. Exhausted beyond my logical capacity after using the wind to suck all the air out of the warehouse fire earlier, my hand was shaking from the exertion of using my powers to their limits.

Still...our lives were on the line, and I had a very basic idea of what to do.

"Hang on to me," I said to Mills, and he looked at me like I was crazy. "Seriously."

"Aw, come on, man," Mills said, easing a little closer and putting one hand on my shoulder. Quite lightly.

"Yeah, that's not going to do it. Might want to get real

secure in your sexuality, real fast," I said, and clenched my fist.

A roaring torrent of wind buffeted by us, swirling in a circle only feet from us. It caught the leading edge of the waves behind us, sucking them up, and the fires that closed in ahead, bringing them around in a swirling elemental maelstrom.

"You think that's going to stop us?" Angelo grinned down dark malevolence. "We should have killed you as soon as we got powers, Mills. You never dealt fair with us —liar."

"I never lied to you!" Mills shouted over the rising winds.

I was having to spool up the tornado around us a lot faster than I wanted to, and it felt a little like lifting max weight after you'd already completely exhausted your muscles. I was running on fumes as I pushed, expanding my tornado out and stacking on wind speed.

"What the...?" Big Bert said behind us. I didn't dare look to see what he was up to, because it was taking all my concentration to spin up this tornado and watch Angelo up front. He was the direr threat anyway.

The winds around us were sucking up all the water trying to pass, and expanding out now, working on Bert and Angelo, each hovering in their respective directions. The vortex was getting strong now, passing from the realm of F5 tornado and into the realm of F6, which was only theoretical because none had ever been recorded.

Except when I made them.

400mph winds blew and consumed the water and fire, swirling them together in a furious blend that created a sizzle and hiss, black smoke as they suppressed one another. Angelo screamed as he got yanked through the air, his power of flight unable to cancel the winds I was sending his way.

"Holy shit!" Mills shouted in my ear. He was clenching tight enough to me to fill my hug quotient for years to come.

Big Bert flew by in front of us, and it looked like— forgive the pun—he couldn't hold his water. His mouth was open and he was screaming. Angelo went by in a blur next, also screaming, flames doused from his skin.

I slowed the winds, turning down the blender I'd created, and then, once I'd reached non-fatal speeds, let them both hit the walls of the warehouse on either side. They each crashed into the concrete block with a sickening thud, and I hoped they were out.

All my energy sapped, I thudded onto my ass, Mills barely keeping me from breaking something as I fell. The edges of my vision were dark and cloudy, and I tumbled over slowly, thanks to his aid, and lay down on the concrete floor of the warehouse.

"Might wanna dial...911," I said, trying to lift my head to look at Angelo and Bert, trying to assess whether they were still threats. I failed, and ended up staring at the warehouse ceiling. Which was rent asunder, I mean completely ripped off. The corrugated metal had a hole in it the size of a...

Well...a tornado.

"How you doing, Mills?" I asked, my voice wobbly.

Mills had a cell phone almost to his ear, but he seemed pretty quiet, not too sanguine. "Still alive," he said finally. "Still ruined, though."

"Could be worse."

"How?" Mills pushed the dial button and a faint voice announced that he'd reached 911 and asked what his emergency was.

"Well," I said, as he started to talk to them, "you could be those guys." I managed to lift my head enough to see—

Angelo and Bert splayed out against the walls on either side of us. I wasn't sure they were even alive, but if they were? They were going to be recuperating for a while.

Chapter 116

Sienna

H oly hell, I was falling.

Then I caught myself on my fingertips, hanging from the latticed support of the tower. It lurched and paused, tipped at a forty-five-degree angle, nothing but the residual remainder of the concrete base holding us upright even this minimal amount.

I looked down, then gulped.

It was a solid five hundred plus feet to the ground.

And I could no longer fly.

"Craaaaaaaaap," I muttered.

Brance was screaming so loud to my left that I could barely hear myself think. Reaching out with one hand, I grabbed him by the arm and swung him over to my back. He anchored on my neck like I was his last chance at holding onto life, because...well, I was.

I clenched my chin to my collarbone to keep him from choking me around the neck, and started to climb down, dropping ten feet at a time, catching myself on the next support, then dropping again.

"Easy does it," I said as Brance's screams gave way to whimpering. "Easy, easy."

"We're going to fall and die," Brance said.

"No one likes a whiner, Brance," I said, his wrist rubbing against my chin. "Get your shit together and put on your big boy pants. Screaming about it is not going to reverse gravity. In fact, if you hit the wrong note right now, it's going to hasten *me* giving way to gravity, and then your survival chances are going to get a lot slimmer, a lot quicker."

"O-okay," he stammered. He was still shaking, but at least he'd stopped crying. "Have you...been in a situation like this...before?" Brance got out between stammers of fear.

"Yeah, this is just like that freaking tower in Revelen," I said. "You know, on the news? When the building collapsed with me inside?" I swung down and caught a lattice of steel, this one white. Some were red, barely visible in the light of a half moon. I'd made it down almost a quarter of the way already by dropping and catching myself. Well, us.

"Oh," Brance said, and his voice dropped an octave or so. "Well, you made it out of that."

"Yes, I did," I said, timing my next swing. I dropped us about twenty feet this time, accelerating things somewhat. "And we'll make it out of this, too, if—"

The tower let up a terrible groan, vibration coursing through the metal and my fingers where they gripped the antenna's structure.

"Uh oh," I muttered. I couldn't drop down aggressively right now, so I dropped down quickly to the next lattice and the one beyond. The tower was shifting, straining—

And I had only come down about a third of the way from the top, still some four hundred feet from the ground.

With a groan, the antenna support finally gave up, and the tower lurched sideways, surrendering to the forces of gravity.

My grip failed as Brance's weight twisted me and I tumbled, Brance still wrapped around my neck, toward the dark fields waiting hundreds of feet below.

Chapter 117

"You okay?" Chandler's voice was distant, far off, as I sat on the hood of the BMW, straining against the desire to close my eyes and keel over right here. Lots more flashing lights surrounded me now, the Brentwood police department out in force at the scene of the antenna crash.

"Well, I didn't die," I said, rubbing my shoulders where Brance had nearly choked me out. He was cuffed, suppressed, and in the back of Chandler's SUV, awaiting delivery to the Nashville jail. "On the other hand, the landing involved me rolling down that hillside over there with the weight of a country music singing fugitive draped around my neck like the heaviest choker necklace ever, so there's that."

"He seemed a little out of it," Chandler said. The AR-15 was still slung around his shoulders, but he had it safetied. He'd told me about Jules and his thugs, how they'd caused this whole messy finish to Brance's story. I'd thought Jules was smarter than that, but it just reinforced my beliefs about anyone deciding crime was the best way to make their fortune being irredeemably dumb.

"Well, he'd just fallen off a damned radio tower," I said, "and I'm pretty sure he and I knocked the breath out of each other—in addition to him trying to choke me, so..." I shrugged. "He's honestly lucky to be alive."

Chandler nodded. "I should get him to lockup." He glanced around the crime scene with great significance. "You sure you're okay?"

My head was a fuzzy mess, and I don't just mean my hair. My brain was spinning from the climb and the fall, the adrenaline and the sudden comedown once it was all over. I glanced at the white sheets draped over the bodies of Jules's criminal sidekicks behind the first silvery Brentwood PD car. "Yeah, I'm fine," I said at last, then forced a smile. "I made it, after all. Not everyone was so lucky."

Chapter 118

Reed

"Messy," Ileona Marsh of the TBI opined, reading over the transcription of mine and Mills's statements about what had happened. She had a furrowed brow as she looked at it. "So you think these two guys were the only ones from the labor group involved in the attacks?"

"I think so, yeah," I said. "They were just mad, and acted out. I don't think they crossed the line into even being homicidal until the last." I shrugged. "Mills's revelation that he was actually broke sent them over the edge." I looked over the twin Murfreesboro police cars where Angelo and Bert respectively cooled their heels, suppressant already dosed in. "My question is—where did they get their powers?"

"It comes from a drug now, doesn't it?" Marsh asked. She had a pen in hand, hovering over the clipboard.

"It does," I said, "but that drug supply was cut off before Revelen fell. My group saw to that. We've noticed a marked decrease in the number of new metas the last couple years." Which had really hit my wallet, obviously. "Where did these guys come from?"

"We'll question them about it," Marsh said, then proffered a hand. "We don't need this kind of trouble in Tennessee, but we sure do appreciate you coming down here to deal with it. Thank you."

"You're welcome," I said, shaking her hand gingerly. She walked off without another word, still reading the report in her hands.

"So," Logan Mills's quiet voice reached me. I turned and found him strolling up, one of those emergency blankets wrapped around his shoulders. "You've got a failing business too, huh?"

"Yeah," I said.

Mills just nodded, slowly. "What do we do now?"

"That's a great question," I said. "I wasn't really ready to fully admit, or talk about it until—well, you know." I smiled at him tightly, and a slow realization dawned over me.

"It was easier once I heard you say it out loud," Mills agreed. "Like a revelation from the heavens. I couldn't deny it anymore."

"Yeah, I had to hire consultants to break it to me," I said. "And even still, I am—was—in denial, sort of."

"Because you think if you just get the right break—just a small one—maybe you can turn it around, right?" Mills asked. Now he was smiling wanly. "Oh, man. How do I even tell everyone...any of this?"

I looked over at the fence that ran along the edge of the Lotsostuff property. Beyond it was a crowd of spectators—some of them the protesters, but buried in there I could see Alan Kwon and Yolanda Biddle. I pointed them out. "You mean the press? I'd suggest, if you're just looking to do a hard-hitting, fair interview? Talk to him. And avoid the hell out of even letting her overhear you."

Mills chuckled. "Yeah. I guess step one is admitting the problem. Getting the word out there. Then maybe I'll wind these things down and...figure out what comes next."

"It's all about the steps," I said. "One after another."

I looked into the crowd, searching for a familiar face.

And found him toward the side.

Harry Graves.

"You bastard," I muttered, pretty sure he knew I was saying it.

This damned thing had never been about Mills or Lotsostuff. Oh, sure, I'd saved his life, but still...

Harry had sent me here...for me.

What was it he'd said? Sienna wasn't here to look after me, so...

"Bastard," I said again.

"I should have a personal life again," Mills announced. "I haven't had one in a long time. A date, even."

"Cuddling up to me during the fight there almost counts, I think. Another few seconds—"

"Hah," Mills said. "But no. Actual intimacy of the emotional kind, I'm talking."

"You'll figure it out," I said, as another thought occurred to me, and I blasted wind beneath my feet. "Good luck, Mills."

Mills just stared at me as I started to blast off. "Where are you going?"

"I have something I have to do back in Minnesota," I called, already surging into the sky. A minute later I was above the clouds, wind blowing me home.

Chapter 119

Brance

The back of the police car was quiet, and Brance was basking in the—well, not silence, because he could hear everything going on outside, but...

He was basking.

Jules had betrayed him, and that stung. He'd let himself get dragged down, though. Fallen for Jules's bull. How could he have not remembered suppressant? Everyone knew about that stuff. He just hadn't thought about it, he'd been running so much. Running scared.

Brance had been ready to die not thirty minutes ago. Now he was facing a prison term of some length, and...

It wasn't that he didn't care, it was just that he could finally see beyond that, however long it lasted, to...

Hope.

Brance opened his cracked lips, split by long exposure to the cold night air and whipping winds up on the tower, and warbled out the opening strains of "Folsom Prison Blues."

He stopped.

No glass shattering.

No screaming.

The door opened, and the TBI cop—Chandler, Brance thought his name was—got in, shutting the door behind him. He looked over his shoulder at Brance. "You going to serenade me on the way?"

Brance hesitated. "I won't if you don't want me to."

Chandler looked him over once. "The suppressant is in, so we should be good." He shrugged. "You've got a nice voice, and I think the Opry is probably off the air for the night so...yeah. Why not?"

"Okay," Brance said, and picked up right where he left off with the second verse.

Chandler nodded along with the beat. "You know, you've got a real love for the music. And it shows."

"Thank you," Brance said, smiling. And then he kept singing.

Chapter 120

Sienna

I'd just gotten back in my borrowed BMW, sliding against the leather seats, when my phone started to ring.

It'd been ringing on and off all night, and I'd mostly ignored it.

My time to ignore it was pretty much over now, though.

Heather Chalke, read the caller ID.

"Yeah?" I answered, feeling about as tired as I sounded.

I could tell Chalke was a little surprised that I answered. "I heard you wrapped up that Tennessee business," she said primly.

"It's done," I said.

"There's a ten o'clock flight to DC," she said. "I'm having my secretary book your flight right now. Be on it. I'll make sure you get the directions to your temporary housing along with your plane ticket."

What the hell else was there to say? "Roger that." I was bone tired, too tired to argue. If I even had an argument.

She hung up, leaving me looking at the time on my phone. It was already almost nine. A ten o'clock flight?

I punched in the GPS directions to my hotel and got on the road. If I floored it, maybe I could collect my battered luggage and make it to the airport in time.

Chapter 121

I dialed Chandler on the way to the hotel, figuring I should at least let him know I was going to be exiting town in a hurry. There was a lock box in the trunk of the BMW; I could drop the firearms that the TBI had been kind enough to lend me in there without fear they'd be stolen—unless the whole car was. Either way, I left him an urgent message as I sped through the night, the Nashville skyline bright, beautiful and growing increasingly closer. It almost seemed to wink at me as I sped toward town, hurrying to get to my hotel.

When I parked, I shot Chandler a follow-up text letting him know, since I hadn't heard from him. He was probably in the labyrinth of the jail, out of service reach. The elevator ride was interminably long, but I made it, opened up my room, and threw all my shit in the suitcase. Two minutes later, I was headed back downstairs, back to my waiting car and hauling ass for the BNA airport with less than an hour to go until my flight.

As I drove, Nashville's skyline winked at me again from the rear view. I gave it one last look, then looked away.

Fortunately the drive to the airport was through almost non-existent traffic, and I made it from downtown in less than ten minutes. My phone lit up as I was about to have to make the fateful choice between the parking ramp and the Departing Flights, and I hit the speakerphone as I was about to commit. "Hello?"

"Hey," Chandler's voice cut through. "I caught a Lyft to the terminal. When you get here, just drive up to Departures and I'll take your car and stuff back to TBI, okay?"

"Sure thing," I said, cutting across three lanes of traffic and into the Departing Flights lane. Fortunately, there was no one for me to cut off.

I slid up to the curb when I saw Chandler wave at me. I put the BMW in park and slid a hand appreciatively over the steering wheel. It had been a long time since I'd driven, and maybe even longer since I'd realized how fun and how freeing it could be.

"Did you enjoy your trip, Ms. Nealon?" Chandler asked, opening my door for me.

I chuckled, handing him the keys. "I sense there's a good time to be had in Nashville—if I was maybe a little less preoccupied with...stuff."

"'Stuff' is always getting in the way," Chandler agreed, pocketing the keys. "You want to, uh...dump the guns in the trunk? I already told the airport police on duty what was up."

"Yeah, sure," I said, and he popped the trunk. I dropped the spare Sig and the HK into the lockbox. "The HK might need to go to forensics for Metro PD," I reminded him. "Because of the house shooting thing."

"I'll make sure everything gets ironed out." He opened the back door and pulled my suitcase out for me, setting it on the curb and pulling up the telescoping handle. What a gentleman. Then he waited, awkwardly clapping his hands together. "So."

"I'm going to miss this," I said, pausing, my hand a couple inches above the suitcase handle.

"The guns? The freedom to do your job?" Chandler asked, little hint of a smirk.

"Also, the lack of bitter winter," I said, "the BMW, the actual freedom...thank you."

Chandler cocked his head. "For what? I mean, all that stuff was easy—"

"For reminding me that I'm a human being and that, occasionally, people are not entirely shitty." I smiled.

His smile disappeared. "Why are you doing this?"

I knew what he meant. "I have to. It's the job."

"Doesn't seem like what you want, though," Chandler said. "What...what do you actually want?"

A long, running answer formed in my head. Something about a normal life, far from the crowds and the pressure of New York and DC. Somewhere quiet, pastoral—in the romantic, poetic sense of the word. Where I wasn't always being told what to do and when to do it.

I said none of it and meant all of it, but buried it inside. "I don't know," I answered instead. Other, darker answers came to me, and those I kept to myself as well, for they were all more immediately likely to come true than any other distant dream.

"I hope you find what you're looking for, Sienna," Chandler said.

"Me too," I said, and started to walk away. "But...I would like one thing from you."

Chandler perked up. "Name it."

"Send me your playlist?" I asked. "I'll admit it—you've got me interested in country music." I held my thumb and forefinger centimeters apart. "A little."

"Sending it now," he said, messing with his phone. I started to walk away, but he called after me. "Oh, and Sienna?"

"Yeah?"

His eyes were glittering. "I suggest you try Johnny Cash's song 'Oney.'"

I frowned. "Why?"

There was a delicious sort of subversive look on Chandler's broad face. "It's about a man on his last day of work before retirement, and he's going to...well...punch the shit out of his annoying supervisor's face on the way out the door. I think you'd like it."

I couldn't help but smile. "It really does sound right up my alley, doesn't it?"

Chapter 122

I was done with checking in my battered bag, the clerk giving it a pitying look before putting it on the carousel, when someone slipped up to me and hung an arm around mine.

Always ready for murder, I turned on this person who'd taken such a liberty with me, only to find a smiling, sweet, benevolent face looking back at me.

Mayor Clea Brandt.

"Looks like someone saved the day," Mayor Brandt said, her arm looped through mine. "I thought I'd walk the triumphant hero to the security checkpoint at least."

"I don't know how much of a hero I was today," I said. "I basically just arrested a couple street criminals, killed some sex traffickers, didn't really help my partner knock off a few gangsters, and talked a whiny millennial down off a falling antenna."

"I don't think many people could have done what you did here," Mayor Brandt said. "And let's face it—even if this was the easiest thing you've done in a while, you do things no one else does. There's real value in that." Her eyes glittered.

"I'm glad someone finds use in it," I said.

"Honey, I guarantee you that more people than me see value in what you do," Brandt said knowingly. "If they didn't, there'd be no demand for your services."

"Maybe not," I said. "But there's a dark aspect that comes with my services."

"Property damage?" Brandt asked.

"No. I mean, yes. But also—I know Foreman has told you I've got an impulsive, wrathful anger. Maybe even a little bit—a tiny smidge—of a god complex."

"You're a woman, sweetheart; we've all got that," Brandt said dryly.

"Mine's worse than most," I said. "People look at me two ways—"

"Black and white," Brandt said, smile disappearing. "Good and evil."

"Yes," I said.

"I see a scale," Brandt said. "I see a young lady striving to balance. Not many have the power you do. There's a weight that comes with that. You carry it well—as well as you can."

"It's heavy," I said. "Other people are adding to it."

"So take some of that weight off." Brandt pursed her lips. "You could find a home here. We could help you reduce the load."

She already knew my answer before I gave it voice. "I can't."

Brandt unlooped her arm from mine. We'd been at the security checkpoint for a few minutes, and I'd barely noticed. "Think about it? The offer's open, if you change your mind."

"Thanks," I said, and started toward the TSA agents

waiting. I turned back, though, one last time. "Really. Thank you."

Brandt cocked her head at me, smiling so sweetly. "For what?"

"For making me feel...human again, for a minute." With that I waved, and didn't dare look back for fear I wouldn't catch my flight. And wouldn't want to.

Chapter 123

Reed

I let myself into my apartment in Eden Prairie after a long, chilly flight across the nighttime sky. Isabella greeted me at the door with a wary look and carrying a gun at her side. I reflected on how many ways my life had changed since I'd met Sienna for the first time all those years ago. I had a girlfriend, and enough worries about our safety that she came to the door armed at night when she heard it opening.

Whether this was good or bad, I couldn't even say anymore. All I knew was that it was how it was.

"How did it go?" she asked.

"Figured it out," I said, closing the door and locking it behind me. She pulled her nightie closer around her, taking care not to go pointing that pistol anywhere dangerous. As a doctor, she had once seemed concerned about the ethics of picking up a gun. Running with me for a few years had erased her reservations, apparently. "Turns out the CEO of that big, huge company was belly up financially and had trouble admitting it to himself."

One of Isabella's eyebrows arched up. "Oh?"

"Yeah, it seemed a little high on the déjà vu scale," I said, shedding my coat. "He was talking about how he'd failed and lost everything in life, and I couldn't help but feel...really bad for the guy."

"How so?" she asked.

"Because he literally spent his whole life on his business," I said. "And now that it's leveled, he has nothing else to show for it. At all. It really made me think."

Pushing a lock of dark hair out of her eyes, she furrowed her brow at me. "What did it make you think?"

"It made me think about what's important in life," I said, taking up her free hand. "About what really matters. And it gave me some clarity on—oh, to hell with it." I dropped to one knee. "Will you marry me?"

She just stared at me for a moment, gun in hand, like she hadn't heard me right.

It took a little while to convince her I was serious.

But then...she said yes.

Chapter 124

Sienna

I settled back on the plane to DC, headphones in my ears, Chandler's playlist downloaded. I scanned it, the anticipation of digging my way through it the only thing I had to look forward to at this point.

Distantly, I heard the flight attendant talking. Ignored it, save for that the flight time was an hour and forty-five minutes.

An hour and forty five minutes and I'd be dealing with Heather Fucking Chalke full-time.

I hovered my finger over the screen until I found "Oney" by Johnny Cash, then pressed it.

It only took a minute of listening to a man scheme about punching his asshole boss in the face, and I was smiling.

Chapter 125

Jaime Chapman

Man, was Chalke in a mood tonight. Chapman watched the words rip across the screen at high speed, the FBI director venting her spleen in near real-time. He checked the clock; hopefully Gwen would be along sometime this evening. She was so hard to predict. That was both a blessing and a curse. It was nice to have a girlfriend he could actually discuss intellectually weighty things with. Be charmed by.

On the other hand, a little more predictability wouldn't have been so bad. As it was, it tended to feel like they were ships passing in the night sometimes, since Gwen tended to be working on her startup until after midnight and Chapman had countless things to do at Socialite or his other companies.

The screen of his cell phone lit up with the conclusion of another long screed from Chalke about her favorite subject: Sienna Nealon.

CHALKE: She needs to produce some useful results soon or I think we're done with her. She's nothing but a pain to me.

BILSON: I have things I can use her for.

This was all so blah blah. Chapman couldn't think of many uses that a political operative like Bilson could get out of Sienna Nealon. Or maybe he just didn't want to contemplate it. Chalke and Bilson were so focused on the hard power world of politics and law enforcement. Chapman preferred soft power.

KORY: Make her available to me for an interview, I'll get mileage out of her. She needs to rehab her image anyway.

JOHANNSEN: Same. I want an exclusive if you're handing out interviews with Nealon.

Hmm, that sucking sound was the press trying to get their piece of her as well. Chapman wore a little smile every time he thought about those leeches. Without the search engines he and others had built, or the desire of people to socially share Kory's hacky, clickbait content, Flashforce would have been out of business years ago. Johannsen's Washington Free Press was struggling. Hell, they'd both be toast in a decade or less.

CHALKE: No interviews, not after the Gail Roth fiasco. Other government parties are interested in her. Probably going to have to bow to them thanks to Gondry's influence soon. None of this has worked out the way I've hoped. She's not serving our priorities.

Chapman pulled up the surveillance report from the Remote Access Trojan—RAT, to him—they'd installed on Nealon's phone via the Cloud. He'd had some of his people monitoring her constantly, checking where she was at all times. Chalke had access to it, but he doubted she availed herself of it.

CHAPMAN: Want some good news?

CHALKE: Dear God, yes. I need some.

CHAPMAN: We own her. She was within however many miles

Murfreesboro is to Nashville—I don't know much about the middle of the country—but it's close, right?

FLANAGAN: 30 miles or so I think, yeah.

Chapman smiled, typing.

CHAPMAN: She never once got close to Murfreesboro. She's that close to her brother and they don't even touch base? She's ours.

CHALKE: I guess that is some small good news.

They went on for a while longer and Chapman paid only small amounts of attention. The agenda was loose tonight, and he got the feeling that some of them were only online because rubbing shoulders with each other was more fun than sitting alone in their apartments on the respective coasts.

Chapman looked at the time again, wondering where Gwen was and how long it would be until he saw her again. Hopefully tonight. Otherwise he'd just be sitting around like the rest of these losers, dateless, on a Saturday night.

Chapter 126

Reed

I was contemplating packing up my desk—an unpleasant prospect, even though I'd finally surrendered to the idea the agency was going out of business—when Miranda knocked on my door. "Hey," I said, glad that she'd spared me—at least for a few minutes—from having to face this. I mean, it was one thing to realize I was going to have to give up on Sienna's dream here (and sort of mine, too). It was another to actually have to start working to clean out my desk. Or tell everybody else we were broke and shutting down.

"So, Tennessee," Miranda said, a folder in her hand.

"Yeah, I just got back," I said, turning my attention back to the empty box on my desk. I'd gotten it from Costco, and it was branded with a vodka company's symbol and name, which I took to be an omen. "I came to some decisions while I was there—"

Miranda shook her head, frowning. "The invoice, Reed. Did you see it?"

It was my turn to frown. "What invoice?"

She lifted the paper. "The State of Tennessee paid us last night. Like...a lot." She smiled. "Enough to float us for ninety days, which means—"

I sat down, heavily, in my chair, weird rush of relief blowing over me. "We're not broke."

Miranda just smiled. "To put it in terms you'd understand...'still flying.'" She waved the paper. "I'll get things disbursed. You might want to get some more work, though. Most jobs aren't quite as generous as this one, and they damned sure don't pay as quickly. I mean, overnight?" She shook her head. "We should work for them every chance we get."

I was left shaking my head, staring at the empty box on my desk. Why had Tennessee paid us so quickly? No one did that. Every state we'd ever worked for waited sixty, ninety days to pay invoices. I thought back to Sienna being up in Nashville and wondered if somehow she'd had something to do with it. What it might have been, I had no idea.

Suddenly, though, the empty box on my desk seemed wildly out of place.

"We're not going out of business," I muttered. Then another thought clicked into place.

Harry had sent me to Tennessee knowing that this would happen. That taking this mission would save Logan Mills's life...and the agency.

"Thanks, Harry." I frowned, wondering if, wherever he was, he could hear me with his weird, future-seeing powers. I kind of hoped he could, and added, "But you're still a bastard."

Epilogue

Julie Blair
Eisenhower Executive Office Building
Washington, DC

The Eisenhower Executive Office Building was a French Second Empire-style office building that stood across Pennsylvania from the White House. It had once been called the Old Executive Office Building, and before that, simply, the State, War, and Navy Building. Now, though, all those departments had their own buildings, and the EEOB, as it was now known, was reserved entirely for the President's men—and women.

And Julie Blair was definitely that. She was a vocal supporter of President Richard Gondry, dedicated and believing.

Which led her to still be sitting at her desk in the EEOB, working for the tenth night in a row well past her kids' bedtime. She massaged her eyes. Moved her glasses up, tried to read through the blur, then slid them back down. Still blurry. This much missed sleep would do that to you, she supposed.

Finally, she gave up.

"It's a non-stop deluge," she said, sinking back in her chair. And it had been. Like someone was just bombarding her with emails on a constant basis to see how many she could answer before breaking.

Wait, what time was it? She squinted at the clock in the corner of her screen. Eleven? Already?

Julie sank back in her seat. She'd worked past her kids' bedtime and hadn't even remembered to call them at tuck-in time.

She stared longingly at the family picture on her desk, trying to remember the last time she'd actually been home for bedtime, and cursed, fumbling for her purse and the cell phone within.

Thirteen missed calls. Five missed video calls.

Burying her face in one hand, she thumbed the screen to call back her husband. The slow beeping would have annoyed her under normal circumstances, but after so many nights of exhaustion, it just made a noise that rolled right past her consciousness almost unnoticed until he picked up. "Hey, honey—" She sat forward, chair squeaking. "I know, I know...well, I thought I was going to get done early tonight, but...you know how it is. Yeah. Something blew up." She massaged the scalp above her eye. "Like it always does, yeah...I know...I'm sorry...did—oh, they asked for me? I'm sorry, honey. What? Oh, he wanted me there to sing to him? I know, I'm...I'm sorry..." She sighed, deeply. "No...no, I don't know when it's going to get any better..."

She nudged the mouse, and her computer screen sprang back from where it had started to fade to black, going to power save mode. Blinking, she stared.

Five more emails had just come in.

"What?" Her voice cracked. She sounded broken, even to her own ears. "Sorry, I just got..." She stared. One of them was from Kathy over at— "No, I'm listening, I'm sorry, hon, I'm just..." She put her head in her hands. "I know. I should be home soon. I just need to wrap up...yeah. Love you, too."

She hung up absently, clicking the email from Kathy. Maybe just one more and she'd head home.

Wiping her bleary eyes, Julie clicked open the email, already mentally composing her reply. By the time she finished reading it, thoughts of going home had already begun to fade as she settled in to try and dig out of yet another endless crisis in a world that seemed full of them.

Author's Note

Thanks for reading! If you want to know immediately when future books become available, take sixty seconds and sign up for my NEW RELEASE EMAIL ALERTS by CLICKING HERE. I don't sell your information and I only send out emails when I have a new book out. The reason you should sign up for this is because I don't always set release dates, and even if you're following me on Facebook (robertJcrane (Author)) or Twitter (@robertJcrane), or part of my Facebook fan page (Team RJC), it's easy to miss my book announcements because … well, because social media is an imprecise thing.

Find listings for all my books plus some more behind-the-scenes info on my website: http://www.robertjcrane.com!

Cheers,
Robert J. Crane

Other Works by Robert J. Crane

The Girl in the Box
(and Out of the Box)
Contemporary Urban Fantasy

1. Alone
2. Untouched
3. Soulless
4. Family
5. Omega
6. Broken
7. Enemies
8. Legacy
9. Destiny
10. Power
11. Limitless
12. In the Wind
13. Ruthless
14. Grounded
15. Tormented
16. Vengeful
17. Sea Change
18. Painkiller
19. Masks
20. Prisoners
21. Unyielding
22. Hollow
23. Toxicity

24. Small Things
25. Hunters
26. Badder
27. Nemesis
28. Apex
29. Time
30. Driven
31. Remember
32. Hero
33. Flashback
34. Cold
35. Blood Ties
36. Music
37. Dragon* (Coming October 2, 2019!)
38. Control* (Coming December 2019!)

World of Sanctuary
Epic Fantasy
(in best reading order)

1. Defender (Volume 1)
2. Avenger (Volume 2)
3. Champion (Volume 3)
4. Crusader (Volume 4)
5. Sanctuary Tales (Volume 4.25)
6. Thy Father's Shadow (Volume 4.5)
7. Master (Volume 5)
8. Fated in Darkness (Volume 5.5)
9. Warlord (Volume 6)
10. Heretic (Volume 7)
11. Legend (Volume 8)
12. Ghosts of Sanctuary (Volume 9)
13. Call of the Hero (Volume 10)* (Coming September 2, 2019!)

14. The Scourge of Despair (Volume 11)* Coming in 2020!

Ashes of Luukessia
A Sanctuary Trilogy
(with Michael Winstone)

1. A Haven in Ash (Ashes of Luukessia #1)
2. A Respite From Storms (Ashes of Luukessia #2)
3. A Home in the Hills (Ashes of Luukessia #3)

Liars and Vampires
YA Urban Fantasy
(with Lauren Harper)

1. No One Will Believe You
2. Someone Should Save Her
3. You Can't Go Home Again
4. Lies in the Dark
5. Her Lying Days Are Done
6. Heir of the Dog
7. Hit You Where You Live* (Coming Late 2019!)
8. Her Endless Night* (Coming in 2020!)
9. Burned Me* (Coming in 2020!)
10. Something In That Vein* (Coming in 2020!)

Southern Watch
Dark Contemporary Fantasy/Horror

1. Called
2. Depths
3. Corrupted

4. Unearthed
5. Legion
6. Starling
7. Forsaken
8. Hallowed* (Coming in 2020!)
9. Enflamed* (Coming in 2021!)

The Mira Brand Adventures
YA Modern Fantasy
(Series Complete)

1. The World Beneath
2. The Tide of Ages
3. The City of Lies
4. The King of the Skies
5. The Best of Us
6. We Aimless Few
7. The Gang of Legend
8. The Antecessor Conundrum

Acknowledgments

Thanks to my editing team of Lewis Moore, Jeff Bryan, and Nick.

A big thank-you to Karri Klawiter (artbykarri.com) for the cover and for being an incredibly patient human being during my regular requests for additional art.

Gratitude to my wife, my kids, my parents and my in-laws for keeping life interesting and running. Love to you all.